continued . . .

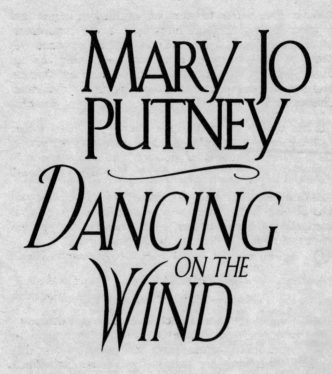

MARY JO PUTNEY

DANCING ON THE WIND

A SIGNET BOOK

SIGNET
Published by New American Library, a division of
Penguin Group (USA) Inc., 375 Hudson Street,
New York, New York 10014, U.S.A.
Penguin Books Ltd, 80 Strand,
London WC2R 0RL, England
Penguin Books Australia Ltd, 250 Camberwell Road,
Camberwell, Victoria 3124, Australia
Penguin Books Canada Ltd, 10 Alcorn Avenue,
Toronto, Ontario, Canada M4V 3B2
Penguin Books (N.Z.) Ltd, Cnr Rosedale and Airborne Roads,
Albany, Auckland 1310, New Zealand

Penguin Books Ltd, Registered Offices:
80 Strand, London WC2R 0RL, England

Published by Signet, an imprint of New American Library,
a division of Penguin Group (USA) Inc. Previously published in a Topaz edition.

First Signet Printing, May 2003
10 9 8 7 6 5 4

To my widely scattered writing buddies, for comfort, laughter, and commiseration. You know who you are.

Prologue

After the funerals he was sent back to school. What else could be done with a boy, even one who had just become the wealthiest child in Great Britain?

The brand-new Earl of Strathmore, Lucien Fairchild, was desperately anxious to return to Eton. There, with his friends, he could try to pretend that nothing had changed; that when he went back to Ashdown at the end of the term, he would find his father and mother and sister still alive and well.

He knew better, of course, but he was not yet ready to accept the finality of death. Perhaps when he turned twelve, it would be easier.

His former title had been Viscount Maldon. The Eton headmaster who greeted his carriage was quick to call him Strathmore, as were the school servants who took charge of his baggage, but behind his back, twice he heard voices murmur, "The orphan earl." Lucien cringed when he heard the phrase. It sounded unbearably pathetic. He resented his cane for the same reason, but at least that would be gone in a few weeks.

It was midevening when he arrived at the boarding house where he was lodged. As soon as he had shed his coat and gloves in his room, he went in search of his particular friends, all of whom lived in the same house. As usual, they had gathered in Rafe's chamber, which was the largest and the warmest.

Lucien limped into the room without bothering to knock. His three friends were sprawled in various positions across the furniture. Nicholas was a viscount, Rafe a marquess, and Michael the younger son of a duke, but those titles were mere courtesy, while Lucien was now a peer of the realm. He wished to God that it wasn't so.

When the door swung open, they all looked up. There was a moment of ghastly silence. They had heard the news, of course.

Lucien's heart sank. Brittle with grief and a primal loneliness that he knew would be with him for the rest of his life, he needed desperately for his friends to be the same. He didn't think he would be able to bear it if they were too embarrassed to treat him as they always had.

Then Nicholas set aside his book and uncoiled from his spot in front of the fire. His Gypsy blood made him more demonstrative than the others, and it was entirely natural for him to drape an arm around Lucien's shoulders and guide him to the fire. "Glad you're back," he said easily. "You're just in time for toasted cheese."

Lucien was deeply grateful for his friend's casual gesture. It made him feel real again. In the last fortnight he had sometimes wondered if he was as much a ghost as his family.

As he folded down onto the rug in front of the fire, the other boys set their books aside. Then they toasted chunks of cheese on long forks. The oozing, savory results were smeared across slabs of bread, a perfect supper for a cold, damp night.

Conversation was casual, mostly school news that had taken place in Lucien's absence. It wasn't necessary for him to talk at all, which was fortunate, because he wasn't sure if he would have been able to speak past the lump in his throat. In time, as the tight knot in his chest began to ease, he was able to contribute an occasional comment. He also found, with mild wonder, that he was hungry for the first time since the accident.

When the cheese was gone, Rafe said, "I found something in town that I thought you might like for your collection, Luce." He got up and rooted around in his desk, then came back and handed over a small object.

It was a windup mechanical tortoise with a miniature bronze mermaid perched on top of the shell. Even his corrosive grief could not prevent Lucien from being intrigued. "It's a real turtle shell, isn't it?" He turned the device over in his hands, studying the fine workmanship, then wound the spring and set it on the floor.

Ponderously the turtle lurched forward. Though it rolled on tiny hidden wheels, the head and legs moved as if it really walked. On its back, the coy mermaid waved her arm back and forth, throwing flirtatious kisses to the watching boys.

Lucien smiled for a moment before reality crashed down on him again. It was his father who had given him his first mechanical toy, and encouraged him to collect and build them. His father, who now lay in the family crypt at Ashdown, his laughter forever silent. Lucien blinked back the tears that threatened to spill from his eyes. If only there really was a fairy land of mermaids and magic where no one ever died.

When he had mastered himself, he said, "Are you sure you want to give this away, Rafe? I've never seen one like it."

Rafe shrugged. "Any time I want to see it, I'll know where to go."

The turtle ground to a stop, so Lucien wound the spring and set it off again. Finally able to make an oblique reference to what had happened, he said in a low voice, "They're calling me the Orphan Earl."

There was a revolted silence before Michael said, "A beastly nickname. Makes you sound like a beggar boy."

The others nodded agreement. Lucien had known that they would understand.

"We need to find a better nickname before that one sticks," Rafe said firmly. "Luce, how would you like to be known?"

Nicholas chuckled. "How about the Serpent of Strathmore? That sounds properly dangerous."

Lucien considered. A serpent, sleek and deadly. Everyone feared serpents. Still ... "Not bad, but not quite right."

"I've got a better idea." Michael grinned and held up the book he had been studying. It was Milton's *Paradise*

Lost. "Since your name is Lucien, Lucifer is a natural choice."

"Perfect," Nicholas said enthusiastically. "Lucifer, the rebellious archangel who would rather reign in hell than serve in heaven. Blond as you are, you'd make a good morning star."

"A dashing name," Rafe agreed. "Personally, I think Milton had a secret fondness for Lucifer. As a character he's far more interesting than God, who acts like a bullying headmaster."

"If we all start referring to you as Lucifer, in a fortnight every boy at Eton will be doing the same." Michael's green eyes sparked with mischief. "The masters will say it's sacrilegious. They'll be *furious.*"

Lucien leaned back against the bed and closed his eyes as he considered. Nicknames were important; being called something stupid like Weezy at Eton could follow a man all his life. Lucifer was a good strong name—a being that could laugh at God would know better than to love too much. And surely a proud, dangerous fallen archangel would not weep at night.

He tried on a cool, ironic expression. Yes, this would do very well. "All right," he said slowly. "I'll be Lucifer."

Chapter 1

Two days had passed, and the time for weeping was over. Now it was time for action.

She had already asked the obvious questions of the appropriate people, and come up empty-handed. There was no evidence beyond her intuition that something dreadful had happened.

Of course, in this instance her intuition was infallible.

At least, thank God, the worst had not yet occurred. If she acted quickly, she might be able to prevent the ultimate disaster. But what could be done? There were no conventional sources of aid in such a situation, and while there were men whom she might ask for help, there were none she dared trust.

She forced herself to stop her frantic pacing around the disordered room, which showed the effects of her futile searching. She was supposed to be a clever woman, so it was time she acted like one.

Seating herself at the desk, she cut a precise point on a quill pen, dipped it into the inkstand, and began to jot down what she knew. First came dates, times, and the answers of those people she had questioned. Then she wrote out her theory of what must have happened. It was supported mostly by half-remembered conversations, but it fit the facts, so she would proceed as if it were true. After all, she had no other theories.

Ink dried on her quill while she pondered what to write next. The critical need was for information; if she could learn exactly what had occurred, she would be able to devise a solution.

Though she was not without allies, the brunt of the investigation must fall on her. Not only were her skills uniquely valuable, but no one else, not even Jane, could possibly care as deeply.

Slowly a course of action emerged, though her face tightened as she listed places to investigate and how she might go about doing so. Some of the necessary methods might prove dangerous, and she knew that she was not a brave woman. But she had no choice; passive waiting would be unbearable.

The boldest idea was stunningly simple. As she wrote it down, she berated herself for not thinking of it immediately.

Her pen began flying across the page as more thoughts tumbled out. Soon she had worked out everything she would need to become another person.

Though perhaps it would be more accurate to say that she would become half a dozen different persons.

Chapter 2

"Stop right there, y'r bloody lordship!"

He halted instantly. Lucien Fairchild, ninth Earl of Strathmore, secret head of Britain's loose-knit intelligence service by profession, and enigma by choice, knew murder when he heard it.

Slowly he turned to face the man who had accosted him, cursing himself for having grown careless since the end of the war. He should have known better. Though the fighting had ended on the battlefields of Europe, the stealthy world of plots, politics, and power was eternal.

He had been walking home from his club and it was late, past midnight. Dry leaves skimmed across the cobblestones, and a block away carriages rumbled through Hanover square, but Lucien was alone in the shadowy street with one—no, two—dark, hulking figures. The faint starlight reflected dully from the long barrels of the two pistols aimed at his heart.

Play for time. Find out who you're facing, and why. "Are we acquainted, sir?" Lucien asked politely.

"Not personal-like, but they say you've been looking for Harry Mirkin for nigh onto two years, so I decided it was time I introduced myself." The man gave a derisive snort. "I'm disappointed. They say you're called Lucifer because you're a dangerous devil, but you're just a whey-faced dandy, too pretty to scare a ten-year-old pickpocket in the East End."

"Sorry I don't meet your expectations. Reputations are often distorted." Lucien gestured at Mirkin with his ivory-headed cane. "For instance, rumor painted you as king of the London underworld. It was said that the French paid you to assassinate the Tory leaders, hoping that the government would collapse and Britain would withdraw from the war. Did rumor speak truly?"

"Aye, that's true," Mirkin said viciously. "And I would've succeeded if it hadn't been for you and your weasel informers. Failure cost me most of my gang, my position in the underworld, and the five thousand gold guineas I would have been paid if I had been successful. I was lucky to escape with my life."

"A good fee for a job, but a poor price for betraying your country," Lucien murmured. "I have wanted to find you, though I can't say that I looked very hard. I've had more important things to do."

"The more fool you for not thinking me important!"

"Obviously I underrated you." Lucien toyed with his cane, surreptitiously loosening the head. "You did a good job of vanishing. What sewer were you hiding in?"

His opponent spat on the sidewalk. "I was in stinkin' Dublin, and it's all your fault. I've come back to take what's mine, and I'm going to start by killing Lord Lucifer, who sticks his nose into things that are none of his concern."

"I'm sure it will do wonders for your reputation when it becomes known that you needed help to kill an unarmed man," Lucien said dryly.

Mirkin waved toward his brawny associate, who stood within six feet of Lucien. "My brother Jimmy here won't give me away. All anyone will know is that you're dead and it's my doing." His voice turned venomous. "Beg for your life, Strathmore. I want you to crawl like the snake you are."

As he tensed for action, Lucien said evenly, "Whatever you say, Harry. Do you want me on my knees?"

There was a brief, predatory flash of teeth. "I'd like that. Grovel well and I may kill you quickly. Otherwise, it will be two bullets in your belly and you'll be weeks a'dying."

Mirkin's pistol lowered slightly as he waited for his enemy's humiliation. And while his guard was down, Lucien dived low and fast into Jimmy. The maneuver was a risk, but with luck he would ruin Jimmy's aim while making Mirkin hold his fire for fear of hitting his brother.

Lucien won the gamble, though only just; as the big man pitched forward onto his assailant, his pistol fired. The ball blasted by Lucien's head and powder grains scorched his cheek.

Ignoring the deafening explosion, Lucien flipped onto his back and yanked the head from his cane, exposing a glittering, razor-edged sword stick. Then he braced the sword stick with both hands so that it pointed straight up at the man falling toward him.

An instant later, Jimmy impaled himself on the blade with an impact that made Lucien's whole frame vibrate. The gunman gave a brief, hair-raising shriek that ended as quickly as it began. Then the full weight of the corpse smashed into Lucien, pinning him to the ground.

Before he could free himself, Mirkin roared, "You bloody, murdering *bastard*!" He reversed his pistol and slammed the butt into Lucien's head, then drew his arm back to do it again. "For that, I'm going to kill you by inches."

Pain exploded through Lucien's skull. Holding onto the consciousness with grim determination, he snapped, "If you succeed, at least you'll have earned my death honestly."

When Mirkin drew his foot back for a kick, Lucien heaved Jimmy's massive body off himself and into his opponent's legs, then lurched to his feet. He spent precious seconds trying to wrench his sword stick free, but it was lodged too firmly in Jimmy's chest. He would have to face Mirkin unarmed.

"You're a tricky bastard, aren't you?" Mirkin raised his pistol. "I'm going to shoot you like I shoulda done in the beginning."

Before he could fire, Lucien lashed out with one foot and kicked the gun from the other man's hand. It flew through the darkness and landed with a metallic clatter.

"By God, if I can't shoot you, I'll rip your head off with my bare hands, you filthy swine!" Mirkin bellowed as he hurled himself forward in a charge that knocked both men to the ground.

Lucien struggled to escape the lethal embrace, but Mirkin had started his criminal career as a thief on the

London docks, and he still had a stevedore's size and brute power. He pinned Lucien to the cobblestones, then locked his hands around Lucien's throat and squeezed with all his might, cutting off air and threatening to crush the windpipe.

As his vision darkened, Lucien heaved himself upward to unbalance his attacker, then jerked his knee toward Mirkin's groin. The other man's instinctive recoil gave Lucien the chance to break away. Cat-quick, he leaped to his feet and caught his enemy's head from behind. With one savage twist, he broke Mirkin's neck.

After the hideous snap, all was silent save for Lucien's ragged breathing. He let Mirkin's limp body crumple to the ground, then stepped back and wiped the sweat from his forehead with one wrist. "In a way you did me a favor, Harry," he panted. "I dislike cold-blooded killing, but for self-defense, I feel no remorse at all."

Men were starting to come from the nearby houses, drawn by the sound of Jimmy's shot. It must have been no more than three or four minutes since Mirkin and his brother had accosted him.

Long enough to kill two men.

Half a dozen neighbors arrived bearing lanterns. One, an acquaintance of Lucien's named Winterby, exclaimed, "My God, Strathmore's been injured. Send for a physician!"

Lucien looked down and saw that his fawn-colored cloak was saturated with crimson. "No need—the blood isn't mine."

"What happened?"

"Two footpads attacked me." Lucien bent and picked up his hat. Now that the crisis was over, he was shaking with reaction. It had been a near thing, a very near thing.

"Shocking that a man ain't safe even in Mayfair," someone said indignantly.

A thin man who had knelt and examined the bodies gave Lucien a strange look. "They're both dead."

"Fortunately, I had my sword stick." Lucien retrieved the two sections of his·cane. After wiping the blade clean on his ruined cloak, he screwed the handle back onto the base.

The thin man glanced down at Mirkin, whose eyes stared glassily and whose neck was bent at a strange, impossible angle. "Very fortunate," he said dryly.

Another voice murmured, "No wonder they call him Lucifer."

Raising his voice to cover the comment, Winterby said, "Come into my house for a brandy while the magistrate is summoned."

"Thank you, but since I live just ahead in the square, I'd rather go home. The magistrate can interview me there."

He took a last look at the bodies of the two men who had tried to kill him. What a strange life he lived, where forgotten business from the past might surface and destroy him at any moment. If Mirkin hadn't felt the need to explain himself, Lucien would be the one lying on the cold stones.

Wearily he turned toward Hanover Square, accompanied by one of Winterby's footmen carrying a lantern. The attack was a forcible reminder that it was time to address some unfinished business. Harry Mirkin had been only an instrument in the hands of another, more powerful figure, an agent of Napoleon who had worked against Britain for years. Mentally, Lucien had dubbed him the Phantom, for he had been as elusive as a ghost, always staying in the background while he worked his mischief.

After Napoleon's abdication in the spring, Lucien had concentrated on monitoring the treacherous undercurrents that swirled around the Congress of Vienna. That work had been more urgent than finding the Phantom, but the Congress was proceeding well, and the time had come to destroy the spy whose activities had prolonged the war and might complicate the peace.

Where to begin? There had been hints that the Phantom was a well-born Englishman, quite possibly someone known to Lucien himself. He would evaluate what little evidence he had, add a dash of instinct, and devise a plan to capture the traitor.

As Lucien climbed the steps to his house, he gave an ironic, self-mocking smile. Even a phantom could not evade Lucifer.

Chapter 3

The time was ripe for burglary. The male guests of Bourne Castle were downstairs drinking and boasting, their valets similarly engaged in the servants' quarters, and Kit Travers was as ready as she'd ever be.

She wiped her damp palms on the drab fabric of her skirt, telling herself that she was Emmie Brown, chambermaid, conscientious and not very bright. Her droopy mobcap reinforced that image, with the added benefit of obscuring her face. No one would ever guess that she wasn't what she appeared to be.

Taking the warming pan in one hand and a lamp in the other, she emerged from the safety of the backstairs into the upper west corridor of Bourne Castle. The wavering light of her lamp revealed a dozen identical doors.

Luckily, it was the house custom to place a card identifying the occupant in a bracket by the door of each guest room. Presumably that was for the benefit of illicit late night traffic. Kit had once heard of an amorous swain in search of his mistress who had burst through a door, crying, "Is Lady Lolly ready for Big John?" only to find that he had accidentally invaded the chamber of the seventy-year-old Bishop of Salisbury. The memory almost made her smile.

Levity faded as soon as she raised her lamp to check the first card. Mr. Halliwell. As far as she knew, he was not a member of the Hellions Club, so she moved to the next door. Sir James Westley. He was on her list, so she set down the lamp and hesitantly turned the knob. The door swung open under her hand.

Heart thundering, she stepped inside, trying to act as if she had every right to be there. Nonetheless, she was relieved to find that the room was as empty as it was supposed to be. She set the warming pan on the hearth, then began searching the clothes press.

Based on the evidence of his clothing, Westley was portly in build and dandyish in his tastes. Swiftly, she searched the hanging garments, paying particular attention to pockets, but she discovered nothing of interest. Then, one by one, she pulled out the trays containing linen. Nothing.

After a quick survey to ensure that everything was exactly as she found it, she closed the press and went to the writing desk. Several letters were tucked in a leather folio. Uneasily conscious of the passing time, she hastily paged through them. Again, nothing seemed relevant.

When there was nothing left to search, she ran the warming pan over the sheets, then departed. The next room housed the Honorable Roderick Harford. Excellent; he was a founder of the Hellions and one of the men she was most interested in.

More secretive than Westley, he had locked his door. Kit glanced left and right to assure that she was alone, then drew out a key that should fit the simple locks on most Bourne Castle rooms. If she should be discovered inside, she could claim that the door had been open, and it would be assumed that the lock hadn't caught properly.

The key worked with a little jiggling. She entered and began the same kind of search she had made of Westley's room. Harford was much taller than the previous man, and more careless of his clothing, with snuff stains on his linen. He should discharge his valet.

How much time had passed? Since all of the guests had put in an exhausting day of hunting, they might retire early. Nervously, she ran her hands between piles of folded cravats. If only she knew what she was looking for!

Once more it seemed there would be nothing of interest. Then she discovered a large, expensively bound book entitled *Concupiscentia* under a pile of shirts in the bottom drawer. She flipped it open, then grimaced. Apparently the Honorable Roderick had a taste for obscene and rather nasty etchings. He was obviously a man to watch.

She was heading toward the desk when she heard a key turning in the lock. For a terrified moment, she thought her heart would stop,. Since the door wasn't locked, the man outside began rattling the key, trying to turn what was already open. Her momentary paralysis ended, and she dived for the warming pan, then flipped back the covers of the bed. By the time the Honorable Roderick Harford entered the room, she was blamelessly engaged in running the hot pan over his sheets.

In person he was even larger than her study of his clothing had implied. "What are you doing here, girl?" he growled in a drink-slurred voice. "My room was locked."

" 'Twas open, sir," she said in a thick country accent. Rounding her shoulders to ruin her posture, she continued, "If you don't wish your bed warmed, sir, I'll be on my way."

"The damned locks have probably been here since Henry the Eighth dissolved the abbeys. Candover should have them replaced," Harford said sourly. He closed the door and crossed the room , his steps a little unsteady. "Don't leave, girl. It's a cold night, and now that I think about it, I could use a little warmth in my bed."

Alarmed by the glint in his eyes, Kit dodged to one side as he reached for her. "I'll be leaving now, sir." She darted toward the door.

"Not so fast, sweetheart." He grabbed her wrist and jerked her to a halt. "You're a skinny wench, but you'll do for a quick blanket hornpipe."

It was easy to show terror. Tugging to get away. Kit wailed, "Please, sir. I'm a decent girl."

"There will be a gold guinea in this for you," he said with boozy cheer. "Maybe two if you do a good job of keeping me warm." He pulled her into a disgusting, port-soaked embrace.

Fighting would be useless against a man twice her size. She forced herself to relax, though she kept her mouth closed tightly against the attempted invasion of his tongue. Taking her stillness as compliance, he mumbled.

"That's better, sweetheart," and moved one hand to her breast. "Show me how warm you are."

She took advantage of his relaxed grip to break away. She had made it to the door and was halfway into the corridor before he caught her again. "Like to play, do you?" he said jovially. "You're livelier than you look."

Panicking, she shoved violently at his chest, knocking him off balance. He clutched at her to save himself from falling, and succeeded in dragging her to the floor with him. They ended sprawled across the doorsill with their heads in the hall, Harford on top. As Kit gasped for breath, he pulled at her bodice, ripping it halfway to her waist. "*Much* nicer than I expected," he said huskily. "Maybe I'll make that five guineas."

She had feared many things of this night, but casual rape by a man who didn't even know her name was not one of them. Terrified, she tried to scream, but her cry was cut off by his mouth.

Suddenly, his imprisoning weight was gone and she could breathe again. Above her a cool voice said, "The young lady doesn't seem interested, Harford."

Kit looked up to see a tall, blond man pinning her attacker to the wall. Though the elegant newcomer seemed to be exerting no pressure, Harford was unable to break free.

"Mind your own business," Harford panted as he tried unsuccessfully to free himself from the blond man's grip. "She's a chambermaid, not a lady. I've never yet met a maid who wasn't flattered when a gentleman wanted to mount her."

"I think you've met one tonight. It would be one thing if she was willing, but it's bad form to rape your host's servants," the cool voice said with gentle reproof. "Candover would be most upset if you succeeded, and you know what a good shot he is."

The words penetrated Harford's drink-sodden brain. "I suppose you're right," he said grudgingly. "A scrawny maid is hardly worth fighting a duel over." The blond man released him, and he shuffled into his room with a yawn. " 'Night, Strathmore."

Kit stiffened. Dear God, her rescuer was Lucien Fairchild, the Earl of Strathmore. A man called, in whispers and after a wary glance in all directions, Lucifer. He and several of his rakish friends were collectively known as the Fallen Angels. She had not known that he was a Hellion.

Yet he could not have been more gentlemanly when he offered her a hand up. "Are you all right, miss?"

Wondering if she had gone from the frying pan to the fire, she took his hand and scrambled to her feet. "Y-yes, my lord."

When she looked into his face, she felt shock of a different kind. Like his namesake, Lucifer, the earl blazed brighter than mortal man. If vice had ruined him, it did not yet show in his face, but his green-gold eyes held the weariness of a man who had seen the flames of hell. She hoped that he was not her enemy, for she guessed that he would be a deadly adversary.

His grip tightened on her hand. "What's your name?"

She was so shaken that she automatically said, "Kit," before she remembered that she had joined the household as Emmie Brown. Furious that she had revealed her true name, she turned her error into a stammered, "Kit-Kitty, my lord."

His gaze ran over. "Perhaps you would be worth fighting a duel over, Kitty."

Realizing that her torn bodice had almost completely bared one breast, she cringed back and used her free hand to pull the ripped fabric over herself.

He immediately released her hand. Reverting to his former detachment, he said, "Get yourself a cup of tea and go to bed, Kitty. A good night's sleep and you'll be fine."

Though she would like nothing better, she said, "I haven't finished my work yet, your lordship."

"The rest of the guests can sleep on unwarmed sheets tonight. I'll explain why to the duke so you won't be punished." His gaze went over her again. "Tell the housekeeper to assign someone older to this particular task the next time a hunting party visits. Now get along with you, Kitty. And for your own sake, learn to sharpen your claws."

Glad to obey, she ducked her head and scuttled away like a girl who had been frightened out of her limited wits. It required no acting skill at all. She turned the corner of the hall and took refuge behind the door that concealed the servants' stairs.

Once she was safe, she sank onto the top step, set down the tools of her trade, and buried her face in her trembling hands. There were half a dozen more men whose rooms she should have searched, but she didn't dare continue. Apparently the party downstairs was breaking up early, and if she met another randy guest, she might not be lucky again.

Furiously she cursed herself for having accomplished so little. She had hoped to learn something that would narrow her search, but it had taken several days to arrange to be hired as a chambermaid and the hunting party was almost over. Tomorrow all of the guests would leave, and she had learned nothing.

Stiffly she got to her feet, feeling the bruises she had acquired when she had hit the floor. She might as well leave tonight, for she would be unable to learn anything more. Emmie Brown, unsuccessful chambermaid, would vanish. The housekeeper would merely mutter about the difficulty of getting good help and say good riddance.

As Kit climbed the dark steps to the tiny attic room that she had never slept in, she swore that she would do better.

She had no choice, for failure was unthinkable.

As he ambled down the corridor toward his room, Lucien thought about the vagaries of nature. The chambermaid was a simple country girl, a vulnerable innocent who was none too quick of mind and who had the bowed shoulders of someone ashamed of her height. Yet for an instant he had seen her face in profile, and it had the purity of a face on a Greek coin. Perhaps that was what had attracted Harford. No, the man probably hadn't noticed; the Honorable Roderick was not the discriminating sort.

Putting the maid from his mind, Lucien entered his bedroom, stripped off his cravat, and bent to build up the fire. Then he settled in a wing chair and contemplated the low flames while his mind gnawed at a random assortment of facts, trying to find some pattern. He was making no progress, so it was a relief when a quiet knock sounded at his door. He called, "Come in."

He was not surprised to see that his visitor was the Duke of Candover. He and his host had had no chance to talk privately during the hunting party. The duke entered carrying two glasses and a decanter in the crook of his arm. "You were so busy analyzing the other guests that you scarcely touched your port, so I thought you might like some brandy before going to bed."

Lucien chuckled. "Very thoughtful, Rafe. I suppose you were also hoping to learn why I asked you to invite such a motley crew to Bourne Castle on short notice."

"Always glad to place my ducal splendor at your service, Luce, but I'll admit I'm curious about what you're up to this time." The duke poured brandy for both of them, handed one glass over, then took the chair on the other side of the fire. "Is there any other way I can help your investigation?"

Lucien hesitated as he decided how much to say. When necessary, he had enlisted old friends, including Rafe, in his intelligence work, but he never did so without good reason. "Not this time—you're a little too respectable. It would look odd if you did anything more than invite the men I'm interested in for a casual hunting party. Speaking of which, thank you for obliging me. Arranging invitations to the famous Bourne Castle has enhanced my status with the Hellions."

Rafe gave a low whistle. "Of course. I had wondered why you asked me to invite those particular men. They're all in the Hellions Club. Why are you investigating the group? I thought it was just a loosely organized collection of rakes who like to fancy themselves as spiritual heirs of the old Hellfire Club, without the criminal behavior."

"That's mostly true," Lucien agreed. "The majority are young men who like to feel dashing and dangerous. After a year or two most outgrow the group's rather childish antics and drift away. But there is an inner circle called the Disciples, and they may be using the drinking and wenching as a cover for other, less acceptable activities." He made a face. "Which means that for the foreseeable future, I'm going to be spending a great deal of time with men of rather limited interests."

"My guests are all Disciples?"

"Most of them are, I think, though it's hard to be sure." Lucien frowned. "A pity that Roderick Harford's brother, Lord Mace, didn't come. I think that the two of them, plus their cousin Lord Nunfield, are the backbone of the organization. I have to win Mace's approval to be admitted to the group."

"Surely you know Mace already? I thought that as a matter of policy, you know everyone in London."

"Not quite, though I try. Mace and I are mere acquaintances—he isn't the sort I would choose as a friend. He's suspicious of everyone, and he seems particularly suspicious of me."

"As well he should be," Rafe said dryly. "I assume there are political implications, or you wouldn't be investigating the group."

"You assume correctly. At least one government official was blackmailed about something that occurred during one of the Hellion orgies. Luckily he had the sense to come to me, but there may be other victims who haven't." Lucien studied the brandy in his goblet. "I also have reason to believe that someone in the group was selling information to the French."

Rafe's dark brows drew together. "Nasty if true, but with Napoleon gone, a spy should no longer be much of a threat."

"During the war, one of my agents in France died because a man in London revealed his identity to Napoleon's police. And there was other damage done." Lucien's eyes narrowed. "The war might be over, but I am not yet prepared to forgive and forget."

"If a Hellion is responsible, he'd better hope for infernal help." The duke smiled. "Even so, I'll back you to win."

"Of course," Lucien said lightly. "As leader of the Fallen Angels, I have first claim on all diabolical aid."

Rafe laughed, and they relaxed into a companionable

silence. As he idly watched the flames, the duke asked, "Did you ever wonder how many pounds of cheese we toasted over fires like this one in our school days?"

Lucien chuckled. "I can't say that I have, but now that you've raised the question, I won't be able to sleep for trying to calculate how much."

Suddenly serious, Rafe asked, "Is it tiring to always have to know the answer?"

"Very," Lucien said tersely, his smile fading.

After a long silence the duke said quietly, "No one man can save the world, no matter how hard he works."

"That doesn't mean one shouldn't try, Rafael." Lucien gave his friend a wry glance. "The trouble with old friends is that they know too much."

"True," Rafe said peaceably. "That's also the advantage."

"Here's to friendship." Lucien raised his glass, then took a deep swallow of brandy. It was ironic that he and his three closest friends from Eton had acquired the nickname of Fallen Angels when they had descended on London after leaving Oxford; except for Lucien himself, they were the most honorable of men. When tragedy had shattered Lucien's childhood, what saved him was the blithe good nature of Nicholas, the calm acceptance of Rafe, the unswerving loyalty of Michael. If it hadn't been for them, loneliness and guilt would have consumed him.

He knew how incredibly fortunate he was in his friends. It was no one's fault that even deep friendship could not repair the damage to a soul that had been torn in half.

As he drained his glass, he remembered the incident in the hall. "I had to separate Roderick Harford from one of your chambermaids, a girl named Kitty. He wanted to expand her duties in a way that didn't appeal to her."

Rafe grimaced. "Harford is an oaf. I hope you won't ask me to invite him here again; that might strain even the bonds of old friendship. Is the girl all right?"

"Shaken but not injured. I told her to skip the rest of her duties and go to bed—that I would make it right with you."

"Very well. I'll speak with the housekeeper in the morning to make sure the girl isn't punished for dereliction of duty." Yawning, Rafe got to his feet. "Will you leave with the others tomorrow, or stay on for a few days?"

"I'll be going back to London. I have a long way to go before I become a real Hellion."

"Oh, I don't know about that. Just think back to that first year when we were all in London."

They both laughed, then Rafe left. Lucien continued gazing at the fire. As a man who disliked excess, he wasn't looking forward to trying to infiltrate the Hellions. Yet he had no choice. Though what he had told Rafe was the truth as far as it went, what he hadn't said was that his finely honed hunter's instincts were in full cry.

The original Hellfire Club of fifty years earlier had been notorious both for its debauchery and for its exalted membership, which included many of the most influential men in England. The club had been founded by Sir Francis Dashwood, a man of great wealth and inventive depravity. Besides raising vice to new heights, members had reveled in mocking religion and had played political games with far-reaching consequences. If not for the Hellfire Club, it was quite possible that the American Colonies would not have revolted and become a separate nation.

The Hellions of the present day made no such exalted claims. In theory, it was only a jolly drinking and wenching society, little different from a dozen similar groups. Yet Lucien sensed there was something very wrong going on behind the group's facade, and he intended to discover what.

A pity that he didn't enjoy orgies.

The next morning the great hall of Bourne Castle was noisy as the guests and their servants prepared to leave. Under cover of the racket, the duke said to Lucien, "I asked the housekeeper about that chambermaid. Harford has cost me a servant—it was the girl's first day on the job, and apparently he distressed her so much that she ran off in the middle of the night."

Lucien thought of the maid's air of vulnerability. "She seemed shy. I hope she has the sense to seek her next job in a quieter establishment. A vicar's manse, perhaps."

"One odd thing—the housekeeper said that the girl's name was Emmie Brown, not Kitty."

Surprised, Lucien said, "Could it be two different girls?"

"No, Emmie Brown was unquestionably the chambermaid you talked to, and there is no other Kitty employed in the household."

Lucien shrugged. "Perhaps Kitty is a childhood nickname that the girl blurted out because she was upset."

It was a plausible explanation. Yet as he drove back to London, more than once he found himself wondering about the girl with two names. It gave her an air of mystery, and he did not like mysteries.

Chapter 4

The next step in Lucien's campaign to become accepted by the Hellions took place the evening after his return to London, when he visited a tavern called the Crown and Vulture, site of the group's monthly carouse. Roderick Harford had invited him to come and said that his brother, Lord Mace, would be there.

A cold rain was falling, and Lucien was glad to enter the smoky warmth of the tavern. The taproom at the front was full of roughly dressed working men. After one look at Lucien's expensive clothing, the bartender jerked a thumb over his shoulder "Yer fine friends are that way."

As Lucien walked down the hall to the back of the building, a roar of laughter met him. The Hellions were in a good mood.

He paused in the doorway to survey the room. It was his first visit to the Crown and Vulture. Lit by a fire and a handful of candles, it was a welcoming scene on a wintry night. About two dozen men lounged around the tables, tankards in their hands. Most were young, but several older men were also present.

There was also one woman, a saucy barmaid who was trading quips with her customers. Tall and voluptuous, she had a heavily painted face and an untidy mass of garish red curls rioting from beneath her cap. Her amazing figure was further emphasized by the apron tied around a remarkably slim waist.

What held the men enthralled, however, was her quick cockney tongue. When a youth asked reproachfully, "Why have you taken an instant dislike to me?" she replied tartly, "It saves time."

A burst of laughter rang out. After it died down, another youth declaimed, "You've won my heart, darling Sally. Come away with me tonight and we'll ride to Gretna Green."

"Go all that way on a bony nag?" She waggled her lush hips suggestively. "I can find me a better ride here in London."

The double entendre produced more hilarity. When it quieted, her suitor said with an exaggerated leer, "You'll find no better rider than me, Sally."

"Be off with you, lad," she scoffed. "You don't know a thing about riding, and I can prove it."

"How?" he asked indignantly.

She tilted her pitcher and splashed more drink into his tankard. "By pointing out that if the world was a sensible place, all men would ride sidesaddle."

Her comment brought the house down. Even Lucien laughed out loud. Having won the encounter, the wench strolled from the room, swaying provocatively. She had an earthy sensuality that would catch the attention of any man.

"So Lucifer has deigned to call. My brother said that you might," a deep voice drawled. "You should feel quite at home amongst the denizens of hell."

Lucien glanced to his right and saw Lord Mace lounging in a corner from which he could watch everything that went on in the room. As tall and lean as his younger brother, Mace was a compelling figure with dark hair and lightless eyes.

Taking Mace's comment as an invitation, Lucien ambled over to the empty seat next to him. "I'll do my best."

He started to say more, then stopped, arrested by an unexpected sight. Behind Mace stood a wooden perch, and on it was a huge hooded bird that moved restively from one foot to the other. "Who is your feathered friend?"

Mace's thin lips stretched into a smile. "That's George, the vulture this place is named for. The tavern owner used to be an actor, and he rents the bird out whenever a theater needs one." He glanced affectionately at the vulture. "Lends a nice touch, don't you think?"

"Definitely atmospheric," Lucien agreed.

Sally appeared with a full pitcher in one hand and a tankard in the other. She plunked the tankard in front of Lucien. "Here you go, my 'andsome lad. Enjoy your devil's punch."

Then she undulated away. Her eyes had been averted, and her face was obscured by her garish hair, but the fleeting glimpse he had of her features showed that she was so heavily painted that she might be trying to cover up smallpox scars. Not that it mattered; few men would bother to look as far as her face.

The tankard proved to contain mulled ale with a hefty dose of spirits added. "I see why this is called devil's punch," he observed. "It burns like the fires of hell."

"After two tankards, you'll be able to recite scripture backward," Mace said with sardonic humor.

"Or I'll think I can, which comes to much the same thing." Lucien nodded toward the barmaid. "Does she ever attend your ceremonies? She looks like a lively piece."

Mace's eyes narrowed. "What do you know about our rituals?"

"Rumor says that the Hellions dress as medieval monks. After a ceremony, each 'monk' chooses a partner from among a group of 'nuns' enlisted from the ranks of London's better prostitutes. It's said that some of the nuns are actually society ladies out for a lark." Lucien gave a wicked chuckle. "I heard that once a monk and nun were appalled to rip off their robes and discover that they were husband and wife."

Mace's heavy brows drew together. "You're well informed."

"When half your members drink like fish, you can hardly expect secrecy." Lucien gave a faint smile. "I thought your group sounded amusing. Life has been getting dull lately, which is why I accepted your brother's invitation."

"We do our best to stave off boredom." Mace studied Lucien's face, frank skepticism in his eyes. "Roderick said that you were interested in joining us. I was surprised. You give the impression of being too fastidious, too much the dandy, to want to be part of a group dedicated to dissipation."

"I enjoy contrasts. I also enjoy intrigue." Lucien made a minute adjustment to his cuff. "Most of all, I enjoy confounding people's expectations."

Mace smiled faintly. "Then we have something in common."

"We have other mutual interests, I think. I've heard that you're interested in mechanical toys." When Mace nodded again, Lucien pulled a cone-shaped silver object from his pocket. "Have you ever seen anything like this? Look through the small end."

Mace raised the cone to his eye and peered inside, then sucked his breath in. "Fascinating. It holds some kind of lens that breaks the world into a number of identical images?"

"Exactly." Lucien drew a second one from his pocket and looked through it. The room immediately splintered into multiple images. "I know a natural philosopher who is interested in insects. He once told me that dragonflies have faceted eyes and must see this way. It sounded intriguing, so I decided to try to reproduce the effect. A lens grinder made these lenses to my specifications, and I had them mounted. For lack of a better name, I call it a dragonfly lens."

He blinked when his casual sweep of the room brought Sally into view. A dozen pairs of lush breasts swayed before him, and a dozen slim waists. The effect was rather overpowering.

"Do you make other mechanical curiosities?" Mace asked.

Lucien lowered the dragonfly lens, reducing Sally to singularity again. "I design and build the mechanisms myself, but I have a silversmith make the exteriors."

"I do the same." Mace gave a small, secretive smile. "Over the years I have created a collection of mechanical devices that is utterly unique. Perhaps I'll show them to you some day."

When he tried to return the dragonfly lens, Lucien waved it away. "Keep it if you like. I had several made."

"Thank you." Mace regarded Lucien thoughtfully. "Would like to attend the next time we have a ritual?"

Success. "I'd be delighted."

Mace raised the lens again and studied Sally. "A rather overblown female. The girl who is usually here is more to my taste—slimmer, less vulgar."

"That's another thing we have in common."

A man approached to talk to Mace, so Lucien relinquished his seat. Tankard in hand, he surveyed his companions. Most of the Hellions reminded him of boisterous university students, more wild than wicked. Across the room a very drunk youth unbuttoned his breeches and said brashly, "See what I have for you, Sally?"

After one bored glance, she retorted, "I've seen better." In the howls of laughter that followed, the beet-faced young man buttoned himself while the barmaid sauntered from the room.

Lucien grinned, then turned his attention to the older Hellions, who included some of London's most notorious rakes. Several were sitting together, so he joined them when Sir James Westley beckoned.

"Glad to see you, Strathmore. Wanted to say how much I enjoyed the visit to Bourne Castle." The stout baronet gave a slight hiccup, then chased it with a mouthful of punch. "Good of you to arrange it with Candover. I've seen him give setdowns that would fell an elephant, but he was a very amiable host."

His neighbor was Lord Nunfield, a cousin of Mace and Roderick Harford who shared the same lanky build. In a bored drawl he said, "You're fortunate to have a friend who lives in such good hunting country, Strathmore." His mouth curled into a characteristic sneer. "I understand that you and Candover have been the *closest* of friends since school days."

The sexual innuendo was unmistakable. With deliberate ambiguity, Lucien said, "You know what school is like."

"Boys will be boys," agreed Harford. His gaze went

to the barmaid, whose breasts bobbled delightfully as she poured punch at a nearby table. "But I think schools should have female students as well. It would make lessons much more interesting."

A spark of interest showed in the eyes of Lord Chiswick, the last man at the table. The son of a bishop, he had devoted his life to breaking as many of the Ten Commandments as possible. "I've been getting bored with false nuns. It might be amusing if our little playmates dressed as schoolgirls at the next service. A delightful contrast of innocence and experience."

Harford nodded thoughtfully. "Worth considering. Makes me think of the gamekeeper's daughter, when I was fourteen." He began to describe the encounter in detail that was as graphic as it was tedious. His anecdote was followed by reminiscences from the others. Even Lucien contributed a story, though his was fabricated from whole cloth; it was not his custom to discuss his affairs with anyone.

It was a dull evening, with the conversation seldom rising above the waist. However, from Lucien's point of view the time was well spent. By the time midnight struck, all of the Hellions seemed to have accepted him as one of their kind.

To counter boredom, he kept an idle eye on Sally during her frequent comings and goings. Tart and teasing, she was expert at amusing her customers while dodging occasional groping hands. She was hardly the sort of female who usually caught his fancy, but something about her intrigued him, an elusive sense of familiarity. Perhaps he had seen her somewhere before.

By one in the morning, most of the Hellions had left and Lucien was thinking that it was time to go home himself. Then he saw the most vocal of her youthful admirers, Lord Ives, lurch to his feet and purposefully follow the barmaid out of the room. Though she seemed quite capable of taking care of herself, Lucien was unable to suppress his protective instincts. After saying good night to those of his companions who were still awake, he rose and quietly followed Sally and Ives.

The old tavern was a maze of flagstoned passages.

Briskly the barmaid went down one, heels tapping, and turned left, then left again, ending in a storeroom half filled with kegs. Apparently unaware that Ives was close behind her, she set her candle on a keg, then stooped to draw off a pitcher of ale.

Lucien paused in the shadowed passage. If his assistance wasn't needed, he would fade away. It would be bad for his pose as a rake if he kept defending beleaguered damsels, and where the Hellions went, damsels appeared to be beleaguered regularly.

As the barmaid straightened, Ives asked in a slurred voice, "If you won't run off with me, pretty Sally, will you at least give me a quick tumble before I go home?"

She started, the ale sloshing from her pitcher, then said good-naturedly, "Even if I was willing, which I'm not, I doubt you'd be much use to me, lad. Alcohol may increase the desire, but it takes away the ability."

Lucien was startled to hear a Shakespearean quote from a barmaid. Still, there was no reason why Sally shouldn't enjoy the Bard as much as an aristocrat.

Less literary, Ives said, "If you doubt my ability, try me and I'll prove otherwise."

Her carroty curls bobbed as she shook her head. "My man is called Killer Caine, and he wouldn't like it one bit if I spread myself around." She gave Ives a playful push. "You go home to your bed, lad, and sleep off the punch alone."

"Give me a kiss, then. Just a kiss."

Before she could reply, he pulled her into an embrace, his mouth crushing hers and one hand squeezing her bounteous breast. Lucien guessed that Ives meant no real harm, but in his drunkenness he didn't realize his own strength, or notice that the woman was struggling to escape. Unpleasantly reminded of the chambermaid at Bourne Castle, Lucien decided to intervene.

He started forward, but before he could enter the storeroom, Sally stamped hard on her admirer's foot.

"Ouch!" Ives yelped and raised his head. Keeping his hand on her breast, he asked reproachfully, "Why did you do that?"

"To get rid of you, lad," Sally said breathlessly.

"Don't go," he pleaded, his hand kneading the ripe globe that filled his palm.

She shoved against his chest and managed to break his hold. Before he could embrace her again, she snapped, " 'Tisn't me you want, it's *these*."

Reaching into her bodice, she wrenched out an enormous bust improver and threw it into her assailant's face. "Have a good time, lad."

Ives released Sally and rocked back on his heels as the soft, pillowlike object bounced off his nose and fell to the floor. After staring in befuddlement at the undulating cotton curves, he raised his gaze to the barmaid. The folds of her bodice now fell loosely over a chest of modest dimensions.

To his credit, the young man began laughing. "You're a false-hearted woman, Sally."

"It's not me heart that's false," she said pertly. "Now get along with you so I can do my work."

"I'm sorry—I behaved badly," he said. "Will you be here next time the Hellions meet?"

She shrugged. "Maybe yes, and maybe no."

Blowing her a kiss, Ives left the storeroom by the other door, which led toward the front of the tavern. Sally was watching him go when she heard Lucien's chuckle. She jumped, then spun and spotted him in the shadows. "If it isn't old Lucifer himself," she said waspishly. "Did you enjoy the show?"

"Immensely." He moved forward into the storeroom. "I had thought you might need help, but obviously I was mistaken."

"Lucifer to the rescue?" she said with heavy sarcasm. "And 'ere I thought you wanted a piece of my padded arse."

Now that the bust improver was gone, it was obvious that only her slim waist had been natural. Take away the hip padding and she would have a lithe, feminine form that Lucien found more appealing than her exaggerated cotton curves. "Why do you conceal a figure that is perfectly pleasing as it is?"

"You may like scrawny females, but most men prefer a buxom wench with a bouncy backside." When he grinned, she said acidly, "You may think it's a joke, your bloomin' lordship, but that cotton stuffing puts three quid a week extra into my pockets."

"I'm not laughing at you," he assured her. "I admire cleverness wherever I find it."

She ducked her head, apparently discomfited by his compliment. In the silence that followed, he was very aware of her innate sensuality, which owed nothing to her fraudulent figure. He was close enough to see that the skin under her heavy paint was unpitted, and he guessed that she was younger than he had first thought. "You'd also be prettier without the paint."

She raised her head and gave him a fulminating glance. "I didn't ask for your opinion, my lord. Believe me, I know me own business best."

Her eyes were clear and light, though he couldn't identify the color in the dim light. Again experiencing a nagging sense of familiarity, he said, "I have the feeling I've seen you before. Have you ever been on the stage?"

She looked horrified. "I may be a barmaid, but there's no call to be insulting."

"Not all actresses are whores," he said mildly.

"Most of 'em are."

Before he could reply, a voice bellowed from the taproom, "Sally, where the 'ell are you?"

She scooped up the bust improver, then ostentatiously turned away. "If you'll excuse me, I have to put me bosom back."

He found that he was strangely reluctant to leave. Sally intrigued him, and he wanted to know more about her. The impulse was dismaying, for he had never been given to seducing servants. Lightly he said, "Tell Killer Caine that he's a lucky man."

Yet as he left the tavern, he found himself hoping that Lord Mace would invite the barmaid to the next orgy, and that Lucien would be able to recognize her in a nun's robe.

Kit leaned back against the kegs, her heart racing. How could she have been so foolish as to trade quips with one of her suspects? Particularly Lord Strathmore, whose lazy-lidded eyes missed nothing, and whose charm made him doubly menacing. The tavern must be haunted by the bawdy spirit of some long-gone barmaid who had taken possession of Kit's wits and tongue, for she had been unable to refrain from bandying words with him.

It must not happen again. Though Strathmore had not recognized her as the chambermaid from Bourne Castle, he had thought her familiar, and another meeting might be disastrous.

She had come to the Crown and Vulture because she thought that an evening working among the Hellions would give her a better understanding of their individual characters. The usual barmaid, Bella, had not wanted to miss such a lucrative party, but Kit had promised to pass along whatever tips she would receive and five pounds over that.

Tempted but wary, Bella had asked why a lady would want to do such a thing. Without so much as blinking, Kit had spun a glib tale about being the sister of one of the Hellions, and having made a wager that she could disguise herself so that her own brother wouldn't recognize her.

Amused by the idea, Bella had told Kit what to do, then introduced her as a cousin who would substitute that night since Bella was feeling poorly. On the whole, the evening had gone well. Kit's witticisms had disguised her lack of experience, and no one had suspected that she was a fraud.

"*Sally!*" the owner bellowed again. "Stop lazing in there and start cleaning the back room."

After molding the bust improver into a convincing shape, she wearily went back to work. It was exhausting to play a part so different from her own nature, but at least, she thought sourly, she was getting used to being mauled by amorous, drunken men. Soon she would be an expert at escaping unwanted embraces.

What would it be like to be kissed by Lord Strathmore? He would smile at her with those amused green-gold eyes, and his touch would be light and sure. A woman might not want to escape him. . . .

The thought made her shiver and quicken her step. One thing she knew: he would not be like the others.

After Kit had cleaned the empty back room, she returned to the main taproom. A few tenacious souls still slouched on settles by the fire. She was preparing to leave when a customer rose and approached. Her wariness dissolved when she recognized the burly, powerful figure. With a surge of hope, she said, "You're up late, Mr. Jones. Have you news for me?"

He shook his head. "Nary a thing since our last talk. I came to escort you home."

Swallowing her disappointment, she murmured, "Bless you. I wasn't looking forward to walking the streets alone."

He cast an amused eye over her as she drew on her cloak. "You've grown, lass. I scarcely knew it was you."

She smiled faintly. "That was the general idea."

He lit the lantern he had brought and held the door open for her. Outside, she shivered and pulled her cloak closer against the chilling mist. "I'll go to Marshall Street tonight."

He nodded and they set off side by side, their way illuminated by the dim glow of the lantern. When they were well clear of the tavern, he asked, "Did you learn anything useful?"

"Only in a general sense. Most of the Hellions seem fairly harmless. My guess is that Chiswick, Mace, Nunfield, Harford, and Strathmore are most dangerous. The first four have a kind of coldness that makes them seem capable of any kind of wickedness." She paused to circle a particularly dank puddle. "I don't know what to make of Strathmore. There is something menacing about him, yet he was ready to intervene when one of the younger men cornered me in the keg room."

Mr. Jones muttered a blistering oath. "You shouldn't be putting yourself in a position where you must suffer such insults, miss."

Her mouth tightened. "I hope you are not going to waste our time by trying again to change my mind."

"I should know better than that by now, shouldn't I?"

he said wryly. "Don't discount Strathmore. He may have
had a chivalrous moment, but of all that lot, he has been
the hardest to investigate. All of my inquiries have come
to dead ends. The man's a mystery, and that makes
him dangerous."

"Your report said that Strathmore hasn't been involved with the Hellions for long, so probably he isn't
the man we want."

"He's been with them long enough," Jones said grimly.
"Not long ago, he killed two footpads, one of them with
his bare hands. At least, he claimed they were footpads.
You keep your distance from him, miss."

She shivered a little, remembering the earl's feline
eyes. "I intend to." After that, there was nothing more
to say. When they reached the little house on Marshall
Street, Kit invited Mr. Jones to have a quick drink
against the cold, but he declined.

"If I don't get home soon, my Annie will become suspicious." He gave a deep, rumbling laugh as he lit Kit's
candle from his lantern. "She thinks that other women
find me irresistible. Does my old heart good."

"You'll let me know if . . .?"

"Aye," he said gently. "If I learn anything at all, I'll
notify you immediately."

Kit locked the door after him, then leaned against it
for a moment, feeling the silent rooms welcome her. As
always, her wrenching fears subsided, and it was possible
to believe that everything would be all right.

She straightened when a small warm body stropped
her ankles, purring loudly. "Don't try to turn me up
sweet, Viola. You're only interested in your supper."

Kit boosted the plump tabby cat onto her shoulder,
then took the candlestick and made her way to the tiny
kitchen at the back of the house. The flat was small but
comfortable, with a sitting room and one bedroom. The
upper floor of the house contained a similar apartment
and was home to actress Cleo Farnsworth. Though Cleo
was actually a little younger than Kit, she was a warm-
hearted soul who mothered both Kit and Viola.

After feeding the cat, Kit built a small fire and wearily
undressed. The flat's most unusual feature was a full wall

of built-in closets. After hanging her garments, Kit opened the left closet, revealing several shelves of blank plaster heads. All but one supported a wig—all colors, all lengths, all styles.

With relief, Kit removed the garish red wig and ran her fingers through her own matted light brown hair. It was equally a relief to remove the padded forms that altered her figure and store them in the next closet, then scrub off her face paint.

Finally, she crawled into bed, where Viola was already snoozing on one pillow. As she waited for sleep, Kit prayed that her dreams would bring the inspiration she desperately needed.

The old man raised his bushy brows when he admitted his visitor. "I'd not have recognized you, my lord. You look like a lamplighter."

"Good. That is what I was trying for." Lucien took off his shapeless cap. "Thank you for receiving me so late."

The old man chuckled as he ushered his guest into the library. "A moneylender grows accustomed to odd hours, for there are many who don't want to be seen. What can I do for you, my lord? I'll not believe you have need of my services."

"You're right—it's not money I need, but information." He withdrew a list from his pocket. "I'd like to know which of these men have had recourse to you or your colleagues. In particular, are there any who needed money only after the emperor abdicated last spring? Or who had occasionally borrowed before, but have needed more lately?"

The old man gave a shrewd glance, but refrained from voicing his deductions. After studying the list, he said, "I'll talk to my colleagues and have some information for you soon." Setting the paper on his desk, he said slowly, "There is a small matter. I hesitate to mention it, but . . ."

When his voice trailed off, Lucien said, "Yes?" encouragingly.

"A young man who owes me a considerable sum of money said that in eastern and central Europe, people like me often become victims of mob violence. A riot, a fire, and in the ashes, all outstanding debts are canceled." He spread his hands, his face troubled. "He pretended it was a joke, but I do not think he meant it as one."

Lucien frowned. "That has not happened in Britain for centuries, but a mob is unpredictable. What is the young man's name?" After it was given, he nodded, his expression thoughtful. "Very well. You need not fear—he won't trouble you again."

The old man said uneasily, "What are you going to do? I would not want a life on my hands, even that of a vicious, greedy young swine."

"Nothing so drastic. Besides, if he were dead, he would be unable to repay you. I know something that will persuade the fellow to behave as he ought."

Looking relieved, the old man said, "Do you have time for a pot of tea, my lord?"

"Not tonight. I've several other calls to make in the East End. I'll come again three nights from now." After a handshake, he disappeared into the night.

As he returned to his library, the old man wondered what sort of calls the earl would be making. Then he shrugged and opened a ledger book. He doubted that his imagination would stretch that far.

Chapter 5

Lucien placed the jumping mechanism inside the silver figurine and studied the fit. A bit too close in one place. Removing the device, he took a jeweler's file and began rasping down the tight spot. He was making a christening gift for his friend Nicholas's expected child and wanted it to be special. He also knew from experience that the concentration required for such work allowed the lower reaches of his mind to stew away until disparate pieces of data formed new patterns.

Unfortunately, tonight his lower mind was making no progress. He was accumulating dossiers on all of the Hellions, a composite of careful financial investigations plus his personal impressions. Yet he was no closer to knowing which of them might be a spy than the day he had begun this quixotic investigation.

His only evidence was a report that had come from one of his agents in Paris. In the files of Napoleon's chief of intelligence, the agent had found several cryptic references to a valuable English source of information. One reference implied that the informant was a member of the Hellions Club. It was all Lucien had to work with. He assumed that the spy was motivated by greed rather than political ideals. That didn't help much; it turned out that half the Hellions had financial problems brought on by gambling and spending beyond their means.

Lucien finished filing, then leaned back and stretched his cramped muscles. Usually he was patient when he had to be, but he felt unaccountably restless. He was getting tired of spending so much time with the Hellions. In the morning he would be leaving for another hunting party, this time at the estate of Lord Chiswick. While not an official Hellion activity, the half dozen other guests were all senior members of the group. They were not a stimulating lot; it took considerable effort on Lucien's part to blend in and behave like one of them.

The image of the saucy barmaid at the Crown and Vulture passed through his mind. With a wry smile, he realized that his restlessness was more basic: his body yearned for a woman. He glanced at the clock and saw that it was eleven o'clock. Not too late to go to one of the discreet brothels that catered to men of wealth and discernment, where the women were warm and willing.

He hesitated, torn between lust and prudence, before shaking his head. His need was not yet strong enough to make such indulgence worth what it would cost him.

For the thousandth time, he wished that he was like other men and could bed a woman without emotional repercussions. Unfortunately, for him that was impossible.

As a lustful youth, he had enthusiastically pursued the pleasures available to a man of wealth. Passion was so intoxicating that it had taken him years to recognize that sexual gratification was invariably followed by depression.

An ancient epigram said *post coitus, triste:* after intercourse, sadness. But what Lucien felt went far beyond the sorrowful sense of mortality that other men sometimes experienced. His attacks of bleakness were deeper, and they lasted for hours, sometimes days.

After probing the darker corners of his mind, he had concluded that the problem was the false illusion of intimacy provided by mating. When the encounter ended and he returned to his essential aloneness, desolation followed.

Once he realized what a high price he was paying for a few minutes of pleasure, he had regretfully chosen a more monastic existence. Occasionally, when passion and his longing for closeness overwhelmed his self-control, he would seek out a woman. He always hoped that this time it would be different; that he would be able to give and receive pleasure and wake with a smile the next day. But that had never happened.

His gaze went to the framed charcoal sketch of himself

and his sister, Elinor, drawn two years before her death. The sketch had been dashed off by the artist who had come to Ashdown, the Strathmore estate, to do a formal oil portrait of the whole family. The painting was handsome, and it had a place of honor, but Lucien preferred the sketch, which did a better job of capturing Elinor's fey, delicate charm.

He studied the two blond heads held so closely together. Both wore the carefree expressions of children who had been born of loving parents and who had never known want or cruelty. It was hard sometimes to remember that he had ever been so happy.

Face tight, he bent over his workbench and reached for his narrowest screwdriver. With enough concentration, he could lose himself again.

Kit had practiced Henry Jones's instructions diligently, and it took her only a few minutes to pick the simple lock on the French doors. After slipping into the dark library, she held her breath and listened hard. Soprano giggles sounded in the distance. Lord Chiswick was nothing if not hospitable; he had brought ten whores all the way from London to entertain his guests. The evening was young, so she should have time to search most of the guest rooms.

She was becoming a better criminal; this time, illegal entry left her merely terrified rather than quivering with panic.

Quietly she made her way up the backstairs to the guest rooms. She had been unable to obtain another chambermaid position, but her inquiries in the village had led her to a disgruntled former footman of Chiswick's. For a modest sum, the fellow had described the customs of the household and sketched a floor plan. He had also told her that Chiswick always brought doxies to his house parties, to the scandal of the neighborhood.

That had given Kit the idea of dressing like a tart and slipping into the house to continue her searches. A blond wig and a modified version of the padding and cosmetics she had worn as Sally made her look like a proper slut.

Any guests who saw her would assume she was part of Chiswick's entertainment.

She frowned when she saw that this time there were no cards to identify the occupants of the guest rooms. She would have to look for identification as she searched.

Palms damp, she glided into the first room.

Lucien knew that the orgy was beginning when the voluptuous redhead seated at his right climbed into his lap. "You look lonesome, ducks," she cooed. "Let Lizzie cure that." She twined her arms around his neck and gave him a wine-flavored kiss.

She was a charming armful who reminded him of the barmaid Sally, though the cut of Lizzie's gown left no doubt that her curves were genuine. As the kiss lengthened, he considered accepting her offer. It had been a long time since he had had a woman—too long. Perhaps Lizzie's jolly directness would prevent him from slipping into melancholy afterward.

But that was desire talking, he realized ruefully. Mindless coupling with a stranger produced the worst depressions. He would regret succumbing to temptation the instant it was over. His interest wasn't great enough to make it worthwhile.

On the other hand, celibacy was conspicuous in the midst of an orgy. If he didn't participate, he must at least give the impression of doing so.

Matters had progressed while he and Lizzie kissed. When a deep masculine groan issued from under the table, Lucien glanced down and saw a woman demonstrating her professional skills on Roderick Harford. His arms around two blondes, Chiswick was weaving his way into the adjacent drawing room, where the carpet was softer and the fire warmer. Nunfield lay on his belly sucking the toes of a dark-haired doxy. The other guests were also pairing off in various quiet corners.

Lucien set the redhead back on her feet and rose from the chair. Then he put his arm around her shoulders and guided her out of the dining room and into the hall beyond.

"You don't like an audience, ducks? Can't say that I

do, either." She cuddled close and began expertly caressing him.

It was almost enough to overset his resolution, but not quite. "Sorry, Lizzie, but tonight I'd rather sleep alone." Gently he detached himself. "I took a hard fall when hunting today and have bruises in all sorts of uncomfortable places."

"Are you sure?" she said coaxingly. "I have to do someone, and you're the best of the lot."

Noticing faint circles under her eyes, he suggested, "Why don't you get some rest, too?"

She hesitated. "If the truth be known, I've had a tiring day and wouldn't mind a solid night's sleep. Still, business is business, and Lord Chiswick likes to get his money's worth."

"Tomorrow I'll tell the others how sensational you were. Chiswick will never know otherwise."

She grinned. "Very well—it will be our secret." Her gaze ran over him admiringly. "I owe you one, ducks. Come see me sometime when we're both feeling more in the mood. Lizzie LaRiche—look for me in the lobby of the Theatre Royal."

He bid her good night and headed to his room, not without a pang of regret. She was an appealing wench, and perhaps he would seek her out the next time lust overcame prudence.

To his surprise a sliver of light showed under the door of his bedchamber. He entered quietly and saw a tall female form on the far side of the room. He assumed she was a chambermaid until he saw the rouge and translucent evening gown. It was another of Chiswick's doxies, this time a tousled blonde. He repressed a sigh; there was such a thing as too much hospitality. His ability to kick pretty girls out of his bed was not unlimited, so perhaps he should surrender to the inevitable.

His amusement evaporated when he realized that she was searching his clothes press. After checking the hanging garments, she closed the upper doors and turned her attention to the linen drawer. There she found a box containing several of his mechanical devices, which he had brought to show Lord Mace.

Before she could open it, he said coldly, "If you're looking for money, you won't find any there."

The girl dropped the box, which fell to the floor and broke open, spilling the contents across the floor. As she whirled toward him, her wayward golden curls danced around her face and her eyes widened with shock. He might have been sympathetic if she hadn't been caught red-handed in the act of theft.

He closed the door behind him, then folded his arms and leaned against it. "Do you always steal from your customers?"

"I ... I wasn't stealing, my lord." Her low, pleasant voice had a broad Yorkshire accent.

"Of course not," he said dryly. "You merely got lost and made a wrong turn into my armoire."

She stared down at her clenched hands. "I ... I was seeking Mr. Harford and didn't know what room he was in, so I looked in the press to see if I could recognize any of the clothes as his."

Perhaps it was true, though he doubted it. However, he thought he had stopped her in time. That scanty costume couldn't be concealing much in the way of stolen goods— it didn't even conceal much of her. He studied her appreciatively. It was hard to be outraged with a woman with such long, elegant legs. "I doubt that Harford is in need of your services. When I last saw him, he was engaged with one of your colleagues."

"Oh." After an awkward pause, she said, "I arrived here late—Lord Chiswick will be cross with me."

Thinking of Chiswick and the blondes, Lucien said, "I doubt that he will notice your absence any time soon."

"Still, I had best find him. I'm sorry I accidentally came into your room. Truly, I wouldn't have taken anything." She began walking toward him, confident that he would step away from the door and let her leave. "Good night, my lord."

He didn't move. As he watched her supple movements, the desire that had been simmering for days began burning hotter, curling through his veins and quickening his pulse. Though the girl was not as flamboyantly attractive as Lizzie, something about her intrigued him. Perhaps it was the improbable contrast of shyness and worldly appearance. Or perhaps it was a quiet dignity that was visible even in these circumstances.

The reasons were unimportant; what mattered was that the longer he looked at her, the less he cared about the consequences of passion. "Since Harford isn't available, you can stay and earn your fee with me."

His words dropped into the silence like a pebble into a pond, sending ripples in all directions. Kit stopped in her tracks. She had been right to fear Strathmore, for his feline, green-gold gaze was mesmerizing. Her pulse accelerated, and she was uncertain whether the cause was fear or anticipation.

He held out his hand. "Come here," he said in a deep, easy voice.

She wanted to run. Instead, as if it had a will of its own, her hand lifted and grasped his. His long fingers twined around hers, and he drew her into his embrace.

She had known this man would be different, and he was. Instead of mauling her, he held her lightly, smoothing her unruly curls, stroking her back, resting his cheek against her hair while she became accustomed to his touch. Her eyes closed. Warmth. Strength. A subtle eroticism that ravished her senses. Slowly her body softened and molded to his.

"What's your name?" he murmured.

She didn't reply, for doing so would destroy the moment. For the first time since starting her quest, she felt safe. She had been so alone, so afraid . . .

He lifted her chin for a kiss. A shiver went through her when their lips touched. Though the kiss was undemanding, she could not have broken away to save her life. It deepened, became a voluptuous mating of lips and tongues, a harmony of pulses. Without an iota of physical force, he was melting her resistance.

The spell shattered when she felt his warm palms on her bare shoulders. Good Lord, he had untied the tapes that secured the back of her bodice, then drawn down the flimsy sleeves of her gown. If she didn't stop him, she'd soon be naked. And it wasn't only her clothing he was stripping away, but her defenses and her sense of purpose. How could she have so easily forgotten that he was one of the enemy? It was not an accident that he was called Lucifer.

With a choked gasp, she shoved herself away, the heels of her hands hard against his chest. "I must go." She tugged her sleeves up again. "I . . . I was engaged especially for Mr. Harford. If he releases me from that obligation, I'll return."

She slipped around him and moved toward the door. In another moment, she would be free. . . .

Chapter 6

Lucien swore to himself as the girl slid away. Why did he have to set his sights on a doxy with an overdeveloped sense of responsibility? He reached out to draw her into his embrace again. "You can look for Harford later, if you still want to."

She gracefully stepped away, turning as she did. For an instant her face was silhouetted against the lamplight. A delicate profile, as pure as a Greek coin . . .

The recognition stunned him. Surely it wasn't possible—the resemblance was mere coincidence.

Instinct said otherwise.

Lust vanished, and he dived after her, catching her arm when she was halfway into the corridor. None too gently he pulled her back into the room and slammed the door, then swung her around so that he could see that unmistakable profile again. "By God, it really is you!"

She tried to twist away. "Let me go! I don't know what you're talking about."

He wondered if Lord Mace could have set her to spy on him. If so, that meant Mace was suspicious about his prospective new member, and the situation was more dangerous than Lucien had realized. But the girl shaking in his grasp did not seem like a hardened spy, or a whore, either. She had kissed like an innocent—an innocent who was learning quickly.

"Don't think you can deceive me again, my larcenous lady." He gripped her shoulder so that he could study her face at close range. With his other hand, he skimmed his fingertips over her features. "Clever how you've used cosmetics to subtly alter the shape and planes of your

face. Your own mother would have trouble recognizing
you. And you've padded your figure again, though not
as obviously as when you were Sally."

Her resistance collapsed, and she stared at him, tears
shimmering in her blue-gray eyes. "The game is up, isn't
it?" All trace of the Yorkshire accent had vanished.

"It certainly is." He released her wrist. "Who the devil
are you?"

She turned away and pressed trembling hands to her
temples.

"I'm not going to hurt you," he said more quietly,
"but I want the truth. What is your real name—Kitty?
Emmie Brown? Or Sally, like the bawdy tavern wench?
Probably none of those."

She sighed and raised her head. "My name is Jane. I
won't tell you my family name. I'm in enough trouble
already."

He suspected that meant that he might recognize her
family; her natural air was that of a gently bred young
woman, the sort usually found in a London drawing
room rather than a theatrical tavern. "Why have you
been haunting the Hellions? Or is it only me you're trying to drive to distraction?"

"It's not you I'm interested in, Lord Strathmore, but
another of your associates."

"Which one?"

She hesitated. "I'd rather not say."

"You're going to have to tell me something," he said
sharply. "Surely you're aware of the penalties for theft.
Since you're pretty, I don't suppose you will end up
dancing on the wind at Newgate, but if I decide to press
charges, you will certainly be transported."

Her face paled. "Please don't turn me over to a magistrate. I swear that I want only what I'm entitled to."

He frowned. "Is your quarry a man who ruined you?"

She began prowling restlessly about the room, her pale
gown fluttering around her ankles. "It was my brother
who was ruined, though I'm affected, too."

"Did your brother lose a fortune at cards?"

She stopped and stared at him. "How did you know?"

"An informed guess," Lucien said dryly. "Gambling is

the quickest road to ruin for a man. But what kind of contemptible young swine would allow his sister to risk herself to save him from his own folly?"

"James isn't like that." She drifted to the fireplace and gazed down at the banked coals. "One couldn't ask for a better or more responsible brother. He's in the army and had come home to convalesce from wounds. Just before he was due to return to his regiment, he was lured into a card game with ... with a certain man. My brother was coerced, cheated, and probably drugged. When he awoke the next morning, the man had a note of hand saying that he would receive title to our family estate if James didn't pay him twenty thousand pounds within sixty days."

Lucien gave a soft whistle. "A bad business if true."

Hearing the reservation, Jane glared at him. "My brother is not a liar, and he did not make up that story in order to excuse his folly."

"If he feels he was cheated, why didn't he challenge the man to a duel?"

"And make a bad situation worse? The man who cheated him"—she gave a humorless smile—"for the purposes of this discussion, I'll call him Captain Sharp—has a great deal of influence. There would have been a terrible scandal that would have ruined my brother's career. James is a good shot and would probably have killed his opponent. If not ..." She shivered. "I don't want to think of the alternative. I told James to return to his regiment because I had a plan that would solve the problem."

"So he went blithely off and left the situation in your hands." Lucien shook his head. "What is your plan—to slide a dagger between your quarry's ribs? Not a good idea."

She began drumming her fingers on the mantelpiece. "Believe me, I don't fancy myself as Lady Macbeth. I've learned that Captain Sharp has done this sort of thing to other young men—usually ones like my brother, who are well-born but not extremely wealthy or influential. It's his custom to keep the notes close, either on his person or in his baggage. I hoped to steal the note back before the sixty days are done."

"You say that as if theft is a perfectly logical solution rather than dangerous lunacy." Lucien tried to decide if she was the bravest woman he'd ever met, or the most foolish. Probably both. "Are you and James twins?"

There was an odd pause before she replied, "No, I'm three years older. What made you think we might be twins?"

He shrugged. "Because you seem to be unusually close."

A shadow crossed her expressive face. "That's because our parents died when we were young. There was only the two of us."

"No other relative to look out for the family interests?"

"A cousin has acted as guardian, but he has lived abroad for several years."

"Perhaps I can help," Lucien offered. Besides doing a good deed, it would also give him more information about one of the Hellions. His guess was that Jane's Captain Sharp was Harford or Nunfield. Both had unsavory reputations as gamesters.

"Don't be ridiculous," she said, startled. "This isn't your problem."

"You would be wise to accept any aid you can get, my dear," he said mildly. "This is what—your third attempt to get close enough to your quarry to steal what you want? Or are there other occasions I don't know about?"

She gave a rueful smile. "You've seen me every time."

"It's a miracle that you haven't been ravished or arrested yet," he said with exasperation. "If you tell me who you're stalking, there's a good chance that I can get you and your brother out of trouble."

Her eyes narrowed. "I see I shall have to be blunt. Your reputation is not precisely pristine, Lord Strathmore. You may think I'm a fool to reject your help, but I would be a greater fool to trust you."

Since he did his best to seem mysterious and faintly menacing, her words shouldn't have stung, but they did.

He said acerbically, "The fact that I haven't turned you over to a magistrate should give you some reason to trust me."

"That's frail evidence since the nearest magistrate is Lord Chiswick," she said sweetly. "As you yourself said, he would not welcome interruptions in the middle of an orgy."

Lucien almost laughed out loud. Now that Jane's initial fright had passed, she was formidably self-possessed. Perhaps she would trust him more if he found a solution to her problem. "You mentioned a guardian. I assume that you are over twenty-one, but what about your brother?"

"He'll be twenty-one in February."

Lucien gave a satisfied nod. "Excellent. Since James wasn't of legal age when he contracted the debt, Captain Sharp can't collect a single farthing from him."

Her eyes widened as hope warred with doubt. "How can that be? Young men often run up gambling debts."

"For honor's sake most youths will pay off their debts if they can. But they can't be legally compelled to do so. In a case like this, where your brother believes he was cheated, Captain Sharp is hardly likely to pursue the matter with your guardian," Lucien replied. "It was foolish of him to waste time on a boy who was under twenty-one."

"He might not have realized. James looks older than twenty, and he has been in the army since he was seventeen." She dropped onto the edge of the bed, her expression stunned. "It never occurred to me that legally he is not yet considered a man."

"I suggest that you get a lawyer with long, sharp teeth to write to Captain Sharp, repudiating the debt. I can give you several names if you don't know who to go to."

"That won't be necessary; I know someone who will do." She gave him a dazzling smile. "To think that I've been sneaking around making a fool of myself when there was no real problem."

"But if you hadn't, I wouldn't have met you, and that would have been a great pity," Lucien said softly.

Their gazes met and a primitive, powerful awareness pulsed between them—male and female admiring each other and wanting to be closer. Jane swallowed hard, her throat going taut, and he knew that she was uncomfortable with her attraction to him. Her eyes held the alarmed fascination of a nervous virgin.

"I must be leaving." She got to her feet and almost stepped on one of the mechanical devices that had fallen to the floor earlier. She knelt and began gathering the scattered toys. "I'm sorry for dropping these. I hope none are damaged."

He came and knelt beside her to help. Their fingers brushed as they both reached for a small black-and-silver penguin. In the instant of contact, he felt a tremor in her hand.

She said quickly, "What does this creature do?"

He took the mechanical penguin and wound the key, then set it on the floor. With a low whirring sound the little creature bent forward, then suddenly flipped backward in a perfect somersault. As it landed on its broad webbed feet, Jane gasped, "I don't believe it!"

Even as she spoke, the penguin did another back flip, then another. Jane sat back on her heels, laughing so hard that she pressed one hand to her midriff. She looked like someone who had not laughed for too long. It made Lucien happy to watch her.

In the last few minutes she had been a frightened innocent, a sensual nymph, and a cool-eyed opponent. Now she was a joyous child. He guessed that all of those facets of her were genuine, but were any of them the deepest, most essential woman? She was a fascinating puzzle, one he meant to solve.

Tears of amusement in her eyes, she asked, "Where did you get this?"

"I designed it and built the jumping mechanism. It's going to be a christening gift for the child of a friend of mine."

Kit picked up the toy and regarded it thoughtfully. "You have unexpected talents, Lord Strathmore. Why a penguin?"

"My friend has a dozen of them on his estate. Probably the only penguins in Great Britain. They're delightful to watch."

She supposed it made sense that Strathmore would have friends as unusual as he was himself. She picked up another of the toys, a rabbit in formal court wear who sat on a chair playing a violoncello. She wound the key and the rabbit began sawing the bow back and forth while a tune tinkled inside the figure. "Charming. Did you make this one also?"

"No, it's French. A friend found it for me in Vienna." He examined the rabbit, then carefully straightened one ear. "This fellow got a bit bent when he hit the floor."

She smiled at Strathmore's concentration. He did not look menacing. Yet even though he had treated her with courtesy—chivalry, in fact—he alarmed her. He was a man of mysterious depths, and she sensed that ruthlessness was as much a part of his nature as charm.

She lifted the last of the toys, wrapped it in one of the squares of velvet that had fallen from the box, and packed it with its fellows. Then she got to her feet and returned the box to the linen drawer. Apparently there was still quite a bit of Emmie and the chambermaid in her. Having tidied up, she said, "Good night, Lord Strathmore. I can't thank you enough for your help."

He had also risen and was studying her face with uncomfortable perception. She wondered uneasily if he suspected that she had been lying through her teeth about her mythical brother and his gambling debt.

"I want to see you again," he said quietly.

His words were more startling than an accusation would have been. Her heart jumped, partly from fear, more because of the shocking knowledge that she also would like to see him. After reminding herself of all the reasons why she couldn't, she said calmly, "That isn't feasible, my lord."

His brows arched, making him look more than ever like Lucifer. "Why not?"

"Because I will not be your mistress, and there is no other possible relationship between us."

Amusement gleamed in his eyes, making them seem more gold than green. "You accuse me unjustly. I haven't made an improper suggestion since I found out that you weren't really a whore. Why can't we be friends?"

It had been easier to deal with the Hellions who merely assaulted her body. She took an unobtrusive step backward. "Friendship between men and women is rare at the best of times, and nonexistent between those of unequal station. I don't move in the same circles you do, my lord, so we cannot be friends."

"Nonsense," he replied, undeterred. "You're obviously of good birth, and while, as you pointed out, my reputation is hardly pristine, I'm still considered socially acceptable. Let me know where to find you, and I will arrange as proper an introduction as anyone could want."

Deciding to take the offensive, she asked bluntly, "What do you want of me, Lord Strathmore?"

"I honestly don't know," he said slowly. "But I intend to find out."

"Prepare yourself for disappointment." She walked around him and headed toward the door. "Unless you are going to hold me prisoner, I will leave now."

"Wait," he ordered.

She stopped, nerves jumping, knowing that she was entirely at his mercy.

To her relief, he said only, "I'll take you downstairs. It wouldn't be safe for you to go alone."

He was right, she silently acknowledged. It was too late to search any more rooms. By this time the first stage of the orgy must be over, and those of the Hellions who could still walk would be heading for the comfort of their own chambers. One of them might be in the mood for a new bedmate.

"Very well," she agreed. "I came in through the library and left the door open so I could leave the same way."

He untied his cravat and tossed it aside, then peeled off his coat. As he started undoing the buttons at the throat of his shirt, he saw her alarmed expression and interpreted it accurately. "We must look as if we have been improperly engaged," he explained, a smile lurking in his eyes.

With his blond hair tousled and his shirt falling open to reveal his broad chest, he was the very portrait of a rake, the kind of man no woman could resist. And he knew how he affected her, damn him. Alone together in this room, both in dishabille, there was almost as much intimacy as if they were lovers in truth.

He surveyed her critically. "You need to look more debauched." He pulled down one of her sleeves. Since the back of her bodice was still untied, the fabric slid easily, exposing her left shoulder. When his fingers skimmed her bare flesh she almost jumped out of her skin.

Feeling her reaction, he hesitated, as if tempted to turn his attempt at camouflage into a caress. The moment hung suspended between them.

Finally, to her relief, he moved away and opened the door. After scanning the hall, he draped an arm around her shoulders and steered her out.

Voices sounded downstairs, but there no one was in sight. Getting into the spirit, she wrapped an arm around his lean waist and tried to look like a satisfied doxy. It was easy to act the part when his warm body was twined around hers. His closeness fueled the fire that had been kindled by his earlier kiss.

Grimly she reminded herself that she only had to hang on to the rags of her composure for a few more minutes. Then she would be free of her alarming companion.

On the ground floor they passed one of the Hellions with a half-naked woman supporting him as the couple headed for the stairs. In the dim light, she had no idea who the man was. A wavering tenor and soprano duet sounded from the drawing room as they passed, singing a song that Kit guessed would be horribly embarrassing if she understood what all of the words meant. But as Strathmore had predicted, she was safe with him. At least, safe from other men; the earl himself was another matter.

She broke away as soon as they entered the library and retrieved the cloak she had hidden behind the sofa. When she was safely swaddled in its folds, she parted the draperies and opened the French doors. The night air was piercingly cold.

He said softly, "I assume that you have a horse or carriage waiting to take you safely away?"

She studied his face. In the moonlight he had a cool, unearthly beauty. What would have happened if they had chanced to meet in a normal, uncomplicated way? Probably he would not even have noticed her. "I have, my lord. You need not concern yourself about my welfare any longer."

Before she could step outside, he caught her shoulders and drew her to him. "My name is Lucien." Then he bent his head and kissed her with calm possessiveness.

How quickly a presumptuous male embrace came to seem natural, then desirable. Her heartbeat accelerated as she kissed him back. Quite clearly she knew that she would never forget this moment or this man. The intimacy of male nearness, the erotic contrast of icy breeze and warm flesh, the soft caress of his breath on her temple when he released her—all were graven on her soul.

"I wonder if your name is really Jane," he said pensively. "Probably not, but no matter. I shall discover who you really are."

His matter-of-factness was the most unnerving aspect of a thoroughly unnerving encounter. "No, you won't," she retorted as fear overcame the haze of sensuality that had enveloped her. "Thank you again, my lord, and good-bye. There is no room in my life for you."

"You will make room," he said absolute assurance. "Until next time, my dear."

She slipped away into the night, pulses pounding as she thought about what he had said about "dancing on the wind." The phrase was a euphemism for dying on the scaffold, which was certainly a possibility if she continued her criminal activities.

But the words also described her quest. She felt as if she were dancing frantically in midair, struggling to stay aloft in a precarious situation where the least misstep would send her plunging to her doom. For that reason, the enigmatic earl was dangerous, for he caused her to lose her balance. She hoped to heaven that their paths would not cross again.

Interlude

The silent, stone-faced maid came, which meant that it was time to prepare herself. After stripping off her regular clothing, she drew on a translucent black silk chemise that left half her breasts bare and fell only to midthigh. Then the maid helped her into the black brocade corset, pulling the laces so tightly she could scarcely breathe.

Next came the black lace stockings that tied to her corset with scarlet ribbons. The long boots over them were made of supple black leather that clung to the curve of her calves. The boots had been specially made with high, thin heels that were difficult to walk in.

She sat still while the maid covered her light brown hair with a luxuriant red wig so long that it brushed her backside. Rouge to make her lips full and cruel and to bring a hectic flush to her pale cheeks. Last of all a black half mask with eyeslits cut at a wicked angle, and elbow-length black kid gloves.

She stood and examined her appearance in the mirror. All black, white, and scarlet, she was a caricature of femaleness with a tiny waist that exaggerated her breasts and hips and indecently long legs. The maid gave a nod of approval and left.

To prepare herself mentally, she stared at the clever, loathsome mechanical device she had been given and thought of what she must do. When she was as ready as she would ever be, she went into the next room and began lighting the dozens of candles that clustered on every surface. When they were all lit, the room had the orange glow of an antechamber to hell.

He would arrive soon. She picked up the whip and gave it an experimental flick. Perfectly balanced. All was in readiness for her premiere. Yet still she tensed when the key turned in the lock. In spite of her study, there was much she did not know.

Quickly she turned her back to the door, as if utterly indifferent. She sensed his entry, heard the key turn again behind him, and listened to the heaviness of his breathing. She toyed with a long tress of false red hair, making him wait.

When his impatience got the best of him, he said huskily, "I am here, mistress. What is your bidding?"

Slowly she turned, using her body to express arrogance, contempt, dominance. He watched her with avid eyes.

When he tried to speak again, she snarled, "Silence!"

The whip twitched in her hand like the tail of an angry cat. As the tension built, sweat appeared on his face and white became visible all around his irises.

With a sudden, fierce movement of her arm, she slashed out with the whip. The vicious crack shattered the suffocating silence. She caught his gaze and said with deadly menace, "Kneel, slave."

Chapter 7

Kit awoke from sleep with a cry. Her heart hammered as she tried to remember the nightmare, but already it was dissolving into fragmentary images. She stared at her hands, half surprised to see them bare rather than clad in black leather.

There had been something important in the dream—desperately important—but it was gone beyond recall. She lit the bedside candle with shaking fingers. The clock showed a little after midnight. She slid from the bed. Her legs folded under her, and she fell to her knees, head spinning. Every bit of energy had been drained away, leaving her helpless as a babe.

When the world around her steadied, she got clumsily to her feet and pulled a robe over her nightgown. Then she went to the kitchen and set a kettle over the fire. Viola, who had been sleeping on the bed, strolled into the kitchen with a questioning meow. Kit scooped the cat up and cuddled her. The warm feline body eased her shattering sense of loneliness, but not enough.

As she waited for the kettle to boil, she heard the front door of the house open. It had to be Cleo Farnsworth, whose presence would be a blessing just now. Kit set the cat down, then hastened across the drawing room and unlocked her door. When she peered into the common hallway, she saw that Cleo, a shapely blonde in her early twenties, was halfway up the steps.

"Good evening, Cleo." Kit tried not to sound forlorn. "Would you like a cup of tea and a bite to eat?"

"Don't mind if I do. There's nothing like treading the boards to give one an appetite." The actress came down the steps and frowned. "You're up very late. Is something wrong?"

Kit was tempted to pour out all her woes, but she managed to control the impulse. "Only a nightmare," she said as she led the way into the flat. "I'm so tired. I feel as if I'm living three different lives, each of them exhausting."

"Well, you are. You've had a busy fortnight."

"It seems like much longer." Kit warmed the teapot and poured boiling water over the tea leaves, then set out cheese, pickled onions, and some sausage rolls that she'd bought at a bake shop. "How did tonight's performance go?"

Cleo shrugged. "Middling. The theater was only half full. I told Whitby it was too soon to stage *The Magistrate* again, but he never pays attention to mere females. I got a good bit of applause for my part, though."

After making short work of a wedge of cheese, two sausage rolls, and half a dozen pickled onions, Cleo pushed back her chair and gave a small, ladylike burp. "Have you decided what you're going to do next?"

"Based on my investigations so far, there are several men whom I consider to be the most likely suspects," Kit replied. "Mr. Jones has supplied me with their London addresses, so I will search the lodgings of each."

"Oh, Kit!" Cleo exclaimed. "That's even more dangerous than what you've been doing. Can't Mr. Jones find a nice reliable burglar who can do the searching for you?"

Kit smiled a little. "I doubt if there are any reliable burglars. Besides, no one but me can find what I'm looking for, because I'm not sure what it is."

"I suppose you're right," the actress admitted. "But how will you do it? Even though Mr. Jones has taught you how to pick locks, you'll still run the risk of walking into servants."

"I'll go over the roofs and through the upper windows. Growing up wild in the country made me quite a good athlete."

Cleo shuddered. "I don't even want to think about it. Still, you've managed so far. Pray God your luck holds."

"My luck has been erratic." Kit fed a bit of cheese to

Viola, who lurked hopefully under the table. "It wasn't so bad when two of the Hellions tried to maul me—they had no idea that I wasn't what I seemed. But one of the cleverer ones caught me rifling his room at Lord Chiswick's and recognized me from earlier encounters. He let me go after I spun a farrago of lies. I don't think he'll mention me to the others, but since he thinks my problem is solved, I'll be in trouble if he sees me again."

Cleo chuckled. "If that happens, I'm sure you can come up with another convincing table. Who was the gentleman?"

"The Earl of Strathmore."

"Strathmore!" Cleo's expressive brows shot upward. "Old Lucifer himself. You do like to live dangerously."

"You know everything about everyone." Kit started to rub the itchy patch on her inner thigh, then stopped herself. She couldn't risk scarring. "What do you know about him?"

"I don't *know* much, but there's no shortage of rumors," Cleo said slowly. "He drifts through all levels of society, from the lowest to the highest. Though he's no gamester, when he gambles he has the devil's own luck, and they say he's ruined more than one man. He was considered one of the greatest catches in the marriage mart when he was younger, but I've heard that the hopeful mamas have given up on him. One has to wonder why, since he's rich, handsome, and eligible."

"None of that sounds very wicked."

"It's true that gossip of that sort doesn't mean much," Cleo agreed. "More worrisome is the fact that once or twice well-born gentlemen have vanished from society without a trace. I heard it suggested that Strathmore might have had something to do with the disappearances, but since he has friends in high places, no one dares accuse him openly."

It was not what Kit wanted to hear. Her mouth tightened. "So he may be a kidnapper, murderer, or worse."

"Perhaps." Cleo's expression turned pensive. "I met him once in the green room and liked him. A very witty man. He could have charmed any woman there into his bed, yet he didn't. I thought it strange, since few gentlemen will pass up a comely actress." Her face became grave. "Don't let him catch you again, Kit. He's a deep one and no mistake. I wouldn't rule out him being the one you're after."

"I liked him, too." Kit emptied the last of the tea into her cup. "Unfortunately."

"How are you coming with your dancing?"

The mere thought made Kit feel even more tired. "I think I have the steps down," she said without enthusiasm.

"Show me."

Kit blinked. "At one o'clock in the morning with me in my nightgown?"

Cleo grinned. "Why not? I'll hum the music." She rose and went into the drawing room and flopped into a chair, then began a wordless croon, her trained voice filling the chamber.

Feeling self-conscious, Kit belted her robe more tightly, then began dancing. It was a lively jig, and as she moved through the steps she began feeling stronger.

When she finished, Cleo said critically, "Not bad, but this time with more spirit. And show some leg, it's what the gentlemen come to see." She began humming again, this time clapping strongly to the beat.

Kit turned her thoughts inward for a moment, telling herself that she was an irresistible coquette, a man's deliciously seductive fantasy. She imagined Lucien Fairchild watching her, his eyes golden with desire. . . .

A wave of heat coursed through her at the thought. She began to whirl about the drawing room, narrowly escaping collisions with the furniture. This time she submerged herself in the music, stamping her heels and spinning so that her robe soared above her knees. She ended with a flourish that changed Cleo's hand claps into real applause.

"Well done, Kit! You'll be a great success."

Kit's temporary high spirits began to fade. Perhaps her dancing would be successful, but that was the least important of her goals. Time was passing with frightening speed, and the crucial, life-or-death goal was as elusive as ever.

*   *   *

Lucien sat down at his desk to outline what he had learned in his investigation of the Hellions, but his pencil strayed and he began sketching. He had a knack for drawing that was useful when he designed his mechanical toys. What emerged on the paper this time was no penguin, but a woman's face.

When he was done, he studied the result. Lady Nemesis, as intriguing as she was elusive.

Mentally he called her Jane, since that was her most recent name. Though they had met three times and shared two really superior kisses, he wasn't sure exactly what she looked like. Were her cheekbones really that high, or had that been a trick of her skillful cosmetics? Was her face a perfect oval, or a little longer? And her mouth—touch had proved the softness of her lips, but he couldn't define the precise shape. The only thing he could swear to was the slim, graceful figure which he found more alluring than Sally the barmaid's artificial curves.

He tried sketching her several ways before giving up. None of the drawings seemed quite right. It was maddening to know that he might pass her on the street without recognizing her.

With a sigh, he leaned back in his chair and propped his feet on the desk. The blasted female was becoming an obsession. He had said that he would find her and he would, though locating a nameless young woman who might be anywhere in Great Britain was akin to searching for a black cat in a cellar at midnight.

But after he found her, what the devil was he to do with her? The raging lust he had felt at Chiswick's had subsided to a manageable level, but he still wanted to bed her and the consequences be damned. He had been depressed before and he would be again; at least brave, clever Jane would be worth the emotional price. But one did not seduce well-born virgins, which she certainly was, in spite of her devious actions.

Women like her were the sort one married.

Which meant that he had no right to seek her out. His gaze went to the sketch of himself and Elinor. He had long ago decided that he would never marry unless he found a woman with whom he could share the profound emotional intimacy that had been absent from his life for so long.

He would be a happier man if he had never known such closeness. Yet though he still ached for the loss, he could not be sorry that he had once had it.

He was returning to business when his butler entered to announce "Lord Aberdare is here to see you, my lord."

"Nicholas!" Lucien rose and shook the hand of his friend, who had entered on the butler's heels. "I didn't know you were coming to London."

"No more did I. But Rafe summoned me here for that vote about the peace negotiations in Ghent that he is putting before the House of Lords."

"Good Lord, he brought you all the way from Wales for that?" Lucien waved his guest to a chair as he re-seated himself. "Mind you, Rafe is right—since the war with the Americans has turned into a stalemate, it makes no sense for Britain to demand territorial concessions. Rafe's resolution requests that the government soften its position and accept existing boundaries, which is the only way a settlement will be reached. But even if the resolution passes, it won't carry the force of law."

"True, but when the House of Lords barks, the government listens, and Rafe needs every vote he can get. That's why he sent for me." Nicholas dropped casually into a chair and stretched out his legs. "It's time to put an end to a war that never should have started in the first place."

"That's certainly true. It was mad to slide into a brawl with the United States when we were fighting for our lives against Napoleon. The sooner we make peace, the better."

"Particularly since our upstart cousins have begun winning the battles," Nicholas said wryly.

Lucien asked, "How is my favorite countess?"

"Clare is as calm as always." Nicholas gave a rueful smile. "I'm the one who is quivering with nerves. She claims that there is no reason to worry because she comes from a long line of sturdy peasant women who were back in the fields cutting hay half an hour after giving birth. No doubt she's right, but I'll be glad when the baby has arrived."

Lucien pulled the mechanical penguin from a drawer. "I made this as a christening gift. You can take it back to Wales with you now."

"What have you done this time?" Nicholas wound the key. When the penguin started doing backflips, Nicholas collapsed back in his chair, helpless with laughter. "What a strange and wonderful mind you have, Luce," he gasped when he could speak again. "Clare will love it. But what will you do to match this if we have other children?"

"Penguins can do other things. Swim. Slide on their bellies. Dance. We'll see when the time comes."

Nicholas reached for the penguin again. As he did, he saw the sketches of Jane that lay on the desk. He lifted one and studied it. "An interesting face. Full of character and intelligence. Are you love-smitten?"

"Absolutely not," Lucien said repressively. "That is merely a female who is more trouble than a sackful of cats."

His friend chuckled. "Sounds promising. When can we expect an interesting announcement?"

Lucien rolled his eyes. "Don't try to persuade me of the advantages of marriage. There is only one Clare, and you found her first. Since I refuse to settle for anything less in a woman, I am condemned to spend the rest of my years a bachelor. Your children can call me Uncle Lucien and talk behind my back about my eccentricity."

Nicholas, intuitive as a cat, must have heard the bleakness under the surface levity, for he gave Lucien a sharp glance. "Apropos of nothing," he said slowly, "Clare said that the reason the Fallen Angels became so close is that none of us had a real family, so we had to invent one."

It was truth so unexpected and accurate that it momentarily silenced Lucien. At length he said, " 'Apropos of nothing,' indeed. What is it like to live with a woman who sees too much?"

"Sometimes alarming." Nicholas grinned. "Mostly wonderful."

Lucien decided that it was time to change the subject before his envy became too visible. "Have you heard any interesting news from your Gypsy kinfolk?"

Nicholas's smile faded. "That's one reason I wanted to talk to you. A distant cousin with whom I traveled on the Continent recently sent a message to Aberdare. He says that there are persistent rumors that Napoleon intends to make a triumphant return from exile."

Nicholas had spent several years wandering through Europe with his Gypsy relatives. The Rom went everywhere and heard everything, and the information he had sent back to London had been invaluable. Hoping that this time his friend might be wrong, Lucien said, "One would expect such rumors about the Corsican. He's a living legend."

"True, but this goes beyond what might be expected," Nicholas replied. "My cousin said that agents of the emperor have been moving secretly through France, testing the temper of the people, and have concluded that the majority would support the emperor again. He has also heard whispers that there are powerful men among the Allies—British, Prussian, and Austrian—who would help because they want Napoleon to return. Apparently they found war to be a profitable business."

"Jackals," Lucien said with barely suppressed violence. The fighting might have ended, but he should have remembered that greed and violence were eternal. It was time to stop thinking about an elusive lady and concentrate on his real work. "Likely the rumors are no more than speculation and idle talk, but one can't take chances. I'll make inquiries. I'll also send word to my counterparts in Prussia and Austria. If there is a plan afoot to restore the emperor, perhaps it can be nipped in the bud."

"I hope so," Nicholas said gravely. "I surely do hope so."

The night was darkly overcast, but dry, perfect for criminal activity. Dressed entirely in black men's clothing and supplied with thin, strong rope and a grappling hook, Kit launched her career as a burglar at the town house of Lord Nunfield. The sardonic, amoral nobleman was one of her prime suspects.

The house next to his was temporarily vacant, so she was able to scale it without fear of being heard. From there it was simple to cross to the roof of Nunfield's house.

Lights in the basement indicated that the servants were spending a quiet evening in their own sitting room. The upper house was dark. After securing her rope around a chimney, Kit looped the line around her body and lowered herself to the level of a back window. It was strenuous work, even for a someone who had always been athletic to a most unladylike degree.

Luckily, the window she had chosen was fastened with a simple latch she could open with a knife. She paused to catch her breath inside, for she was panting heavily, as much from nerves as from exertion. This time if she was caught, there would be no way she could explain away her presence.

When her pulse steadied, she set to work. She had become adept at searching, and she was able to go through the upper floors of Lord Nunfield's modest dwelling very quickly. Though she paid particular attention to the master's bedchamber, she checked every room.

It all went flawlessly. Unfortunately, she found nothing of interest. By the time she leaned out the window and caught her dangling rope, she was inclined to think that Nunfield was not her man. Her next sortie would be to the town house of Lord Mace.

As she scrambled up onto the roof, she told herself that the evening had been successful in one respect: this time she hadn't been caught by the alarming Lord Strathmore.

For that, at least, she could be grateful.

Rafe's proposal to make a speedy settlement with the United States brought a surprisingly large number of peers to the House of Lords. The issue produced a brisk and occasionally virulent debate. Rafe himself was eloquent in promoting his resolution, and Lucien and Nicholas also gave brief speeches of support.

Debate continued until past midnight. When the matter was put to the vote, Rafe waited stone-faced, as if indifferent to the result. Lucien sat on his friend's right and kept a running tally of the results. It was going to be close, very close, and the chamber was silent with tension.

The resolution carried by a single vote. As a babble of voices rose, Rafe permitted himself a jubilant smile. "A good thing you came, Nicholas."

"Let's hope the resolution does some good." Nicholas clapped Rafe on the shoulder. "Well done. I was afraid that the crush-the-colonials crowd would win."

Rafe turned to Lucien. "Care to come to my house to celebrate? Perhaps we can do a little plotting about other kinds of pressure that might be brought to bear on the government."

"I'll join you later." Lucien scanned the crowded chamber. "There are some people I want to say hello to."

Lucien had not been surprised to see that Mace and Nunfield had attended, nor that they voted against the measure. He made his way through the crowd of peers to them.

Mace raised his brows when Lucien joined them. "You really favor surrendering to that rabble of Americans?"

"The issue is not surrender but compromise," Lucien said as they stepped to one side of the stream of men exiting from the chamber. "I see no point in continuing a useless war."

"It sounds as if you have dangerously liberal tendencies," Nunfield said with mock horror. "You probably read radicals like Leigh Hunt and L. J. Knight and agree with them."

"Sometimes I do." Lucien gestured at the crowd. "Peace shouldn't be a radical issue. Most people here have relatives on the other side of the Atlantic. I do myself. We should be making the Americans our friends, not burning their capital."

"It's true that they gave us tobacco, and for that we

owe them something. Speaking of tobacco ..." Mace produced a gilt snuffbox and opened it with an elegant flip of his left hand. After inhaling a pinch, he gave a sigh of pleasure. "Delightful. Almost as pleasing as nitrous oxide. Have you ever tried that?"

Though Mace's expression was casual, there was a note in his voice that made Lucien realize that the question was significant. "No, but I've heard of it, of course. I understand that inhaling the gas produces an effect like intoxication, only without the headache the next day."

"It's even better," Mace assured him. "Unlike alcohol, which often makes one morose, nitrous puts a man quite in charity with the world. That's why it's sometimes called laughing gas. I have a chemist who makes nitrous for me, and occasionally I invite a few friends over to enjoy it with me. In fact, I'm doing so tomorrow night. Care to join us?"

"I'd love to," Lucien replied, not entirely truthfully. "It's one of those things I've always wanted to try."

"Until tomorrow, then." Mace nodded and went on his way.

As Lucien went in search of Rafe and Nicholas, he permitted himself an inward smile of satisfaction. Nitrous oxide had a reputation for loosening tongues and inhibitions, so he might learn some interesting things from other guests at the party. By the same token, he would have to make sure that Mace didn't learn anything from him. A good thing that Lucien was experienced at keeping his own counsel.

Chapter 8

Lucien deliberately went late to Lord Mace's nitrous oxide party. It was only two blocks from Strathmore House to Mace's home, so he walked. Since the weather was unseasonably cold, more like January than November, he had the streets to himself.

The draperies were drawn at Mace's, making the house so dark that it appeared unoccupied. However, an impassive butler answered Lucien's knock promptly, took his cloak, and guided him to the drawing room. The dim lamps illuminated about a dozen people, mostly male but including several women. What distinguished it from other social gatherings was the rapturous smiles and the large leather bladders all of the guests held and periodically inhaled from. Footmen moved about quietly, bringing new containers when guests signaled for replacements.

Lucien scanned the room, looking for his host. Several guests were talking and laughing together, though there was a disoriented quality to their conversation. Others, perhaps more intoxicated, had turned inward to trancelike states, more interested in their own sensations than their surroundings.

In a corner Lord Nunfield lounged in a chair, alternating sips of wine with inhalations from his gasbag. Closer to hand, Lord Chiswick sat on the floor with a giggling woman sprawled across his lap. He raised his deflated bag and waved it at a footman. " 'S empty," he said querulously. "Need more."

The servant silently brought another bulging bladder and exchanged it for the empty one. After sucking greedily at the pipe stem, Chiswick's expression dissolved into a beatific smile.

Mace's cool voice said, "Glad you made it, Strathmore."

"Thank you for the invitation."

Lucien turned and found that his host had a flushed face and pupils dilated so widely his eyes appeared black. If nitrous oxide caused that, it explained the low light level.

"You'll have to work hard to catch up with the others," Mace said. "Come in here where it's quieter."

He led the way into an adjoining reception room, and the two men settled into a pair of leather-covered chairs. A servant promptly brought over two of the leather bladders.

Lucien examined his, guessing that it held a volume of about a gallon. "How is the gas produced?"

"By heating some substance—ammonium nitrate, I think," Mace explained. "I won't let the chemist make it here, of course, because sometimes the stuff explodes. Go ahead, try some."

Lucien adjusted the pipe stem, then began inhaling the gas, hoping that it wouldn't rot his brain. After emptying the bladder, he said, "It's relaxing, but nothing more."

Mace took away the original gasbag and handed his guest a new one. "It takes several minutes to feel the full effect."

Midway through the second bladder, Lucien began to feel light-headed, though not unpleasantly so. He inhaled again and vibrant tingling pulsed through his body, dancing along his veins and thrumming in his extremities. Colors seemed brighter, and he felt exhilarated, intensely alive. "Interesting. I'm beginning to understand why you like this."

"It gets even better," Mace said as he signaled for more. "If nitrous was easier to obtain, drink would go out of fashion."

Lucien laughed, for the comment seemed very humorous. He hadn't felt so carefree since he was a boy.

Mace lifted a notebook and pencil from the table beside him. "Describe the sensations you're feeling. My chemist is compiling data on how different people react to nitrous."

"It's like ... being music." Lucien groped to explain the unexplainable. "A friend once took me to Westminster Abbey to hear Handel's *Messiah*. The building resonated with the sounds of hundreds of instruments and singers. This is rather like that."

"Are your ears ringing?"

Lucien considered. "Yes, pounding in rhythm with my heartbeat."

Mace continued to ask questions, though sometimes Lucien lost track of them. Time blurred as one container of gas after another was placed in his hands. He noticed that Mace was inhaling the nitrous at a much slower pace. Though it was obvious that the other man wanted him intoxicated, it didn't seem worth worrying about. Once or twice Lucien tried to collect his scattered wits, but he couldn't quite remember why he should try. He took things too seriously—all his friends said as much—so he should seize this opportunity to relax and enjoy himself.

A small corner of his mind stood aside, watching, but it had no power to act. It simply observed.

After a number of questions about reactions to the gas, Mace casually asked, "Why do you want to join the Hellions Club, Strathmore? I'd like the truth this time."

"I want to know ... to know ..." Lucien's mind temporarily went blank, and he could not remember what it was that he was determined to learn. In the seconds while he searched for the answer, he recognized the hard glint in his host's eyes. Mace had been waiting for this moment.

It was not unexpected. What shocked Lucien was that, in spite of years of practice at keeping secrets, he wanted to blurt out the truth. The normal walls of judgment and inhibition had vanished, and his tongue was ready to say that he was looking for a spy and intended to destroy the man when he found him.

The part of his mind that stood to one side said coolly that if he gave that answer and Mace was the spy, there was an excellent chance that Lucien would not survive the night. An accidental death would be easy to arrange. A slip on the icy cobblestones—an assault by unknown robbers—and he would be gone. Society would be shocked and regretful, for a day or two.

Struggling to avoid giving an answer, Lucien mumbled, "Sorry—the ringing is getting worse. Makes it hard to hear properly."

Mace sharpened his voice. "Tell me what you want to learn."

"I want to learn . . ." Grimly Lucien tried to focus his fragmented mind, to connect with that small part of himself that still had clarity. He rubbed his hand into his forehead and couldn't feel the pressure of his own fingers. *Think, dammit!*

He doubted that he could lie, even to save his life, but with a wash of relief he saw that he could offer lesser truths. "I wanted to learn . . . more about you and the others. Sometimes I get . . . very tired of myself. Too serious. I envy those who can live for pleasure, because I don't know how." And those were things he had never seen in himself, he realized with mild wonder.

Mace repeated his question several different ways, but now that Lucien had worked out his answers, he was able to reply more easily. At length Mace leaned back and regarded him through half-closed eyes. "Congratulations, Strathmore, you've just passed the Hellion test. No one can be initiated into the group without undergoing trial by nitrous oxide, for it seems to make men unusually candid."

Grateful to be able to lower his guard, Lucien asked, "Does anyone ever fail?"

"Not usually, but you might have. I wondered why you wanted to join us—complicated men make me wary. But I can understand being bored with too much sobriety. We will cure that. For men of wealth and breeding like us, pleasure is a duty." Mace inhaled deeply from a fresh bladder of gas, and his bloodshot eyes glowed with inner fire. "Simple animal satisfactions are available to all, but refinements of ecstasy require talent and imagination. You will learn, Strathmore, you will learn."

Mace rose and signaled to a footman to bring them two fresh gasbags. To Lucien he said, "Since you will be one of us, I can show you something special."

Dizziness swept through Lucien when he stood. He caught the back of his chair. After his head steadied, he followed Mace from the room. He felt nothing when his thigh struck the sharp corner of a table. In fact, he could not feel his body at all. He was not so much numb as disconnected. Very strange.

Halfway up the staircase, he turned and looked down at the foyer floor. If he fell down the steps and smashed into the marble squares, he wouldn't feel that, either.

"C'mon," Mace said, his impatient voice faintly slurred. "You're one of the few who can fully appreciate these."

Lucien obediently continued up a second flight of stairs and along a corridor that led to the back of the house. There Mace unlocked a door that opened into a room with a worktable in the center and glass cases lining the walls.

As Mace lit a lamp, Lucien said rather unnecessarily, "You keep your collection of mechanicals here." He looked into a case and saw a group of three figures, one of which appeared to be in the process of chopping off the head of another. "Bavarian?"

Mace nodded. "John the Baptist being beheaded. Very rare. But it's nothing compared to the ones I design myself." Using a small key that doubled as a watch fob, he opened the one cabinet that had opaque doors. Then he brought out a mechanical device and set it on the table. After a lengthy key winding, he stepped back so that his guest could see the device clearly.

It consisted of two exquisitely sculpted figures, a naked woman and an equally naked man lying between her legs. With a metallic rasp of gears, they began fornicating.

Lucien stared at the bare, pumping male buttocks and the female arms that flailed in mock ecstasy. The sight triggered an inner coldness so profound that even the euphoria generated by the gas could not dispel it. Mace's prized "toy" was a caricature of sexuality, a symbol of the mindless, mechanical copulation that Lucien loathed in real life. In his present uninhibited state, he wanted nothing more than to sweep the ugly thing to the floor and smash it to pieces.

The impulse was so strong that his arm trembled with the effort of holding it still. In a voice of careful neutrality, he said, "I've never seen anything like it. Excellent craftsmanship. You have an ... ingenious mind."

"There cannot be another collection on earth like this. I design the devices and build the mechanisms, and a metalsmith makes the figures." Mace brought out another specimen. This one showed a woman with two men, each of them behaving in a most imaginative fashion. "I find the work ... exciting."

Lucien inhaled from the new bladder of gas, but it could not completely eliminate his distaste. Fortunately, Mace didn't look at his guest; he was too absorbed in admiring his little monstrosities. All Lucien had to do was make appropriately admiring remarks about the craftsmanship, with an occasional questions about unusual technical aspects.

When all of the devices were set on the table, they represented a gallery of sexual variations. Mace said in a roughened voice, "Help me wind them so all will operate at once."

Reluctantly Lucien complied, starting with a woman and a stallion. He hated touching the devices, but by ignoring what the figures represented, he managed his share of winding.

After the two men had worked their way from one end of the table to the other, there was perhaps ten seconds when all of the devices were working, filling the room with a chorus of mechanical buzzing. One of the figures—Lucien wasn't sure which—contained a small horn that crudely simulated bleats of rapture.

Mace stared at his prizes until the last one wound down. "I'm going to get one of the women downstairs," he said thickly. "Care to join me?"

Lucien bit back an honest reply. "No, thank you. I'm still dizzy from the gas."

Mace ushered his guest outside. "Dizziness passes quickly," he said as he locked the door. "If you need to lie down, the room across the hall is for guests."

Craving solitude, Lucien accepted the suggestion. The guest room was blessed quiet and dark. He found a chair by tripping over it and sat down. By the time he finished the last of the nitrous oxide, he was serene again. His mind drifted, afloat in a sea of unearned pleasure.

A rattle at the window roused him from lassitude. He glanced over and saw a lean black figure silhouetted against the glass like a human spider. An improbable sight; perhaps the gas was causing hallucinations.

The left-hand casement swung open, admitting a blast of frigid air along with a nimble human form. The burglar landed with a soft thump, then stood still, the labored sound of his breath filling the room.

A rational man would think twice about going after an intruder who might be armed, particularly if it wasn't even his own house. But Lucien was not rational at the moment. He rose and lunged at the burglar. He would have been successful if he hadn't bumped another chair in the darkness. It clattered to the floor, throwing him off-stride and alerting his quarry.

The intruder gave a sharp gasp of alarm, then dived out the window and vanished. Lucien blinked at the black rectangle of night sky and wondered if he had imagined the whole thing. But the window was certainly open. He leaned out and discovered a rope swaying two feet in front of him. Glancing up, he saw the dark shape of the burglar clambering onto the roof.

Driven by the same instinct that had sent him across the room, Lucien caught the rope and swung outdoors. As he climbed swiftly upward, the mental observer registered a bitter wind, but he felt no discomfort. The exhilaration of the drug still pulsed through his body, and he ascended as effortlessly as if he had wings. Even the awkward task of scrambling over the eaves onto the roof was accomplished with ease.

He released the rope and knelt on the flattened edge while he reconnoitered. The roof was shallow enough to walk on if care was used. Where was the burglar? Not to the right, where a broad expanse of slates stretched emptily. The fellow must have gone left, where a thrusting gable offered concealment.

Lucien's guess was confirmed when he realized that a faint slithering sound was the rope being pulled up and to the left. By the time he noticed, the end of the line was out of his reach.

The burglar must be just on the other side of the gable. Lucien swarmed upward, using the angle between main roof and gable to brace hands and feet and knees. As soon as he lifted his head above the peak of the gable, he was blasted by the full force of the wind. He ducked and steadied himself with a hand on the ridge pole while he looked for his quarry.

Though his black clothing rendered him almost invisible, the burglar was betrayed by his own swift movements. He had crossed Mace's roof and was halfway over the next house as well.

Lucien followed, the hunter instinct singing in his veins with the same exultation that he felt when soaring on horseback over fields and fences. He laughed aloud as he glided over the treacherous slates. Foxes and thieves were only an excuse; what mattered was the pursuit.

The god of the hunt protected him so that he could travel at a speed that swiftly closed the distance between him and his quarry. His mind scarcely connected with his body, he flung himself from gable to chimneys and onto the roof of the next house.

The thief glanced back and spat out an unintelligible oath when he saw that he was still being pursued. Then he launched himself over the gap that separated the second house from the next in the row. On the other side he caught at what appeared to be a rope that he had left earlier. After regaining his footing, he darted across the slates and vanished over another gable, taking the rope with him.

When he reached the edge of the roof, Lucien leaped over the gap without hesitating., But his luck had run out. The roof was pitched more steeply than the previous two, and his feet went out from under him when he landed. He hit hard and rolled, then began sliding down the slates on his belly.

He tried to stop his descent, but there was nothing to cling to. His fingertips skidded over the icy film that cov-

ered the slates. With a sense of mild wonder he realized
he was plunging inexorably to his death. The drug that
clouded his mind bestowed a careless blessing by also
blocking fear and pain.

Yet though his mind was indifferent to imminent
death, his body reflexively fought for survival, scratching
and clawing at the flat, slick stones. On the very edge of
the roof, his flailing hand found a small decorative stone
rim. It slowed his slide, and he found himself teetering
precariously on the edge, his head and shoulders suspended over three and a half stories of dark nothingness
as he clung by his fingertips.

Gravity was his enemy, and very soon it would defeat
him. It was a damned foolish way to die.

A sharp voice barked, "Catch this!"

Lucien looked up and had a brief impression of something flying toward him from the shadows cast by a clus-
ter of chimneys. Before he could register what it was, a
bristly rope end struck him in the face. He lost his tenuous grip on the eaves and plunged headfirst from the
roof.

As he fell, by sheer luck he managed to catch the rope
with his left hand. The line went taut, and his fall ended
with a jerk that tore viciously at the muscles of his arm
and shoulder. He ended up swinging one-handed over
the void, the wind whistling around him. At first he simply hung there blissfully, entranced by the sheer improb-
ability of his situation.

Reality intruded when he realized that his strained
fingers were gradually losing their grip. He caught the
rope with his other hand and clambered upward with the
same bizarre buoyancy that had gotten him into this fix.

After he hauled himself safely onto the slates, he
crouched on his hands and knees and fought for breath.
He felt no pain, yet his body insisted on shaking
violently.

A low voice cut across the wind, saying, "Thank God!"
What a very peculiar burglar. Lucien must meet him.

He scrambled up the roof to the chimneys, supported
by the rope. By the time he reached his destination, the
thief was retreating, but still close enough for Lucien to

grab the back of the man's jacket. "Not so fast, my larcenous friend. I must thank you for saving my life."

The thief tried to tear himself free, but he lost his footing on the icy slates and crashed back onto Lucien. Together they fell into the safe angle between chimney and roof, Lucien on the bottom, his quarry sprawled full-length on top of him.

After Lucien caught his breath, he realized that there was something very familiar about the lithe shape of the thief. And also about the elusive, spicy fragrance of carnation, which was not at all what one would expect of a housebreaker.

He had recently met someone else who wore the scent of carnations. With a feeling of inevitability, he yanked off the black scarf that concealed the burglar's features. The pale oval face was instantly recognizable even in the dark.

Lucien grinned as he settled the long, delightfully feminine length of her against him. "So we meet again, Lady Jane. Or whatever you're calling yourself tonight. It's beginning to seem that we are fated to be together."

"This is farce, not fate," Jane snapped.

She punctuated her remark with an elbow in Lucien's belly as she tried to break free. It would have hurt if his body and mind were properly connected. "You must have a passion to be transported to New South Wales," he remarked as he used a firm embrace to immobilize her arms, "or you wouldn't have broken into a house where a party was in progress."

"I thought Lord Mace must be away because most of the windows were dark." Deprived of her arms, she tried to knee him in the groin.

Fortunately, he was holding her close enough so that she didn't have the leverage to do any damage. "You're very strong for a woman," he said rather breathlessly. "Of course if you weren't, you wouldn't be swinging over the rooftops of London like a demented monkey."

"You should talk! You were taking insane chances. It's amazing you didn't fall sooner." The heels of her hands and her elbows ground into him as she tried to slither from his arms. "Let me go, you big oaf!"

"But I don't *want* to let you go," he said with breath-taking simplicity. "And at the moment I'm doing only what I want."

"I should have let you fall off the roof!"

"Very likely," he agreed. "But since you didn't, I have a better idea."

He kissed her.

Chapter 9

Infuriatingly, Kit found herself responding to Strathmore's kiss. It was madness when they were sprawled on an icy roof and she had just committed a capital crime, yet the man's humor and sensuality were irresistible. His arms were a warm haven against the cruel night, his mouth and teasing tongue an invitation to erotic pleasures.

As her body softened, he released his steely grip and began caressing her. Even with layers of winter clothing between them, her skin tingled wherever he touched her. One large hand glided over her hip and under her coat, then began stroking the small of her back with a gentle rhythm that eased her tense muscles. Inch by inch, lips and hands and torso, she yielded, instinctively molding her body to his.

She didn't realize that he had tugged her shirt loose from her breeches until his bare hand touched her naked back. It would have been one more sweet delight if his fingers hadn't been ice cold. Mood shattered, she gave a squeak of shock and broke away. "This is absurd," she said crossly, as if she hadn't been an enthusiastic participant. "You can stay here if you like, but I'm getting off this roof before I freeze to death."

He raised his hand and brushed her cheek with gossamer tenderness. "I'll keep you warm."

As he tried to draw her face down for another kiss, she hastily pushed herself upright and sat back on her heels against the chimney. He was different tonight, moving and speaking with a lazy deliberation unlike the focused intensity of earlier occasions. Guessing the reason why, she said tartly, "You're drunk. No wonder you're behaving like an idiot."

He ran his fingers through his tousled hair. "Not ... not drunk," he said with precision. "Nitrous oxide."

That explained why she hadn't tasted alcohol when they kissed. "Degenerate," she muttered. "Though what else could one expect of a Hellion?"

"It's interesting stuff," he protested. "Makes one very frank. And frankly, my little felon, I want you." He sat up and reached for her again. "I've never kissed a criminal before."

She didn't know whether to laugh or push him down the slates. She settled for batting his hand away. "I'm not little—I'm as tall as many men. Now I'm going to take the rope and get down before whoever lives in this house hears us scampering overhead and sends for the watch."

He laughed. "The watch has too much sense to be out on a night like this."

"Then we should show equal sense," she retorted. "Are you capable of climbing down without breaking your neck?"

He considered carefully. "I think so."

It was not a reassuring statement, but his strength and instinct for self-preservation and athletic skill had saved him before. Since climbing down the back of the house would put them in a walled garden, she took one end of the rope, checked that it was still securely tied to the chimney, then crawled to the side of the house that overlooked the alley.

No one was in sight and the windows were dark, so she wrapped the rope around her waist and prepared to descend. "When I reach the ground, I'll tug on the rope twice," she said to Strathmore, who had followed her. "Then you come down, and for heaven's sake, be careful."

After the tricky maneuver of swinging from roof to rope, she descended in a controlled slide, her leather gloves protecting her hands from being rasped raw. She reached the ground safely, only to slip on a patch of ice

directly under the rope, Luckily she was still holding onto
the line, which kept her from falling.

She stepped away cautiously, then signaled to Strathmore. As soon as she was on the ground, she would be
away at a speed that would do credit to a frightened
hare. The tipsy earl would be on his own, and good
riddance.

He made the descent so quickly that she wondered
about the condition of his bare hands. Telling herself
that it was none of her concern, she gathered herself for
flight. Then Strathmore hit the ice below the rope and
went down hard. She winced at the violence of the impact. "Are you all right?"

"I believe so." He started to rise, then went down
again as his right ankle folded under him. "Then again,
maybe I'm not."

"Damn!" Kit said with feeling. "Have you broken
your leg?"

"I don't think so." He probed the limb in question.
"This ankle gives way whenever it's abused. In a day or
two it should be fine." With the aid of the rope he pulled
himself up, then leaned heavily against the wall of the
house.

"Does it hurt badly?"

"My dear, nothing hurts at the moment." He chuckled.
"I could have my foot hacked off with a dull knife and
not notice. If I'm ever forced to submit to the surgeon's
knife, I intend to saturate myself with nitrous oxide first."
He took a cautious step and went down to his knee.
"However, though my ankle doesn't hurt, it's showing a
certain stubbornness about walking."

Kit sighed. "I'll help you to Lord Mace's front door.
Please don't knock until I've had a chance to get away."

"I appreciate the offer," he said politely, "but I'd really rather not return to Mace's house."

"If you stay outside in your condition without so much
as a cloak to keep you warm, you'll be dead before
dawn," she pointed out, trying to hold on to her temper.

"I live about two blocks away. Don't worry, I can hob-
ble that far on my own." He attempted to demonstrate
and almost fell again. If not for the wall, he would have.

Resigned, Kit slung his right arm over her shoulders. He was very large and very solid. "I'll help you home, if you think you can stay out of further trouble for that long."

"No guarantees, my dear." In spite of everything, there was laughter in his voice.

Trying not to think of the lean, hard length of his body, she headed toward the street. They must look like two drunks helping each other home. "If you hadn't interfered," she said acidly, "I would have been able to leave at my leisure and escape with my rope. Now I'll have to buy a new one."

"I'll buy you another." He considered. "Then again, maybe I won't. The last thing I want is to encourage you in your life of crime. Not that you need any encouragement. I'd wager that you didn't ask for directions to my house since you already found out where it is while planing your burgling schedule. Am I right?"

Since he was, she didn't dignify the remark with an answer.

At first he kept up a flow of nonsensical chatter, but soon he fell silent, his breath becoming more labored. At least the vile weather meant the streets were deserted.

Half a block from their destination, they hit another patch of ice and both of them went down. Kit wasn't hurt, but the earl gave a sharp gasp. As she helped him up, he muttered, "The effect of the nitrous oxide is wearing off. Unfortunately."

The last two hundred yards seemed endless. When they finally reached his house, she frowned at the high marble steps. "I'll ring for your servants. It will take a couple of footmen to get you up to the door."

"There's a better way," he panted. "Down the alley."

By the time they reached a ground-level door at the rear of the house, she was so tired that she wasn't sure who was supporting whom. When he ordered, "Turn your back for a moment," she obeyed without even trying to cheat and steal a peek.

There was a sound of rasping stone, followed by a key grating in a lock. She turned back, curiosity revived. "If you keep a key hidden behind a brick, you must do this regularly. Why don't you use the front entrance like a proper earl?"

"I like to come and go unobserved sometimes." He opened the door into a drab hall lit by a small oil lamp.

"I'm beginning to think you're as big a sneak as I am." She helped him inside, thinking that it was dangerous to feel such comradeship with a suspect. "Since there's a cane in the corner, I assume that you can get upstairs on your own." She lifted the cane and handed it to him. "Good night, Lord Strathmore."

She had left escape too late. Before she could take a step, a long, powerful arm wrapped around her waist, stopping her in her tracks. "Not so fast, my felonious friend."

She tensed for battle, but he said reassuringly, "Truce, my dear, at least for tonight. It would be ungentlemanly to turn you over to the law when you saved my life."

"Then what do you want?" she asked warily.

"I want you to come upstairs and warm yourself so that you don't end up frozen in a gutter somewhere."

The earl was right; now that his warm body was no longer draped over her, she was shivering uncontrollably. After he closed and locked the door, she accompanied him up the stairs.

Though Strathmore leaned heavily on the cane, he managed quite well without Kit's help. She wondered if he had exaggerated his injury in order to get her to come with him. Very likely; it was obvious the earl was devious—exactly the sort of villain she was hunting for.

Yet in spite of her misgivings, she could not fear him. She felt an odd kind of rapport between them, a sense that they were kindred spirits. Rationally, she knew that the feeling was an illusion brought on by her need for companionship. She had never been good at being alone, and it was hideously tempting to turn her problems over to someone else. If only she dared trust Strathmore! She might take the risk if hers was the only life at stake, but she could not gamble with the safety of another.

Yet even if the earl was a monster, for tonight she was safe; rescuing him had given her a margin of grace. She winced at the memory of her terror when he was sliding to his death. Alarming and inconvenient Strathmore might be, but she didn't want him dead.

When they reached the next floor, he led her to the library, where the coals of a banked fire glowed. Kit went to the fireplace and knelt to build up the fire while Strathmore used the lamp to light a branch of candles. Then he limped to a cabinet and brought out a brandy decanter and two glasses. He poured a generous measure into each glass and emptied his in a single gulp. After refilling it, he sat in one of the wing chairs that bracketed the fireplace and began to wrestle with his boots. The left one came off easily, but the one on his injured leg proved more difficult.

Once the fire was burning briskly, Kit took a mouthful of brandy. The potency made her blink, but it certainly was warming. After a more cautious sip, she went to help the earl.

As she bent to grasp the boot, she felt a light touch on her head as he pulled her scarf down around her shoulders. "This is finally your real hair color, isn't it? Pretty."

She looked up and her breath caught. His eyes were golden, the warmth more intoxicating than brandy.

Trying to sound nonchalant, she said, "It's merely light brown, as undistinguished as hair can be."

He brushed back the strands which had escaped from the knot at her nape. "You do your hair a disservice. It's like shot silk, shimmering with streaks of amber and bronze."

She shivered when his fingertips grazed her temple. As a rake, he was first class. Determinedly she bent and tugged at his boot, but without success. Hearing his sharp, painful inhalation, she said, "It might be best to cut this off."

"And ruin my best pair of top boots?" he said, scandalized. "Try again. I'll survive."

Kit shrugged, then pulled with all her strength, almost landing on the floor when the boot suddenly came off. A spasm crossed his face and he bit off an oath.

Gently she touched the swollen ankle. "Are you sure this isn't broken?"

"Quite." He removed his cravat and used it to fashion a crude bandage around the ankle. Then he pulled up an upholstered stool and rested his injured leg across it. "As I said, this has happened before. It's only a sprain."

"A pity you don't have any more nitrous oxide to blot out the pain."

He made a face. "It was an interesting experience, but not one I care to repeat. Nitrous makes one lose control, which is not a state I enjoy."

"That news does not surprise me." Feeling a need to fuss, she found a folded blanket on the sofa and spread it over the earl. Then she took off her damp coat and scarf, retrieved her glass and settled in the chair on the opposite side of the fire.

Strathmore slouched back with a sigh. "What a very strange night this has been." He cocked an eyebrow at her. "I must congratulate you on your lying. I pride myself on being able to read people well, but you certainly fooled me at Chiswick's house. What the devil are you really up to?"

Her mouth tightened. "I should have known that you invited me in for an interrogation. It would have been wiser to take my chances with the cold."

"I'd have to be dead not to be curious," Lucien said dryly. "You were very convincing as a distressed sister. Do you really have a brother?"

She glanced down at the glass in her hands. "If I was convincing, it was because there was a . . . a core of emotional truth in what I said. However, the story was false. I have no brother, in the army or otherwise."

"Then why are you stalking the Hellions?"

She looked up again, her expression challenging. "Why should I answer your questions?"

"Does the fact that I am twice your size and notoriously ruthless count for anything?"

Sudden laughter lit her grave face. "Not tonight, my lord. Quite apart from having called a truce, you can't move fast enough to catch me."

He gave her a ferocious scowl. "It's a sad day when a man can't get any respect in his own home."

When she laughed again, he asked softly, "Who are you?"

She almost answered, but caught herself. "Diabolical man! Trying to disarm me with humor." She set her brandy glass down with a clink. "But you won't catch me that easily."'

"Ah, well, it was worth a try." His levity faded. "There may be a truce between us tonight, but I can't allow you to continue your criminal activities. Quite apart from being illegal, housebreaking is a damned dangerous pastime."

"If you're so moral, why are you a Hellion?"

He had wondered when she would point that out. "I'm not an official member of the club, though I will be soon."

Surprised, she said, "Why are you bothering to join? That lot hardly seem to be your sort."

"I have friends of many kinds. The Hellions are amusing, in an uncomplicated way. For more cerebral companionship, I look elsewhere." He regarded her thoughtfully over the rim of his glass as he took a sip. "My excuse is low tastes, but what is your interest in the group? You've been amazingly persistent."

Indecision on her face, she rose and began prowling about the room, moving with lithe, unconscious grace. The masks she had worn in their previous encounters had dropped away to reveal a glimpse of the real woman.

Yet still she was a paradox. In his work he had met more than his share of daredevils—usually male but sometimes female—who thrived on danger and taking risks. Jane was not one of that number, for she seemed to find no pleasure in her bold feats. There was a diffidence about her that was very real, yet it was coupled with the steely, bone-deep strength that had sent her into the lions' den time and time again.

Decision made, she swung around to face him. "Since there is a truce between us, and you are not yet an initiated Hellion, I will tell you the truth. You show signs of a conscience—perhaps what I say will persuade you to withdraw from the group."

The nitrous oxide must still be affecting him, for he said irrepressibly, "The truth will be a pleasant change."

She scowled. "This is not a laughing matter. I am a journalist. I write essays and articles for several periodicals. I have been working on an exposé of the Hellion Club. In theory it is no worse than any other group of privileged, debauched men, but I have received information that some of their practices surpass the wickedness of the original Hellfire Club."

"Such as?"

"Kidnapping and murdering innocent young girls as part of their ceremonies," she said bluntly.

He sobered instantly. "Appalling if true."

"I'm quite sure it's true."

He thought of the members he knew. Impossible to believe that young Lord Ives, for examples, would condone ritual murder. "I have trouble believing that most of the Hellions would participate in such activities."

"You're probably right. I think that the viciousness is limited to an inner circle."

"The Disciples?"

She gave him a hard look. "You are familiar with them?"

"I know only that the Disciples exist, not their identities or what their purpose is. Do you think they are using the larger group to disguise their activities?"

"Exactly. I have some evidence, but I want more before I write my article."

"What kind of evidence have you found?"

"I met a girl who managed to escape from where she was being held prisoner. She told me what she had heard from her abductors and from some of the servants. Because her information was limited, I have been trying to learn more."

He drummed his fingertips on the arm of his chair. "It's rare enough for a young woman to be a journalist, but to pursue a topic like this strains credulity."

"In other words you think I'm lying again?" she snapped. "If there were more female journalists, there would be more writing on such subjects. England is full of women and children who have been brutalized, a situation many men consider normal."

Her words burned with conviction. They also produced a faint echo in the back of his mind. Something he had read ... "What is your name? Perhaps I have seen some of your articles."

"Since no female essayist would be taken seriously, I write under several different names, depending on the publication."

That was plausible; most of the scribblers who wrote for the diverse, lively popular press had multiple identities. "I read widely. What is a name that you use regularly?"

She hesitated. "Do I have your word not to reveal it?" After he nodded, she said, "For the *Examiner*, I am L. J. Knight."

"Good God!" he exclaimed. The weekly newspaper she named was noted for its courage and reforming zeal; in fact, the two brothers who edited it were currently in jail for their disrespectful treatment of the Prince Regent. "L. J. Knight, the radical firebrand, is a young woman?"

"One doesn't need to be either male or old to see that there are many things in our society that need changing. In fact, my youth and sex are advantages, for I see the world differently from male writers," she said coolly. "I was twenty when I first submitted an essay to the *Examiner*. Leigh Hunt bought it immediately and asked for more."

Still not quite believing her, Lucien said, "I'm surprised that I've never heard that L. J. Knight is female."

"I communicate with Leigh Hunt and my other editors by post or special messenger."

Wanting to test her, he said, "I thought you were a bit hard on Lord Castlereagh in that piece you did on him last summer."

"You have confused me with another journalist. I've never written about the foreign minister." The ironic gleam in her eyes showed that she had recognized the attempted trap.

He considered more brandy, but decided that he

needed all of his wits. "Have you learned much by burgling the Hellions?"

"Not as much as I would have if you didn't continually get in the way," she said, humor tempering her exasperation. "However, housebreaking is only part of my investigation. Evidence is mounting, and soon I'll be ready to write my piece."

"What have you learned?"

She shook her head. "I would be a fool to say more."

He studied the slim, feminine figure with respect. It took courage to challenge wickedness armed with only a pen. "My dear, you are a constant source of surprises."

"As are you. For a professional wastrel, you have a remarkably inquisitive mind." She cocked her head. "Do you call all women 'my dear'?"

"Only those I like. Which is quite a number, actually."

"One would expect that of a rake."

"I said like, not lust after," he said dryly. "Those are two entirely different things."

"It's rare, I think, for men to genuinely like women. Why are you different?"

"When I was a child, my closest companion was female," he replied after an infinitesimal pause. "Besides, I still don't know your true name, so 'my dear' is safely neutral."

She smiled a little. "I actually am named Jane."

"Lydia Jane Knight? Or Louise or Laura?"

"I've told you as much as I intend to, my lord, so you can stop asking questions." She gave him a level look. "Now that I've told you the truth, do you understand why I have been investigating the Hellions?"

"Yes, but I still don't approve. You're playing with fire."

"Then perhaps I'll burn." She stood and donned her coat, which had been gently steaming by the fire. "So be it. Good night, my lord."

As she started wrapping her scarf around her head, Lucien hauled himself from his chair, grabbed his cane, and limped over to her. "Not yet. As I said once before, I want to see you again. Where do you live?"

She sighed. "You're very persistent."

"It's a quality you should understand. And that is hardly the only thing we have in common." He raised his free hand and gently stroked the tender curve of her jaw with his knuckles. "We are not enemies, you know."

She stepped back. "I am less sure of that than you."

"Can you deny that there is an attraction between us?"

"Even I am not that good a liar," she said sardonically. "But attraction is a small, unimportant thing. It may be hard for you to believe that a woman can be more interested in justice and the life of the mind than in men, but that is the case with me. We live in different worlds, Lord Strathmore."

"Is this small and unimportant?" He drew her into his arms and kissed her, not with the drug-hazed delight he had felt on the rooftop, but with the emotions that had been building since they had met. Passion, yearning, hope.

Her hands came to rest on his forearms, opening and closing spasmodically as his hand circled her breast. Through the layers of fabric he felt her nipple hardening against his palm. She filled his senses, touch and sound and scent.

When he bent his head to kiss her throat, she whispered, "Don't, Lucien. I . . . I can't afford to be distracted by desire. You're just giving me more reasons to avoid you."

The delicious sound of his name on her lips obliterated the sense of her words. When she took a halfhearted step backward, he followed, then gasped as agony jolted through his forgotten ankle. "Damnation!" Sweat filming his brow, he caught a chair to save himself from falling. "Remarkable how pain overcomes lust."

"If I'd known that, I'd have been tempted to kick you in the ankle earlier." Pulling her coat tightly around her, she headed for the door. "It's time for me to go."

He lifted a lamp and followed her. "I'll light you out." He gave her a smile that was as dangerously seductive as his kisses. "With a cane in one hand and a lamp in the other, there isn't much I can do in the way of seduction. Though if I think about it, perhaps I could come up with something."

"Then don't think about it," she said. Yet when they reached the stairs, she silently took the lamp so he could grasp the railing. It was another example of the odd way they worked together, an instinctive harmony she had known with only one other person.

They did not speak until they reached the side door. He turned the key in the lock, but kept one hand securely on the knob as he asked, "Where do you live, Jane?"

In the lamplight, his eyes were lucent gold. She was no match for a man like this, she thought despairingly. He was a master of mysteries she had never learned, and he used his knowledge with ruthless gentleness, beguiling rather than compelling her.

Knowing she must leave before her last grain of sense disappeared, she said rapidly, "Wardour Street. I have a flat at number 96. But what I said earlier was the truth, Lord Strathmore. There is no place in my life for you."

"Places can be created." He released the doorknob and stepped back, allowing her to slip past him.

The weather was even worse than earlier. Luckily her destination was only a few blocks away. As she made her way through the silent streets, she found herself wondering again what it would be like to be free to reciprocate his interest. If his intentions were honorable, not villainous ... if she successfully completed her mission....

Yet no matter how hard she tried, she could not imagine them together in any meaningful way. She had played a variety of roles and would play more, but none of her identities belonged in the Earl of Strathmore's wealthy, glittering world.

Chapter 10

After Jane left, Lucien was so tired he could barely manage the three flights of stairs to his room. Yet when he dropped into the bed, ankle throbbing, he felt deeply pleased. His mystery lady had admitted to a mutual attraction, and while she was still doubtful, the first steps toward a more rewarding relationship had been taken. Jane. He turned the name over in his mind. He didn't really see her as a Jane, but he was becoming accustomed to the name. Jane, quietly sensual, diffident but determined, with a tart tongue and the heart of a lioness.

It had been a pleasure to see her without wigs and cosmetics. Finally, he had an authentic face to visualize. He liked her softly waving hair, and her unpainted complexion had the delicate translucence of pearl. Most of all, he liked the intelligence and individuality that radiated from her now that she was no longer in disguise. He drifted off to sleep thinking of clear gray eyes and the soft warmth of her slim body.

The nitrous oxide left a parting gift: a restless night full of lurid dreams. The first was of passion with Jane, who was a dozen women in one while always gloriously herself. Yet after matchless fulfillment, she began to dissolve in his arms. He tried to hold her, but she vanished into the shadows, leaving him alone with a soul-destroying sorrow.

He awoke at dawn drenched with sweat. The images were already fading away, leaving only a haunting sense of loss. Perhaps the dreams were a warning to avoid Jane in the future. The more he wanted her, the more it would hurt if emotional intimacy proved unattainable. It was no accident that he had led a life of near-celibacy for years, and surely it would be wiser for him to continue on his solitary way.

His mouth thinned. It was too late to turn back—whatever the cost, he must continue his pursuit, for Jane had taken possession of his mind and imagination as no woman ever had. He would take his chances.

As he rang for tea, he told himself dryly that if there was a message in his dreams, it was to keep away from nitrous oxide. The brief euphoria had come at an exhausting price.

Lucien's ankle had improved overnight. After a thorough soak and expert bandaging by his valet, he could walk well enough to go out. As a concession to his injury, he rode in a closed carriage rather than driving himself.

Inevitably, his destination was Wardour Street. It was in Soho, an area known for artists, writers, eccentrics, and foreigners, just the sort of place where one would expect to find an independent woman such as Jane.

As he climbed from his carriage, cane in hand, anticipation bubbled inside him like champagne. He hoped she was in; if so, he would ask her out for a drive. It would be a pleasure to see her in daylight instead of the dead of night. Their relationship to date couldn't have been more nocturnal if they had been bats.

He grinned when he saw that the other side of the street boasted a tavern called the Intrepid Fox. It seemed appropriate, though Jane would more properly be called an intrepid vixen.

His anticipation began to fade when he studied number 96. It appeared to belong to a single household rather than being divided into flats. Still, appearances could be misleading. He gave a sharp rap with the brass knocker.

A trim parlor maid answered the door, her eyes widening as she saw the elegant gentleman on the steps. Using his most ingratiating smile, he said, "My cousin asked me to pay a call on her friend Jane at this address, but I'm afraid that I don't remember the young lady's last name. Is Miss Jane in?"

"Oh, there are no young ladies living here, sir." The parlor maid giggled. "Except me, of course, but I'm a

Molly, not a Jane. Are you sure you have the right address?"

Cold rage washed through him, and his hand tightened on the cane. The devious little witch had made a fool of him again. He stood very still until he had mastered himself enough to say evenly, "Very likely I made a mistake. Perhaps number 69 is the house I want. If not, I shall write my cousin and ask for clarification."

With a polite tip of his hat, he turned and limped back to his carriage. Bloody hell, how could he have been so stupid as to believe she had told the truth? He'd like to blame the nitrous oxide for his misjudgment, but the real intoxicant was Jane, or whatever her name was, the only woman he had ever met who could turn his brain to rubble.

As he climbed into the carriage, he ordered his coachman, "Head for Westminster Bridge. I want to go to Surrey Gaol."

Leigh Hunt glanced absently up from his desk when the cell door creaked open. Recognizing his visitor, he stood with a pleased smile. "Strathmore, good of you to call."

The two men shook hands. Having visited the editor before, Lucien was not surprised by the rose-trellised wallpaper that brightened the stone walls, nor by the blue sky and clouds painted on the ceiling. Leigh Hunt was not the man to let a small thing like incarceration spoil his enjoyment of life.

A guard entered with a large vase of flowers. "I saw a vendor with these and thought you might enjoy them," Lucien explained as the guard set the vase on top of the pianoforte.

"Thank you." The editor stroked the bright petals of a chrysanthemum. "They are splendid for so late in the year."

"You're due to be released soon, aren't you?"

"February." Leigh Hunt grimaced. "And counting the days. I've made this cell as comfortable as possible, but when all is said and done, it's still a prison." He waved toward a chair. "Please, sit down and tell me what's happening in town."

"Since you are editing the *Examiner* from this cell, you probably know more than I do. Still, you may not have heard ..." Lucien recounted several anecdotes his host would enjoy.

Gradually Lucien worked the conversation to the subject that had brought him to the jail. "By the way, I heard a rumor that one of your writers, L. J. Knight, is really a woman."

Leigh Hunt laughed heartily. "What utter nonsense!"

"I thought the story seemed unlikely," Lucien agreed. "What is Knight really like? From his idealism, I assume he's young."

"I really don't know. I've never met him in person; we deal through the post."

Interesting. Lucien asked, "Knight lives in the country?"

"No, he's a Londoner."

"So it is possible that Knight could be a female who uses a nom de plume to conceal her sex."

The editor shook his head. "Theoretically possible, perhaps, but no woman could write such powerful, well-reasoned essays."

If Leigh Hunt had ever met a female like Jane, he might be less sure of that. Of course she might have lied about being L. J. Knight, but Lucien was inclined to believe her; her zeal and knowledge of public affairs had been convincing. "Do you think Knight would mind if I called on him? I'd like to shake his hand. I don't always agree with his opinions, but he has an insightful mind. It's a pleasure to read his essays."

Leigh Hunt frowned. "I doubt if he would welcome visitors. I believe his health is poor, so he lives very retired."

Lucien gave a small nod. To be an invalid was the perfect disguise for an unconventional woman, and exactly the sort of cleverness he would expect of Jane.

"I wouldn't want to overtax the fellow's strength," he said piously, "but I have a proposal for him. The war is over and it's time for Britain to look ahead. I'd like to publish a pamphlet about my economic and social ideas. However, I'm an indifferent writer so I need to hire someone to present my views effectively. If you can give me Knight's address, I'll send a note and ask if he would consider the project. If he's not interested, I shan't disturb him."

The editor hesitated. "Knight has always refused to allow me to call. Still, it's a rare scribbler who isn't interested in more work, especially with a gentleman as generous as you. His address is 20 Frith Street."

Soho again. Lucien did not think it was a coincidence. Since Jane had also come up with a Soho address when he had pressed her, there was a good chance that she lived in the area. That narrowed his search down to manageable proportions. He steered the conversation to other subjects, and after a few more minutes he took his leave.

On the ride back to London, he weighed what he had learned. In his work he had met many kinds of liars, including those who told falsehoods for sport, and those who could not tell illusion from reality. Jane was not like that; her lies were told for a purpose. He supposed he couldn't blame her for lying about where she lived since he had been pressing her to reveal what she preferred to conceal. But though his anger lessened, his determination to find her did not.

It was late, so the visit to Frith Street must wait until the next day. He wondered what he would find there; devious Jane probably had her mail sent someplace other than her home. But the address might lead to something else.

Since nothing more could be done about her for the time being, he turned his thoughts to the Phantom. A French spy was more important than finding one maddening young lady.

His head knew that, but his heart didn't.

Wearing a drab cloak and a deep poke bonnet that shadowed her face, Kit entered the greengrocer's shop. The owner, a stout, middle-aged woman with a pleasant face, was busy with an elderly customer, but she gave Kit a quick smile of welcome.

Kit busied herself inspecting the produce until the other customer was gone. Then she said, "Good morning, Mrs. Henley."

"It's good to see you again, miss. It's been too long," the other woman said affably. "What's your pleasure today?"

"A dozen leeks, please, and two pounds of those fresh Brussels sprouts." As Mrs. Henley selected the vegetables, Kit murmured, "Someone might come by and ask about L. J. Knight. Probably a very charming, very persuasive gentleman."

Mrs. Henley said, "Don't worry, lass, he'll learn nothing from me."

"The less you say, the better, for he's a clever fellow."

Another customer came into the shop, so Mrs. Henley said in a louder voice, "Would you like some of these oranges, miss? They're a bit dear, but ever so sweet."

"They do look good," Kit agreed. "I'll take six."

When the oranges had been added to her basket, she handed over the money for her purchases. Concealed among the smaller coins was a gold guinea. Softly she said, "This is to cover the cost of forwarding the mail. I don't want to collect it in person for the time being."

Mrs. Henley gave a conspiratorial smile as she pocketed the money. Then she turned to her new customer.

Soberly, Kit left the shop. She should never have told Lucien—she gave herself a mental shake and changed the name to Strathmore—so much. Granted, not all of it was true, but she didn't think it would take him long to separate the wheat from the chaff. He might be questioning Leigh Hunt right now, which would lead him straight to Mrs. Henley's shop.

He would also, she feared, be furious at her deception. It was ironic that she, who had always had a passion for the truth, was now telling so many different lies that it was hard to keep them all straight. That she had no choice did not make her feel much better.

With a sigh she set aside her concerns about Strathmore. It was time to start worrying about what she would be doing that night. It wouldn't do to get her anxieties mixed up.

Lucien was not surprised to find that number 20 Frith Street was a combination greengrocer's shop and postal receiving office. With a steady stream of mostly female customers coming and going all day, it would be easy for Jane to collect her letters unobtrusively.

When the customers realized that a man—not only that, but one of obvious wealth and position—had entered the shop, they began exchanging nervous glances. One by one, they hastened to complete their business and leave, though not without studying the intruder. He stood calmly, his hands folded on the head of his cane, but he found it secretly amusing that he could clear a shop by his mere presence.

When the other customers had left, the shopkeeper turned to him, showing no surprise at the sight of a fashionable gentleman among the baskets of turnips and potatoes. Very likely Jane had warned her that Lucien might come looking for L. J. Knight. "What can I do for you, sir?" the woman asked. "Some nice oranges, perhaps?"

To his regret, she did not look easily bribable. Any information he got would have to come by misdirection. "I'm looking for my uncle. He's a delightful old fellow, but not as steady as one would like. Periodically he runs away from home. I've heard that this time he has taken a flat in Soho and is having his mail sent to this address. His name is L. J. Knight. Does he collect his letters here?"

She looked startled, as if she had been expecting a different question. "Your uncle's name sounds familiar, but I can't put a face to him."

Lucien gave the woman a disarming smile. "May I be candid with you? We're afraid that this time the old boy has run off with an adventuress. Perhaps she is collecting his mail. Is this woman familiar?" He drew a sketch he had done of Jane from an inside pocket.

If he hadn't been watching the shopkeeper so closely,

he would have missed the slight, involuntary widening of her eyes. Lucien was willing to swear it was recognition.

After a moment she said, "Perhaps I've seen her, but I can't say for sure. It's not a memorable face."

Lucien did not agree with that, but it was true that Jane had no single feature that was distinctive. It would take an exceptional artist to capture her uniqueness, and his talent was not equal to the task.

Handing back the sketch, the shopkeeper remarked, "She doesn't look like an adventuress."

"That is what makes the woman so dangerous. Though she looks like butter wouldn't melt in her mouth, she has an alarming reputation. We fear she might injure Uncle James when she realizes that he has no money in his own right."

A spark of amusement showed in the shopkeeper's eyes as she recognized that Lucien was spinning tales. "If the girl becomes difficult, no doubt your uncle will come home."

"I hope so. He has not always shown good judgment where females are concerned." Lucien wondered wryly if he was talking about his mythical uncle or about himself.

After thanking the shopkeeper for answering his questions, he left. He could have a watch set on the shop, but doubted it would do much good. Jane was too clever to come in person now that Lucien knew about the place.

It would be more productive to have one of his inquiry agents ask for her around Soho, armed with the sketch. Though slow, such work often yielded results. In time he would find her.

But what would he do with her when he did?

Interlude

When she heard him enter the anteroom, she drained her tea and very carefully set down the cup. Then she stood and shook out the black hair that fell straight as a waterfall to her waist. Tonight she wore a black lace costume that fitted her like a second skin from deep décolletage to thigh-high boots. The open patterns of the lace teased the eye, pretending to reveal more of her body than they actually did.

Her lips tightened when she heard the small whirring sound from the next room. Grasping a whip, she swaggered out with the arrogance of a cavalryman. "Touch nothing without my permission, slave," she snarled as she slashed at his wrist.

Though it was the softest of the whips, the lash still raised a welt. He flinched and set down the mechanical device, but his eyes were glowing as he dropped to his knees. "I humbly beg your pardon, mistress."

She kicked him in the face, a glancing blow that avoided his eye and would leave only a slight mark. "I do not accept your apology, slave. You must be punished. Strip off your clothing so that you are as naked as other beasts."

He obeyed, his hands clumsy with eagerness as he bared his strong, leathery body. Then he crouched on his hands and knees. She laid the whip across his spine with furious strength. He gasped and raised his head to stare at her, pupils dark.

She had gone too far, too soon. This was the most difficult part, holding back while she slowly raised the level of pain. If she proceeded too quickly, she would lose him, and a great deal more.

She cracked the whip again, more gently, and he relaxed with a rasping moan of pleasure. As carefully as an artist painting a portrait, she began flicking the lash all over his body, monitoring his degree of arousal with hawklike intensity.

She also cursed him, calling him every filthy name she knew, telling him what an utterly loathsome creature he was. Her diatribe added fuel to the flame of his excitement.

When the soft whip reached the limit of its effectiveness, she exchanged it for one with a harder thong that raised blood at every blow. He began to writhe under the rhythm of her whip, welcoming strokes that would have been too painful earlier. Finally, she was free to strike with the full viciousness of her rage. She slashed him again and again, violence possessing her until she was scarcely human. His mewling cries became louder and louder, filling the room until his sweat-soaked body began shuddering with ecstasy.

Then it was over, and he lay sprawled on a sheepskin rug, his blood staining the white wool, his whole body limp with repletion. "You are superb, mistress," he panted. "Superb."

Choked with self-loathing, she spun on her heel and stalked from the room.

Chapter 11

Kit awoke shivering, her body drenched with sweat. It had been the most vivid nightmare yet, and it left her feeling nauseated. She tried to make sense of the images, but without success; the nightmare was so alien to her experience that it was like trying to understand Chinese. Only the emotions were recognizable: rage and anguish so intense that they threatened to drown her.

Viola rose from the foot of the bed and strolled up the blankets with a soft meow. Kit almost cried with relief when the cat gently butted her cheek in an unmistakable request for breakfast. The normalcy of the cat's plea helped Kit counter the torrent of misery that had engulfed her.

First she relaxed, muscle by muscle, until her shivering stopped. Then she filled her mind with positive emotions—peace, love, hope—until all of the wretchedness was washed away.

When calm had been restored, she climbed from the bed and drew on a robe against the chilly morning air. Then she draped Viola over her shoulder and headed to the kitchen, telling herself determinedly that she was making progress. She had gotten through the previous night without disgracing herself, and she had had the opportunity to study one of her suspects closely enough to eliminate him. Though that was negative information, it was another small step forward.

She fed the cat, put on the kettle, and brought out a loaf of bread. Then, as she lifted a knife to cut a slice, her mind suddenly flashed an image from the nightmare.

Though the details were vague, it was clearly some kind of mechanical toy. She froze, knife poised in midair

and stomach churning. She knew only one man capable
of creating such a device. Dear God, don't let it be Lucien, she prayed. Please don't let it be him.

Yet if it was . . .

She stared blindly at the glittering edge of the blade.
Even if the man she sought was the Earl of Strathmore,
she would not be deterred from her goal.

Glumly Lucien eyed the piles of information he had
gathered on the Hellions. It was a positive embar-
rassment of riches about their finances, their politics,
their love affairs, their public vices, and secret virtues.
Yet he knew no more after sifting through the material
than he had deduced through pure intuition. Most of
the Disciples had chronic financial problems. Several had
direct access to government secrets, and all moved in
circles where information might be gleaned from the
careless words of officials. Any one of them might have
taken French money.

He wasn't doing any better in his search for his mystery woman. For two days his investigator had been can-
vassing Soho with the sketch of Jane. Some residents and
shopkeepers thought she looked familiar, but no one
could put a name or address to her. Perhaps the flaw
was in the sketch, but he suspected that the problem
was her chameleonlike ability to look very different at
different times.

On impulse he decided to put his papers away and go
to dinner at his club. An amiable evening among friends
might clear his fuzzy thinking.

Business and pleasure combined when Lucien found
Lord Ives at his club. Though he did not suspect Ives of
being the Phantom, there was always a chance that the
youthful Hellion would say something interesting about
other members of the group. More to the point, Lucien
enjoyed the younger man's company. Anyone who could
laugh at himself after being whacked in the nose with a
bust improver was worth cultivating.

Over the port, Ives said, "I'll have to leave soon. I'm
going to the theater tonight."

"Drury Lane?"

"No, the Marlowe, that new place on the Strand. Have you been there?"

"Not yet, though I've been meaning to attend," Lucien said with a stir of interest. "I've heard that it's giving the two royal patent theaters a run for their money."

"It's true—they're first-rate at comedy." Ives grinned. "And they have the most luscious opera dancers in London."

"You have your eye on one?"

"I've had more than my eye on her," Ives said with a touch of endearingly youthful pride. "Would you care to join me tonight? I'm not meeting Cleo until afterward, and I'll have the whole box to myself. Tonight there will be a performance of the company's most popular play. I can vouch that it's very diverting."

"I'd like that. I've always enjoyed the theater, but lately I've been too busy to attend."

The younger man began discoursing knowledgeably about the stage, past and present. Clearly the subject was a passion with him. He also mentioned that he had met Lord Nunfield through a mutual interest in the theater, and that acquaintanceship had led Ives to the Hellions.

As they finished their port, Lucien remarked, "The theater is a special place, and its people are a special breed."

"I admire the carefree way they live their lives," Ives said pensively as they left the club dining room. "Wouldn't it be wonderful if all females were as uninhibited as actresses?"

"I'm not sure the world is ready for that." Lucien signaled for their hats and cloaks to be brought. "When you marry, will you want your wife to be as free as an opera dancer?"

Ives gave a rueful smile. "Point taken."

Each man took his own carriage so they could leave separately later. They reunited in the box lobby of the theater and went up immediately since the performance had already begun.

Only the two theaters that held royal patents, Drury Lane and Covent Garden, were allowed to present "serious" drama. Other theaters, such as the Marlowe, skirted the law by including music and dancing so performances could be billed as concerts. Lucien and Ives took their seats as the house orchestra finished a spirited rendition of Handel's "Water Music."

After the music came the main event. According to the playbill, the title was *The Gypsy Lass*. It was an enjoyable bit of nonsense that started with a dashing young nobleman called Horatio being disowned by his stern father, the Duke of Omnium, after a wicked cousin made it appear that Horatio had disgraced the family name. Brokenhearted, the young man went into the wilderness, where he was saved from death by a troop of Gypsies.

When Horatio joined his new friends for a feast around the campfire, Ives said quietly, "In a moment a chorus of girls will come out and dance. Cleo will lead the line."

Brilliantly costumed and jingling with coin necklaces, the girls pranced onstage. Cleo was a lively wench with a pretty face and a saucy eye. As she raised the tambourine over her head, which did impressive things to an already impressive figure, she glanced up at their box and grinned at Ives. She looked like the delightful answer to a young man's prayer.

Then the chorus fell back a few steps and another Gypsy girl spun onto the stage to dance a solo. Her appearance produced a wave of applause. The newcomer was not a great beauty, but she had in full measure the indefinable quality that makes the best performers able to rivet the attention of everyone within sight.

The girl pivoted and leaped joyously across the stage, her skirts rising to reveal a delicate gold chain around one shapely ankle. As the tempo increased, her skirts floated higher, allowing tantalizing views of her calves and an occasional glimpse of a knee. She had truly superior legs.

When the girl glided to a halt, her gaze met that of the enraptured Horatio. The two stared at each other. She had an elegant profile, as pure as a Greek coin. . . .

Lucien inhaled sharply, paralyzed by shock so intense

it was physical. It wasn't possible, it bloody wasn't possible. Tightly he asked, "May I borrow your opera glass?"

Ives handed the glass over obligingly. The magnification proved that Lucien's eyes had not betrayed him. The long limbs and classic profile were unmistakably Jane.

His knuckles whitened around the opera glass. The woman he had thought to be a reserved, idealistic bluestocking was an *actress*. An actress, moreover, who was not the least bit shy about exposing an indecent amount of her lovely body to a theater full of strangers.

He handed the opera glass back, allowing only mild curiosity in his voice. "Who is the solo dancer?"

"That's Miss James—Cassie James. She plays Anna, the romantic interest. She's very good, isn't she?"

She was more than good; she was stunning as she whirled back into action. There was a glow about her that lit up the stage, eclipsing the other actors.

As mesmerized as Lucien, Horatio rose from the campfire and began dancing with Anna. Flirtatiously, she tossed her black hair and flounced the foaming layers of her skirts as she danced, her hem going higher with every turn.

"Any moment now, we should see the famous tattoo," Ives said softly. "Watch for it above her right knee."

Sure enough, her skirts swirled high enough to expose a design on her inner thigh just above the knee. The sight provoked a deafening roar of male approval from the audience.

Anna obligingly flounced her skirts again, provoking more shouts. Lucien wanted to grind his teeth. "What is the tattoo, a flower?"

"No, a butterfly."

Ives handed back the opera glass, and on Anna's next kick Lucien was privileged to view a frivolous black-and-scarlet butterfly etched on the silken flesh of her inner thigh. He wanted to swath her in a cloak that would cover her from chin to toes. He wanted to wring her untrustworthy neck. He also wanted, rather desperately, to press his lips to that teasing, maddening butterfly, then let them drift higher. . . .

Feeling on the verge of suffocation, he closed his eyes

until he could breathe again. As he opened them, the curtain was descending for the interval. He turned to his companion. "Tell me about Cassie James."

"Taken with her, were you?" Ives grinned. "Well, they say she's destined to be as successful in comedy as Mrs. Jordan was. She started on the stage in London three or four years ago, I believe, but had only minor parts so she went to the provincial circuits. Two years ago I saw her in the Theatre Royal in York in a production of *She Stoops to Conquer,* and she was excellent. The manager of the Marlowe decided Cassie was ready for London, so he hired her for this season and wrote *The Gypsy Lass* for her. Both she and the play have been a great success."

Lucien didn't give a damn about her theatrical triumphs. "Does Miss James currently have a protector?"

"Not that I know of. I think she's the sort who prefers having a variety of lovers."

"Details, please."

"You really *are* interested, aren't you? Sorry, but I honestly don't know who has bedded her—she's fairly discreet for an actress. In York I saw her in the green room being rather brazen with some colonial—a Canadian, I think, or perhaps an American, but I have no idea what his name was." Ives thought a moment. "Nunfield was after her. I was with him the night she made her London debut this past September. He acted just as you're acting now."

Lucien's feeling of suffocation returned. "Did he succeed with her?"

"I don't think so, but again, I couldn't swear to it. I know he was prepared to offer her a very generous carte blanche."

Lucien wondered how many men "Jane" had lain with while acting like a distressed gentlewoman with him. *Acting.* That was the key. It explained the wigs, the makeup, the ability to assume different personalities. Even Ives, who knew Cassie James, rising comic actress, hadn't recognized her when he had made that drunken advance to Sally at the George and Vulture.

The only real question was why had she been stalking

the Hellions. One nauseating possibility was that she was Nunfield's mistress and had been spying on the group at his request, either for information or because the two of them found the idea perversely amusing. Or perhaps they had been lovers, and he had dismissed her, and now she was seeking some kind of revenge.

One thing was blindingly clear: once again, she had made a complete fool of Lucien.

The interval ended, and the next act of *The Gypsy Lass* began. Romance blossomed between Anna and Horatio, and they were on the verge of a Gypsy wedding. Then the Duke of Omnium appeared and begged his son's forgiveness for believing the wicked lies told by the cousin.

After reconciling with his father, Horatio asked Anna to be his bride, offering her luxury and a future as the next Duchess of Omnium. Tears in her eyes, she declined the offer because of her humble birth, saying she was unworthy to be a duchess.

As the two lovers were about to separate forever, the King of the Gypsies made a grand appearance, accompanied by the whole chorus of tambourine-thumping opera dancers. The king explained that Anna was really the daughter of an earl who had been stolen as an infant because of her exquisite beauty. Her breeding established as suitably aristocratic, Anna accepted Horatio's offer. The play ended with the whole cast, including the Duke of Omnium, dancing merrily around the campfire.

As Gypsy lore the play was ludicrous; Lucien made a mental note to tell Nicholas to see it, since his friend would find the depiction of the Rom uproarious. But as entertainment it worked, and Cassie James was the best part.

After the cast had made its bows and left the stage, Ives said, "I'm going to find Cleo now. Do you want to go down to the green room with me, or shall we say good night here?"

Lucien stood and lifted the cloak he had tossed over an empty chair. "I shall accompany you to the green room. I cannot tell you how much I am longing to meet the talented Miss James."

Chapter 12

The green room swarmed with exuberant actors, actresses, and their friends. The after-performance tumult always made Kit uneasy, so she held court with her back to the wall. A dozen men stood in a half circle in front of her, offering extravagant compliments and vying for her attention.

She had become adept at the suggestive banter that gentlemen enjoyed. When one admirer said, "You were like an angel tonight, Miss James," she replied mischievously, "If that's true, the angels had better reform."

The crowd around her laughed. A dandyish fellow said soulfully, "Are you sure you won't accept my carte blanche? I long to become your protector."

She eyed him thoughtfully. "Men are always trying to protect me. I can never figure out what from."

The group started offering boisterous suggestions of just which of them she most needed to be protected from. As they tossed names back and forth, she kept one eye on the rest of the green room, watching for surprise, or shock, or some other reaction that might be significant to her search.

Lord Ives had come, and he was now leaving the room with a smiling Cleo tucked under his arm. From what Cleo said, he was a decent young man. She saw no other Hellions. Those who were theatergoers must have long since seen *The Gypsy Lass*, so she was unlikely to learn much tonight.

She brought her attention back to her admirers when a sober young man tried to press a religious tract into her hand. "The theater is no life for a decent woman," he said earnestly. "Read this, and you'll see the error of your ways."

Declining the tract, she said with a wicked smile, "To err is human—and it feels divine."

In the roar of laughter that followed, the earnest young man beat a hasty retreat. A dignified older man said, "Goodness, but you have a quick tongue."

She batted her lashes extravagantly. "Goodness has nothing to do with it."

More laughter. She glanced across the room to see if anyone new had come in, then stiffened in shock. Lord Strathmore was stalking through the crowd toward her with the single-minded intensity of a hungry leopard.

She gave an inward curse. She should have known her luck wouldn't last; Strathmore had an uncanny ability to locate her.

Her instinct was to bolt, but she quelled it. She would never be able to move quickly through the press of people. Besides, she was better off staying in the green room. He couldn't do anything too dreadful in such a public place.

She underestimated him.

While she was trying to gather her wits, Strathmore reached the inner circle of the group around her. He was in his Lucifer mode, radiating such an aura of menacing force that the other men instinctively drew back.

Yet his manner was unexceptionable when he spoke. "You were magnificent tonight, my sweet." He raised Kit's chin and gave her a light, possessive kiss, as if they were established lovers.

Impossible not to respond to his warm lips, but she distrusted his glittering smile. She flattened her spine against the wall and wondered what mischief he was planning. "I'm glad you enjoyed the show," she said warily.

"You are a continual astonishment, my dear," he said in a husky, intimate voice. "Every time I see you perform, I feel that I've just met a fascinating new woman."

While she was trying to think of a suitable response for his double-edged words, he opened the cloak that had been draped over his arm. The voluminous garment

was large enough to wrap around her twice. In a flurry
of swift movements, he did exactly that, pulling her away
from the wall and swaddling her so tightly in the heavy
folds that her arms were pinioned to her sides.

She sputtered, "What the devil are you doing?"

"You complained that I was becoming predictable,"
he said silkily, "so I decided to remedy that." He swept
her up in his arms and brushed a kiss on her lips, deftly
lifting his head away when she attempted to bite him.
"Tonight, we recapture romance."

Outraged, Kit tried to struggle free, but she was helpless in the cocoon of dark fabric.

One of her admirers said jovially, "I knew a prime
piece like Cassie must have a protector, but I had no
idea you were the lucky man, Strathmore. No wonder
she's refused the rest of us."

"I'm very aware of my good fortune." His tender tone
was belied by the dangerous green light in his eyes as he
gazed at her. "There's not another woman in England
like Cassie James."

Their progress across the green room was accompanied
by ribald suggestions for what his ladybird might find
romantic. Kit tried to wriggle free, but his arms held her
against his broad chest as securely as iron bands. She did
manage to ram an elbow into his solar plexus, and he
winced at the blow, but his smile never faltered.

Under his breath he said, "I wouldn't advise you to
make a scene, my dear."

A quick glance at the laughing men around her made
her realize that an appeal for help would do her no good.
Any protest would be seen as part of a teasing game
between lovers.

An obliging visitor opened the door for Strathmore,
who gave a nod of thanks and stepped into the hall. His
footsteps echoed hollowly as he carried her from the
empty theater. Even if she screamed, no one would hear
her over the noise of the green room.

When they reached the side door, the porter made a
deep bow. "Your carriage is waiting, my lord."

Strathmore inclined his head. "Thank you, Smithson."

Kit tried to struggle free, but with no more success

than before. "Help me, Mr. Smithson," she said urgently. "This is no game—I'm being kidnapped."

The porter smiled indulgently as he let them out. "His lordship told me about his plans earlier, miss. Enjoy yourself. You work hard, and you deserve a bit of fun."

Strathmore's carriage stood directly outside, the horses' breath cloudy in the cold night air. Smithson opened the door and lowered the steps for them. After the earl lifted Kit into the carriage and deposited her on the leather seat, he tossed a gold coin to the porter.

Kit used the moment that his back was turned to try to free herself from the enveloping cloak, but before she could make any progress, Strathmore climbed in beside her and slammed the door. The carriage immediately began rolling along the rutted alley that led to the Strand.

As the motion pitched Kit against the side of the vehicle, her fear flared into sheer panic. Through all of their improbable encounters, she had not really believed that Strathmore would hurt her, but now she wondered if her judgment of him had been dead wrong. In a matter of moments, she had gone from safety to imprisonment. So swiftly, so easily. He could murder her tonight and throw her body in the Thames. If her disappearance were ever investigated, all he would have to do is say that they had had a splendid night and he had left her in perfect health. No one would ever doubt a fine, upstanding nobleman who could lie with such elegant ease.

Her hands clenched into fists underneath the cloak, and she bit her lip until she tasted blood. She had never felt so helpless, so much at a man's mercy. Frantically, she reached out to the source of strength that had never failed her.

When she found what she was seeking, a thread of calm began to twine through her terror. She was not alone. Her breathing deepened, and her fear subsided to where she could think again. She must be strong, the equal of the man who had captured her.

Closing her eyes, she created a new role for herself: that of a worldly, sophisticated actress who was afraid of nothing. When she thought she could be convincing, she opened her eyes and said coolly, "Do you make a habit of kidnapping women, my lord?"

"Not as a rule," he said with matching coolness, "but it seemed appropriate since the female in question is apparently incapable of telling the truth."

"My honesty or lack thereof are none of your business." Her tart words were undercut by a lurch of the carriage that caused her to roll against the seat. Without the use of her arms, it was impossible to maintain her balance.

Strathmore caught her shoulders and tucked her back into the corner, where she could brace herself against the vehicle's motion. "Remember that Lucifer is the Prince of Lies—surely that gives me dominion over you," he said as he settled back on his side of the seat. "You're one of my most devoted followers."

"In a pig's eye," she said inelegantly. "My most devout wish is to avoid you."

Her ongoing struggles finally paid off, and she freed herself of the cloak. As she pushed it away, he said, "I suggest you keep that on. The door on your side is locked, so you can't escape that way, and it's deucedly chilly tonight."

Plague the man, he was right; it was bitterly cold, and her Gypsy costume had not been designed for warmth. She wrapped the cloak around herself again. In the process she stealthily tested the door handle on her side, but it was indeed locked. With a sigh, she settled back into the corner and wrapped the cloak more tightly. The heavy wool folds carried the faint, tangy scent of his cologne. "Where are you taking me?"

"To supper. Anyone who worked as hard as you did on that stage must have a fearsome appetite."

The answer was so prosaic she almost laughed. Her fear receded further. "You're right—after a performance, I'm always ravenous. But why didn't you simply ask me to go out with you? I do not appreciate being manhandled."

"No?" he said with biting sarcasm. "I understand that quite a lot of men have handled you."

She gasped, then retorted, "Again, what business is

that of yours? You are not related to me by blood or marriage, and you have no right to censure my actions."

"I'm not censuring you," he said coolly. "In fact, I'm delighted to be free of the strictures of respectability. It was damned limiting to think you were virtuous. Now I can try more powerful persuasions."

"If seduction is your aim, you've set about it very badly, my lord," she said with awful formality.

Before he could answer, the carriage rumbled to a halt and a footman opened the door. Strathmore climbed out, then assisted her with as much courtliness as if she were an honored guest rather than a virtual prisoner.

As Kit stepped down, she discovered that they were in front of the Clarendon Hotel. At least he had been serious about feeding her. Hastily she rearranged the cloak so that it made a high cowl around her neck, obscuring her face. The last thing she needed was to be recognized by someone else.

A firm hand on her elbow, Strathmore escorted her up the steps. Inside, he said to the deeply bowing maître d'hotel, "A private dining room, Robecque, and a swiftly served meal suitable for a hungry lady. With champagne."

Robecque hesitated, distress on his mobile face. "I am most sorry, Lord Strathmore, but I believe that all of the private rooms are reserved," he said in a heavy French accent.

Strathmore arched his brows. "Oh?"

The Frenchman reacted to that single, softly uttered syllable as if a knife had been laid against his throat. "This way, my lord, my lady," he said instantly. "I have just recalled a room that is available."

He led the way along a private corridor to a small, lavishly furnished chamber. "Champagne and a suitable repast shall be brought directly."

After Robecque had bowed and left, Kit said ironically, "I presume that you just bullied the poor man out of a room that a lesser mortal had reserved for tonight."

"Very likely." Unperturbed, Strathmore removed the cloak, his fingers grazing her bare forearms for an instant.

She shivered and stepped away.

"My need was greater," the earl explained as he hung the garment on a hook in the corner.

"And your purse deeper." Feeling that taking a seat would put her at a disadvantage, she prowled around the room, her full Gypsy skirts swishing around her ankles as the thick carpet soundlessly absorbed the impressions of her light slippers. She had dined at the Clarendon once or twice on special occasions, but had never visited a private parlor. It was a world of winter roses, sparkling crystal, and the soft sheen of waxed wood.

Her gaze went to the velvet-covered chaise longue tucked in a corner, then shifted away. Nothing was missing for those who had come for a luxurious assignation.

The door opened and a platoon of servants entered. While one lowered the small chandelier and lit the candles, another built up the coal fire. A third opened a bottle of champagne and the last rolled in a heavily laden cart with wisps of steam trickling out from under silver covered dishes. The food smelled heavenly, and it had arrived so quickly that Kit suspected they had received someone else's dinner.

Strathmore said to the waiter in charge, "Thank you, Petain. You may go now. We shall serve ourselves, so your presence will not be needed for the rest of the evening."

The waiter bowed, then led his troops from the room. When they were alone, Kit said, "Considering the service you receive, I'm beginning to wonder if you own this place."

He shrugged. "I was once able to do a small service for the maître d'hotel. He has not forgotten."

"I assume that means he lost a fortune to you at the card table and you generously chose not to send him to debtor's prison."

"Something of the sort." He pulled a chair from the table and made a gesture of invitation. "Shall we begin?"

Deciding that she might as well make herself comfortable, she tugged out the hairpins that secured her black wig. After removing the wig and hanging it on a hook beside the cloak, she shook out her own hair, then ran her fingers through it to loosen the flattened tresses. She guessed that she must look like a dandelion that had gone to seed. Yet there was admiration in the earl's eyes when she took her seat.

He poured champagne for them both, then raised his glass to her. "To the most talented, devious female I've ever met."

"Is that a compliment or an insult?"

He smiled a little. "A mere statement of fact." He looked civilized and heart-stoppingly handsome. She would have believed him to be a complete gentleman, if not for the chancy light in his green-gold eyes.

Uneasily aware of the sexual tension between them, she tried her own champagne. Bubbles danced across her tongue, then tingled into her blood, relaxing her tense muscles. Feeling more at ease, she turned her attention to the food. It tasted even better than it smelled. After sole with sage and artichoke, braised leeks, chicken in apricot sauce, and pistachio cream, she felt better prepared to face her adversary.

He had eaten very little and was leaning back in his chair, one leg crossed over the other, his hair gleaming in the candlelight like spun gold. Now that she had recovered from the strains of performing, she was intensely, physically aware of him. Every time they met, their interaction was more profound, and she wondered uneasily what this evening would bring.

Hoping to keep the mood lightly social, she said, "Thank you for an excellent dinner."

"I've always found that it's more productive to question someone who isn't hungry." He sipped at his champagne. "And I have quite a quantity of questions to ask you."

She took a deep breath, then laid her knife and fork neatly across her plate.

The battle was joined.

Chapter 13

Kit raised her gaze to his. "I have nothing to say to you."

"What, no more fanciful tales to spin? I'm disappointed," he said with delicate sarcasm. "You're one of the most creative liars I've ever met."

"You should talk," she retorted. "I doubt that you have an honest bone in your body. You had everyone in the theater convinced we were lovers."

"I'm honest when it's convenient and doesn't cost me anything," he said blandly. "We have much in common. Are you sure you can't conjure up another cheated brother or journalistic investigation for me?"

She shook her head. "I'm tired of lying. As I said earlier, I am under no obligation to answer your questions, so I won't. I give you my word that I do not intend harm to any innocent person. More than that I will not say."

"I wish I knew what you consider guilt and innocence." He studied her face. "Clever of you to pretend to be L. J. Knight. Since no one knows what the fellow looks like, your claim is hard to refute. It might even be true, though I wouldn't bet a ha'penny on it. It's more likely that you are merely a regular reader of Knight's work. Care to comment?"

"I'd rather ask a few questions myself." Her eyes narrowed. "I think you have secrets of your own, for your behavior is hardly that of an honest, upright citizen. Why are you so determined to interrogate me?"

"I find it hard to restrain my curiosity about a female who routinely practices fraud, burglary, and assorted other capital crimes." He accompanied his explanation with a smile that made her breath falter.

Even if Strathmore wasn't the villain she sought, he was certainly a threat to her and her mission. That being the case, why was she still drawn to him? The memory of the kisses they had shared was as vivid as the flames burning on the fireplace grate. As warming, too.

She must leave before the atmosphere became any more intimate. "If you think I'm a criminal and have the evidence to prove it, you should call a magistrate," she said steadily. "But if you decide to hand me over to the law, remember that I am not without influential friends who would come to my assistance."

That produced a dark flash in the depths of his eyes. "It would be a waste to send you to prison, my dear. You wouldn't like it, and you would be of no use to me there."

"I assume that your purpose is seduction, but I must decline the honor." She rose to her feet. "I'll see myself out."

When she moved around the table toward the door, he raised a hand. Though he didn't touch her, she came to a halt, caught in the web of his formidable concentration.

"Seduction implies taking advantage of a reluctant or defenseless female," he said. "You are neither of those things."

"Thank you, I think," she said dryly. "But I have already declared my unwillingness, Lord Strathmore. Do you intend to keep me here by force?"

Softly he said, "I don't think force will be necessary."

He was seated, which made him seem less threatening. But his eyes—ah, his eyes were still dangerous, for they promised delights that would strip her soul bare. Steeling herself against his potent allure, she said, "If you hope to persuade me into your bed, think again."

He gave her a lazy smile. "I have infinite patience, as long as I get what I want in the end." He took her hand, linking his fingers through hers. "You refuse to call me Lucien."

She swallowed hard, trying to resist the subversive effects of his warm clasp. "To use your given name would imply an intimacy between us that I want no part of."

"No?" His gaze holding hers, he drew her toward him, then raised their joined hands and kissed the inside of her wrist, his tongue tracing the blue shadow of a vein.

The effect was shocking, causing every cell in her body to thrum with desire. She tried to edge away, yet though his hold was gentle, it was inexorable. He began caressing the sensitive hollow of her palm with his thumb, and she could not summon the will to free herself. A little desperately, she said, "To be an actress does not make a woman a whore, my lord."

"No, but it implies that a woman might be ... less conventional than most." He gave a slow smile. "And the one thing I do know about you is that you are not conventional."

He increased the pressure on her hand, yet it was the golden light in his eyes that drew her toward him. Her breath quickened, as much from anticipation as alarm.

He had an uncanny ability to read her mood, for instead of a kiss, he pulled her into his lap. "You must be tired." Softly his arms came around her. "Should I call you Cassie, or Jane?"

"Cassie is a stage name. I really am named Jane."

He began to knead the nape of her neck with gentle skill. "Jane. Such an undistinguished name for a remarkable woman."

"I'm not remarkable—merely good at creating illusions," she said, and then wondered why she had said so much. He was even more dangerous than she had realized, for he made her want to trust and confide. It seemed utterly natural to have his arms around her, to rest her head against his shoulder. She wanted to pour out her fears and bask in his strength, for she was tired—so infinitely, painfully tired—of her lonely struggle.

Though she was not fool enough to yield to her treacherous craving for union, her initial stiffness soon dissipated. She drifted, content to be in his arms, vaguely aware of the rich scents of food and flowers, the distant sounds of talk and laughter. But that was mere background for the profound reality of Lucien. He filled her senses, his quiet breath stirring tendrils of hair at her temple.

As he had said, he was patient. For a long time he simply held her, slowly massaging away the tension in her taut muscles and tendons. His warmth and desire surrounded her, a crucible that gradually raised her temperature to match his.

She scarcely noticed the first soft contact of his lips on her forehead, or how it became a delicate tracing of the planes of her face. A gossamer caress on her closed eyelids; a teasing, erotic exhalation into her ear. Finally, the light pressure of his forefinger under her chin tilted her head up, and with seamless ease his mouth claimed hers.

The velvet stroke of his tongue soothed the raw place where she had bitten the inside of her lip in the carriage. Hard to remember why she had been so frightened of him. Her hazy pleasure thickened, became a craving, when he cupped her breast.

His kiss deepened, exploring, evocative. He slid her Gypsy blouse from her shoulder and she welcomed the cool touch of air and the warm comfort of his hand.

As he teased her nipple to hardness, he murmured, "Since Jane is too plain, I shall call you Lady Jane."

How had he known? The thought jarred her out of her flowing contentment. She raised her head, shaken, and realized her foolishness. "I must go."

"Not this time, Lady Jane," he said huskily.

He bent his head and pressed his mouth to her breast, the lapping rhythm of his tongue matching the pounding of her blood. Her body arched, and she twisted in his lap, guiltily aware that she was not trying to escape, but to offer herself more fully.

One of her heedless movements tilted him off balance and they almost fell. His reflexes saved them from crashing to the floor. After a swift recovery, he swept her up in his arms and carried her the short distance to the chaise longue.

He laid her full-length on the padded surface, then sat on the edge of the chaise beside her. Holding her gaze with his own, he pulled her blouse from her shoulders, then untied the front laces of her corselet. Below it her chemise rose and fell with the quickness of her breathing, until he pushed her garments down to her waist. He brushed aside her modesty with equal ease, for her shyness vanished in the glow of his admiration.

He cupped her newly freed breasts in his warm, strong hands, then leaned forward to suckle them. She gave an involuntary whimper and closed her eyes, deluged by delirious new sensations. The faint prickliness of his chin against her fragile bare skin; his teeth nipping with exquisitely judged force; his hands skimming her limbs and torso as if seeking to memorize every curve and texture. Her slippers had gone missing, and the velvet was a voluptuous caress under her bare feet as she shifted them with restless yearning. There was only him, only this moment . . .

Yet that was not true. There were far more important things in her life than the gratification of lust. In a frantic bid for sanity, she drew up her legs and braced her hands against his shoulders, pushing him away. "Stop! You frighten me."

He went very still, then lifted his head, frowning as he studied her face. "Not, I think, with physical fear."

"No," she said honestly. "I fear going too fast. Doing something I will regret."

The corner of his mouth turned up ruefully. "Will it make you feel better to know that you frighten me equally? You are going to cost me dearly, Lady Jane. In fact, you already have."

It gave her a sense of power to know she could affect such a man. And yet . . . "It may make me feel better, but not safer."

"Is that why you keep running away from me? For you can't deny that there is something very intense between us." As he spoke, his hand glided down her left leg from knee to foot.

A disorienting shiver ran through her as his thumb made slow, circular motions on the arch of her foot. "I won't deny there is attraction," she said, a catch in her voice, "but that doesn't mean I'll surrender to it."

Yet her words were belied by the irresistible impulse to touch. Her hands softened their resistance and moved down his shoulders, feeling the hard muscles beneath his elegantly tailored clothing. She brushed aside his coat and ran her palms down his ribs and narrow waist, her hands open and hungry.

He didn't mock her weakness, merely smiled into her eyes with quiet triumph as he stroked her leg again. This time the direction was upward and the movement raised her voluminous skirts to expose her anklet. His gaze went to the shining gold. "This does a splendid job of drawing attention to your lovely legs," he said as he followed the circle of gold links around her ankle with a fingertip.

She inhaled sharply, her toes curling into the velvet and her fingers into his ribs. "The anklet belongs to the Gypsy maiden. The plain Jane who is the real me would never be so bold."

"Plain Jane?" His glance was quizzical and a little mocking. "A gold chain can be removed, but this"—he lifted her skirts higher to reveal the butterfly tattoo above her right knee—"exists only to drive men mad. And it has maddened me."

He leaned forward and traced the image with his tongue, his warm breath whispering along her inner thigh. Her eyes widened and her lower body tensed with craving. "Lucien," she gasped. "Oh, God, Lucien . . ."

The restraint that he had shown dissolved in an instant. He stretched out alongside her, his taut body molding her soft curves. As he kissed her with fierce carnality, his hand moved upward between her thighs, burning across sublimely sensitive skin to the hem of the short drawers she wore when doing her provocative dancing. A warm, broad palm drifted over the light fabric. Fingertips found the open seam and probed through soft curls into moist, heated feminine folds. Sliding deep, profoundly intimate. Sweet, drugging torment.

She whimpered helplessly as passion raged through her, making a mockery of morals and judgment. She could not bear this tumult, this wildness, could not bear it . . .

Release, when it came, was shattering. She cried out, the sound smothering in the depths of his mouth as he drew her essence into himself. He was absorbing her, yet

at the same time making her more fully herself by un-
locking hidden desires.

She came to her senses slowly, her lower body pulsing
with aftershocks of fulfillment. She was physically sated
as never before, and the process had drawn her to Lucien
in a way she could not have imagined before this
evening.

That recognition was followed by furious self-
reproach. Dear God, how could she have been so mad?
She could not afford to lose herself in him. Even if she
didn't have a desperate mission to fulfill, it would be the
height of idiocy to allow a rake to become master of her
soul. She had been criminally weak to allow such
intimacy.

And the intimacy was about to become greater. He
caught her hand and drew it to the ridge of hard male
flesh that pressed against her thigh. Through the layers
of fabric that separated them, she felt a hot, insistent
throbbing.

Cautiously she squeezed. He groaned and rocked
against her hand, his eyes closed and his breathing rough.
There was deep satisfaction in pleasuring him, and in
seeing that he was as defenseless as she had been a few
moments before. Dimly, she sensed that this mutual vulnerability was a crucial element of the lovers' bond.

Her musings ended when he started to undo the buttons of his breeches. He wanted to complete their union,
and she yearned for that with matching intensity. She
longed to enfold him, to make him part of herself, to
cause him to lose himself in ecstasy.

But she dared not. *She dared not.*

Her racing mind sought and found the necessary excuse. She whispered, "Not yet. I ... I must take
precautions."

His dazed eyes opened, golden with passion. "I'll take
care." His feather-light fingertips brushed her temple. "I
would never harm you."

His tenderness was as potent a weapon as desire.
Breathlessly, she wriggled away before her resolution
crumbled again. "It will be better if you don't have to

withdraw," she promised when he stretched out his hand to draw her back.

He laughed a little and his hand dropped. "Obviously you know that that is an almost irresistible argument."

Hating herself, she got to her feet and touched his tangled hair. He looked less intimidating than usual—no longer Lucifer but Apollo, born of the sun.

Regret pierced her, yet her wicked, lying tongue continued, "I'll only be a minute ... I have what I need with me, and there's a retiring room just down the hall." Hastily, she tugged her disarranged clothing into some semblance of order.

His smile was a caress. "Hurry back, Lady Jane."

She bent forward and kissed him. "I will," she said huskily. "I ... I hate leaving you, even for an instant." And that, at least, was the truth.

He settled back on the chaise and rested one arm across his closed eyes. Though he gave the impression of being relaxed, his body was still taut, unfulfilled.

She would never see him so trusting again. Even if they did met in the future under less troubled circumstances, he would never forgive her for what she was about to do.

Before remorse could totally unravel her resolve, she darted across the room, retrieving her slippers and sliding her feet into them as she went. She hesitated when she saw the cloak and wig that hung on wooden pegs by the door. She was going to have to walk home, and she would need the cloak to prevent freezing and to cover her absurd, conspicuous Gypsy costume. The wig couldn't be abandoned, either. Silently she lifted both items, then slipped out the door.

The corridor was empty, so she tugged the wig on and hastily shoved her hair under it. Then she wrapped the cloak around her so thoroughly that no one would recognize her.

Almost no one—she ran into the maître d'hotel as she was on the verge of exiting through a side door. His eyes sharpened at the sight of her dishevelment and solitary state, but he was too discreet to comment. "I hope my lady enjoyed her dinner?"

Donning her most patrician manner, she inclined her head and said in French, "The food was superb, monsieur. As always."

A pleased light in his eyes, he swung the door for her.

Before stepping out, curiosity prompted her to say, "Lord Strathmore mentioned that he had once done you a small service."

The Frechman's professional manner fall away. He said intensely, "It was not small, mademoiselle. He brought my family safely out of France. For that, my life is his for the asking."

It was one more shock in a night that had already had too many. As she set out for the nearest of her abodes, she silently cursed the earl for his complexity. Though she suspected that he had done many things that would not bear close examination, it was entirely believable that he could act with generosity and heroism. But how the devil had he managed to rescue people from France when the Continent had been closed to the English for most of the last two decades? Perhaps he augmented his income with smuggling or something equally villainous.

Despite the intimacy they had just shared, he was still a man of mystery. And mysteries were dangerous.

Images of Jane haunted Lucien as he awaited her return. Her lithe limbs, her mesmerizing diversity, the soft, smoky-sweet sensuality of her responses. She intrigued him as no woman ever had, and he ached to possess her. Perhaps in the intensity of mating he would finally touch her quicksilver soul.

He wondered about the fact that she carried the means of contraception with her. With most women he would have assumed that was a sign of promiscuity, but in the case of Jane, it might only mean that she was too intelligent to let herself be caught unprepared. Yet he could not rule out the possibility he was fooling himself because he didn't want to think that tonight was merely one more casual episode in the life of a free-spirited actress. He was reluctant to analyze his own feelings, but they were most assuredly not casual.

His fingers drummed restlessly on the chaise as he

wondered how long she would be. It had been several minutes. Ten, perhaps? Certainly five. It seemed longer. He never should have let her out of his sight.

Never should have let her out of his sight . . .

His eyes snapped open, and with sudden, shattering certainty, he knew that she was not coming back. The selfish little trollop had taken her satisfaction, then left him to burn. Christ have mercy, how could he have been so stupid? What was it about this one female that could consistently beguile a mind usually notable for wariness? He had never been violent with a woman, but if Jane were present, there was a very real possibility that he would make an exception.

If she had been present, he wouldn't be feeling violent—at least, not in that way.

Bloody *hell*! He swung to his feet, furiously grabbed the edge of the dinner table, and hurled it to the floor. The dinnerware hit with a satisfying crash of splintering crockery and jangling silver. His mouth twisted as he watched wine splash across the oriental carpet. This would undoubtedly prove to be the most expensive dinner of his life, in every possible way.

There was a discreet tap on the door, followed by the maître d'hotel's voice. "Is everything all right, my lord?"

Grimly, Lucien straightened his clothing and his expression. He'd be damned if he would let anyone guess what that little witch had done to him.

As he crossed the room, his anger flared again when he saw that she had stolen his cloak and repossessed her wig. The cold-blooded, scheming, light-fingered . . .

Opening the door, he said, "A small accident, Robecque. I was abominably clumsy. Send me the bill for the damages."

The Frenchman surveyed the wreckage, keeping his thoughts to himself. "As you wish, my lord."

Lucien paused in the doorway. "Did my lady friend leave safely? I disliked letting her go alone, but she's a headstrong wench—very fond of her independence."

"A woman to remember," Robecque said admiringly. "Her French is exquisite. As good as yours."

"She's a woman of infinite talents." And the next time they met—as they surely would—she would pay for what she had done tonight.

Chapter 14

Like his quarry, Lucien was rather good at altering his appearance. He was disguised the next morning and looking for a hackney coach on Oxford Street when he saw the Duke of Candover approaching. Feeling mischievous, he said with a thick Yorkshire accent, "Excuse me, sir, but is the English Opera House near here?"

Looking pained at being accosted by a stranger, Rafe said coolly, "Five minutes' walk ahead, on the left."

Lapsing into his natural voice, Lucien said, "Many thanks, your grace."

Rafe halted, then swung around. "Luce, is that you?"

"In the flesh," Lucien replied, "and gratified that you didn't give me the cut direct when I asked you for directions."

The duke snorted and fell into step beside him. "What are you up to this time?"

"A bit of investigation, though I'd thank you not to announce it to all of Mayfair."

"How do you do it?" Rafe asked in a quieter voice. "Obviously darkening your hair and wearing spectacles and shabby clothing make a difference, but those things are superficial." He gave his friend a searching glance. "Your features are the same, yet you look shorter and broader than usual, and entirely forgettable. If I hadn't known you since I was ten years old, I would have no idea who you are."

"A disguise starts in the mind," Lucien explained. "Wealth and power and position endow a person with a kind of confidence that is unmistakable. Putting those things aside and thinking of oneself as insignificant and financially insecure creates a very different aura."

"I suppose it would," Rafe admitted, "though I can't imagine wanting to do so. I quite enjoy wealth, title, and power."

"You play the role of arrogant aristocrat so well that it would be a crime to drop it," Lucien agreed. "Speaking of which, we had better separate. It might damage your reputation for hauteur if you're seen speaking to such an undistinguished character as James Wolsey of Leeds."

"I am perfectly civil to the lower orders, as long as they show proper deference," Rafe said blandly. "Be sure to tug your forelock when you leave."

Lucien grinned. "I've heard that the negotiations in Ghent are going better."

The duke nodded. "With luck we'll have peace with the Americans by Christmas."

"Amen to that." After a parting nod, Lucien hailed a hackney and rode to the Marlowe Theater. There he introduced himself as a journalist writing an article about Cassie James. The young lady had often pleased audiences in the north, and readers there would be interested in her London success.

His presence was accepted casually, and he spent several hours wandering about asking questions and taking notes. He was very skilled at extracting information; unfortunately, no one had anything useful to say. It was universally agreed that Miss James was a charming young lady, not high in the instep at all. Very professional, too.

However, she liked her privacy more than most. No one knew where she lived or any details of her personal life beyond the fact that the night before, her aristocratic lover had swept her from the green room, and a rare sight it had been. Though it had been assumed she had a protector, they'd not known the fellow was of such exalted rank. The lass had done well for herself, and more power to her.

Lucien took a certain satisfaction that no one recognized James Wolsey as the Earl of Strathmore. It was the only satisfaction he was finding in his day's work.

Even the theater manager was unable to help. During a break from rehearsing a new production, which seemed to consist of bellowing insults at clumsy dancers, he ex-

plained that Miss James played small roles in a number
of different plays, but her understudy would be filling in
for a week or two because Miss James had asked for
time off to visit an ailing aunt. A satirical edge in his
voice suggested that he considered the aunt to be fic-
tional; he had been in the green room the night before
when his rising young star had been carried off.

However, the girl would be back for the next performance of *The Gypsy Lass,* since that was her most important role. Mr. Wolsey should be sure to tell his
readers that another play featuring Miss James was in
development. She would play a breeches part, and it was
safe to predict that all London would soon be worship-
ping at her dainty feet.

No, he had no idea where the young lady lived. Considering what temperamental creatures most actresses
were, he thanked his lucky stars that Cassie kept herself
to herself, showed up when she said she would, and never
threw objects at her long-suffering manager. Now if Mr.
Wolsey would excuse him, he must get back to work.

Lucien left the theater, frustrated but unsurprised.
Once again, Lady Jane had covered her tracks well.

He arrived home to find that in his absence, an anonymous youth had delivered a parcel. He opened it in his
study and found his missing cloak and an unsigned note
saying, "Whatever else you may think of me, I am not
a thief."

It did not improve his mood to see evidence that in
her own weird way, Jane was honest. He was tempted
to throw the cloak against a wall, but refrained; the heavy
wool fabric would not have smashed in a satisfactory
fashion.

Besides, he had already indulged in far too much emotion where Jane was concerned. It was high time he set
lust aside and analyzed the woman objectively, as he
would any other target of investigation. He tossed the
cloak over the sofa, then sat at his desk with a sheet of
foolscap and a pencil.

To begin with, what did he really know about her?

The one indisputable fact was that she was an actress,
a worldly woman who was brilliant at assuming roles all

the way from shy innocent to committed intellectual crusader.

She was also like him in many ways—too damned much so, since that similarity underlay both his obsession and his anger.

They were both devious, capable of lying with utter conviction. In his case he was convincing because there was always a purpose to his deceptions; he genuinely believed that he was acting for the ultimate good of his country.

There must be a similar core of sincerity in Jane, or she would not be such a persuasive liar. In fact, she had said as much when explaining why her story about a nonexistent brother was so convincing. That underlying honesty was why he kept believing her over and over again.

What was driving her to repeatedly risk her life and reputation? He wrote down the key question and underlined it twice. If he knew the answer, he would finally understand her.

He thought back on the stories she had spun. First she had been a sister trying to help a younger brother, then an essayist determined to expose the rape and exploitation of defenseless young women. The common theme was protection, and her passionate caring had been utterly convincing.

Ergo, her maddening, unpredictable behavior was probably caused by a desire to protect someone. Could the person she was trying to help be a lover?

His mouth tightened. He didn't like the thought, but a lover who was in trouble would explain the ambivalence of her reactions to Lucien. Being torn between attraction to one man and fidelity to another could easily produce fevered kisses alternating with wild flight.

For a moment, a vision of her with another lover almost destroyed his dogged detachment. It took time to suppress the image enough for him to proceed with his analysis.

Her persistent attempts to spy on the Hellions indicated that her goal lay within that group. Apparently one of the members had something she wanted, and she had not yet found what she was seeking.

If he stayed close to the Hellions, she would probably appear again, but he was tired of waiting. Thoughtfully he tapped the end of his pencil on the leather surface of the desk as he considered other avenues of pursuit.

Jane had been very knowledgeable about the writings of L. J. Knight. Her claim to be the writer was probably false, but she might move in circles where the man's work was routinely discussed. Perhaps she frequented the salons where writers, artists, actors, and assorted other eccentrics rubbed shoulders and talked about life, politics, and art. In such a place she would have learned that the essayist was a recluse and that she could safely claim his identity, at least temporarily.

He had always enjoyed the salons himself—they had the liveliest conversation in London—but he had been too busy to visit any of them recently. It was time to make the circuit again. He would start at Lady Graham's. She was a wealthy widow with liberal opinions and a gregarious nature, and her fortnightly gatherings drew some of the most interesting and controversial people in Britain. Surely there he could find someone who knew a rising comic actress.

He laid down his pencil, feeling that he had finally made some progress. But it was time to set aside the mystery of Jane and prepare for dinner with Lord Mace. With luck, tonight he would be told when the next Hellion ritual would be held. On that occasion, he could be formally admitted into the group. That should bring him closer to finding the traitor.

As he tied his cravat, he smiled wryly. Perhaps Jane would turn up tonight, her leggy frame and mobile features disguised as one of Mace's footmen. If she did, this time he wouldn't be fool enough to let her out of his sight.

Chapter 15

As soon as Lucien stepped inside Mace's house, a dark, heavy cloth was dropped over his head and a voice—Roderick Harford?—said portentously, "The moment of truth has arrived, Strathmore. To become a Hellion, you must undergo initiation. Do you choose to go forward into the unknown, or will you withdraw and never become one of us?"

Lucien suppressed a sigh. He should have known the Hellions would do something juvenile like this. "I wish to be part of your fellowship," he said gravely, "so I shall proceed."

"Obey all orders," Harford intoned. "Expect only the unexpected, and let the hellfires transform you."

Anonymous hands tugged the dark fabric down over Lucien. Apparently it was a shapeless, hooded robe that completely covered the face. After his hands were loosely bound in front of him, he was led through the house and outside to a carriage. A low voice warned him of steps and turns, but it was disorienting to be without sight. Cynically he guessed that the treatment was designed to undermine a man's confidence and make him more susceptible to whatever nonsense followed.

The carriage ride was long and took them out of London. No one spoke, but humans are seldom totally silent. From the sounds of breathing and shifting weight, he guessed that three men accompanied him.

Eventually the carriage lurched to a stop, and someone helped Lucien climb out. The chill wind carried the damp, earthy scents of the country and the sound of lapping waves. After a short walk over soft turf, he was urged into a flat-bottomed boat. It had the narrowness

of a punt, designed to be poled through shallow waters.
It rocked precariously when he stepped inside, so he sat
down quickly.

Three more lurches as the others climbed in. The punt
was pushed from the bank, and it glided smoothly
through the water. Ahead of them a church bell began
to toll somberly, as if counting the years of someone who
had just died.

The journey was short and soon the punt crunched
into gravel. The passengers disembarked, Lucien banging
his shin on the gunwale in the process. More men waited
on the shore, for he heard shufflings and a muffled cough.
It was a much larger group, perhaps two dozen people.
Someone turned Lucien to the right, then tugged at the
head of his robe. It fell away, and suddenly he could
see again.

On the hill above sprawled a medieval castle, the full
moon gilding the ancient stones with cold, uncanny light.
The mournful, doom-laden tolling of the church bell
made Lucien's hair prickle. He schooled his face to mask
his reaction. It was merely theater, but damned effective.
If he were superstitious, he'd be frightened half out of
his wits.

Surrounding him were perhaps thirty men wearing
deeply hooded white robes and clasping tall, lighted candles. They looked like a conclave of ghosts. His own robe
was black, presumably because of his novice status.

The nearest man was Roderick Harford. Raising his
arms, he cried, "What is our password?"

The false monks chorused, "Do what thou wilt!"

"What is our goal?"

"Pleasure!"

"Come, then, brothers, to our sacred ritual."

A man wearing a medallion around his neck started
up the hill and the rest of the group fell in behind him,
marching single file. The wind whipped the flames of
their candles, sending wild shadows careening across the
landscape. Harford gestured for Lucien to join the end
of the line, bringing up the rear himself.

The castle was surrounded by high walls. A heavy iron
gate admitted the marchers into well-kept gardens. The

path wound between shrubs and dimly glimpsed pieces of statuary. As nearly as Lucien could tell in the dim light, one statue was a twenty-foot-high marble phallus. Pure wishful thinking, no doubt.

Their destination was the chapel, which appeared to be the only building intact. As they neared, he saw that the doorway was bracketed by statues of a naked man and an equally naked woman, each holding a finger to the lips in the sign of silence. Both were so well-endowed physically that the average person would feel sadly inferior. Carved above the entrance were the words, *Fay ce que voudras*. Do what thou wilt. The phrase had sounded familiar earlier, and now Lucien recognized it as the motto of the original Hellfire Club. He wondered what Jane would think of all this masculine self-indulgence, then suppressed a smile at the thought.

The iron-banded door swung open with a squeal, and the procession entered the chapel. Braziers glowed around the sanctuary, filling the air with eye-stinging fumes of incense. Though care had been taken to maintain an atmosphere of crumbling antiquity, Lucien guessed that the structure had been recently restored. Certainly the dozen stained glass windows depicting the apostles in lewd acts were new and undeniably imaginative.

He glanced upward and saw that the vaulted ceiling had been decorated with an equally obscene fresco. As with the rest of the abbey, the images were an eclectic blend of Christian and pagan. Goat-footed satyrs coupled with angels and lustful monks pursued Greek nymphs. The Hellions obviously liked variety.

As the monks formed a circle around the edges of the room, Harford whispered, "Walk to the altar rail and prostrate yourself. After the priest bids you to rise, stand at the railing throughout the ceremony. Address the priest as Master."

Lucien obeyed with the irreverent thought that if he had known he would have to wait so long for his dinner, he would have eaten first. Prostrating oneself on cold stone was no fun on an empty stomach.

A door behind the altar opened and footsteps approached with a rustle of brocaded scarlet robes. Lucien refrained from looking up, but Mace's husky voice was readily recognizable when he asked, "Do you understand the gravity of what you are about to undertake, Novice?"

Trying to feel a proper sense of awe, Lucien replied, "I do, Master." The flagstones were gritty beneath his cheek.

"Rise and face me, Novice." After Lucien obeyed, Mace continued, "Do you swear solemn allegiance to this brotherhood, knowing that falseness will bring the curse of the Hellions down on you?" His words rolled like thunder, and there was danger in his eyes.

Lucien's levity vanished. Reminding himself never to underestimate the other man, he said, "I do so swear, Master."

Mace's gaze probed and judged. Finally he nodded. "So be it." He turned and used a candle to ignite a fire in a stone basin atop the altar. The acrid scent of burning herbs joined the heavy incense.

The service that followed was not a black mass, but a strange mixture of pagan and blasphemous Christian, both portentous and self-mocking. Speaking in Latin and French as well as English, Mace's voice rose and fell in a rhythm that wove a potent spell of mystery.

As the smoke thickened, Lucien began to grow light-headed. He guessed that the burning herbs included narcotics such as belladonna and henbane. The pungent blend produced a receptive state where it was easy to believe that mystical powers were being invoked. He forced himself to take rigorous mental notes, for analysis kept him detached. He preferred it that way; sacrilege had never been his style.

At the climax of the ritual, Mace cried, "Thou art one of us!" He dipped his fingers into a black chalice, then sprinkled brimstone-scented brandy over Lucien in a parody of baptism. "Within the fellowship of Hellions, our new member will be known by the mystical name of Lucifer."

"Welcome, Lucifer!" the monks chanted.

Mace turned and flung a handful of powder onto the altar fire. Violet flames shot up toward the ceiling while clouds of smoke swirled in all directions. Above the altar the smoke thickened into a menacing shape, as if the devil had come to call. The air in the chapel became electric with tension.

Mace raised his arms and barked an unintelligible phrase. The diabolical figure began to dissolve, and with it the tension that had gripped the onlookers.

Lucien admitted to himself that the smoky apparition had been a good effect. Given a bit of time, he didn't doubt that he could reproduce it himself. Apparently, Mace was using his technical skills for something more than obscene toys.

Mace lowered his arms, the exalted glow fading from his eyes. "Come, brothers, and let us feast."

A monk pushed aside a black drapery in the corner, revealing a passage that led into a banqueting hall. Instantly the solemn atmosphere was replaced by a cheerful babble of voices as the Hellions streamed into the hall and sprawled on the Roman-style couches that lined the walls.

As Lucien hesitated, Mace gestured toward the head of the room. "Come sit beside me, Lucifer." He settled onto his own couch. "What do you think of the service?"

"Impressive," Lucien said truthfully as he reclined on the leather squabs. "It's certainly not as simple as the devil-worship of the Hellfire Club. It must have taken considerable study to weave together such a unique blend of classical, Christian, and pagan customs."

"I knew you would be capable of appreciating the multiple levels of meaning. Not all of our members are as learned." Amusement showed in his eyes. "Certainly one must give the devil his due, but Satanism is too banal, a mere reversal of Christian customs. It's far more intriguing to invent one's own religion."

He was describing his research when a bevy of serving girls swirled into the hall, garbed in translucent silk costumes that revealed every enticing curve and cleft. Only their faces were invisible, concealed behind elaborate feather masks.

Nunfield had taken the couch on the other side of Lucien. As the serving girls entered, he said, "Tonight's theme is Turkish. Personally, I like it when the tarts dress as nuns—the habits leave so much to the imagination. But many of our brethren prefer the obvious." He beckoned to a server carrying a jug. The woman leaned forward and poured wine into their goblets, her lush breasts swaying behind the veils that floated above her torso.

"Lovely creatures, aren't they?" Appreciatively, Mace caressed a round buttock. The woman gave a throaty chuckle and rubbed against his hand. "Roderick is in charge of arranging for the girls, and he has excellent taste."

"Are they professionals?" Lucien asked, unsurprised to learn that Roderick was chief pimp.

"Most are, but not all." Mace gave a satyr's smile. "Some are women of the highest rank, the sort one might meet in the queen's drawing room. That is why they are masked. If you had a sister, you might find her here. Or a wife."

Lucien suppressed a surge of distaste. "A tantalizing thought. What a pity that I have neither."

Mace raised his goblet. "To debauchery!" After a challenging glance, he drained his cup with one swallow. Lucien did likewise. When in Rome . . .

Another serving girl arrived bearing a platter of steaming sausages that had been shaped to resemble phalluses. Lucien took one and bit off the end. The things he did for his country.

The feast rapidly degenerated into a latter-day version of a Roman orgy. Whenever possible, the food was formed into suggestive shapes, and wine and spirits flowed freely.

As the night progressed, giggling serving girls were pulled onto the couches. Some of the couples, including Nunfield and a busty brunette, engaged right there; others rose and stumbled off toward the private chambers that lined an adjacent hallway. After Mace disappeared with one of the women, Lucien rose and surreptitiously slipped away into the gardens, feeling that he couldn't bear another minute of the fetid atmosphere.

The chilly air was refreshing, though he still felt dizzy from the amount of alcohol he had consumed. Matching

Mace drink for drink was enough to strain even the hardest head.

He wandered through the moonlit paths, automatically noting the layout in case the knowledge might someday prove useful. When he climbed a stone staircase to the top of the wall, he discovered that the castle was not on an island. The water that he had crossed was a moon-silvered river that curled halfway around the hill. The castle itself was probably a remnant of Norman times that had been rebuilt by the Hellions.

The gardens were beautifully laid out, though the obscene statues rapidly became tedious. Once he turned a sharp corner and walked into a marble Venus who was bending to remove a thorn from her foot. She had been placed in midpath so that any newcomer would collide with her naked buttocks.

He found that he was not the only wanderer when he came across Lord Ives contemplating a statue of Zeus raping a swan. Lucien gestured toward the figures. "Call me a puritan, but I can't imagine becoming aroused by a swan. Unless I was a swan too, of course."

The young man grinned. "Leda would have been safe from me as well. Those Greek gods were a randy lot."

The men fell in together and continued along the path. Lucien said, "Taking a break to regain your strength before the next encounter?"

Ives hesitated, then gave an embarrassed laugh. "I was considering going home early, actually. You'll probably think I'm foolish, but I didn't really enjoy myself with the girl I chose. I kept thinking I'd rather be with Cleo."

"I don't think you're foolish." Lucien thought of Jane, who had more sensuality in one teasing glance than all of the underdressed serving girls put together. "Passion without emotion might satisfy the body, but the pleasure is gone as quickly as it came, leaving emptiness."

"That's it exactly. I'm glad I'm not the only one who feels that way." Ives grimaced. "If Cleo learned that I had bedded another woman, she'd leave me. She's not a Cyprian, you know. There are other men who would be willing to pay more for her favors, but she chose me because she preferred my company."

"If you feel strongly about the girl, perhaps you should drop out of the Hellions."

Ives nodded as if the suggestion confirmed his own thoughts. "I think you're right. It's foolish to risk losing something valuable for the sake of a few minutes' pleasure with a female whose name I won't remember in the morning."

Deciding to do some research, Lucien asked, "Do the Hellions take the rituals seriously?"

"Perhaps Mace does a bit—he's a pagan at heart—but it's really only for amusement. Most of us joined for the entertainment and the girls."

Their meanderings had brought them back to the chapel, where the sounds of carousal had faded. In the west the moon was setting. "When and how do people go home?" Lucien asked.

"Most sleep off their excesses here, but I'm going to leave now. Would you like to go back to London in my curricle?"

Lucien hesitated, tempted, then shook his head. "That would be uncivil for my first time. I'll stay until the others leave."

The men said their farewells and Lucien reentered the banqueting hall. After the freshness of the night, the rank, overheated atmosphere was choking. Sleeping bodies littered the couches and floor, male and female tangled together. In one corner, Westley lay on his back giggling while a nude woman trickled wine into his mouth. No one else seemed to be awake.

Lucien was looking for a quiet spot to sleep away the rest of the night when Nunfield emerged from one of the private rooms, moving with the exaggerated care of the extremely drunk. Clinging to his arm was a lusty-looking wench wearing a half-mask of pheasant feathers and not much else.

"Lucifer! I've been looking for you." Nunfield hiccuped. "You've got to go with Lola. She's 'ceptionally skilled."

"Thank you, darling," she purred, her eyes gleaming behind the slits of the mask. "I do aim to please." She stretched out a sinuous hand and caught Lucien's wrist.

"Come with me and I'll try to live up to Nunny's recommendation."

Lucien was looking for a way to refuse when he saw the sharpness of Nunfield's gaze. To decline would be conspicuous, so he must appear to go along with the suggestion. Once he was alone with the woman, he would disengage as he had done at Chiswick's house. Donning the facade of drunkenness, he said with heavy gallantry, "It will be my pleasure, Madame Lola." He offered his arm and almost overbalanced in the process.

Deftly she caught his elbow and guided him toward a private chamber. He felt Nunfield's gaze boring into his back as they crossed the hall, picking their way around slumbering bodies.

The chamber contained a chaise wide enough for two. Lola tossed aside her mask and pushed Lucien down so that he was sitting on the edge. Then she straddled his lap and wrapped herself around him for a fevered kiss. As Nunfield had said, she was exceptionally skilled. Yet he sensed that under her extravagant display of passion was a nature as cold and calculating as that of a reptile.

Feeling repelled, he broke away and said blearily, "A pity I didn't meet you earlier, Lola, before I used up all my energy." He gave a hiccup for good measure. "Sorry. Sh ... should have drunk less."

He was about to remove her from his lap when she ran a hand down his torso. The unprincipled brigand attached to his body began to harden under the expert manipulation of her fingers.

She gave a crow of satisfaction. "Don't worry, mate, there's life in the old lad yet. Lola will take care of everything." From the flinty light in her eyes, he guessed that she secretly despised men and enjoyed seeing them helpless in the throes of lust. Most men would not notice or care about her private opinions, for her blatantly carnal behavior was the stuff of male fantasies. But not of his. Oh, God, not his. He wanted to walk out, yet he knew he should maintain his rakish role.

While he teetered between duty and inclination, Lola pressed him back across the chaise. Then she lifted the hem of his monk's robe and attacked the buttons of his trousers. When her heated mouth closed over him, raw desire surged through his veins, paralyzing his judgment and will. It had been a long time, too long, since he had lain with a woman, and his body would no longer be denied.

Lola's ministrations brought him to culmination in a matter of minutes, yet there was nothing satisfying about the physical release. No sooner had his ravening hunger been appeased then desolation overwhelmed him.

What was he doing here with a vulgar tart? Why did he think his hidden schemes were necessary to his country? Britain had survived centuries without him and would endure long after he was gone. He was a fool to think his actions could ever make a difference; his life's work was as futile as cold ashes.

He tried to counter his despair by invoking the memories of friends and family, but he instantly stopped, feeling too soiled to be worthy of the recollections. What would Jane think if she saw him now? His stomach churned at the thought, leaving the bitter taste of bile in his mouth.

To continue such thoughts would lead to madness. Painfully, he clamped down on his emotions, forcing them back into the hidden chamber that had saved him time and time again.

When a semblance of sanity had returned, he opened his eyes. Lola was sprawled on the chaise beside him, looking sleepy and pleased with herself. Though he couldn't bring himself to touch her, he made the sort of remarks a man was expected to make under such circumstances, thanking the woman who had served him and flattering her skill. Her report to Mace and Nunfield should be unexceptionable, and that was what mattered. Wasn't it?

As soon as he decently could, he got the hell away from the tawdry woman and the sordid room. A pity that he could not escape his own tarnished spirit so easily.

Chapter 16

It was midafternoon by the time Lucien finally returned home, and he was sick to death of pretending to be a libertine. His first action was to take a long, hot bath, as if he could scrub away the spiritual pollution of the Hellion orgy.

• Though he would have preferred a quiet evening at home, tinkering with some new mechanical device, it was the night of Lady Graham's salon, so he must venture forth. He consoled himself with the thought that a dose of witty conversation would dispel his depression even if he didn't find any clues to the whereabouts of Cassie James.

When he entered Lady Graham's substantial town house, his hostess greeted him with a fond smile. "Lucien, what a pleasant surprise. I've missed your wicked sense of humor."

He gave her a light kiss. "It's been too long. I can't imagine what I was doing that seemed so important that it left no time for enjoyment."

Lady Graham gave him a shrewd glance. "Very likely it really was important, and absolutely not the sort of thing you'll talk about. Come and meet some of my other guests. There's a good turnout tonight. You're acquainted with many of the people here, but I guarantee you'll see some interesting new faces. My bluestocking friend Lady Jane Travers, for example, I've known her since my come-out thirty years ago. She doesn't choose to move in fashionable circles so you've probably never met her. She has a very droll sense of humor and strong opinions about how the government should be run. Look for a redheaded woman who is six feet tall."

"She sounds like a veritable Amazon. No doubt she is a proponent of the theories of Mary Wollstonecraft Godwin?"

Lady Graham's brows arched. "Of course, any intelligent woman is. And you agree, you radical in dandy's clothing. You once spent a whole evening arguing for female rights against some dreadful Tory, so don't try to pull the wool over my eyes."

He laughed. "I should have known you'd remember that." As his hostess guided him to the drawing room, he asked casually, "Does the actress Cassie James ever attend your salons?"

"No, but I wouldn't mind if she did," Lady Graham replied. "I saw her at the Marlowe in some Gypsy piece—a very talented girl. We'll be hearing more of her." Noticing a young man who was at loose ends, she beckoned him over. "Mr. Haines, there's someone here I'd like you to meet."

After introducing the two men, Lady Graham abandoned Lucien while she went to greet another guest. Mr. Haines proved to be an aspiring poet who was keen on discussing the merit of Byron's new epic poem, *The Corsair*. Since Lucien hadn't read it and had a low opinion of Byron's self-aggrandizing poetry, their conversation was a short one.

Lucien spent the next hour working his way through the main drawing room, listening more than he talked. The topics of conversation were varied, ranging from heated discussions of Czar Alexander's politics to the imminent success of the peace negotiations and Miss Austen's latest satiric novel.

He enjoyed the talk, but his oblique inquiries about Cassie James bore no fruit. Everyone had heard of the actress and a number of guests had seen her perform; however, no one claimed any personal acquaintance.

Investigation was usually a tedious, unproductive business, so he accepted his lack of success philosophically and moved into the adjacent salon, which was smaller but equally crowded. As he did, Lady Graham materialized at his elbow. "Let me introduce you to Lady Jane, who's over there in the corner. She's interested in the theater, so she might be acquainted with that actress you asked about."

Lucien easily picked out Lady Jane, for she stood half a head taller than the group clustered around her. Her red hair had faded to auburn and was streaked with silver, but she was still a handsome woman.

Standing half-concealed at her side was a younger woman in a gray gown. She was easy to overlook, for her eyes were cast down and she had the colorless manner of a poor relation. Next to Lady Jane she appeared short, though she must be above average height. He would not have noticed her at all except that her stillness was noteworthy in a room full of animated people.

The young woman stepped back and turned slightly to avoid being hit by an enthusiastically waved hand. She had a lovely profile, pure as a Greek coin. . . .

Lucien stopped dead in his tracks. *No, it wasn't possible, not again.* "That girl beside your friend," he said tightly. "I believe I've met her before. Who is she?"

"What girl?" Lady Graham halted also and followed the direction of his glance. "Oh, you mean Lady Kathryn Travers, Jane's niece. Not really a girl, of course. She must be all of twenty-four and quite on the shelf. A pleasant young woman, though she never has anything to say for herself. Her parents are dead, so she lives with Jane now."

Pure, scalding rage burned through his veins. He had thought he was beyond surprise where she was concerned, but once again the little witch had caught him off guard. Her new role surpassed even her own deceitful standards. It was the ultimate effrontery: a shameless actress masquerading as a proper young lady. Not only that, but as a member of the aristocracy!

As always, her acting was pitch perfect. If he hadn't known her so well—hadn't held her in his arms and kissed her lying lips—he might have been fooled, for her present demeanor was so reserved that she seemed like a stranger. Yet her face was undeniably that of Emmie and Sally and Jane and Cassie James.

He had a fleeting image of her lying beside him, half-naked and with passion-hazed eyes. He had believed in her then, but no longer. This time he would not be gullible.

In a voice showing only mild interest, he said, "Of course, Lady Kathryn Travers. I wasn't sure I recognized her at first. Such a quiet young woman. But a fine mind under her shyness."

"I'm surprised you ever had the opportunity to meet her," Lady Graham commented. "As I'm sure you know, the family is an old one, but the male Traverses have always been known for wildness, and none of them ever had a penny to bless himself with. There was no money to give Lady Kathryn a London come-out, and her present life with Jane is very quiet."

"Nonetheless, I have had the pleasure of making her acquaintance." With a glittering, dangerous smile, he started cutting through the crowd. "And I can't tell you how much I look forward to renewing it."

When they reached the group in the corner, Lady Graham said, "Jane, I'd like you to meet a friend of mine, Lord Strathmore. Lucien, Lady Jane Travers."

When Lucien's name was pronounced, Lady Kathryn's head swung around and her slim body stiffened. Only someone watching as closely as he would have noticed, for her face was without expression.

Lucien bowed over Lady Jane's hand and said all that was proper. She was almost as tall as he, and her gray eyes were shrewdly capable. "A pleasure, Lord Strathmore," she said. "You've given some noteworthy speeches in the Lords. Have you ever considered taking a government office?"

"Never," he said promptly. "It's much easier to point out what is wrong than to make it right."

Lady Graham laughed, then continued, "Of course you already know Lady Kathryn Travers."

Genially he said, "It's been too long, Lady Kathryn."

Her brow furrowed. "Have we met, Lord Strathmore?"

Resisting the temptation to compliment her on an artful display of perplexity, he gave an elaborate sigh of regret. "How lowering to discover that you don't remember an occasion that is graven on my memory. We were having *such* a fascinating discusion when we were interrupted."

She made the mistake of looking directly at him. Though she had been able to school her face, she could not quite conceal the tension in her eyes, or the rapid pulse beating in her throat. A lesser woman would have taken flight.

Glancing at the older women, he said smoothly, "I was much taken by Lady Kathryn's exposition of Mary Wollstonecraft Godwin's theories. Her thoughts on the education of women were most intriguing. In fact, I'm considering introducing a bill in the Lords to address some of the inequities Lady Kathryn raised, so I must talk with her again. If you'll excuse us?"

Not waiting for a reply, he caught Kathryn's elbow with an iron grip and drew her across the crowded room. If he recalled rightly, there was a study at the back of the house where he should be able to wring her neck in complete peace and privacy.

As he marched his reluctant companion into the empty corridor, she tried to resist, saying, "Lord Strathmore, it's hardly proper for me to go off alone with a stranger."

He gave her a hard stare. "I don't know what we are to each other, but we are definitely not strangers." When she looked like protesting again, he said in a dulcet tone, "Shall I raise my voice and tell the room how lovely your naked breasts are? Or the sound you made when I kissed the tattoo on the inside of your thigh?"

She stopped dead and flushed violently. Then her face turned white and her resistance collapsed.

He towed her into the dimly lit study and slammed the door behind them. When he let her go, Kathryn immediately retreated to the far side of the study, rubbing her elbow and watching him as warily as if he were a fugitive from a lunatic asylum.

"Is Lady Jane your accomplice or another victim of your lies?" He lit a taper from the low-burning lamp and used it to ignite the branches of candles set about the room; he wanted to be able to see every nuance of expression on her deceitful face. "I wouldn't put it beyond

your powers to convince an innocent woman that you
are a relative she didn't know she had."

He blew out the taper with a sharp puff of air. "You
even appropriated her name. I've been thinking of you as
Jane ever since you insisted that the name was genuine.
However, I must admit that Kathryn suits you better
than any of the other things you've been calling
yourself."

"I don't know what you're talking about," she said
shakily.

The tears trembling in her gray eyes were a masterly
touch, but instead of being mollified, his anger erupted
again. "What, no Gypsy dancing, no passionate quest for
social justice? Not even a barmaid's suggestive quip?"
He paced toward her purposefully. "I'm disappointed.
Surely you can come up with a new story—probably half
a dozen of them. Perhaps you're a Napoleonic spy who
has fallen on hard times since the emperor abdicated. Or
are you the persecuted ruler of a Balkan kingdom who
is trying to regain her rightful throne?"

She darted behind the sofa. "I think you're mad, Lord
Strathmore. Or very, very drunk."

He circled behind the sofa after her. "I assure you I
am not drunk, and if I'm mad, it's you who have caused
me to lose my wits."

She retreated again. "Stay away from me!"

"Don't be hen-hearted. The one thing I do expect
from you is brazen courage."

She dashed around the far end of the sofa before he
could reach her. "I'm not who you think I am!"

He paused and made an elaborate show of examining
her. "Same face, same figure, same coloring." His mouth
hardened. "And the same lying gray eyes. Only the name
has changed, and that doesn't count since you've claimed
a different identity each time we've met."

She tried to slide away again, but the room was too
small. In two swift steps he had cornered her. She flattened her back against the wall and quavered, "What are
you going to do?"

"The idea of murder is tempting." He reached for her.

"But I'll settle for completing what was interrupted when you ran away the last time we were together."

"Don't touch me!" she cried. "I'll ... I'll scream for help."

"The way everyone out there is chattering, you won't be heard." As soon as he touched her, he realized how much of his anger was frustrated desire. He wanted her—dear God, how he wanted her, even though he couldn't trust her an inch.

He enfolded her in his embrace, needing to feel the slim length of her body against his. "Don't fight the inevitable," he said softly.

She tried to wriggle free. "There is nothing inevitable about this!"

"No?" Gentle but implacable, he held her captive in the circle of his arms. "Relax, my dear. I won't hurt you, because I can't stay angry with you, no matter how hard I try."

She made a choked sound and hid her face against his shoulder. He stroked her back, patiently waiting for the intense mutual attraction to work its magic. Gradually, her rigid body began to soften, becoming all warm, carnation-scented femininity.

He rested his cheek against her coiled hair, suspended in a curious state between peace and crackling desire. "A pity we can't be like this all the time," he murmured as he skimmed his hands over the familiar, supple curves of her back and waist.

His words jarred her out of her compliant state. She planted her hands in the middle of his chest and shoved herself away. "We shouldn't be like this at all!"

He braced his hands against the wall on both sides of her so that she could not escape. "Is the problem another man in your life? Tell me so at least I'll understand what I'm up against."

"You don't really want me!" she said vehemently.

"You're wrong. I want you very much." He brushed his fingertips over her cheek in a feathery caress. Her complexion had the smooth, fragile delicacy of a blossom. "And this time, I intend to have you."

"No!" She bit her lip, as if wrestling with a decision.

.

At length, she took a deep breath, then said unevenly, "I didn't want to tell you this."

"Tell me what?" he said encouragingly.

She gave a twisted smile. "I fear, Lord Strathmore, that you have confused me with my sister—my identical twin sister, Kristine."

Chapter 17

After a startled moment, Lucien laughed out loud. "I'm glad to see your imagination hasn't failed yet, but surely you can come up with something better than a mythical twin sister. That's a plot device from a Gothic novel."

"Kristine is not mythical—she is a comic actress who performs as Cassie James. You obviously know her, but you most assuredly don't know me." She swallowed hard. "So for pity's sake, don't blame me for whatever you think my sister has done."

Lucien hesitated. Damnation, but the girl was convincing. He studied her earnest face. Every feature, line, and hollow was exactly as he remembered. The soft brown hair that glinted with gold and the slim, graceful figure were equally familiar. There was no sign of the bawdy vitality of Sally or Cassie James, but her demeanor was similar to that of "Jane" when she had claimed to be a young lady trying to help her brother.

Based on her record, Lady Nemesis was quite capable of acting the role of shy Lady Kathryn Travers, poor relation. She had also, briefly, responded to his embrace as naturally as if it was familiar. Yet there was something in her voice that caused him to wonder if she might possibly be telling the truth.

There was one way to find out, for even a consummate actress would have trouble concealing her identity in a kiss. He drew her close and bent his head.

Before their lips could touch, she jerked back and hit him with a ringing slap across the cheek. "How dare you, sir!"

Yes, she was strong. Yet what caused him to release her was not force, but the note of outraged virtue in her voice. It was hard to believe that even the most gifted of actresses could sound so much like an offended virgin.

Cheek stinging, he scrutinized Kathryn's face once more. Yet even though he used all his trained powers of observation, she still looked exactly like the duplicitous minx who had brought chaos to his orderly life. Except, perhaps, there might be more vulnerability in the depths of those clear gray eyes than he had seen before. "No twins are truly identical," he said slowly. "There are always subtle differences, yet I see none in this case. And believe me, I speak as one who has studied you with great concentration."

She blushed and ducked her head as if embarrassed by the warmth in his eyes. "All of our lives, people have said that Kristine and I are the most identical twins they've ever seen," she said haltingly. "But believe me, if Kristine was here, you could tell us apart instantly. You'd never notice I was in the room, because she has the kind of vitality that draws every eye."

"Many actresses and actors have that ability, and they can turn it off when they choose to," he said, unimpressed. His eyes narrowed. "When Lady Graham introduced us, you recognized me, though you tried to conceal your reaction."

"That wasn't recognition, but alarm," she said tartly. "You were glaring at me as if I were a cockroach."

"Surely not a cockroach," he said with an involuntary smile.

"Your expression was enough to terrify any innocent female." She went to stand by the fire, her head bowed. "I don't know what is between you and Kristine, and frankly, I don't want to know. My only desire is to be left in peace."

"I'm still not convinced that you have a sister." He folded his arms and leaned against the wall, regarding her thoughtfully. "Since my experience is that you are a fluent liar, I'll need stronger evidence than your unsupported word."

She raised her head and gave him an icy glance. "I can't see why the burden of proof should be on me. I was minding my own business when you assaulted me."

Good God, what if she really was an innocent stranger who had never seen him before? An appalling thought. "If you're telling the truth about having a twin sister, I'll owe you a groveling apology."

A hint of smile showed in her eyes, as if the prospect pleased her. "Prepare yourself to be humbled, Lord Strathmore, because Kristine is as real as you are."

As she became more relaxed, Kathryn paradoxically seemed both more and less like the woman he knew. She had the familiar quicksilver intelligence, yet it was coupled with a cool reserve that was new to him. Of course, an actress could simulate that.

He was more likely to get information by being conciliatory instead of accusing. "I know it's an impertinence on my part, Lady Kathryn, but would you be willing to explain why you and your sister are leading such different lives?"

At the implication that he had accepted her story, she relaxed even more and took a seat by the fire. "It's really quite simple. My father was the fourth Earl of Markland. The Traverses have never had any distinction apart from charm, wildness, and a tendency to produce identical twins. The family seat, Langdale Court, was in Westmoreland."

He took the chair opposite her. "Was?"

She sighed. "My father inherited a load of debts and promptly piled on a mountain of his own. The house was falling about our ears when we were growing up. My mother died when we were ten, and after that we ran wild. If some of the ladies in the neighborhood hadn't taken an interest in us, we would have been complete heathens. Papa managed to hold off the bailiffs when he was alive, but after his death five years ago, the estate went to auction, the title went to a second cousin in America, and Kristine and I were left penniless."

"Your father was so irresponsible that he made no provisions for your future?"

"Thinking about the future was not in his nature," she said dryly. "I suppose he thought that eventually he would dower us with the winnings from some card game, but he never got around to it. My mother was a vicar's daughter who was disowned after eloping with my father, so there was no help from her side of the family either. Kristine and I were in the position of any other young ladies of good birth and no fortune."

"Which is not a good position at all."

"Precisely. One can marry, find work, or become a poor relation existing on charity."

"Marriage would seem the logical choice. You' are both very attractive young women."

"It takes a great deal of beauty to overcome the lack of a dowry," she said cynically. "And there were ... other reasons."

He wondered what they might be, but refused to let himself get sidetracked. "Is that when you came to live with Lady Jane?"

She nodded. "Fortunately, Aunt Jane had inherited a modest independence from her grandmother, enough to maintain an establishment here in London. I was happy to accept when she offered us a home, since I don't think I would make a very good governess, and I certainly wasn't qualified to do anything else."

When she fell silent, he prodded, "What about Kristine?"

She gazed into the dancing flames. "My sister is ten minutes older than I, and she inherited both of our shares of the Travers charm and wildness. She's too headstrong, too independent to settle for a quiet life with a blue stocking aunt. She had always loved acting and performing, and she often organized plays and concerts. So she decided to throw propriety to the winds and try for a career in the theater."

"And so the two of you become classic examples of good twin, wicked twin."

Missing the irony in his tone, she said sharply, "Kristine is not evil, simply braver than most. She would never take the coward's way out."

Was that how Kathryn saw her own life—as the coward's way out? "The theater may not be evil," he said mildly, "but it is an unusual choice for a gently bred girl. Her reputation would be destroyed."

"Kristine said what use is a reputation when it comes

to putting food on the table? If she was going to be poor, she might as well enjoy herself. She chose to use a stage name to avoid embarrassing the family, not that there is much family left to embarrass. It took her several years, but as you know, she's now doing very well."

"Do you keep in close touch with her?"

Expression troubled, Kathryn turned her gaze back to the fire. "Though Aunt Jane has radical political views, her personal moral standards are of the highest. She strongly disapproved of Kristine's decision and forebade her the house. That made it ... difficult for me to see my sister."

"In other words, you had to choose between your twin and having a roof over your head," Lucien guessed. "Difficult."

"Not at all. Kristine effectively made the decision for both of us, just as she always made decisions in the past."

The pain in her voice cut too close to the bone for Lucien's comfort. "Surely she misses you as much as you miss her."

Kathryn's face shuttered. "That is neither here nor there, Lord Strathmore. You wanted to know why my sister and I lead very different lives, and now you do. I'll thank you not to spread the information. Jane would not like it to be public knowledge that Cassie James is really a black sheep Travers."

"Your aunt sounds like a bit of a tyrant."

"She has been very good to me," Kathryn said with even greater coldness. "I will not countenance criticism of her."

He admired her loyalty and hoped it was rewarded in kind. Despite her prickliness, there was a vulnerability about Kathryn that made him want to protect her—even though he was still not convinced that she wasn't a bald-faced liar.

"Though actresses can happen in even the best-regulated families, I understand why Lady Jane would rather not advertise the connection. However, since you are identical twins, trying to conceal the relationship seems like an exercise in futility."

She shrugged. "Not really. While we are generally con-

sidered attractive, we have no single, distinctive feature
like red hair or unusual height. When Kristine performs,
she wears costumes and cosmetics so that she scarcely
looks like herself, much less like me. Since my circle of
acquaintance is small, there are few people in a position
to notice the resemblance. No one has made the connection yet.''

He smiled. ''I take your point, but you do yourself and
your sister less than justice. Though your features may
not be flamboyant, the total effect is ... memorable.''
His gaze went to the heavy coil of hair at her nape. If
loosened, it would fall past her waist. ''For example, your
hair might be dismissed as merely brown, but it is still
lovely. Thick, shiny, and shimmering with gold
highlights.''

She touched her head self-consciously, then stopped in
midgesture. ''I should have thought of it sooner—our
hair is the one obvious difference between my sister and
me. Mine has never been cut, but Kristine shortened hers
to make it easier to wear wigs.'' A triumphant gleam
showed in her eyes. ''Even the cleverest of actresses
couldn't grow this much hair in the interval since you
last saw my sister, Lord Strathmore. Does that finally
convince you that we are two different women?''

A vivid mental image of soft hair brushing Cassie
James's shoulders flashed through his mind. He uttered
a mental oath. Damnation, but his brain was failing. He
should have noticed himself. A different apparent hair
length was not absolute proof that he was dealing with
two separate women, but it came close. ''You could be
wearing a switch of false hair.''

She rolled her eyes. ''You're a suspicious man, but
even you must admit that if I am using a switch, it is an
exact match for my natural hair.''

She was correct again; her warm, subtly gilded brown
tresses were entirely consistent. Half joking, he said,
''For proof positive, I would have to pull out the pins so
your hair could fall freely.''

Her eyes narrowed like an aggrieved feline. ''Enough,
Lord Strathmore. A certain amount can be forgiven because you confused me with my sister, but I will not

permit further assaults on my person. Surely, even rakes know that the rules are different for actresses and ladies."

He had to laugh. "You've routed me completely, Lady Kathryn. One last question before I take my leave. Besides her acting, does your sister write political essays under the name L. J. Knight?"

Kathryn's brows arched. "Of course not. She is an excellent actress, but certainly not a writer. What ever gave you such a foolish idea?"

"Kristine did."

"She must have given a truly superior performance if she convinced you that a twenty-four-year-old girl could write with the perception of L. J. Knight."

"She's a very persuasive young woman." Making a guess based on something he had heard in her voice, he asked, "Do you know Mr. Knight yourself?"

"Not personally, but Aunt Jane does. According to her, he is an aging invalid with a sharp tongue and little patience for human foibles. They deal very well together."

If Kathryn knew that about Knight, undoubtedly Kristine did too, which would explain why she had known it was safe to claim his identity. It all made sense.

Getting to his feet, Lucien said, "You've been very helpful, Lady Kathryn. I'm sorry if I distressed you earlier."

"That's not a true groveling apology, but I will accept it anyhow." She gave him a level look. "You're not going to hurt Kristine when you find her, are you?"

"No." He smiled wryly. "Besides, I haven't the foggiest notion where she is. Unless you can tell me?"

"Even if I knew, I wouldn't tell you, Lord Strathmore. I may not approve of the life Kristine has chosen, but she is still my sister."

He had not expected anything else. "Very well. Until next time, Lady Kathryn."

"I sincerely hope that there will never be another time," she said with a return to her earlier acerbity. "Considering the length of time we have been closeted together, it would be best if we left separately. I'll wait here for a few minutes."

He hesitated as if on the verge of saying something more, then settled for a bow and a formal farewell.

After the study door closed, Kit leaned back in her chair, shaking. Had Strathmore believed her? He had seemed to, but she was unsure; he was a difficult man to read. She wondered what he would do with the information he had pried out of her. Though he might not be an enemy, that didn't mean that he wasn't a danger.

Danger . . .

She shivered as a disturbingly vivid memory of how it had felt to be in his arms flashed through her mind. Dear Lord, she should have slapped him sooner instead of clinging to him like ivy! She had not behaved at all like the prim, ladylike Kathryn Travers who had inherited a double share of propriety. But she had felt so good, so blessedly safe, that she had been temporarily paralyzed. The Travers part of her was shameless.

She found herself rubbing the itchy spot inside her thigh, and instantly dropped her hand. Thank heaven he hadn't seen the tattoo. If he had, she would *really* be in trouble.

Chapter 18

Lucien had trouble falling asleep after he returned from the salon. When he did, his dreams were disturbing. He found himself trapped in a swirling, featureless fog that hid all landmarks. As he inched his way forward, knowing that he had a vital mission to perform, he suddenly saw his lovely, elusive Lady Nemesis just ahead of him, her slim body clothed only in mist. Her beauty caught at his heart.

She smiled and extended her hand. He stepped forward eagerly, but before they could touch, her expression changed to horror. She turned and fled. Ignoring the menacing shapes that surrounded them, he raced in pursuit, determined to claim her. She led him to a castle built of stones as dark as death. Sensing that it would be disastrous to enter, he called a warning, but she plunged recklessly through the black arch.

Grimly, he followed. He emerged into a bright chamber filled with mirrors, every one of them reflecting a different image of her. She was a frightened chambermaid, a worldly, provocative actress, a cool intellectual—every guise he had seen and many that he had not.

And through the hall echoed the desolate sounds of a woman weeping with anguish.

Desperate to help, he reached out to a sad-eyed image—Kristine? Kathryn?—and banged his hand into the cold, impervious surface of a mirror.

Behind him a husky voice whispered, "Help me, Lucien—in the name of God, please help me."

He whirled about, but could not tell which of the glittering reflections was real. Increasingly frantic, he searched through the hall until his lungs burned and his hands bled from smashing into an infinity of mirrors. But he could not find the warm, flesh-and-blood reality of the woman he sought—only mirrors and cruelly mocking images.

He awoke, shaking and possessed by a feeling of doom, though he wasn't sure if the doom was his or hers. Perhaps it was mutual. He forced himself to lie back on the pillows and relax, muscle by muscle.

As his breathing steadied, he had the wry thought that at least he wasn't experiencing the paralyzing emptiness he had known after the sordid encounter with Lola. With his Lady Nemesis, the problem was not too little emotion, but too much, most of it frustration.

Though Lucien was nine-tenths convinced that his quarry was Kristine Travers, a volatile actress with a very proper twin sister, he was too experienced to accept Kathryn's story without confirmation. His Great-aunt Josephine, the dowager Countess of Steed, might be able to tell him what he needed to know. She had a very long ear for gossip; it was a family trait.

Fortunately, his aunt was willing to receive him at an unfashionably early hour. Tiny and silver-haired, she sat by a fire, swaddled in shawls, when he was shown into her morning room. "Ring for tea, my boy," she ordered. "Then come here and give your old aunt a kiss."

After he had obeyed, she waved him into a chair opposite hers. "Have you come here to tell me that you are on the verge of matrimony?"

He laughed. "The answer is the same as always: no. I promise that if I ever change my mind, you'll be one of the first to know, but for now, you'll have to content yourself with sprigs from other branches of the family tree."

Lady Steed nodded her head, unsurprised. "Then you're probably here to pry facts from my doddering old brain."

"Doddering—you? Your mind and memory are as sharp as a Florentine dagger."

She tried to scowl reprovingly, but couldn't conceal her smile. "What do you want to know this time?"

"You have friends in Westmoreland, don't you?"

"The Miltons, near Kendal. The dowager and I have been bosom bows for almost sixty years. I visit them for a fortnight every summer on my way to Scotland. The current viscount is my godson." She peered balefully over her gold-rimmed half-spectacles. "Lord Milton married at twenty-two and has three sons now. There's a man who knows his duty to his family."

Ignoring her gibe with the skill of long practice, he asked, "Did you ever meet a Lord Markland there?"

"Oh, yes, a charming man, though quite worthless. His estate was only a few miles from Milton Hall." She sniffed. "All he could manage to produce was a pair of twin daughters. After he died, the title went to an American cousin, so I expect it's effectively extinct. As I understand it, Americans don't hold with such things as titles."

Before she could digress into the virtues of the hereditary aristocracy, Lucien said, "Tell me about the twin daughters. Did you ever meet them?"

"Almost every time I visited the Miltons. They were a lovely pair of girls, Kristine and Kathryn, both with a *K*. The Traverses have always been known for having odd kicks in their gallops." She shook her head. "Markland neglected his daughters shamefully. Anne Milton was fond of the girls, so she did her best to teach them how to get on in society."

"The twins were identical?"

She nodded. "As like as two peas in a pod. I've never seen such a resemblance. For all the times I met them, I never could tell them apart. Very different temperaments, though. Lady Kristine was the older, and she was wild, like her father."

The tea tray arrived and the countess poured for them. "Kristine's exploits were notorious throughout the county. Swimming naked in the river at midnight, climbing cliffs, wearing breeches to ride with the local hunt, arguing logic with the vicar until the poor man didn't know whether he was coming or going. She should have been a boy."

That certainly explained where she had developed the skills for burglary and roof running. "What about Lady Kathryn?"

"She took after her mother, a vicar's daughter, and was a very proper young lady. She was always trailing along behind her sister, trying to keep her out of trouble. A sweet child, but easy to overlook—Kristine did all the talking for both of them." Lady Steed lifted the silver tongs and dropped a chunk of sugar into her cup. "People made allowances for the girls because of the way they had been brought up. There was no real vice in them, but Kristine was definitely headed for trouble. Probably eloped with the first man who asked her, or went on the stage, or did something equally disreputable."

Lucien's brows arched. "Do you really think she might have become an actress?"

She chuckled. "I doubt that even Kristine would be so lost to propriety as that, but she was very good at theatricals. She and Kathryn were always staging plays with the other young people in the neighborhood. They were a particular success in *A Comedy of Errors* and *Twelfth Night*."

Lucien smiled at the thought. "One seldom gets to see those plays done with genuine twins rather than false ones. Presumably Kristine was Sebastian to Kathryn's Viola?"

"Yes, and she made a very dashing fellow. One could hardly blame Olivia for losing her heart." The countess sipped her tea pensively. "Wherever Kristine is now, I'm sure she's up to some kind of mischief. That girl needed a strong man in her life." After a moment's reflection she added, "And her bed."

Lucien grinned. "Don't think you can shock me with your bawdiness, Aunt Josie—I'm already inured. Do you know where the twins are now?"

"They left Westmoreland after their father died and the estate was sold. It must have been about five years ago. They went to London to live with their aunt." Lady Steed pursed her lips. "Markland left them quite penniless. No amount of charm could compensate for such shocking irresponsibility."

"Do either of them have Jane as a middle name?"

"As a matter of fact, they both do. Kathryn Jane Anne

and Kristine Jane Alice, I believe. Apparently Markland had asked his sister to be godmother to his first child, and he saw no reason to change merely because his wife presented him with twins." She shrugged. "Or perhaps the parents thought the girls should have identical initials along with everything else."

He remembered "Cassie James" swearing that Jane really was her name. So that time, at least, she wasn't lying. The little witch had a devious mind. Of course, he already knew that.

As he was ruminating, Lady Steed said, "An interesting phenomenon, twins. As infants they often develop their own secret language from baby talk." Seeing Lucien's expression, her gaze dropped. "Of course you know that already. At any rate, the Travers girls had private nicknames for each other. I noticed once when they were chattering together."

"Do you know what the names were?"

"I believe they were Kit and Kara." The countess bit her lip. "No, that's not right. Kira, that was it. Kit and Kira."

Lucien's interest quickened. "Which was which? The sounds are similar enough so that the proper names and nicknames could be combined either way."

"Kit is usually short for Kathryn." His aunt's brow furrowed. "That can't be right—Kit was doing most of the talking, so she would have been Kristine."

"Kit is a nickname for Kristine as well," Lucien said. The first time he had met her, at Rafe's hunting party, she had identified herself as Kitty. It must have been the automatic response of a girl who thought of herself as Kit. In fact, her exact answer had been "Kit . . . Kitty," as if she was belatedly changing a telltale slip to a stutter. "So Kathryn is Kira."

With the issue of names settled, he moved to a more important question. "Did either of the girls have suitors?"

"Not serious ones. Everyone in Westmoreland knew they didn't have a penny to their names, so they weren't really eligible. Oh, plenty of young men flirted with Kristine and the minx flirted right back. And once Anne

Milton said there was a widower who thought Kathryn would make a suitable stepmother for his five children, but I never heard of anything significant."

He grinned at her affectionately. "If you didn't hear, it didn't exist. I never cease be be amazed at how much you know."

She cocked her head to one side like a sparrow. "I've answered all of your questions, but I don't suppose you would answer mine if I asked what you were up to this time."

"Suffice it to say that I wondered whether I was dealing with one woman or two." He rose to his feet. "Thank you for verifying that the Travers *are* twins. I'm in your debt."

"You can discharge it by telling them to call on me if they're in London," she said promptly. "Separately or together. I would enjoy renewing the acquaintance."

"I'll do that," he promised as he took his leave. Issuing his aunt's invitation would give him an excuse to call on Kathryn. She might not want to see him again, but she was still his best lead to finding Kristine.

Wanting to stretch his legs, he dismissed his carriage and started to walk home. He was acting very strangely about Kristine—Kit. He turned the name over in his mind, thinking it a good fit. A name with sharp edges, like hers. He hoped to God he wouldn't have to learn any new names for her; he was confused enough already.

Even though he was finally making progress, he felt a deep sense of disquiet, and he didn't know why. He suspected that it wouldn't go away until he caught up with Kit once and for all.

Chapter 19

The next step was to visit the very proper Lady Kathryn Travers. He had learned Lady Jane's address from Lady Graham, so that afternoon he paid a call. The Travers house was located between Mayfair and Soho, respectable but modest. The door was answered by a saucy chambermaid. Her brows rose when he presented his card. "Cor, a blooming lord."

"Very little blooms in December," he said gravely. "Especially not lords. Is Lady Kathryn home?"

"If she isn't home to you, she's a bloody fool," the maid said irreverently as she led him to the drawing room.

A few minutes later, Kathryn entered, her expression hostile. "I hoped I had seen the last of you, Lord Strathmore." She did not ask him to sit down. "Have we anything more to say to each other?"

"Well, I do owe you a sincere apology for the way I treated you. Shall I get down on my knees?"

He made a move to do so, but she stopped him with a wave of her hand. "Don't be foolish," she said irritably. "That would only ruin fifty pounds worth of expert tailoring. I gather that mature reflection persuaded you that I was telling the truth."

"That, plus a visit with my aunt, the dowager Lady Steed."

Her expression became even warier. "I didn't know that Lady Steed was your aunt."

"Great-aunt, to be precise. She issued an invitation for you to call. She'd like to see you and your sister again."

Before Kathryn could reply, a large tabby wandered into the drawing room and began twining around the visitor's ankles, leaving drifts of fur in its wake. Lucien glanced down in time to see the cat hook a claw into his polished boots. "I might as well have groveled. By the time this feline finishes with me, all of that expensive tailoring will be ruined anyhow."

Kathryn lost some of her dignity as she swooped forward and retrieved the animal. As she banished it, protesting, from the room, she said, "I'm sorry, my lord. Like all cats, Sebastian has an instinct for being where he is least wanted."

"I presume that Kristine has a cat called Viola?"

She stiffened. "How did you know that?"

"I didn't," he said mildly. "It was merely a joke derived from Aunt Josephine's saying that you and your sister enjoyed acting in the Shakespearean plays that featured twins."

Her manner eased fractionally. "We had a natural advantage in that area. As for the cats, we got kittens from the same litter. Since she named hers Viola, my tom became Sebastian."

He was glad she was softening, though the cat deserved more credit than his own fabled charm. "My main reason for calling concerns your sister. I'm afraid she may be in trouble."

Her eyes narrowed to slits. "Explain yourself." She had a remarkable range of suspicious expressions.

Choosing his words carefully, he said, "When I met Kristine, she was engaged in ... fraudulent and illegal activities. I don't think she is a criminal in the usual sense, but I fear she is involved in something that could be dangerous."

A faint sigh went through Kathryn. "You're probably right, but what do you want me to do about it?"

"I understand why you don't want to reveal her location to me, but please, send her a message," he urged. "Whatever the trouble is, I think I can help."

Her gray eyes ice-cool, Kathryn asked, "Are you one of Kristine's lovers?"

So Kathryn could be as bold as her sister. "No, I am not," Lucien said evenly. "I'll admit that I wish I was, but my first concern is her safety. I think she is venturing into deeper waters than she realizes."

Her face suddenly older than her years, Kathryn said, "I wish I could help you, Lord Strathmore, but I honestly have no idea where Kristine is. I wish to God that I did."

Her words were utterly convincing, and Lucien sensed that she was as concerned about her sister as he was. "Come for a drive with me. The day is more like October than December, and the fresh air will do you good."

When she hesitated, he said, "How much trouble can I cause in an open curricle when I have my hands full of reins?"

A hint of a smile showed in her eyes. "A persuasive argument. Very well, I'll get my cloak and bonnet."

Both garments, predictably, were dark, sober, and practical. Though Lady Kathryn might not feel that she would make a good governess, she dressed like one. Lucien was fascinated by how she could look so much like her sister, yet be restrained to the point of near-invisibility.

As if reading his mind, she said, "Kristine could wear this same cloak and look so dashing and fashionable that everyone would stare at her. She told me once that a good actress should be able to walk down a street and be seen, or walk down the same street and *not* be seen. She could do either." Kathryn smiled ironically. "When my sister doesn't want to be seen, she pretends that she is me. Then no one notices her."

"Surely the reverse must be true," Lucien said as he helped her into his curricle. "If you want to be seen, all you have to do is walk down the street pretending to be her."

She settled her skirts primly about her ankles. "I would never wish to attract that kind of vulgar attention."

He studied her from the corner of his eye as they drove through the busy London streets. She sat silently, feeling no need to fill the air with chatter. Though her manner was more reserved than her sister's, she shared the same marvelous, heart-catching profile. The sight of her made him ache for Kit.

When they reached the relative peace of the park, he asked, "Did you ever resent your sister for dazzling everyone?"

"How can one resent the sun for shining?" she answered. "Besides, Kristine enjoyed being the center of attention and I didn't, so there was no competition between us."

"Never?" he asked skeptically.

"Never." She glanced at him askance. "I'm not sure if a non-twin can understand this. Because we are similar in so many ways, a compliment to her pleases me as much as if it were made to me. I have always delighted in her achievements."

She sounded sincere, yet he had the impression that she was not telling the whole truth. Surely there must have been times when Kathryn had yearned for attention.

She continued, "The reverse is also true. Once a stuffy widower who was considering me for his next wife claimed that I was far prettier than Kristine. Even if the idea hadn't been nonsense, I would have been angry. How could he expect me to take pleasure in a compliment made at my sister's expense?"

"That was clumsy," Lucien agreed. "Yet it is not impossible that the fellow might have honestly found you more attractive. The glory of the sun does not lessen the loveliness of the moon."

She gave him a quick, startled glance. Then her gaze fell to her gloved hands. "You have a glib tongue, my lord."

"Yes," he admitted, "but that doesn't mean I don't sometimes tell the truth, as I just did."

Sudden laughter lit her face, and for a moment it was as if Kit was sitting beside him with all her teasing, volatile charm. Lucien's hands tightened on the reins, confusing his horses, and he reminded himself this was not the sister he wanted.

Yet while Kathryn did not have her sister's radiant sensuality, there was an intriguing hint of passion lurking beneath her proper surface. A good thing she was the sort of respectable female that a gentleman could court but not seduce. Otherwise, he might have been tempted to further their acquaintance, and his life was confused enough already.

Kit was a different story. Having chosen to kick over the traces of conventional morality, she was fair game. If—when—they became lovers, it would be as equals.

Yet he was still acutely aware of the woman sitting beside him. With an inward smile, he told himself it was a good thing Kathryn had a strong right arm and was willing to use it. No, it was his right cheek that had stung, so she must have struck him with her left hand.

He asked, "Kira, are you and your sister both left-handed?"

Her previous wariness returned. "Why did you call me that?"

"My aunt said that you and Kristine called each other Kit and Kira. I used your nickname because I like it."

"Lady Steed noticed a great deal," she said repressively. "But those names are private to my sister and me. It sounds strange to hear 'Kira' on a stranger's lips."

"I'm sorry," he said meekly. "I'll restrict myself to calling you Kathryn if you prefer."

"Lady Kathryn, if you please. We are not on familiar terms with each other."

"Yet."

She gave him a straight look. "I am not Kristine, Lord Strathmore, and I don't appreciate being used as a tool to help you find her."

He was surprised at how much he disliked the fact that she felt that way. He pulled his horses to a halt on the side of the track so he could give her his full attention. "It's true that I want to find your sister, for selfish reasons as well as disinterested ones. But you are an intriguing woman in your own right. I think we could be friends, if you would allow yourself, instead of growling like a cornered wildcat."

She looked away. "I'm sorry if I have been rude. The fact that my father was an unreliable sort has tended to make me suspicious of male intentions."

"I have no dishonorable intentions where you are concerned, and I would enjoy your conversation even if you didn't have a twin sister. Could that be considered a basis for friendship?"

"Perhaps ... perhaps it could," she said uncomfortably. "But I don't know if I wish for friendship."

"You're a hard woman, Lady Kathryn,"

"I prefer it that way, my lord." As if needing to change the subject, she asked, "Do you have a brother?"

"No." It was Lucien's turn to be uncomfortable. He started the curricle forward again with perhaps too much concentration on his horses. "I had a sister, but she died very young."

"I'm sorry," she said with genuine sympathy. "A sibling can be one's best ally against a difficult world, for no one else can ever so completely understand the forces that mold us for life."

"I adopted three brothers at Eton, and they've served me well," he said lightly.

She gave a faint sigh. "A family that one chooses must be more satisfactory than the sort one inherits."

"Usually it is, but when there are problems, they are as painful as with blood kin," he said, thinking of the trouble Michael had caused the previous spring. "Since you know Kristine better than anyone, surely you have some idea where I might look for her. I have reason to believe she might be living in Soho."

"She had a flat there once, but no longer," Kathryn replied. "I don't believe she is performing for the next week or two, so she may have left London." She gave him an unreadable glance. "If you learn anything, will you let me know?"

"I was about to ask the same thing. Surely she is more likely to communicate with you than me."

Kathryn stared down at her hands, which were clamped tightly in her lap. "We are no longer as close as we once were. Though I would be pleased to hear from her, I don't expect to."

He thought of the complex ties that bound twins and ached for Kathryn's loneliness. It must be difficult to live on the charity of a strong-minded aunt, cut off from her sister, who had been her closest friend. And it would be worse yet to feel that sister no longer cared for her.

Deciding he had upset his companion enough for one day, he turned the conversation to literature as they drove back to Lady Jane's house. When Kathryn was relaxed and discussing an abstract topic, her dry wit was very amusing.

He was pensive as he drove away. In her own way, Kathryn was as enigmatic as her sister. She was also, he realized unhappily, almost as alluring. He wanted to fan that hidden spark of passion into a flame. He wanted to kiss away her wariness and make her laugh without restraint. He wanted ...

Damnation! He didn't know what he wanted. No, that wasn't true. He wanted Kit, and in his frustration he was transferring that desire to Kit's twin. Granted, the similarities between them were tantalizing, yet the differences were far more significant. The women were individuals, each with her own dreams and fears. To confuse them in his mind would be a denial of their essential humanity.

Besides, Kathryn was entirely too rigid for Lucien's taste. He reminded himself of that—repeatedly.

By the time he arrived home, his normally even temper was thoroughly foul. He needed to find Kristine before he turned rabid. Unfortunately, the progress he thought he had made had turned out to be an illusion. He was no closer to finding his Lady Nemesis than he had been before meeting Kathryn.

Interlude

She waited for him by the door. The instant he stepped into the anteroom, she cracked the whip across his shoulders. He spun around, surprised and aroused. Tonight she wore virginal white, like the innocent girl she was not, and a white veil floated over the soft, false blond curls. But her satin gown was only long enough to brush the tops of her thighs, and her long legs were encased in leather and black lace. "You look especially beautiful tonight, mistress," he breathed.

"Silence!" She stretched sensually so that the white satin strained across her breasts. "Of course I am beautiful, but I am not for the likes of you, slave. You must not touch me. You cannot look at me. You may not even think about me."

"You are cruel, mistress," he whimpered. "I can't help but think of you, and of the ecstasy I find in serving you."

She choked back the bile that rose at his words. When she had mastered her voice, she spat out, "Insolent swine! You must be punished for your presumption. Come into my dungeon."

Though he obeyed eagerly, he paused for a moment by the evil little mechanical device. She slapped the whip handle across his knuckles to start him moving again.

In the center of the rough-hewn stone chamber stood a large wooden frame. Touching him as little as possible, she shackled his wrists and ankles so that he was spread-eagled on the frame.

Then she raised the hardest-edged whip she owned

and used it to strip him naked. Endless hours of practice had made her an expert, and her control was exquisite. She knew exactly how much pressure was required to rend fabric, and how much more to graze the flesh beneath—how to raise a welt, and how to draw blood. Soon rents in his garments revealed the sweat-filmed skin below, and crimson stains marred the white linen remnants of his shirt.

She gauged her progress by watching his organ swell against the tattered fabric of his breeches. The more of his clothing she shredded, the harder he writhed against his bonds and the louder his moans for release.

Not until he was fully naked did she apply the final, vicious slash across the buttocks that she knew would bring him to orgasm. He gave a drawn-out wail of animal need, his hips pumping wildly as his seed spurted in a silvery arc. Then his whole body went slack, and he hung limply from the shackles, only the heaving of his chest showing that he still lived.

She drew the whip through her trembling fingers and wondered how long it would take him to die if she knotted the leather thong about his throat. The murderous impulse was so intense that she could taste it. His face would turn purple, and he would thrash in terror when he realized that this time there would be no escape, but he would be helpless before her lethal rage.

Quickly, before she could act on her desire, she whirled away and fled from the dungeon.

Chapter 20

Kit awoke with a smothered scream, her fingers cramped from her vicious knotting of the leather. Horrified, she looked at her hands in the dawn light. She half expected to see ridges gouged in the flesh, but they were empty. She had not really murdered anyone. It had only been another ghastly nightmare.

They were coming more often now, each uglier and more upsetting than the last, but this was the first time she had dreamed of murder. She tried to remember the face, but it was too distorted—by rage? by fear?—to be recognizable.

Staggering from her bed, she made her way to the washstand and cracked the film of ice that covered the surface of the water in the pitcher. Then she splashed her face and hands, feeling like Lady Macbeth in her frantic desire to cleanse herself.

As she blotted her face dry, she tried to remember the dream more clearly, but she could see only fragments, nothing specific enough to identify. She had dressed and was in the process of combing her hair when a vivid image suddenly appeared in her mind. It was of an indecently dressed female slashing a whip across the naked body of a man.

It took her a moment to realize that she was seeing not real people, but mechanical figures. They were exquisitely detailed, right down to the hand-painted scarlet stripes on the man's back. A tinkling baroque tune acccompanied the rhythmic rise and fall of the whip. She was seeing a music box—an obscene, clever music box that nauseated her.

Strathmore made mechanical devices. Would a man

who crafted backflipping penguins also build such an appalling piece of perversity? She told herself that there had to be other men with such skills, but Lucien was the only one she knew, and he was a Hellion and therefore suspect.

More than once she had been tempted to tell him the truth and beg for his help, for he would be far more capable of achieving her goal than she was. The vision was a harsh reminder that she dared not trust him, no matter how much she wanted to.

It was a relief when a knock sounded on the door. The caller would be Henry Jones, who had sent a note the day before requesting this early meeting. Hair still loose, she opened the door eagerly. "Have you learned something?"

"You're in luck, lass. Most of your Hellion friends will soon be spending a few days at Mace's estate, Blackwell Abbey."

She took his cloak. "Will it be one of their gentleman-only affairs?"

"Not this time. It's a Harford family tradition to hold a masked ball shortly before Christmas. Gives 'em a chance to show how much more money they have than the neighbors, I expect. Most of the county will be invited. Blackwell Abbey is a great sprawling place, so there will be dozens of guests and even more servants." He sat down with a gusty sigh and accepted a steaming cup from his hostess. "Thank you, lass. There's nothing like a spot of tea after a long night prowling London's underbelly."

After pouring a cup for herself, she sat opposite her guest, her face thoughtful. 'With so many guests, it will be easy for me to blend in."

He said gloomily, "Care to tell me what you have in mind?"

"I think there's a good chance that Roderick Harford is the man I want. If I can see him again, I should know for certain."

"Why not just knock on Harford's door and ask him flat out if he's your villain?" Henry asked with heavy sarcasm.

"I considered that, but I don't think it would be a good idea," she said seriously. "Alerting him to my suspicions would be dangerous, and not only to me."

Jones began to toy with the handle of his cup. "It's been weeks now. Have you considered that it might be ... too late?"

"It's *not* too late!" she said hotly. "I know that as surely as I know that I'm sitting here."

Yet as she thought of the dream, she knew with cold, terrifying certainty, that time was running out.

Though Kit had become expert at infiltrating the residences of the rich and famous, her illicit skills would not be needed this time. From the concealment of a small gazebo, she watched the swirling figures in the ballroom of Blackwell Abbey. Clearly it was a great occasion in the neighborhood.

Despite the late autumn chilliness of the night, couples overheated from dancing, and for other reasons, frequently emerged onto the stone terrace outside the ballroom. All wore half masks and dominoes, the voluminous cloaks derived from the robes of medieval clerics.

The masks gave a heady sense of anonymity, and the laughter and teasing remarks that floated into the night simmered with undercurrents of naughty excitement. Most of the guests went back inside after a few minutes and a few kisses, though some of the more hot-blooded ones left the terrace to seek privacy in the shadowed gardens. Kit hoped that the pleasure gained would be worth the risk of lung fever.

About midevening, when champagne and dancing had worked their magic on the guests, she removed the blanket wrapped around her shoulders and dropped it to the floor of the gazebo. Anyone finding it would think the scratchy wool square had been used by a fornicating couple from the ball.

As she shook out the folds of her midnight blue domino and checked that the matching half-mask was secure, she concentrated on the personality she was assuming for the occasion—confident, experienced, more than a little brazen. Then she crossed the garden to the terrace, a cat's-paw breeze fluttering the silk domino around her.

She knew that she looked like any other female guest. Nonetheless, she felt as conspicuous as Daniel advancing into the lions' den when she entered the ballroom. A few steps inside the door, she halted and languidly wielded her lace fan in front of her face as she studied her surroundings.

All was as expected: heat and sweat, a clamor of music and voices, a shifting pageant of swirling silks. Black was the most common domino color, but there were enough brighter hues to create a rainbow effect. The center of the room was occupied by dancing couples while other guests talked and flirted around the edge. Refreshments were laid out in an adjacent salon, and somewhere there would be a card room for gamesters.

Luckily, she had attracted no special notice. She scanned the crowd for Lord Strathmore, who would surely be here. It was not hard to locate him, for his height and blond hair were too distinctive to be concealed by a cloak and half mask. He was dancing with a woman whose domino was tossed back to reveal a dramatic crimson gown and an even more dramatic figure.

Exactly the sort of trollop most men couldn't resist, Kit thought acidly. The earl's own domino, mask, and exquisitely tailored garments were black, the starkness broken only by white linen and his own fair coloring. A perfect portrait of Lucifer out for a lark. As soon as she identified him, Kit turned and went in the opposite direction.

She had taken great pains to give herself an appearance that he had never seen. Her height couldn't be disguised, but she had put tiny pebbles in her kidskin slippers to alter her walk and posture. Her hair was a soft, ashy blond and her low-cut, ice blue gown clung to a figure that had been carefully padded to appear lush, though not as voluptuous as Sally the barmaid.

She had chosen to wear blue because the shade brought an aqua tint to her gray eyes. Below the mask the subtle use of cosmetics had changed the contours of her mouth and cheeks. She had also drawn age lines on her face, then powdered herself heavily as if trying to conceal them. The effect was of a woman of mature years who was trying to appear fifteen years younger. Even Strathmore would be deceived. Nonetheless, she would take no chances.

It was harder to locate Roderick Harford, whose appearance was less distinctive than Strathmore's. As she prowled the perimeter, looking for him, a portly gentleman approached and asked, "Lady of midnight, will you dance with me?"

To refuse might draw unwelcome attention, so she accepted with a gracious simper. The tune was a reel, and she danced her partner to exhaustion. At the end, between heaving breaths, he asked her to join him in the supper room. She did, but after a single glass of champagne, she smiled and slipped away.

She accepted another dance with someone who looked as if he might be Harford. He wasn't. Another man she asked herself, but he was also a false lead.

Four more dances and two more glasses of champagne brought her no closer to her quarry. She began to feel anxious, for the crowd was thinning as the local guests left to drive home before moonset. If she couldn't find her quarry, she would have wasted this perfect opportunity.

She was about to go in search of the card room when she heard Harford's voice. Turning quickly, she spotted him saying good-bye to a group of friends. As soon as he was alone, she approached and purred, "I am looking for a brave knight whose lance is strong and true. Are you such a man?"

After a surprised moment, he gave her a delighted leer. "You'll find no bolder bedroom warrior than me, milady."

She fluttered the lace fan provocatively across her face. "Then dance with me, Sir Knight."

"With pleasure." He drew her onto the floor as the musicians struck up a waltz. From his breath, it was obvious that he had been drinking heavily. Trying not to think of the time he had mauled her when she was a chambermaid, she cooed, "I'm so glad that the sweet young maidens have been taken home by their mamas. All that innocence becomes oppressive."

"Couldn't agree more," Harford replied. "M'brother, Mace, feels that it's family duty to entertain the neighborhood every year, so I spent the first half of the evening dancing with every wallflower in the county. But now duty is discharged, the little girls are gone, and we can do as we please. For the rest of the night there will be only extra long waltzes. So much better for getting acquainted, don't you agree?"

"Indeed." She stroked his right shoulder with her fingertips. "I always adore meeting a new knight."

He responded by pulling her much closer than the twelve inches that was considered proper in most ballrooms. Throughout the dance the suggestive banter continued, Kit acting as blatant as she knew how and Harford responding in kind. But as she had feared, the ballroom was too distracting for her to get a clear sense of whether he was the man she had been seeking. She would have to risk being alone with him.

The music ended. Pressing his hand meaningfully, she said, "Will you show me your lance later?"

He gazed appreciatively down the front of her dress. "Come into the garden and I'll do it right now."

"Too cold," she said with a moue of distaste.

"I suppose we can find a closet somewhere, though some of 'em are already occupied. Could be embarrassing."

"Why does it have to be a closet? A real knight takes his time—that's what chivalry is all about." She batted her lashes, hoping that the mask wouldn't destroy the effect. "Can't we go to your room and do it properly?"

He hesitated. "Since I'm one of the hosts, it's a little early for me to leave for good."

She stroked his chin with her folded fan. "Why don't we meet in your room in an hour?"

"Good idea." He produced a key from an inside pocket. "My rooms are in the west wing, last door on the left. There's no card on the door, but you can't miss it. Why not go there now and wait for me?"

It was an amazing piece of luck. She took the key and

made a show of dropping it into her bodice. "You can
play hunt-the-key when you come upstairs." She rapped
his knuckles playfully with her fan. "Just don't forget
and bring another lady back, or you may have a dragon
to slay."

He laughed and squeezed her backside as she turned
away. Her relief was enormous as she made her way
across the dance floor. With luck she might learn everything she needed merely by being in his room. That
would certainly be simpler than waiting for his return,
then having to devise a way to escape his clutches.
Though she had sworn to do whatever was necessary,
the thought of lying with the enemy made her gag.

She was almost out of the ballroom when the musicians began playing another waltz. Behind her a deep,
familiar voice said, "May I have this dance?"

And before she could protest, she was in the arms of
the Earl of Strathmore.

Chapter 21

Of *course* Strathmore would find her, Kit thought with furious exasperation. The two of them could be dropped into the vastness of the Sahara and be drawn together like opposite poles of a magnet. But there was no sign that he recognized her, which was all that mattered. With only a few square inches of her face visible and that altered by cosmetics, her current disguise was one that even Strathmore would be unable to penetrate.

That didn't mean she should give him the opportunity to try. She altered the set of her mouth to mimic the delicately voluptuous poutiness of a Frenchwoman, then said with a Parisian accent, "I 'ave promised thees dance to another man, monsieur."

"When the fellow finds us, I shall yield to his prior claim," Strathmore said in fluent French. "But until then, it would be a pity to waste the music."

Since he did not release her, she was forced to follow him into the pattern of the dance—the wicked, scandalous waltz, which was condemned by high-minded citizens because it stimulated impure thoughts. Since Strathmore had that effect on her all the time, heaven only knew what a waltz would do.

She had the sense that he was watching her with unusual intensity. Did he have any suspicions? She tried to read his expression, but his black half mask made that impossible.

Their steps matched perfectly. Again she was unsurprised; ever since their first meeting, they had been caught up in a different kind of dance. They glided across the floor in silence.

Conversation was essential, for silence made her too

aware of his nearness. Without removing her left hand from her partner's shoulder, she opened her fan and began cooling her face while she tried to think of something innocuous to say. She should not have had that third glass of champagne, for her usual powers of invention seemed to have failed her.

He solved the problem by asking, "When young French ladies are taught to dance, are they also taught how to fan themselves without missing a step? It's a clever trick."

She gave a trill unlike her usual laughter. "Frenchwomen are full of clever tricks, monsieur." Too late she realized that her remark was the kind of brazen flirtation she had been using on Roderick Harford.

"Splendid. I find tricky females irresistible," Strathmore said blandly.

He drew her closer so that their bodies were lightly touching. Every movement of the dance became a caress—a brush of her breasts against his chest, over even as she became aware of it; the whisper of his breath against her temple; the pressure of his knee as it skimmed her thigh; a grazing of pelvises that sent heat coiling through her limbs.

Though each contact was fleeting, the overall effect was powerfully erotic. She wanted to twine around him, to turn those teasing touches into a fierce embrace. Precise, physical memories of their supper at the Clarendon Hotel caused color to rise in her cheeks. She ducked her head, grateful that Strathmore could not read her mind.

He murmured into her ear, "You dance well, madame."

"As do you, monsieur, but you are too close for propriety," she said with gentle reproof.

She tried to move farther away, but his firm clasp on her hand and waist prevented that. "Propriety at midnight during a masked ball is a very different matter from propriety at high noon in a drawing room, madame. Look around you."

It was true that many couples were locked more tightly than she and her partner. But none of the other men, she was sure, had Strathmore's ability to make a woman's bones turn to taffy....

"You remind me of someone," he said thoughtfully.

Mental alarms went off, yanking her from her languid mood. "A good memory, or a bad memory, monsieur?"

"Both. A most delicious female, but maddeningly elusive. She was much of your height"—his cheek brushed her hair—"and as as delightful to hold as you"—he pulled her more closely in demonstration—"and she was graceful, like you." He gazed down into her eyes with a shrewdness that frightened her. "I wonder if your kisses are like hers."

Before he could act on his last comment, she pulled away, saying frostily, 'Only a most stupid man tries to compliment one woman by comparing her to another."

"You're quite right. I have been too often stupid about women." He raised her hand and kissed her gloved fingertips. "Forgive me. I shall try to be wiser."

More double meanings. Clearly he suspected her identity, but he was not sure. Thank God for the mask and her careful disguise. However, the intense attraction throbbing between them could not be concealed, and the longer they were together, the more suspicious he would become. "I do not think that continuing to dance with you is wise, monsieur."

"Why should we be wise?" His right arm slid around her waist and his domino enfolded her like protective wings as he drew her back into the waltz. She caught her breath at the sweetness of his embrace. She had been right to be wary of silence, for without words to protect her, she had no defense against him.

Torn between longing to stay and the knowledge that she shouldn't, she compromised by vowing to leave as soon as the dance ended. But the music flowed on and on, far longer than a normal waltz, weaving a web of sound and desire. Gradually, the frantic beat of fear that had driven her for weeks eased, soothed by the warmth of his closeness. Her eyes drifted shut, and her cheek came to rest against his shoulder.

Dimly she knew that their dance was an act of mating as explicit as if they were lying naked on satin sheets, yet she could not break away. They glided through the turns of the waltz, their dominoes floating about them as diaphanous as mist, black and midnight blue swirling together.

Finally—yet too soon—the music stopped. They halted beneath a chandelier, their gazes locked as if bound by a sorcerer's spell. Behind his mask, she saw that desire had turned his eyes as golden as new minted coins.

She wondered what her own eyes showed, and knew that she must leave *now*. "Good night, monsieur," she said, her throat dry.

As she turned to go, he caught her wrist. "Don't leave yet," he said thickly. "Or rather, let us go together."

She twisted away from his grip. "Sorry, but I have already made plans for the rest of the night."

Hot wax spattered across her cheek from one of the candles above. She raised her hand, but his fingers were there first, gently rubbing away the fragments of cooled wax. "Come with me now. Surely your 'other plans' can wait for an hour."

He spoke with the calm confidence of a man who did not doubt that in an hour he could make her forget all other obligations. But hers were more significant than mere fornication, as alluring as that might be. She shook her head. "I'm sorry, monsieur, but honor forbids. Perhaps another time."

She sensed the flex of his fingers barely in time. Before he could pull off her mask, she slapped his hand away with her fan, shattering the ivory blades and ripping the delicate lace. "Do not seek to change the rules, monsieur," she snapped. "Such intimacy as we have shared is possible only because we wear masks. If I do not satisfy you, go seek the lady you think I resemble. She might be more accommodating."

"I can't help but wonder if I have found her," he said softly. "Though the appearance is different, the spirit is the same. Can there be more than one woman who shimmers with such a flame, and kindles such desire?"

Damnation. In spite of her best efforts, Strathmore was three quarters convinced of her identity. But not quite sure; if he had been, he would already have hauled her from the dance floor to a more private place.

Attack was safer than defense. She uttered a very French oath learned from the Parisian girl who had been her nursemaid, then turned away, her domino flaring wide. "You become tedious, monsieur. Do not trouble me again."

As she moved away, languidly rolling her hips in a manner quite unlike her usual walk, she could feel his gaze boring into her back. It took all of her willpower not to bolt. Only the knowledge that flight would confirm his suspicions kept her steps slow and steady.

She joined the largest group of people so that the earl would lose sight of her, then slipped out of the ballroom. When she was safely out in the foyer, she leaned against a wall, shaking. How could she have been such a fool as to let that happen? She should have walked away as soon as he accosted her. And how long had she been with him? Harford had intended to return to his room in an hour, and half of that must have passed. There was no time to waste.

Quickly she removed the pebbles from her slippers, for they were uncomfortable, and it was no longer necessary to alter her walk. Then she made her way upstairs at a speed just short of a run. Several times she saw other couples in corners or entering a bedroom, but all were too intent on their own concerns to pay attention to her.

Blackwell Abbey was U-shaped with a center section bracketed by two shorter wings. Dozens of identical doors opened onto the dimly lit corridors. To prevent guests from embarrassing errors, elegantly written cards announced who was in each room. She warily eyed the door marked with Strathmore's name, even though she knew that he must still be downstairs.

She reached the end of the corridor and fished out the key, then spent two frustrating minutes trying to open the unmarked door. Perhaps Harford was playing some kind of idiotic game with her.

Could she have come to the wrong place? She thought about it and realized that she had gotten her directions reversed and come to the east wing instead of the west. Mentally cursing herself, she retraced her steps, instinctively circling wide around Strathmore's door. Right around the corner, along the main corridor, right again. Last door on the left.

This time the key turned smoothly, and the door swung open to reveal a sitting room. She stepped inside with relief, then locked the door behind her so that she would have warning of Harford's return if she wasn't gone before he came upstairs.

A single candle lit the room. She studied her surroundings, wondering what to look for. Once before she had searched a room of Harford's, but then he had been a guest in someone else's house. This sitting room and the adjacent bedroom were places where he actually lived for part of the year, and he must have imprinted himself deeply into his surroundings.

She began searching. The bookcase contained an impressive array of salacious books, repellent and of no value to her. She opened the wardrobe and ran her hands between the garments, trying to find traces of some undefinable essence. Then she turned to his desk and began searching his papers with frantic haste while she prayed that he would stay longer at the ball than he had intended.

The desk contained two drawers full of bills, none of them paid. Another drawer contained highly explicit love letters written in different feminine hands. She skimmed them quickly, but it was all rubbish. Even the doggerel verse about "Roderick's remarkable rod" scanned badly. Obviously, Harford did not favor women with intelligence.

In the center drawer was a journal containing terse notes. She studied them for a few minutes and realized with distaste that it was a record of the women he had bedded, complete with evaluations of their skills and willingness to indulge his sometimes peculiar tastes. If she were actually the trollop she pretended, she would be destined to end up in these pages. He would have made a note of her tattoo.

She flipped through all of the entries for the last several months, but found nothing to confirm her suspicions. She was leaning over to pull out the lowest drawer when an angry voice barked, "What the hell are you doing?"

She jerked upright, heart hammering, and saw Harford glowering in the doorway. Dear God, why didn't it occur to her that he might have second key? She must brazen it out. "Looking through your desk, of course," she said innocently. "I became bored waiting, monsieur, so I decided to explore."

"Next time, don't explore a man's desk," he said, his irritation fading with the quick mood change of the drunk. "You're French? I didn't notice that earlier."

Damnation, she had spoken in the character she had created for Strathmore! "In a bedroom, I am always French," she said throatily. "The French may be our enemies, but they are masters at the art of making love."

"Oh, I don't know about being our enemies. Napoleon's a damned clever fellow, far superior to our own royal family. We haven't seen the last of him." Harford removed his mask, then unfastened his domino and dropped it over a chair. "Start undressing. I want to see if your face is as good as your tits."

It was the moment she had been waiting for. She stepped full into the candlelight and reached for her mask. Though her hair color was different, he would surely recognize her if he was the man she sought. She revealed her face, watching him with hawklike intensity as she waited for the reaction that would tell her all she needed to know.

Nothing! Not a flicker, not a widening of the eyes, only the careless comment, "A bit long in the tooth, but you'll do for a night. I've found that older females make good bedmates because they're so grateful."

A cold knot formed in her belly. He wasn't the one. *He wasn't the one!* She could not have explained how she knew, but she was positive. Though he might be involved in a tangential way, he was not the prime villain.

She had learned what she had come for. Now the trick was to escape without getting raped. "It isn't kind of you to mention my age," she complained as she edged toward the door. "A proper knight wouldn't say such a thing."

"Stop babbling about knights." He pulled off his coat and untied his cravat. "You came here to get bedded. I'm willing to oblige, but don't waste my time with female nonsense."

"You're not chivalrous at all." With a flounce she reached for the doorknob. "I don't think I like you anymore."

Moving with a speed that belied his drunkenness, he seized her shoulders and swung her around to face him. "You're not going anywhere," he growled. "It's too late for me to find another woman, so you're going to stay here and get exactly what you asked for."

His hot, wine-soured mouth clamped over hers. It was horribly like the incident at Bourne Castle when he had thought her a chambermaid. Suppressing her distaste, she made a sound deep in her throat, as if aroused by his crude embrace, and wrapped herself around him.

He groaned when she rubbed her hips against him, then began impatiently undoing his buttons. She waited until he was pulling his breeches down and off-balance. Then she shoved him violently in the chest. He crashed backward into the desk, then went sprawling on the floor.

Not stopping to see if he was hurt, she bolted out the door. The west wing ended to the left, so she turned right toward the main corridor. She was just swinging around the corner when she heard a bellow of fury followed by pounding footsteps. No doubt it was fortunate that he wasn't dead, but it was a pity he hadn't been knocked senseless.

"You'll pay for that, you little slut!" echoed through the halls above the sounds from the ballroom. Ordinarily, this much racket would bring people, but she supposed the other guests were too busy dancing, drinking, or fornicating to notice.

Knowing that he would be able to see her as soon as he turned the corner, she slowed long enough to try the nearest doorknob. Locked! She began running again, heading for the stairs to the ground floor. Once she got through the ballroom and into the garden, Harford would never find her.

Her plans changed when she saw Lord Mace and two

other men talking at the foot of the steps. Perhaps she would be safe if she went to them, but she wouldn't have bet a ha'penny on it.

She swerved and continued along the corridor with the speed she had learned running over the Westmoreland fells. A few seconds after she turned the corner into the east wing, the pursuing footsteps stopped. Harford called, "Mace, did a woman just run down these stairs?"

"No," his brother replied. "What the devil are you up to?"

"Chasing a sly, troublemaking little tease," Harford said viciously. "I'll make her sorry she ever met me."

"Well, chase her more quietly, Roderick," Mace drawled. "There may be a few guests trying to sleep."

Gasping for breath, Kit used the brief reprieve to test the doors in the east wing. One was Strathmore's, the next two were locked. The fourth opened, and she breathed a sigh of relief which lasted until she heard the fevered sounds of a couple in the throes of passion. She retreated hastily, shutting the door behind her.

Harford's steps were approaching rapidly. In a few seconds he would turn the corner and see her. Frantically, she scanned the corridor. Another dead end. One of these blank doors probably led to a service stairway, but she didn't know which, and time was running out.

With her goal still unachieved, it would be disastrous to let Harford catch her. At the very least she would be beaten and raped. The worst didn't bear thinking of.

There was only one hope. Please God, let him be there and willing to help her in spite of all she had done to him.

With a feeling of doomed inevitability, she pivoted and fled straight to Strathmore's door.

Chapter 22

After his encounter with the lady in the blue domino, Lucien returned to his room, seething with a combination of physical and mental frustration. He had told his valet not to wait up, so after removing his domino and mask, he built up the fire, then poured himself a small glass of brandy and sat down to think.

There was no rational reason for his suspicion that the lady in blue was Kristine Travers; apart from height, there was no real resemblance between the two women. Nonetheless, he had been unable to shake the persistent feeling that it had been her laughing at him from behind that mask. Perhaps it was obsession that made him see her everywhere; that, and the knowledge that she was a mistress of disguise.

Yet he had gone thirty-two years without being attracted to a woman as intensely as he was to Kit. It made sense that he would also find her identical twin alluring, but it was hard to believe that a total stranger could also arouse him in precisely the same way. If he hadn't made a fool of himself with Kathryn Travers, he would have forcibly removed the mysterious lady's mask. A good thing she had disappeared into the crowd before he had succumbed to temptation.

With a wry smile, he finished his brandy. It was hard to be rational when waltz music from the ball throbbed through the air. Every rippling measure reminded him of how his last partner had felt in his arms. Maybe the lady in blue was a damned Travers cousin, which was why she affected him the way Kristine and Kathryn did. In the morning he would ask a few questions and see if he could find out who the lady really was, but now it was time for bed.

After he removed his coat and boots, he remembered that he hadn't locked the door on his return. He crossed the room and was reaching for the key when the door swung violently open, almost hitting him in the face. And headlong behind it came Lady Nemesis wearing the blue domino, ash blond curls, and false age lines of his earlier dance partner.

Eyes enormous, she gasped, "Harford's right behind me. Please ..."

Explanations could wait. He instantly swung the door shut and turned the key in the lock. "Get into the bed and pull the covers over your head. Then stay put and don't talk."

As she dived for the bed, he stripped off his cravat and threw it aside, then yanked his shirt loose so that it hung over his breeches. As he was unfastening his collar button, a fist struck the door and Harford's voice barked, "Open up!"

"Go away," Lucien called back, his voice sharp with irritation. "I'm busy." As he spoke, he used one hand to rumple his hair and the other to twist a pinch of skin on his neck, leaving a red mark that looked like a love bite.

Harford bellowed, "Dammit, Strathmore, let me in!"

"All right, all right," Lucien said testily. "I'm coming." He scanned the bed, where Kit was a long, curving shape under the blankets. She was covered except for a fold of blue silk that hung down one side of the bed. He shoved the telltale fabric under the blanket, then ambled across the room, taking his time.

After snuffing all but one candle and donning an expression of intense exasperation, he opened the door. "Is the house on fire? I can't imagine anything else so important that it can't wait until morning."

In the hall was Roderick Harford, his eyes furious and his clothing disheveled. "I want the woman you have with you!"

Lucien's brows arched. "You can't have her. She's mine, and I'm anxious to get back to what we were doing."

"The teasing bitch tried to rob me! I caught her searching my desk, as bold as brass."

"Oh?" Lucien folded his arms and leaned against the door frame. "It can't have been recently, because I've been keeping her busy for the last half hour or so."

"But I just saw her come into this room!"

"Not in here," Lucien said positively. "Your ladybird must have gone through a different door. They all look the same."

Expression belligerent, Harford tried to shove past. "I want to see who's in your bed, and I'm not leaving until I do."

Lucien's arm whipped across the doorway, stopping the other man in his tracks. "I really can't permit that," he said in a voice of dangerous softness.

"I'm not asking your permission, Strathmore!" Again Harford tried to bull his way through.

Lucien grabbed the other man's right arm and yanked it up behind his back. When Harford began thrashing violently, Lucien twisted his wrist to a point on the edge of excruciating pain. "If you insist, I'm afraid that I shall have to call you out," he said coolly. "That would be regrettable—it's damned bad form to kill the brother of one's host."

Brought back to a realization of the circumstances, Harford stopped struggling. Lucien released his wrist, but the other man was not done yet. Furiously he said, "You and that slut are working together, aren't you?"

Lucien's eyes narrowed. "You are beginning to irritate me, Roderick. I am respecting the lady's privacy for reasons that have nothing to do with you."

"Why?"

Lucien rolled his eyes heavenward. "Quite apart from normal gentlemanly behavior, there is the regrettable fact that not all husbands are tolerant of their wives' amusements."

After another silence Harford gave an embarrassed laugh. "A married woman. I should have thought of that."

"Yes, you should have. Now kindly seek your felonious female elsewhere. The next door to the left is a servants' stair, isn't it? Perhaps she went that way."

Harford's brow furrowed. "I guess she must have. In dim light and at a distance, it was hard to tell which door she opened." As he turned to go, he added gruffly, "Sorry. I was out of line."

"Apology accepted. Just don't bother me again tonight." Lucien swung the door shut and locked it, then slid the key under the cushion of a nearby chair.

This time, by God, she was not going to get away.

He listened to the sound of Harford's retreating footsteps, then the faint creak of the door to the service stairs. With his usual curiosity, Lucien had explored the stairwell soon after he had arrived. Harford would wander for a long time in the bowels of the house before finally giving up in frustration.

Turning to the bed, he said, "You can come out now."

Expression wary, she pushed back the covers and sat up, surrounded by drifts of bed linen and blue silk. The atmosphere vibrated with complicated emotions: anger, deceit, desperation, and desire. Most of all, desire.

But for Lucien, anger was a damned close second. "So it really was you earlier," he said, his voice low and hard. "I'm glad to know that my instincts were sound. What have you to say for yourself this time?"

She grimaced. "That facing you under these circumstances is in some ways worse than having to deal with Roderick Harford." With a cavalier lack of respect for the expensive silk, she wiped off most of her cosmetics with the hem of her domino. Looking slightly smudged and much younger, she added wryly, "I've provoked him only once."

Her humor raised his anger another notch. "Perhaps you should have taken your chances with him. You asked for my help, but it comes at a price. And this time, my deceitful lady, I am flat out of gullibility."

Her expression became grave. "Given what you've endured from me, that's hardly surprising."

During the long silence that followed, he saw a shimmer of changing emotions in her eyes: regret, doubt, longing, and finally determination. Her hands locked in her lap. "I know that payment is long overdue," she said quietly. "Once you wanted me in your bed. If that's still true—well, I'm here."

Once again she astonished him, this time by her sheer, arrow-straight directness. He drew an unsteady breath. Though he disliked the implication that her offer was rooted in obligation rather than desire, there was no question of his refusing. Gentlemanly compunctions were a feeble consideration when set against the passion smoldering in his veins. "You had better mean it," he said tightly, "because this time you won't be allowed to change your mind or cry for mercy."

"If anyone cries for mercy, it won't be me, Lucien." She stretched out a slim, strong hand. "I've had enough of lies. It's time for some honesty."

He knew with absolute certainty that this time she would not run away. Yet she looked brittle, her eyes still haunted by the aftermath of her encounter with Harford.

Lucien frowned. Fear made a poor bedmate. He wanted her to be as hungry, as vulnerable, as he was. That meant he must control himself while bringing her to a fervor that matched his own. But restraint would not be easy.

In the silence that stretched tautly between them, the lilting music below was clearly audible. Of course, he thought with relief; dancing would re-create the enchantment that had bound them together earlier. He reached out and clasped her hand. "Dance with me, my lady."

After a startled blink, she slid her beautiful long legs over the edge of the mattress and kicked off her slippers. She released his hand, then curtsied gracefully, as if they had just been introduced. "It will be my pleasure, Lord Strathmore."

"Though we have not been properly introduced," he said with matching formality, "I believe that you are Lady Kit Travers?"

She straightened, a smile lurking in her eyes. "I knew it was only a matter of time until you learned who I am. Jane is one of my middle names, though."

"I've thought of you by a hundred names—Lady Jane—Lady Nemesis—Lady Quicksilver. But Kit is better, crisp and unconventional, like you." He tugged off her blond wig. Then he loosened her hair into a silky cloud, each gentle, circular stroke of his fingertips a caress.

"Mm-m-m." She gave a slow smile. "That feels lovely. No wonder cats like having their heads scratched."

She was still wearing her kidskin gloves, so he lifted her left hand and peeled the glove off. Then he kissed the fragile skin of her inner wrist. Her fingers curled, and her quickening blood pulsed warmly against his lips.

When he did the same with her right hand, her fingertips fluttered across his cheek. "Lucifer, light-bearer," she murmured. "Bright son of the morning."

"Now much fallen from heaven, I fear." He placed one hand in the small of her back. Her spine was vibrant with supple strength. Intertwining the fingers of his free hand with hers, he swept her into the pattern of the waltz. "But I have a glimpse of paradise before me now."

She colored and dropped her eyes. In the candlelight, her hair was a cinnamon-tinted halo. With more space than on a crowded dance floor, they could move freely to the rhythms of the music, their bodies speaking directly to one another. The crimson-patterned carpet was lushly sensual beneath their stockinged feet as they glided across the chamber.

Though her dancing was adept, as befitted a professional, at first there was a stiffness in her movements, as if her mind and body were not quite in tune with the music. But as they circled the open area of the room, the music began to work its magic and the strain faded from her muscles and her face.

Their partnership became fluid harmony. He was intensely, physically aware of the lithe feminine body beneath the blue domino. The reverse was also true, for each of his movements produced a matching response in her, a dynamic, constantly shifting balance between male and female.

As they came to the end of the room, he untied the ribbons of her domino with one hand. The silk billowed outward on the turn and floated obliquely down until it crumpled into the angle between wall and floor. Her bare shoulders glowed like warm cream. His mouth went dry. Not yet. Not ... yet.

Her eyes had drifted shut so that she was following his lead purely through touch and movement. She was thistle-light in his arms. He found it oddly moving that she was placing herself entirely in his hands, at least for the moment.

Now that he had relaxed her, it was time to make her tense again. He bent forward and kissed the tender angle between her throat and jaw, lapping upward to the elegant curve of her ear. Her breath caught, and her lips parted as he spun her about in a fluid circle.

What would it take to open her eyes? With an extravagant swoop, he tilted her backward over his arm, supporting all her weight. At the same time he thrust his leg between hers so that they were intimately locked together. Her startled eyes flew open, and in the clear gray depths he saw the passion he had wanted to invoke.

She recovered from her surprise in an instant. "Sir," she said demurely, "I believe that we are closer than is proper."

As she spoke, she slowly squeezed her thighs around his. Heat curled through his belly. Breathlessly he said, "Indeed we are." He swept her upright again and swirled her across the room. "And we are going to get closer yet."

He began to improvise steps that were too shamelessly erotic to be performed in public. Her pliant dancer's body adapted to his effortlessly, as if she was an extension of him. Their bodies met in full-length caresses, then separated, only to come together again with greater fire. They became part of the music, its beat thrumming in their blood as they performed their ardent mating dance.

When the music downstairs ended, they merged into an embrace, swaying together in the center of the chamber. They kissed ravenously, and she rolled her pelvis into his with wicked provocation. He groaned as he felt himself harden against the yielding cradle of her hips.

The time for restraint was over. He unfastened the ties that held her gown at the back so that the garment fell away from her body. Eyes smoky with desire, she gave a seductive shimmy. The gown rippled downward over her arms and hips until it pooled at her feet, leaving her clad only in her chemise and the artfully padded corselet that disguised her own slim figure.

His gaze holding hers, he unlaced the front of her corselet. The garment fell open and revealed her breasts as softly arching shadows beneath the sheer lawn of her chemise. He cupped her breasts, teasing her nipples between thumb and forefinger. Her eyes widened, and she ran her tongue over her lips as the sensitive nubs hardened.

Every movement of her body signaled desire. Yet the sight made him realize that desire was not enough. Even more than passion, he wanted an emotional intimacy that would reach all of the lonely places deep in his soul.

As he removed her corselet, he tried to catch her gaze, fiercely willing her to look at him, to share the mysteries of her elusive spirit.

Instead, she stepped forward and slid her arms under his loose shirt, wrapping them around the bare skin of his waist as she hid her face against the triangle of bare chest where his shirt gapped open at the front. Her breasts flattened against his chest as she smoothed her palms over the tight muscles of his back.

Reluctantly admiring the deftness with which she had evaded his gaze, he skinned her chemise up over her head and tossed it away. "You're wearing too much."

"You are, too," she retorted. She pulled his shirt up over his head, then tossed it away. " 'Pleasing was his shape,' " she quoted huskily, " 'and lovely.' "

He had to laugh at the rich absurdity of her imagination. "As I recall, Lucifer was in the form of the serpent when Milton said that."

"Isn't there a serpent somewhere near?" She took advantage of his shirtless state to press scalding kisses to his bare chest.

Her hands skimmed under the waistband of his breeches. He gave a harsh exhalation, and his hands tightened convulsively around her buttocks. The ripe curves fitted perfectly into his palms. Half lifting her from the floor, he molded her malleable flesh against the hard angles of his body.

She bit his shoulder, and the last of his control disintegrated. After ripping off his breeches and drawers, he swept her to the bed. They tumbled onto the mattress with an impact that made the bedframe shriek.

He bore her backward into the pillows, wanting to absorb her into himself, to feast on her intoxicating femaleness. Her mouth met his, open and demanding. They twisted together like wildcats, her hips grinding into his.

Feverishly he buried his face in the scented cleft between her breasts—tangy sweet, salt and carnations. He could not get enough of her.

As he sucked her nipple into his mouth, her whole frame shivered, her head thrown back and her chest heaving with raw demands for breath. She wore only her silk stockings.

Unable to resist the delicious curve of her abdomen, he trailed kisses down it, his breath skimming over the sensitive skin. She moaned and caught his head between her hands, pressing his face into her belly. Her satiny warmth intoxicated him.

He pushed himself up and moved between her legs, his thighs spreading her knees wide to receive him. As he did, he saw the butterfly tattoo hovering teasingly just above her ribbon garter. He leaned forward and pressed his lips to it, and felt her thrumming life force against his tongue. She gasped and spasmodically crushed handfuls of blanket in her fists.

His fingers slid through gossamer tangled curls to the hotly moist folds below. She whimpered with delirium when his fingers stroked, probing and preparing. Shaking with urgency, he positioned himself so that he was pressing into intimate heat.

Her back arched in readiness and her silk-clad ankles wrapped around his as he braced himself over her. Then, with a single eager thrust, he entered her.

She cried out—a sound of shock, not pleasure—and her nails ripped his back as she spasmed with pain.

He went rigid, the muscles of his arms and shoulders

like granite, and stared down at her in disbelief. "Jesus bloody *Christ*!" he exploded, his eyes changing from the lucent gold of passion to the glittering green of anger. "Why didn't you *tell* me?"

Chapter 23

Shaking, Kit closed her eyes. Perhaps this was another nightmare and soon she would wake. But the masculine weight and texture of the body pinning her to the bed, the sharp, intimate discomfort, were inescapably real.

She opened her eyes. Taut and dangerous, Lucien loomed over her, the powerful breadth of his shoulders limned by candlelight. "I ... I didn't think you would have to know," she whispered. "I didn't realize how much it would hurt."

He dropped his head forward and rested his brow on her collarbone as a shudder went through him. After a long moment, he sighed and raised his head again. "It would have hurt a great deal less if I had known in advance. Even the most skilled of actresses can't fake everything, kitten." His angry shock had passed, leaving rueful tenderness in its wake. He bent forward and touched his lips to hers in a feather-light kiss. "I'm sorry. I should have known that nothing would be simple where you are concerned. Try to relax now. The worst is over."

He was right. The tearing pain had lasted only an instant, and the uncomfortable sense of being over-stretched was also ebbing. He didn't move, simply continued to soothe her with delicate nibbling kisses on her face and throat. His urgency had been transformed into patience, though the perspiration that sheened his torso testified that his restraint did not come easily.

Her body began to accept his alien presence as natural. As it did, the sensual craving that had vanished when they first joined started to build again. Very carefully she curled her hips upward. There was no pain, merely a new kind of compression that was ... intriguing.

She moved again with more force. He gasped, and she felt the silky-steel length of him throbbing inside her. "You'd best be careful," he panted, "because I am very close to the breaking point."

"Break away, Lucien," she said huskily. "But you'll have to tell me what to do."

"Just . . . just move against me rhythmically."

He pressed deeper into her. She matched the movement, feeling the flex where they were joined. Sharp pleasure tingled through her in newly discovered places. "Like this?" she asked breathlessly.

"God, yes," he groaned. "*Exactly* like that."

He thrust forward again, and this time her body responded instinctively, already understanding what her mind had not yet mastered. The rhythms were as integral as her marrow. A queer aching. Slick friction and liquid heat. Wanting. *Needing*.

He made a suffocated sound and began driving into her, his muscular frame and implacable strength imprisoning her with a finality that was also liberation. This was not the considerate lover of the Clarendon, slowly bringing her to fulfillment, but a man demanding what was his right. He filled her arms and her senses, taste and touch and heat. She was no longer alone . . .

With sudden panic, she realized that he was penetrating her spirit as deeply as her body, stripping away her painfully constructed defenses. She tried to withdraw to the safety of being an observer, but it was impossible. She was utterly vulnerable, needing his warmth and strength with a desperation that shattered her will.

He slid his hand between them and touched her intimately, producing a violent pleasure that hurled her into the maelstrom. When she cried out, he buried his face in the angle between her head and shoulder. Air rushed into his lungs, and a savage shudder passed from him into her. She nearly danced out of her skin, out of control, ravaged as much by the searing force of his spirit as by the tumult of physical release.

The storm passed, leaving her shivering with shock. Dear God, if she had known, she would have dived out the window rather than let him touch her. She should have guessed that asking his help would irrevocably change the balance between them. Instead, she had willingly—eagerly—trusted him with her body, thinking that she would still be mistress of her soul and her secrets.

She had been mad to believe that she could withhold any part of herself once they became intimate. Fearfully, she recognized that anything he asked of her, she would give. And may God have mercy if he was unworthy of trust.

As she tried to choke back her tears, he rolled onto his side and gathered her against him. His hands skimmed over her, as gentle as they had previously been demanding. Quietly he said, "It's always been you, every time, hasn't it?"

She nodded, her face pressed against his collarbone.

"And you're Kathryn, not Kristine." It was a statement, not a question.

Reflexively trying to keep him at a distance, she asked, "Why do you say that?"

"My head accepted that you must be two different women, but my instinct disagreed." Her discarded chemise had chanced to land on the bed, so he used it to carefully blot the small amount of blood between her legs. "You did an excellent job of playing the role of a worldly actress, but even at your most brazen, there was an underlying shyness. I wondered about it a little."

She made a face. "As you said earlier, there is a limit to what acting can do. I can mimic Kira very well, but I can't always make myself enjoy it."

"The final proof was your virginity. Kristine may be many things, but I doubt that virgin is one of them." He grimaced. "If I had listened to my intuition rather than logic, I wouldn't have hurt you as much."

"Virginity is nature's bad joke on womankind," she said gloomily.

He grinned, then stretched out beside her and propped his head on his hand. "I was told you were always tagging behind your sister. The implication was that you were a poor second to her, but that wasn't true, was it? Anything Kira did, you did equally well. When she played Sebastian, the male twin, in *Twelfth Night,* you were Viola, which is actually the larger, more vital role. When she went swimming nude in the river or galloping in breeches with the hunt, you were right beside her, equally brave and equally athletic. And given the nature of identical twins, I'll wager that you instigated your share of mischief."

She stared at him, shocked to her toes. "How do you know that? No one else has ever realized, even Aunt Jane. Everyone assumed that Kira was always the leader."

"Because identical twins are simultaneously alike and different, some people have trouble dealing with them," he said obliquely. "It's easier and more convenient to put them in pigeonholes. The bold twin, the shy twin. The good sister, the wicked sister." His eyes sparked with amusement. "My guess is that Kira is less wild than generally presumed, and that you are less respectable, despite the splendidly straitlaced performance you gave as Lady Kathryn."

"You're right that many people preferred to think of us as opposites rather than variations on a common theme," Kit agreed. "There are also what Kira and I used to call 'those people'—the ones who would only talk to one of us and would ignore the other as if she didn't exist. We used to joke about that."

"You probably also played games with your identicalness, and laughed between yourselves about the world's gullibility."

She smiled a little. "When someone said, 'Kristine's ribbon is red and Kathryn's is blue,' we'd switch ribbons and mannerisms as soon as the person turned away. But we *are* different in many ways. As I said at Jane's, Kira has the kind of charm and vitality that can light up a whole theater. She has always been outgoing and far more willing than I to try something new. I'm the prim and proper one."

He cocked his brows with exaggerated disbelief. "Prim? Proper? Is this the female who has been leading me a merry dance across the rooftops and bedrooms of London?"

"That has been necessity, not choice," she said bleakly.

His amusement vanished. "This is all about Kira, isn't it? Something has happened to her."

The fear that had eased a little during their teasing conversation flared again, clutching at her belly like an icy talon. "My sister is none of your business."

In a calm, implacable voice, he said, "Tell me."

She rolled away and sat up, wrapping the sheet tightly around her body. "Why do you want to know?"

"You wouldn't have risked coming to this ball and going off with Roderick Harford if you weren't desperate. You need help, Kit. Why not accept mine?"

She looked away, knowing that she feared him and not wanting to explain why.

As if reading her mind, he asked, "Why won't you trust me?"

"I can't afford to make a mistake," she said tightly. "There's too much at stake."

"I would never harm you or your sister, and in your heart you know that."

She did know, but the knowledge did not eliminate her wariness. She temporized with part of the truth. "I've never found men very trustworthy. My father could charm the scales off a snake, but heaven help anyone who dared rely on him."

"I am not your father." He took her cold hand, his warm clasp engulfing her fingers. "I try very hard to do what I say I will, and I'm generally considered quite good at solving problems. Why not let me try to solve yours?"

Against her will, she found herself blurting out what she would have preferred to keep secret. "It isn't you that I distrust, but myself. I'm not good at being alone, Lucien. For the first eighteen years of my life, Kira was always there. We were more like two halves of a whole than individuals. We knew that we needed to separate and develop our own lives, but I've done a rotten job of becoming independent. I feel incomplete, like a ... a vine casting about for a pole to wrap myself around. I don't think you would like that. I don't like it about myself."

"You underestimate your strength, Kit. What you are worrying about might never come to pass." His thumb made slow circles on her palm. "Don't let your fears of what might happen stand in the way of helping Kira."

Her resistance collapsed. She buried her face in her hands, thinking that he had gone right to the heart of the issue. Kira's safety was far more important than the likelihood that Kit would make a fool of herself by falling in love with the rich, powerful, rakish Earl of Strathmore.

Besides, she had the uneasy feeling that if she didn't tell him what was wrong, he would reach inside her mind and pull the facts out directly. And she really could not bear to have him invading her thoughts more than he already had. She raised her head and said wearily, "It's a long story."

"Then we might as well get comfortable." He got out of bed and pulled a shirt from the wardrobe. "Put this on. It's easier for a man and woman to talk sensibly when they're dressed and vertical."

She emerged from her sheet and complied. The voluminous folds of his shirt covered her almost to her knees. absurdly, she still wore her stockings, so she stripped them off and tossed them in the general direction of her other scattered garments. Then she settled cross-legged on the bed.

Lucien donned a luxurious blue wool robe that made his hair glow like spun gold. After building up the fire, he dug a flat silver flask from his baggage, poured some of the amber contents into two glasses, and handed one to her. "Drink this."

Meekly she obeyed. The brandy couldn't touch the cold knot in her belly, but it did help steady her hands.

He settled beside her on the bed and leaned back against the headboard. "What has happened to Kira?"

She stared into her glass. "I don't know, and I'm not sure where to begin."

"Wherever you like. We can sit here all night if necessary, and the nights are very long at this time of year."

"Most of what I told you at Jane's was true." She made a face. "Though I slandered Jane herself. She's not the tyrant I led you to believe. Without her cooperation I could never have done what I've been doing."

"She didn't forbid Kira her house?"

"No, though it's true that she was not enthralled by my sister's choice of career. Well, neither was I. But Kira was hell-bent on treading the boards, so I accepted it. We kept in fairly close touch, writing each other every week when she was working in the provincial theaters. When she was in London, we would see each other every week or two, usually when we were going to the market." Kit hesitated, wondering if anyone who was not a twin could understand. "Not necessarily to talk, just to . . . see each other. It wasn't ever arranged. We just . . . knew when it was likely that our paths would cross."

She glanced at Lucien's face, but he accepted that matter-of-factly. "Kira lives in Soho?"

Kit nodded. "She owns a small house and uses the ground floor for herself. The upstairs flat is rented to a friend of hers, another actress named Cleo Farnsworth."

When she fell silent, he prompted, "When did you discover something was wrong?"

"On our birthday, the twenty-first of October. We always celebrate it together. *Always*. When she was working in the provinces, she would come to London. Once when she couldn't get away, I took the mail coach all the way to Yorkshire so that we could be together. This year we had arranged to meet at her house for a quiet dinner." She swallowed the terror that came with the memory. "The night before, I had had a nightmare and woke up feeling horribly anxious, but I didn't connect it with Kira. Yet the minute I let myself into her flat, I knew that something was dreadfully wrong."

"Were there signs of a struggle?"

"No, just . . . emptiness. Horrible, echoing emptiness, even though everything was exactly where it should be." Kit's hands locked around her brandy glass. "The only thing wrong was that her cat, Viola, was ravenous, as if she hadn't been fed that day.

"After I fed Viola, I went upstairs to talk to Cleo, whom I had met several times. At first Cleo thought I was Kira and scolded me for missing a rehearsal. When I explained that I was Kathryn, Cleo became worried, too. She said Kira had left the Marlowe as usual after performing the night before, and Cleo hadn't seen her since. But Kira *never* misses rehearsals. She must have been kidnapped on her way home."

After a brief hesitation, he said gently, "Presumably you have considered the possibility that she was murdered by footpads and her body dropped in the river."

"You think she's dead, don't you? Well, she *isn't*," Kit said fiercely. "You may not be able to understand this, but having a twin is like being connected to another person by an invisible cord. On some level, I'm always aware of Kira. If she died, I would know instantly. She is unhappy, sometimes terribly frightened, but she is as alive as I am."

She expected skepticism, but he said only, "If that is the case, abduction is certainly the most likely possibility. Do you know of anyone who might want to kidnap her and why?"

He actually believed her! Almost dizzy with relief, she replied, "The last time I had dined with Kira, a month or so earlier, she had casually mentioned an admirer who was determined to make her his mistress. She made a joke of it, but I thought at the time that she wouldn't have mentioned the fellow if she hadn't found him disturbing."

"So you think the man decided that if she wouldn't come to him voluntarily, he would take her by force," Lucien said with a frown.

"It's the only explanation that makes sense. The risk to him would be minimal—no one would be very surprised at the disappearance of a young actress," she said with more than a trace of irony. "Since all actresses are considered trollops, everyone would assume that she had run off with some man who had made her an irresistible offer."

"When Kira mentioned the man, did she say anything else that might help you identify him?"

"No, but she has always used a small notebook to remind herself of engagements and things she wanted to remember. After she disappeared, I searched her flat until I found it. Most of it was irrelevant, but there were several exasperated comments about a man who wouldn't take no for an answer." Kit's face tightened.

"Kira called him Lord Hellion. She also made several critical remarks about the Hellion Club."

"No wonder you've been stalking the group." Lucien frowned. "But why have you been taking such appalling risks? Surely you could have engaged an expert, a Bow Street Runner perhaps, to search for her."

She gave a humorless smile. "That's exactly what I did do. Mr. Jones tried his best. He found a drunkard who thought he'd seen a woman forced into a carriage not far from the Marlowe Theater on the night Kira disappeared. But it was raining, and the man couldn't supply any details about the woman or the kidnappers. Mr. Jones hasn't been able to learn anything more even though he has informants all over London. It is as if Kira has vanished from the face of the earth."

"So you decided to take matters into your own hands, risking your life and liberty in the process."

"The best way to learn about Kira's life was to enter it—to become Cassie James and meet the people around her," Kit said defensively. "Since Cleo was the only one at the Marlowe who knew Kira had a twin, it never occurred to anyone that I wasn't the real Cassie James. I'd seen Kira perform often, so it wasn't difficult to pretend I was her."

" 'Not difficult' to pretend that you were the most exciting young comic actress to appear in London in years," Lucien murmured. "That must be a masterpiece of understatement."

"I couldn't have done it without Cleo's help. She told me everything I needed to know about the rest of the Marlowe's company and how to behave backstage. As for the actual impersonation, you were exactly right when you said that if Kira pretended to be me when she wanted to be ignored, I could pretend to be her when I wanted to be noticed." Kit smiled wryly. "I can maintain the illusion of being Kira for several hours, though it's exhausting to have to sparkle all the time."

He shifted position, causing his robe to gap distractingly open over his chest. "What about the famous tattoo?"

Kit forced her gaze away from the fascinating view of

golden hairs dusted across his muscular torso. "I went to the same man who had done Kira's." She rubbed at the spot. "It's still a little itchy."

He brushed aside the hem of Kit's shirt and studied the butterfly that danced on her inner thigh. "I should have guessed when I kissed your tattoo and found that the design was raised slightly. Someone once told me that a new tattoo looks embossed, but I had forgotten." He traced the outline of the butterfly with a fingertip. "When I'm around you, my mind doesn't work very well."

That made two of them. His touch made her insides go hot and shivery. She inched away and tugged the shirttail over her tattoo again. Trying to ignore her acute awareness of her companion, she continued, "When Kira went on the stage, she cut her hair to shoulder-length to make it easier to wear wigs, so I had Jane chop mine the same way. I had a hairpiece made from what was cut off and always wore it when I was being Kathryn."

He grinned. "So if I had investigated your chignon, I would have learned the truth. No wonder you were so frosty that day."

"Kathryn is frequently frosty," she said at her most Kathrynish. In a normal tone she added, "It worked, didn't it?"

"So it did," he agreed. "Is Kira really left-handed?"

"No, she's right-handed. We're mirror images of each other—even our cowlicks go in opposite directions. I had to lie since you had seen me being left-handed when I was playing Kira. No one else noticed the difference."

"Leading two lives must have kept you busy."

"To say the least." She brushed her hair from her eyes. After the first shock of losing most of a lifetime's mane, she had found the lighter weight liberating. "I could never have managed without the help of Jane and Cleo and Mr. Jones. I moved back and forth between being Kathryn and Kristine, staying at whatever house was most convenient."

"Has your impersonation produced any results?"

She sighed. "Not really. I've studied every man who came near Cassie James, particularly in the green room after performances. I had hoped to see a false note or a shocked expression by someone who knew that I couldn't possibly be the real Cassie James, but had no such luck."

"Perhaps the man who abducted her hasn't been to the Marlowe lately so he doesn't know that Cassie James is still performing."

"That's what I think." A cynical edge came into her voice. "If the fellow had seen me and guessed that I was Kira's twin, I probably would have been abducted as well. My sister and I learned early that some men are fascinated by the thought of bedding twins. After my father's death, one of his creditors offered us a thousand pounds to lie with him."

Lucien's eyes narrowed into tigerish slits. "Give me his name and I'll challenge the swine. I'm quite a decent shot."

Kit blinked. "You mean that, don't you? No need. Kira responded by pouring a pot of tea into his lap. We thought it was a suitable response to the insult."

"I should have guessed that the two of you could protect yourselves."

"In the past, but not this time." She looked down into her glass and swirled the brandy. "It was a long shot that I would locate the villain by performing as Cassie James. That's why I began infiltrating the homes and gatherings of the Hellions."

"What exactly have you been looking for? Did Kira leave some telltale hint in her diary?"

"I'm afraid not." Kit slid from the bed, knowing that he would definitely not be able to comprehend her explanation. Mr. Jones and Cleo hadn't; even Jane didn't truly understand, and she had known the Travers twins since they were born. "At first I wasn't sure myself, but gradually I realized that I'm looking for a ... a kind of a psychic imprint—a feeling that a man has been very close to Kira. I feel like a hound casting about for a scent, except that what I'm looking for isn't physical."

"Can you explain that better?" Lucien asked, intrigued.

She hesitated. "It's a recognition of Kira's presence, I

suppose. I've always been able to go into a house or shop and know if she had been there recently."

"Fascinating. Can Kira do the same with you?"

"To some extent, but not as well." She gave a lopsided smile. "It's strange—when we were younger and read far too many Gothic romances, Kira and I would make plans about what we would do if one of us was abducted by a wicked prince. In retrospect it seems prescient, though really it was only an imaginative game. We would swear to think hard about the villain so our twin would be able to recognize him for what he was. When we went riding, one of us would mentally choose a hiding place for a message and the other one would have to guess the spot. We both got very good at knowing what the other would do."

Lucien finished his brandy and put the glass on the night table. "Has your stalking produced results?"

"Not as much as I'd like," she said ruefully. "I was able to eliminate most of the younger Hellions right away. It's harder with the older ones, the Disciples. I have the feeling that Kira knew them all and didn't like any of them."

She began pacing around the chamber. "I came to Blackwell Abbey because I thought Harford might be the villain. I couldn't get a clear reading in the ballroom, so I agreed to meet him in his room. When I did, I realized that he wasn't the one. I'm sure he's met Kira, but I'm equally sure that he isn't holding her captive. If he had her, he would have reacted when I took my mask off."

"What about Lord Mace?"

"He's another chief suspect. I had hoped to find traces of Kira here, but I'm willing to swear that she never set foot in Blackwell Abbey. She was never at Chiswick's estate, either."

"The man who abducted her didn't necessarily take her to his own home."

"Too true." Kit rubbed her temple, trying to relieve the ache that came whenever she thought about her sister's disappearance. "There are far too many possibilities. Yet I don't know what else to do. Men as powerful as the Disciples can't be accused without rock-solid evidence, and I have none. All I have are my own instincts. And I'm terrified, because I have the feeling that time is running out."

"Your bond with your twin is the best tool we have," Lucien said thoughtfully. "We must find a way to utilize it."

She felt an enormous sense of relief at how naturally he had taken on her problem. Lucien would be a formidable ally. He also had a remarkable understanding of her connection with Kira.

Uncanny, in fact. Her eyes narrowed as she regarded him. "How do you know so much about twins?"

His gaze slipped away. After a slight, almost unnoticeable pause, he said, "I've always found the phenomenon intriguing, so I talk with twins whenever I meet them."

Now that she was not thinking about Kira, she realized that the current between her and Lucien ran both ways; just as he seemed able to sense her emotions, she had some understanding of his. And there was something here, something important ... "There's more to it than that. Tell me, Lucien."

His eyes closed, and his face spasmed. Then, as unable to withstand her questions as she had been unable to withstand his, he said painfully, "I mentioned once that I had a sister who died. Elinor was more than a sister. She was my twin."

Chapter 24

Kit stared at him, aghast. "Dear God, you had a twin sister who died? How did you bear it?"

"Very badly." His usual calm disintegrated, leaving his face stark and vulnerable. "It was like ... being torn in half."

She sucked in her breath, then wordlessly crossed to the bed and embraced him.

His arms crushed around her, and he buried his head against her breasts, his whole body trembling. He did not weep. It might have been less dreadful if he had.

Over and over she smoothed her hand over his hair and the rigid back of his neck. She guessed that he had seldom, if ever, discussed his loss. She also had a strong sense that it was time that he did. When his grip on her began to loosen, she whispered, "Tell me about Elinor."

Slowly he pushed away and got off the bed. "Linnie was half an hour younger than I. I'm told that the doctor thought she would not live to see dawn, but she confounded everyone's expectations. We weren't identical, of course, but we looked very much alike, except that she was so much smaller that people assumed she was a year or two younger."

He drifted across the room, his bare feet soundless on the thick carpet. "My earliest memories are all of her. Always there, always smiling. She was quiet and looked so ethereal that she scarcely seemed to be of this world, yet she was clever and very perceptive. When we were four or five, I remember hearing her nurse say that Lady Elinor was on loan from the angels and she wouldn't be long in this world.

"I swore that I would prove the nurse wrong, that I

wouldn't let Linnie die. I had a sixth sense where she was concerned—if she was in trouble, I always knew. When she was ill, I ... lent her my strength. Once I bolted off my rocking horse and ran down the hall and caught her just before she could fall out a window. She had become careless while trying to lure a bird indoors."

He smiled a little. 'She always knew about me, too. Once when I was tossed by my pony and knocked senseless, she led my father straight to me. Other people thought that I was the 'dominant' twin, but it wasn't like that. Though she was quiet, she was in charge. It was almost impossible for me to refuse her anything. She had a mischievous streak, but when we got into trouble, I always insisted that the fault and the punishment were mine since I was the elder. She didn't like that, but I couldn't bear to see her punished, so on that issue, I got my way.

"I thought that I could always protect her." He stopped at the window and parted the draperies with one hand so that he could stare out into the featureless night. "But I failed."

"How old were you when you lost her?"

"Eleven." There was a long silence before he began to speak again. "My parents were indulgent, but they insisted on sending me away to school when I was nine even though I begged to be tutored at Ashdown with Linnie. Being separated was the most harrowing experience of my life. We were literally pulled out of each other's arms, both of us weeping hysterically. It was upsetting for my parents, especially my mother, but I was the next Earl of Strathmore and the Earls of Strathmore have always gone to Eton and that was that. I spent the first weeks at school crying every night, with Linnie doing the same at Ashdown. We wrote each other every day. I lived for her letters."

The thought of the children being wrenched apart made Kit shudder. At least she and Kira had been grown when they were separated. "As a twin, you were used to sharing and closeness. Perhaps that was why you made such deep, lasting friendships at Eton."

His forehead furrowed. "I never thought of that, but

you might be right. Certainly I was lucky in my friends. I met Michael first, about a fortnight after I started school. He found me crying in a corner of the chapel. Most boys would have mocked me, but Michael only asked what was wrong. I told him that I missed my twin sister. He thought about it, then said that his older brother was a beast, and would I be interested in becoming foster brothers?" Lucien smiled a little at the memory.

"After that, Eton became more bearable. Linnie and I adjusted to being apart, though neither of us liked it. The separation was harder on her, I think, because she didn't have new friends and activities to distract her. When I came home on school holidays, she was so fragile that she seemed almost transparent. But her spirit was never diminished. She was like a flame that was too bright for the lamp."

"Did she die of an illness?" Kit asked quietly.

"An accident. A stupid, ghastly accident." Lucien's fingers clenched on the velvet curtain. "It was near the end of the Christmas holiday, almost time for me to go back to Eton. We had made a family visit to some cousins and were returning to Ashdown in one of those great, heavy traveling coaches. There were some Roman ruins not far off the route. Linnie wanted to see them, so I nagged my father to take us. He agreed finally—I could be very persistent. If I hadn't been . . ." His voice trailed off, and his face became dead white.

"The coach crashed?"

He swallowed hard. "It had been rainy for days, and the ground was very soft. We were traveling up a steep track beside a lake when the earth collapsed under the weight of the coach. We tumbled down the hill, the horses screaming and thrashing in the traces. The driver and guard were thrown clear, though both were injured. Inside the coach it was pure chaos with the four of us crashing into each other."

He dropped the curtain and turned back to the room. "The carriage rolled into the lake. One of the windows had shattered and water was pouring in. I don't remember thinking about my parents at all. They were both knocked unconscious by the fall, I think. They never had a chance. I grabbed Linnie and dragged her out the broken window. The water was freezing, and I was numb in seconds. My ankle was struck by the thrashing hoof of one of the horses, but I didn't feel a thing.

"I managed to swim to shore with Linnie, even though our wet clothing was so heavy I was afraid it would drag us to the bottom. The wind was bitter, bitter cold. She was still breathing, but I knew she would die if I didn't get her to shelter quickly. We had passed a cottage not far back, so I tried to carry her there. I remember being furious at being slowed down by my ankle, which wasn't working properly. I didn't learn until later that a bone was broken. I mistreated the ankle so badly that day that it still troubles me sometimes.

"The cottage was within sight when Linnie raised her hand and touched my face. She gave me the sweetest, saddest smile. I knew she was saying good-bye. And then . . . and then . . ." His voice broke, and there was a long silence before he said in a barely audible whisper, "I felt the moment when her spirit left."

Once again Kit went to him and gathered him close, her heart aching. "It wasn't your fault," she said vehemently. "If not for your care, Linnie might never have lived to the age of eleven. You did everything humanly possible."

"But it wasn't enough," he said bleakly. "It's absurd, isn't it? A grown man mourning a child who died more than twenty years ago. I lost my parents and my childhood on the same day. It was dreadful, but I survived, and in time most of the pain faded. Yet the grief for my sister is always there."

"Linnie was your twin, your other self," she said, tears in her eyes. "A Gypsy woman once told Kira and me that twins were those who had been very close in an earlier life. It's a bond that stretches beyond death."

"You understand," he said shakily. "I think only another twin could. That's why I've never spoken of this to anyone. Oh, Kit, Kit . . ."

His mouth came down on hers, and he kissed her with a kind of desperation. The powerful emotions that both had experienced flared into passion, his robe falling away, her shirt yanked over her head. A few short steps to the bed, then his weight crushed her into the mattress. Her hands moved over his body, learning what pleased him. His heated mouth found secret, sensitive places, igniting a hunger that would have shamed her if she had not been beyond shame.

Then union, as natural as breathing. An intimate soreness was drowned by her arousal, enhancing the pleasure that was almost pain. The poignancy of mutual comfort. Then raw, blinding madness swept her up until she shattered. She clawed at him, her body convulsing as he plunged into her again and again.

Afterward they lay silently in each other's arms, drained. She was empty of everything but a mild sense of wonder and a deep contentment that filled every cell of her body and every haunted corner of her mind. For the first time since she and Kira had gone their separate ways, she felt whole.

It was a dangerous thought, one she quickly suppressed. Contentment was safer. Tenderly she stroked the small of his back. She had not known that a man's body could be so beautiful, just as she had never understood how a woman could throw away her reputation and her future for the sake of passion. It was still a foolish thing to do, but heaven help her, she did understand.

Lucien eased his weight down beside her, saying huskily, "This could become addictive."

She smiled a little, understanding the need to speak lightly of something so immense.

Absently, he twined her hair around his forefinger. "We're going to have to get married, you know."

His words were like a blast of icy water in the face. "What!" She would have jerked upright in bed if his arm had not held her down. "You're mad!"

"Not in the least," he said calmly. "You know the rules as well as I do. When a gentleman compromises a lady, only his name will mend the damage. Hence, I am offering you mine."

Struggling to collect her chaotic thoughts, she asked, "Would you be saying this if I were Kristine?"

"The situation would be different. Your sister chose to turn her back on convention. You did not—you've been living an entirely respectable life with your aunt." He smiled and traced the edge of her ear with a fingertip. "You said yourself that a gentleman does not treat a lady the same as an actress. In spite of our irregular activities, you are certainly a lady, and I am nominally a gentleman. Ergo, marriage."

In spite of his light manner, she knew that he was speaking in dead earnest. She sensed he had a need to protect others, particularly women, that was rooted in his failure to save his sister. That was not, she suspected, a good basis for marriage.

The candlelight played over his muscular body and made a silver halo of his hair. He was glorious, a naked, indecently masculine angel who had abandoned heaven so that he could master the arts of earthly sensuality. What would it be like to be his wife, to experience passion and intimacy again and again?

It was a dangerously seductive vision. Grasping for rationality, she said, "You're not very convincing as a defender of conventional morality, Lucien. You don't believe in society's rules, and you certainly don't always follow them."

"I might not always follow the rules," he admitted, "but I do believe in them. Social condemnation is very real—the lives of rulebreakers are wrecked every day. I'm not going to let you be ruined because I heedlessly took your virginity."

"At heart I'm as unconventional as Kira—I've simply lacked her courage and her opportunities," she said tartly. "What happened tonight was every bit as much my doing as yours, so you needn't sacrifice yourself on the altar of gentlemanly honor."

He shrugged. "It would be no great sacrifice. As my female relations point out frequently, it's high time I married, and you are an entirely eligible bride." His hand skimmed over her belly, the warm palm coming to rest on the silky curls between her thighs. "Besides, there is always the possibility of a child. That is one consequence that could not be easily concealed."

To bear his child ... The idea was so alarmingly attractive that it was well-nigh irresistible. "The chance of that happening after a single night is remote," she said firmly. "Time enough to worry if it happens."

As he opened his mouth to continue the argument, she mentally reached out to Kira, seeking the strength to refuse Lucien again.

Kira wasn't there.

Chapter 25

Horror blazed through her. She went rigid. *"Kira!"*

"What's wrong?" Lucien said sharply.

"I can't find Kira!" she gasped, feeling as if she was suffocating. "I reached for her, and she isn't there."

His eyes molten with intensity, Lucien caught her gaze and clamped his palms to her temples, his deep strength flowing through her. "Close your eyes, relax, and breathe deeply," he ordered. "One. Two. Three. *Breathe,* dammit! One—two—three—four—five . . ."

She forced herself to follow his rhythm. When her breath had steadied, he said softly, "Try again."

Frantically she delved inward, seeking the life essence that was as familiar as her own. With a relief as disabling as her earlier fear, she located the gossamer bond that connected her with her twin. It pulsed strong and steady. "She's all right," Kit whispered brokenly. "Nothing has happened to her."

"Thank God." Lucien tucked the covers around her shivering body, then pulled her against his own warmth.

She opened her eyes and saw in his face how deep his concern had been. Like no one else she had ever met, he was capable of understanding the terror she had just endured.

He said soberly, "I think we should get married as soon as possible. It will make it easier to search for Kira."

"No, Lucien," she said in the tone her sister would have recognized as immovable. "Don't you see? What just happened was because passion flooded my senses. I can't risk that happening again. You said yourself that my connection with Kira is essential for finding her. If we become lovers, I may lose that."

"I was talking about marriage, not an affair," he pointed out, his face unreadable.

"Marriage would be even worse." She closed her eyes, not daring to look at him. "Lucien, I can't lie with you again, or think about the future, as long as Kira's life is in danger." Her voice broke. "And if she dies, I might not have a future, because I can't imagine living in a world bereft of her."

"One learns how to endure," he said in a voice that wasn't quite cool enough to mask the pain. "But I understand your point. Very well, all marriage plans are postponed until we've found your sister. But I warn you, when the time comes, I don't intend to take no for an answer."

She smiled at him wryly. "After you've had time to think it over, I'm sure you'll recover from your attack of gentlemanliness. I'm an eccentric bluestocking, you know, not at all suited to be countess to a dashing man about town like you."

"In other words you're afraid I'm too frivolous to tolerate your career as a political and social writer. Actually, that's one of your charms," he remarked. "Marrying a woman who wears as many different faces as you would be like having a whole harem in one wife. There would never be a dull moment. And I agree with most of your opinions, except when you're being deliberately provocative."

She stared at him, off balance again. "What do you mean?"

"I didn't quite believe that Kristine was L. J. Knight, but such work suits Kathryn right down to the ground." His mouth quirked up. "Am I wrong?"

"No," she said ruefully. "Everything I said about being a journalist was true. Knight was my mother's maiden name. I'm beginning to think that you're never wrong."

"This from the woman who tied me in knots for weeks."

She studied his face, again feeling the sense of a current running between them. She had always thought there was a discrepancy between his public face and his real self, and now she was certain. "You're not the idle gentleman you pretend to be, are you? I should have realized earlier that the way you observe and analyze isn't casual at all. What is your purpose?"

It was his turn to look off-balance. "I had the vain hope that you might not work that out," he said after a slight pause. "Suffice it to say that the war with France made information valuable, so I've learned to pay attention and pass on material that might be of interest to the government."

"If you say so," she said skeptically. "I would have thought it more likely that you're some sort of master spy who hides behind a facade of frivolity."

His eyes became greener. Another person might not have noticed, but to Kit it was proof positive that her guess had hit the mark. "So that's why you wanted to become a Hellion," she said triumphantly. "It explains a great deal."

"Peace, woman." He gave a sigh of comic defeat. "I'm going to have to confess, aren't I?"

"I think it only fair. After all, tonight my life has been examined to a fare-thee-well."

"There's no official name for my position, but I've been quietly involved in intelligence work ever since I left Oxford. A friend once said that I'm like a spider sitting in the middle of a vast web, munching on reports that come from all over Europe."

"You don't look like a spider. Nowhere near enough legs."

He grinned. "I sometimes look into domestic matters when there are international implications. In this case, I have reason to believe that one of the Hellions has been a French spy for years. With rumors that Napoleon might try to seize power again, it's particularly important to stop the fellow. So far, though, I've had no success." He scowled ferociously and slid his hand under the blanket so he could caress her breast. "Most of my attention has been taken up by a certain maddening female."

She laughed, then caught her breath when he rolled her nipple between thumb and forefinger. Unhappily, she caught his hand and lifted it out from under the blanket. "Don't, Lucien. Passion is a luxury I can't afford just now. The connection between Kira and me is not as strong as when we were younger, and I daren't do anything that might weaken it further."

He settled his hand on her torso again, but this time quietly on top of the blanket. "The bond seems remarkably strong, considering that you've been living apart and pursuing different interests for years."

"It wasn't geography that weakened the link, but the fact that after we separated, Kira started keeping things from me." Kit gave a wintry smile. "I expect she thought I was too innocent to hear the gritty reality of an actress's life. It was frustrating—I could dimly sense her emotional ups and downs, but usually didn't know enough to interpret them."

His brows drew together. "That could be useful. Did you sense anything that happened to her during those years that might be relevant to her disappearance?"

"The most notable event was a period when she was blazingly happy. It ended very suddenly, and after that she was wretched for a long time. I think she fell in love and it ended badly." Kit sighed. "She refused to discuss it, or even admit that there was a man, but she has never been quite the same since. She lost some of her sparkle."

"It must have hurt to be shut out," he said softly.

Kit didn't answer. In this instance, she wished that Lucien was a bit less sensitive. It had been hard to know that her twin was hurting; it had been even harder not to be allowed to help.

"We've been assuming that Kira's 'Lord Hellion' is the villain, but perhaps that's wrong," he continued. "Could this affair of Kira's be a factor?"

She thought about it, then shook her head. "I don't think so—it happened two or three years ago. Besides, my feeling was that he left her, not vice versa, so he's unlikely to kidnap her from unrequited passion."

"Did you notice any times when she was frightened?"

"Only when she was about to go on stage for a new show, and that kind of fear has a different flavor from fear for one's safety." Kit made a face. "I've learned stage fright well since I started performing in Kira's place."

"Do you enjoy acting? You do it magnificently, with the same ability to bewitch an audience that you say Kira has."

"That isn't my ability; it's borrowed from Kira." She pondered. "The applause is exciting, and I'm glad to have had the chance to experience it. It helps me understand Kira better. But to perform well, it's necessary to bare one's inner life, which I hate. I'm much happier behind the scenes."

"Obviously you were born to be a writer, just as Kira was born to be an actress." He brushed his knuckles tenderly under her chin. "Twins are even more interesting for their differences than for their similarities. If you think of anything else that could be relevant, make a note and tell me later. I might see something that you are too close to notice."

They lay together in silence for a little longer. Kit wondered sadly if they would ever be like this again. Finally, she sat up and swung her feet to the floor. "It's time for me to leave. Dawn can't be far away."

He sat up also, his face grave. "I find myself deeply reluctant to let you out of my sight."

"Not surprising, based on your experience." She stood and pulled her rumpled garments on. "But don't worry. You were right earlier—I need all of the help I can get, so I promise not to vanish again."

"Where is Kira's house?"

It was a test, and she met it without hesitation. "Number 7 Marshall Street. I divide my time between there and Jane's. I always stay at Kira's when I'm performing."

His face eased. "When I leave here, I have to make a quick trip to Ashdown, but I should be back in London late Tuesday."

"I'll be doing *The Gypsy Lass* again that night. Why not meet me in my dressing room afterward?" Her eyes twinkled. "This time I'll go to supper with you voluntarily. No kidnapping required."

"Kidnapping you was particularly inappropriate under the circumstances. No wonder you were furious." He regarded her thoughtfully. "Did you suspect me of being the one who had abducted your sister?"

"Not really. I knew that I should—the information about you was rather ominous—but I didn't really believe that someone who kept rescuing me from drunken Hellions was a villain." Her mouth quirked. "Besides, if you and Kira had met, you would have gotten on smashingly. No abduction would have been required."

"I'm glad to know that my sterling qualities shone through." He stood and began putting his own clothing on. "I'll see you Tuesday night unless the roads are especially bad. If I don't arrive within half an hour of the end of the play, assume that I was held up. I'll call at Kira's house the next morning." He chuckled. "Do you realize how seldom we have seen each other in daylight? It's like the courtship of two owls."

She cocked her head as she tied the ribbon of her crumpled domino. "Is this a courtship?"

"It must be, since soon we will be standing at the altar."

He crossed the room and reached for her. She sidestepped nervously. "I shouldn't kiss you, Lucien. As I said earlier, passion is too distracting."

He paused in midstep. "I thought the ban was on more intimate activities."

She blushed and looked away. "With you, even a kiss is enough to scramble my wits."

He sighed. "Flattering but frustrating. It's going to be very hard to be around you and not touch, kitten."

"I'm too tall and too serious to be a kitten."

"Nonsense." He grinned. "You're a very convenient size, and I think you're absolutely hilarious." Before she could protest the remark, he drew her into a hug. "Tonight is already a flat loss in terms of you keeping your sensory channels clear," he said into her hair. "Would another kiss be that much worse than what we've already done?"

He must have known that she could not resist him when he was so close. "Perhaps . . . ," she said hesitantly, "a kiss will be all right." She lifted her head and pressed her lips to his. His mouth welcomed hers, warm and

deep. He was the whole world, strong as the earth, and
as essential. She clung to him, shaking, for long seconds
after the kiss ended.

His own breath uneven, he said, "We will find Kira,
and then you will marry me. Accept it, my dear tiger
kitten, because we've gone too far to turn back." He
kissed her again, this time lightly. "I look forward to the
next time I can compromise you."

She smiled a little sadly as she emerged from his embrace. She wished she could believe they had a future
together, but she couldn't.

No one saw them when Lucien escorted Kit through
the silent house to an unobtrusive exit. She had insisted
that she would be all right, but it was hard to let her go,
and impossible to sleep when he returned to his room.
Restlessness and yearning churned in his veins. Still,
though the emotions were far from comfortable, they
were a great improvement over the black melancholy
that had followed intimacy in the past.

She filled his mind; maddening, quicksilver Kit, with
her courage and loyalty, her wicked intelligence and her
flowering sensuality. There was a tantalizing possibility
that with her he might find the emotional intimacy that
had been absent from his life since Elinor's death.

Such closeness wasn't there yet, and it might never be.
Kit's first allegiance was to her twin, and dead or alive,
Kira might stand permanently between Kit and himself.
But at least there was hope. It would be worth marrying
Kit for that, quite apart from marriage being the honor-
able thing to do.

It was going to be *very* hard to keep his hands off her
while they searched for Kira.

He smiled into the darkness. Kit could not have found
a better motivation for him to find her twin quickly.

Interlude

Worse than the fear, almost as dreadful as the degradation, was the boredom. Strange how even horror could become banal. Sometimes she thought she would go mad from isolation. She supposed that she should be grateful that her prison was so comfortable, but it was still a prison.

How long she had been locked in her lightless room? Weeks, certainly, perhaps months. It was hard to keep track of time. She yearned for the sight of the sun, or a rain-soaked sky.

Her only diversion was a small shelf of books, none of which she would have allowed in her home if she'd had a choice, but of choices she had none. The nauseating volumes had been essential at teaching her to understand something of her captor's perverse mind. She had also studied them religiously to glean ideas of what she might do to him. He thrived on novelty, and the day he became bored with her, she was a dead woman.

She was restlessly pacing around the sitting room when the hard-faced maid arrived. The massive armed guard who stood outside was briefly visible when the iron-bound door swung open. Knowledge of that guard was all that had kept her from making a desperate attempt to escape. She had not endured what she had to vainly throw her life away. If she waited, eventually a better opportunity would come.

The maid said, "He'll be here in an hour. He wants you to wear the furs."

She nodded wearily. Her captor was particularly fond of that costume. With the help of the maid, she *donned the outfit. First a tight red satin garment that resembled an elaborate French corset. Then the inevitable black boots and lace stockings. Finally, a sable cape that swirled dramatically when she stalked about with her whip.*

If . . . when . . . she escaped from this place, she would be happy to wear plain white muslin for the rest of her life.

She was adjusting her silver blond wig when the maid suddenly spat out, "You think you're safe because he likes what you do to him, but you'll see. In a fortnight you'll end up just like the others."

She spun on her heel and stared at the maid. "What 'others'? And what happened to them?"

The maid gave an ugly smile. "Do you think you're the first he brought here? As for what happens—you'll see, you filthy slut." The maid rapped on the door, and the guard let her out.

Her cold hands clamped about the handle of her whip. She had always known that there could be no good end to her captivity, but time was running out faster than she had realized.

A fortnight. Silently, she vowed that when the time came, she would not go tamely like a lamb to the slaughter.

Chapter 26

The Gypsy Lass went well even though nightmares had disturbed Kit's sleep again the night before. As she danced through her role, she wondered if Lucien had arrived early enough to be in the audience. She suspected that he was present because she felt that someone was watching her with more than usual intensity. She hoped he enjoyed the view of her tattoo.

The performance left her exhausted and drenched in sweat, so she bypassed the green room. Her dressing room was tiny, but all hers since she was now a lead attraction with the company. She removed her black wig, washed off her face paint, and changed from her costume into a dress of Kira's, which was more dashing than her own wardrobe. Though she dared not risk intimacy with Lucien again, she did want him to be tempted. She was discovering that prim Kathryn had a shameless streak.

She smiled as she brushed out her hair. The three days since she had seen him seemed like forever. Perhaps they couldn't touch—or at least, only a little—but it would be wonderful simply to be with him. In his presence it was possible to believe that all would be well.

Her musing was interrupted by a knock at the door. She leaped up from the dressing table. Lord, she was acting like a giddy girl! But Lucien wouldn't mind.

Her greeting died on her lips when she threw open the door. It wasn't Lucien. Instead, a tall, dark-haired man stood in the shadowed hall. Her first reaction was a sense of familiarity, but when she looked more closely, she realized that he was a complete stranger.

He wasn't the first admirer of Cassie James to find his way to her dressing room, and he wouldn't be the last.

She swallowed her disappointment and gave him a friendly smile, the way Kira would have. "Good evening. Did you enjoy the play?"

"Enjoy the play?" His mouth twisted. "I scarcely noticed it. All I saw was you." Without waiting for permission, he moved past her into the dressing room.

Obviously, he knew Kira well. In the brighter light, Kit saw that his features were good, but he was thin to the point of gauntness, and a menacing scar curved from his temple into his overlong hair. He was poorly dressed, his garments ill-fitting and shabby, yet paradoxically he carried himself like a man of consequence. She tried to match his appearance to the brief descriptions that Cleo had given her, without success. Of course, Cleo couldn't know every man Kira had ever met.

Deciding that casual friendliness was the best approach, Kit said, "It's been a long time."

"It's been an eternity." He turned his palms upward. "You win, sweetheart. I surrender—foot, horse and cannon."

It was worse than she had feared, for clearly he had known Kira *very* well. When she hesitated, wondering about the best way to respond, he said with painful humor, "I know I look like something your cat left on the doorstep, but surely you haven't forgotten what you said the last time we saw each other. Perhaps you need a reminder."

Before she could guess his intention, he stepped forward and wrapped her in a crushing embrace. There was raw hunger in his kiss, and a possessiveness that was a little frightening.

She shoved him away, saying flippantly, "Don't rush your fences. As I said, it's been a long time. Tell me where you've been and what you've been doing." She retreated across the room, wondering how long it had been since the end of the performance and whether there was still a chance that Lucien might come. "Would you like a glass of sherry?"

He stared at her, feverish emotion in his brown eyes. "Don't you care that I risked my life to come here? You're acting as if this is a damned drawing room."

As Kathryn, she would have made soothing noises, but tonight she was Kira. She retorted, "And you're acting as if you own me. Well, you don't, and if you won't behave in a civilized manner, I'll have to ask you to leave."

A long moment of silence throbbed between them. Then he said softly, "So you want me to be civilized." He picked up the chair at her dressing table. She thought he was going to ask her politely to sit.

Instead, he raised the chair above his head, then smashed it viciously into the wall. Shards of wood flew in all directions, bouncing crazily and shattering her dressing mirror. "Sorry, Kira, but I'm in no mood to be civilized," he said, his voice all the more frightening for its restraint. "I would never have survived the last two years if I hadn't become a savage, and savagery is not something one can put aside like an old shirt."

She flattened her back against the wall, her heart pounding as she considered shouting for help. No, she would never be heard above the racket in the green room.

Then she caught her breath. He had endured savagery for two years. . . .

The pieces snapped into place. This must be the man Kira had fallen in love with, which was why he had seemed familiar even though Kit had never met him. Perhaps he hadn't left her sister voluntarily, but had been sent to prison. His present fury made it easy to believe that he was a criminal, or perhaps mad. Either possibility would explain Kira's misery and refusal to discuss her heartbreak.

"I'm sorry for what you've had to endure," she said, trying to sound conciliatory. "Tell me about it."

"I didn't come here to talk about my bad luck," he growled. "I came here for you."

She hesitated. If her sister was in love with this man, Kit couldn't send him away. She must confess who she was and hope that he would honor her confidence. Perhaps he might even know something that would help in the search for Kira.

Too much time had passed while she thought. "You're

trying to think of a tactful way to say that feelings change
in two years, aren't you?" he said, anguish in his face.
"Well, mine didn't, and they never will."

It was indecent to let this stranger bare his heart to
the wrong woman. She raised her hand to cut off his
words. "Please, don't say more. I'm not who you think
I am."

Before she could say more, his expression changed.
"No, you aren't," he said bitterly. "I thought you were
loving and honest, even though you were an actress, but
you're as much a whore as the rest of your breed. Very
well, I'll treat you as one. I'm afraid I don't have the
price of a night with me, but surely I have some credit
left from the gifts I gave you before."

He trapped her against the wall and kissed her again,
this time with punishing force. Though she fought him,
his thinness disguised sinewy strength. His hips ground
into hers, and he clamped his hand on her breast. She
bit his tongue.

He jerked his head back and growled, "You little
bitch!"

She tried to wrench herself away, but he caught her
and pinned her to the wall. They stared at each other.
In his burning eyes she saw the struggle between rage
and reason.

With a harsh squeal the door swung open. Kit and her
assailant both looked up to see a travel-stained Lucien.
Summing up the situation instantly, he strode into the
room, his eyes feral. "Let go of her *now*!"

"So this is why you're playing Miss Modesty!" the
dark-haired man exploded. "I taught you too well. I
should have known that once you discovered the delights
of fornication, you wouldn't be able to keep your legs
together. How many lovers have you had in the last two
years? Or have you lost count?"

Before she could answer, he released her and sprang
across the small room to make a wild swing at Lucien.
Kit cried out, but Lucien had already reacted. In one
fluid motion he sidestepped the blow and smashed a hard
fist into his assailant's jaw. The man made a gurgling
sound and dropped like a felled ox.

Lucien stepped over him and gathered Kit close. "Did he hurt you?"

"N-not really." She buried her face against his shoulder, wishing he could touch every part of her at once. He smelled of mud and horse and safety.

Lucien kissed her forehead and stroked her back and shoulders, kneading the fear from her muscles. "Who is he?"

She gave a shaky laugh. "We never did get to introductions, but I think he must be the man Kira fell in love with several years ago. She would never have made him free of her nickname if she weren't serious."

Lucien studied the dark-haired man, whose temporary stupor was passing. "His manners need work."

"He was badly upset." She shivered. "But I'm very glad you arrived when you did."

The man sluggishly pushed himself to a sitting position. A bruise was rapidly forming on his jaw. "Go ahead," he said wearily. "Call the watch or the magistrate or whatever the hell you use for police in London. I really don't care."

Lucien looked at him narrowly. "From your accent, you must be American or Canadian."

"American." The stranger gave Kit a satiric glance. "Naturally, you're too clever to tell the current lover about the former ones."

"If you don't stop making insulting remarks to the lady, I'll break your jaw," Lucien said pleasantly. Releasing Kit, he reached down and hauled the other man upright. "Do you have anything to drink, Kit? I think this gentleman could use some refreshment."

She went to the cabinet that held the sherry. Trust Lucien to notice the subtly un-English accent. Thinking that he could also use something after his long journey, she poured two glasses and gave one to him and the other to the stranger, who was now sitting on the chaise, his head bowed. "Brace yourself," she said. "I'm not Kira, I'm her twin sister, Kit. Obviously she never mentioned me."

His head snapped up, and he stared at her incredulously. Then he lifted his free hand and skimmed his fingers over her face. "Oh, God," he whispered. "It's true—you're not Kira." His face grayed. "I'm sorry, so sorry. If I'd known, I would never have behaved as I did."

"I would hate to think you considered that an acceptable way to treat my sister," she said crisply. "Of course, if I were Kira, I would have behaved differently myself."

He couldn't meet her eyes. "For two endless years the thought of Kira kept me alive. I expected you ... her ... to fall into my arms. When you treated me like a casual acquaintance, I ... I went a little crazy. I hope you can forgive me."

She studied his pale face. Poor devil. "Forgiven and forgotten. But who are you?"

"Jason Travers." His mouth quirked. "Rather belatedly at your service."

"A relative?" Lucien asked.

Kit's eyes widened. "I believe this must be the American second cousin I mentioned—the one who is now the fifth Earl of Markland."

Lucien whistled softly. "Interesting. The fact that he's a peer could be useful if the authorities discover his presence." To the American, he said, "You just escaped from the hulks?"

Kit exclaimed, "Those ghastly prison ships moored out in the Thames? Surely not!"

Jason smiled humorlessly. "I'm afraid so—Hades afloat. Yesterday I had an opportunity to go over the railing, so I did. Damned near froze, got dragged down by debris in the filthy water, and almost didn't make it to shore." He regarded Lucien warily. "How did you figure that out? And who *are* you?"

"Lucien Fairchild, the future husband of the young lady you were mauling." Lucien held out his hand. "You look like a man who has been on prison rations. Since there are some American prisoners of war on the hulks, it seemed a likely explanation."

Jason shook the proffered hand, then took a swallow of sherry. He was trembling and appeared on the verge of collapse.

Lucien said to Kit, "We should take him to my house, I think. Obviously he needs food, clothing, and rest."

She nodded agreement. Her new-found cousin looked up in confusion. "You're not going to send me back to the hulks? The last I heard, our countries were at war."

"God willing, not for much longer. It was a damned fool war to begin with. And frankly, I wouldn't send a rabid dog to the hulks." Lucien helped the American to his feet. "Can you walk? Good—carrying you would be a bit conspicuous." He put his arm around Kit's waist, and the three of them went outside, where his carriage waited right outside the stage door.

Half an hour later they were in the kitchen of Strathmore House. Kit noted that Lucien was surprisingly familiar with the area for a peer; midnight raids on the larder must not be uncommon. He even found a pot of soup. Kit heated it while he rummaged for bread, cheese, and a steak and kidney pie.

In spite of his obvious hunger, Jason Travers was unable to eat much. After pushing away his soup bowl, he studied Kit. She became aware of his gaze and glanced up inquiringly.

"Sorry," he apologized. "I know you're not Kira. If I hadn't been expecting to see her, I would have realized the moment I laid eyes on you. Yet the resemblance is astonishing."

"You're not the first to be confused," she remarked. "Even our father couldn't tell us apart."

"Then he wasn't paying attention." His hands tightened around his mug of ale. "Where is Kira? I assume she must be in some kind of trouble."

Tersely, Kit explained about her sister's disappearance and her own impersonation. Jason's face darkened as she spoke. When she finished, he said with barely suppressed violence, "Damnation, I've felt that something was wrong for weeks, but assumed it was one of the strange fancies one gets in prison." He rubbed the scar on his temple, which was visibly throbbing. "I suppose that was why I risked trying to escape—I knew I had to find her."

Recognizing a distress that nearly equaled her own, Kit said reassuringly, "Wherever she is, she is in good health—I would know if she weren't. And we're doing everything we can to get her back."

"Tell me what I can do," he said, his expression like granite.

"Don't worry," Lucien said, pouring more ale for each of them. "You'll be conscripted if necessary. First we have to locate her. But now it's your turn to talk."

"Yes, I'm curious how you met my sister."

Jason closed his eyes briefly, marshaling his thoughts. "Four years ago your family solicitor notified me that I was the new earl. Because of the late earl's improvidence, there was no financial legacy, so I scarcely paid attention to the letter. My grandfather was a younger son who had emigrated to America and maintained only the most tenuous connection with his family. As an American I couldn't hold the title, so the whole subject was of only intellectual interest.

"However, when business called me to Britain, I found I had a certain curiosity about where the family came from. After I'd finished in Liverpool, I traveled up to Kendal. The current owner of the estate showed me around and invited me to dinner. I looked at the parish church with all of its memorials to dead Travers and rode through the hills and generally found it an interesting trip." He made a face. "I see why my grandfather left, though—it was the dampest, grayest place I've ever seen."

Kit smiled. "Westmoreland is wet even by British standards, but one grows accustomed. The countryside is very beautiful."

"In a bleak sort of way," he agreed. "I was about to leave when the innkeeper told me that one of the late earl's daughters had just arrived at the inn. He said Lady Kristine was visiting because she and her sister had been slowly paying off their father's debts, and that she had probably come to make the last installment and thank the creditors for being patient."

Lucien cocked an inquisitive brow at Kit.

"Not Papa's gambling debts," she said. "His ghastly gamester friends can fry in hell for all we care. But we felt an obligation to pay the tradesmen. We would have been in rags and living on porridge if the Kendal shop-keepers hadn't extended credit to the family."

His eyes glowed with the tenderness that turned them gold. "What an honorable pair you are."

She traced a figure eight in spilled ale. "Kira did more than I; successful actresses earn more than scribblers."

"All the more credit to you." He took her hand under the table, his fingers lacing through hers.

"The innkeeper spoke very highly of you both," Jason said. "Since I was curious about my English cousin, I asked for an introduction to Lady Kristine. She was . . . not what I expected." A reminiscent smile played around his lips.

When the silence became lengthy, Lucien said, "We may assume that the stars stopped in their courses and angelic choirs sang?"

Jason pulled himself back to the present. "That's a fair description. I followed her to York, where she was performing. For the next weeks . . ." His voice thickened, and he stopped.

"Did Kira want marriage, but you couldn't bring your-self to marry an actress?" Kit asked, an edge in her voice.

"No!" He gave her a fulminating glance. "I did pro-pose to her—in fact, I damned well got down on my knees and begged—but she refused to marry me unless I settled in England. I don't know whether she wanted to be a countess, or whether she was enjoying her career too much to leave, but I couldn't agree to give up my home and country."

"Not an easy choice," Lucien agreed.

"We had an almighty row. I told her if she changed her mind, she knew where to find me in Boston. She answered that if I changed *mine,* she'd welcome me back with open arms, but otherwise never to darken her door again."

"No wonder you were so angry when you showed up and my arms weren't open," Kit said.

He ran a distracted hand through his dark hair. "I haven't known a moment's peace since I left York. After I got through cursing Kira, I missed her horribly. So I started to think seriously about moving back to the old country even though, like any good American, I despise the British government. It's rotten to the core."

Kit shot a glance at Lucien, who had spent much of his life defending that government. He said only, "There are many here who would agree with you, but a government is not a nation."

Jason gave a lopsided smile. "True, and when I thought about it, I realized that I like the English as individuals. Since I don't have any close family left in America and my business, which is shipping, could be run as well from Britain as Boston, I decided to go back to Kira, hat in hand, and offer to settle here. Then the war broke out. I volunteered my services, and a few months later I was a prisoner in one of the hulks, living on swill and praying that I wouldn't die of jail fever."

"The hulks are the vilest prisons in Britain," Kit said gravely. She had written several furious articles about how inhumane they were. "You're lucky to have survived."

"Believe me, I know," Jason said with an involuntary shiver.

Lucien commented, "You were a privateer captain?"

The American stared at him. "You must be a damned uncomfortable man to know. How did you guess that?"

"Only someone captured at sea would be likely to end up in a British prison rather than in Canada," Lucien explained. "You mentioned that your business was shipping, and you seem like the sort who prefers giving orders rather than taking them. Hence, a privateer seemed probable. Still, I'm surprised that an officer was sent to one of the hulks."

"The captain of the frigate that captured the *Bonnie Lady* took a personal dislike to me and used his influence to see that I was sent to the rottenest prison available."

"You said that you escaped over the side and swam to shore," Kit said. "How did you manage for money and clothing?"

"I broke into a used clothing shop near the waterfront and outfitted myself with the best I could find," the American said uncomfortably. "By chance, I also found some money hidden under a pile of shirts."

"If you remember the name and location of the shop, I'll send payment for what you took," Lucien said.

Jason gave him a quick glance. "I would appreciate that. I swear I'll pay you back."

Lucien made a deprecatory gesture. "After the peace treaty. What happened then?"

"I was going to take a coach to York in the hopes that Kira was still playing the northern circuit, but at the coaching inn I saw a playbill posted for *The Gypsy Lass,* starring Cassie James, so I went to the theater." He sighed, his face haggard. "I thought my luck had changed. Instead . . ."

After another silence, he said, "That sounds ungrateful. Believe me, I appreciate how fortunate I am that you aren't sending me back to that hellhole."

Lucien smiled a little. "Since we are practically related by marriage, it would be bad form for me to permit you to starve on a godforsaken tub on the river." He stood. "You look dead on your feet. Get some rest. We'll talk again in the morning."

Kit took the American's thin hand in hers. "We'll find her, Jason—or die trying."

"Let us hope it doesn't come to that," Lucien said quietly.

Kit cleaned up after the meal while Lucien took Jason off to a guest room. When he returned, he wrapped his arms around her as if the action was as natural as breathing. She leaned into him, her fatigue and tension dropping away like petals falling from an overblown rose.

"Do you resent his closeness to Kira?" he asked.

"My newfound cousin was right—you know too much." She hesitated, trying to find the right words. "I like Jason . . . he seems an honorable sort and obviously he loves Kira deeply. If I read her feelings correctly, she loves him just as much. God knows that I truly want her to be happy."

She gave a soft, unhappy exhalation. "But at the same time, I *do* resent his coming between us. After she met him, she started shutting me out. She had every right to do that. And yet . . ." Kit hid her face against his shoul-

der and said wretchedly, "She never even told him we
were twins! That has been the most significant fact in my
life, yet she didn't think it important enough to tell him."

He stroked her head tenderly. He was getting very
good at soothing her, she thought with a touch of
hysteria.

"Perhaps the omission wasn't because the relationship
was unimportant to her, but because it was too important," he suggested. "I suspect that one reason identical twins like to confuse others is because it keeps people
at a distance and protects the uniqueness of the twin
bond. You are an aspect of Kira's life that is so special,
she probably didn't dare share it until she was sure of
him. Because of their different nationalities, she may
have had misgivings about the relationship from the first,
so she didn't tell him."

The constriction in Kit's throat eased. "I don't know
if that's true, but it's a very nice explanation. I like it."
She looked up at him. "Where did you learn to be so
kind?"

Though the question was rhetorical, he replied, "From
Linnie. Not only did she have a gentle spirit, but she
taught me something of how the female mind works."
His voice became self-mocking. "I also know that if she
had grown up, fallen in love, and married, I would have
resented her husband. Not because of any perverted
physical jealousy of my sister, but because I would fear
the loss of the special closeness between us."

And he had lost that closeness for all time when he
was no more than a child himself. The thought made Kit
feel ashamed of her own complaints. She hugged him
harder, wishing she could change the past so that Elinor
had survived. "You would have overcome your jealousy
and wished her well with a full heart."

"You'll do the same." He nuzzled her hair. "It's very
late. Why not spend the rest of the night here with me?"

When she hesitated, he said, "Only to sleep, Kit, I
swear it. I don't want to do anything that might jeopardize your connection with Kira. But it's been a long,
tiring day, and I would rest much better if you were
beside me."

"I'd better not. What would your servants think?"

"They were all chosen for their ability to be discreet," he said lightly. "And they might as well get used to the sight of you since you're their future mistress."

He must have felt her tense, because he put his hands on her shoulders and examined her face. "It hasn't escaped my attention that when I mention marriage, you react like a rabbit that has been cornered by a ferret. Is the prospect of being my wife so distasteful?"

Lucien would be easier to deal with if he were less perceptive. Again choosing her words with care, she said, "It's not distasteful, but the possibility seems unreal. I can't see beyond Kira's disappearance to a time that is normal again."

"And that is as much as you're going to say, isn't it?" he said dryly. "Very well, I won't nag you. But I'm not going to change my mind, and I can be amazingly persistent."

"I know, to my cost." She rested her forehead against his cheek. "You're amazing in quite a lot of ways."

"Stay with me," he said softly. "Please."

It was as hard to deny him as it was for her to disagree with Kira. And the brazen truth was that she wanted to be with him as much as he wanted her. "Very well," she whispered. "I'll stay."

Chapter 27

In deference to the circumstances, Lucien produced two of his seldom-used nightshirts. Kit's enveloped her from chin to well past her toes. She looked delectable as she nestled against his side and quickly fell asleep. Though he was tired from a long day on muddy roads, he stayed awake longer, savoring the pure sweetness of having her with him.

Was her reluctance to marry general, or specific to him? Perhaps a bit of both. He'd have to convince her that he had no intention of clipping her wings and turning her into a domestic sparrow. She could be as much of a radical thinker under his roof as she was under her cousin's.

He dozed off, only to come awake with a jerk when Kit gave a choked scream and struck out with her left fist, almost smashing him in the eye. He caught her wrists to stop her flailing. "Kit, wake up! You're having a nightmare."

Her eyes opened, but she continued to struggle. "Kit, it's Lucien and you're safe," he said sharply. "You're safe."

Her thrashing stopped. "Lucien?" she whispered uncertainly.

"I'm here, Kit," He released her wrists and lit the candle on the night table. "Describe your nightmare."

"It was dreadful. I ... I was wearing some strange, indecent costume, and I was flogging a man. He hung in chains, writhing as I struck him again and again." She gave a shuddering sigh. "Even though I was furious with myself, I reveled in every blow. The strangest thing of all was that I had the feeling ... that he was *enjoying* it." She covered her face with chilly hands. "Do dreams reveal our inner natures? If so, mine is loathsome."

"Sometimes dreams show us ourselves," he said slowly. "But they can tell us other things." He stacked several pillows against the headboard to support himself, then cradled her against his chest. "Tell me any other details you remember before you forget them."

"A closed space—suffocating. Sweaty heat. The decor is elaborate and very vulgar." Fretfully, she undid the button that secured the throat of her nightshirt. "I'm wearing tight black boots with insanely high heels and a peculiar garment like a . . . a black satin snake skin. And a long wig. Red, I think."

"What did the man look like?"

She rubbed her temple, then shook her head in frustration. "It's fading away. I'm sorry. I need water." She sat up and swung from the bed, then collapsed onto the carpet.

"Kit!" Lucien dived from the bed and scooped her into his arms, then laid her on the bed and pulled the covers up.

She was white and trembling all over, but she managed a feeble smile. "I'm all right, truly. This has happened before. I'll be fine in a few minutes."

He paused, arrested, on the way to the washstand. "How often does it occur?"

"In a milder form this sort of thing has happened all my life." She exhaled wearily. "Lately it's been much worse. Now I'm not simply tired, but so drained I can scarcely stand, as you saw. The nightmares are new, too. I suppose both things are a result of worrying about Kira."

"Perhaps." He poured a glass of water and brought it to the bed. "Have all the nightmares involved whipping someone?"

She thought. "I . . . I think so."

He supported her while she drank, then gently laid her back against the pillows. As he went to build up the fire, he asked, "Is it possible that instead of dreaming, you are sensing Kira's actual thoughts and experiences?"

"I shouldn't think so," she said doubtfully. "Sensing

her emotions is a long way from being able to read her mind."

"Think back. The whip you were using—was it in your right hand or your left hand?"

She stared at her hands and her face paled. "The right—Kira's hand, not mine." She looked up at Lucien, her face perplexed. "But the images are nightmarish, unreal. Kira would never deliberately torture someone."

He said soberly, "You said that you felt the man was enjoying it. Perhaps he wanted her to whip him."

"No one could possibly enjoy that kind of pain!"

"Not necessarily." He sat on the edge of the bed and held her hand between both of his. "The roots of desire are complex and mysterious, Kit. For some, pleasure and pain are so closely intertwined that they find the right kind of pain exciting."

Seeing her disbelief, he said, "I know it seems implausible, but right here in London there are brothels that specialize in whipping. I know a woman who owns one, and an extremely good living she makes from it."

Kit bit her lip, journalistic curiosity overcoming her personal feelings. "Has she ever explained why men come to her?"

"Dolly says that many of her customers are very powerful, influential men who carry heavy responsibilites. Being in a situation where they are helpless and the only purpose is sex arouses them. Similarly, there are women who like to wield a whip because it is one time when they can dominate a man totally and be thanked for it."

"I suppose that makes a weird kind of sense."

"Don't expect too much logic—it's not a rational subject," he said dryly. "There are both men and women with these specialized tastes, and some take turns at both ends of the whip. And it isn't only whipping. Dolly has customers who talk rapturously about being spanked by nursemaids or schoolmasters when they were children, and ever since they've been looking for the same kind of pleasure-pain. Others—" He halted. "Never mind. I'm sure you get the general idea."

Kit's hand clenched his. "Do you think Kira has been kidnapped and forced to work in that sort of brothel?"

"It's unlikely—such places don't need to kidnap employees. There are society women who sometimes go to Dolly's and work for free." He shifted uncomfortably, wishing he didn't have to explain such things to Kit. "I think your original idea was right. Kira was abducted by a man who was obsessed by her. However, instead of standard rape, he has ... more unusual tastes. Once she was his captive, he could explain what gave him pleasure and make it clear that it is in her interest to please him."

"Oh, God!" Kit pressed the back of her hand to her mouth, expression nauseated. "That's revolting."

"There are worse things that could have happened to her," he said gravely. "It would explain why you sense she is physically well even though she is emotionally distressed."

Kit frowned. "If such a man is aroused by being helpless, what is the point of holding her captive? He would still be in control even if the whip is in her hand."

Lucien shrugged. "Perhaps he is incapable of ever allowing himself to be completely helpless, so he creates an illusion of submission while still retaining the ultimate power."

Looking as if she wasn't sure she wanted to know the answer, she asked, "Have you ever done such things, Lucien?"

He smiled and shook his head. "Dolly has offered to demonstrate the exquisite pleasure of being dominated by an artist like her, but I declined. The only pleasure I've ever found in pain is relief when it stops."

Since Kit still seemed baffled, he added, "Many things that are considered perverse are merely extensions of behavior that is accepted as normal. Most sets of lovers play in ways that mutually please them—teasing, or mock wrestling, or pretend seduction, for example. Some people just go further."

She made a face. "Much further. Still, explained like that, I can understand a little better. Do you think Dolly will tell you the names of her customers?"

"I doubt that she would give them to me outright, but she might confirm names that I suggest to her. Remember, though, there is no guarantee that the villain is someone who has patronized her establishment."

"It's a start. Ask her about Mace, Chiswick, Nunfield, Westley, and Harford. Though I don't think Harford is the abductor, he might be involved indirectly." Looking stronger, she pushed herself to a sitting position. "What made you suspect that my nightmares were coming from Kira?"

"Linnie and I used to have the same bad dreams sometimes, though we didn't realize it until we were nine and compared notes after a difficult night. Also, there was the matter of lending strength. Remember that I said I did that with her?"

"Yes, but I wasn't sure what you meant."

His gaze became unfocused. "It's hard to explain. When we were small and she was ill, I would sit on her bed, hold her hand, and tell her to take some of my energy. It was a kind of game, yet it seemed to work. She would convalesce more quickly, while I would tire more easily. That bond held even when I went away to school. Sometimes I would wake unrested and later learn that Linnie had been ill." He cut the memory off before it could become painful. "Is it like that between you and Kira?"

"Perhaps it is, without either of us recognizing it. When I'm in a difficult situation, I'll consciously reach out to Kira. I think of myself as seeking emotional support, but perhaps I've also taken physical energy without meaning to."

"And now the current has reversed because your sister is in trouble, and she is drawing on your strength to help her endure." He grinned suddenly. "Can you imagine how strange this conversation would sound to a non-twin?"

"It makes perfect sense to me." Kit fell silent, her expression intent. She looked slim and fragile within the voluminous folds of his nightshirt. With the collar unbuttoned, the garment opened to a point well below even the most daring of evening gowns. His gaze fastened on the shadowed cleft that was teasingly revealed. He was acutely aware of the body beneath the white linen. Because they had been lovers, he knew the winsome line of her waist, the shape of her soft, unsupported breasts, the tender warmth of her inner thighs.

His mouth became dry. Though he had always been good at waiting for what he wanted, that ability seemed to have deserted him. Passion was a fever and Kit the only cure. More than anything on earth he wanted to make love to her, not only to slake desire, but to deepen the closeness he longed for.

It didn't help to know that he had the power to seduce her away from her determination to avoid physical intimacy until Kira was found. It would be so easy; a light kiss, a stroke down the graceful arc of her back, a hand on her knee. Each caress would lead to another. Soon her passion would be the equal of his, and she would welcome him with innocent fire.

And after, she would despise him for his shortsighted selfishness. Mentally uttering every curse he could remember, he forced himself to raise his gaze and ask evenly, "What are you thinking? You have a speculative gleam in your eyes."

"The Marlowe is going to perform *Scandal Street* for the first time on Friday," she replied. "It's a play that has been popular in the provinces, and this will be its first performance in London. My part is small, so Cassie James isn't featured on the playbills. Do you think you could invite the chief suspects to be your guests at the theater? You could watch when I make my first appearance and see if anyone seems unduly surprised."

"A good idea, except . . ." He frowned. "If the kidnapper sees you, he will know that you must be Kira's twin. As you yourself said, some men are stimulated by the prospect of bedding identical twins. That might put you in danger."

"If I'm abducted, too, at least I'll find Kira."

"Don't joke about it, Kit," he said sharply. "If something happens to you . . ."

Whatever she saw in his face made her gaze drop. For a moment scalding emotions hovered in the air. By unspoken consent, they both retreated. He said, "Tomorrow I'll try to arrange a theater party. From now on I don't want you to go anywhere alone. Can your Bow Street Runner act as an escort when I'm not with you?"

She nodded. "I think so. He's been as protective with me as a sheep dog with an errant lamb."

"A man of sense." Lucien regarded her speculatively. "I've been wondering. Do you think you could consciously communicate with Kira? If it's possible, perhaps you could learn something about her captor and where she is being held."

"Do you mean that the next time I have a nightmare, I should try to ask Kira questions?" She frowned. "I don't think I can control my dreaming like that. Even if I could, I doubt the results would be very helpful. The nightmares are only hazy images and a sense of her emotions."

He studied her expression, wondering if she was in a daring mood. "Rather than waiting for another nightmare and hoping for the best, we could try mesmerism."

Her brows shot up. "I thought that was mere quackery."

"I'm not convinced that Dr. Mesmer's animal magnetism exists," he admitted, "but his techniques can induce a sleeplike state in sensitive people. If you could establish contact with your sister that way, I could ask questions through you."

"You know how to mesmerize someone?" When he nodded, she began to laugh. "Lucien, where do you learn such things?"

"In this case, from a physican who had studied with Mesmer and went on to develop methods of his own. I thought it sounded interesting, so I asked him to teach me. I don't know whether mesmerism will help you reach Kira, but I'm reasonably sure that trying won't hurt."

"Very well." She rubbed her palms along her thighs nervously. "What should I do?"

He frowned. "You must be exhausted. Perhaps we should wait until tomorrow, when you've had some rest."

"Fatigue lowers one's mental barriers. I think the chances are best when Kira and I are both tired." Kit made a rueful face. "I know I am, and if she has just endured a session with her captor, she is, too. It's worth a try."

"Very well. Make yourself comfortable."

While she settled back among the pillows so that her upper body was slightly elevated, he took a candle from the branch on the night table, then held it several feet in front of Kit at a level where she could see it without strain. "Ready?"

She nodded and smoothed the blankets over her hips, but there was anxiety in her eyes.

"There really isn't much to this. You might not notice anything at all," he said in a deliberately casual manner. "All you have to do is relax and look at the flame. Steady, bright, burning away all of your worry and fatigue, leaving peace and calm. You're tired, very tired, and now you can relax. You feel very light and very tranquil, like a feather drifting in the breeze." He continued in a similar vein, making his voice soft and flowing, like warm, smooth molasses.

As he had suspected, Kit was a good subject. Muscle by muscle her tension disappeared, leaving her face peaceful and her gaze steady on the flame. When he thought she was ready, he said, "Your left arm is very light, so light it wants to float up into the air. Let it float free."

Slowly, her arm rose until it was a foot above the blanket. "Good, very good, Kit. Now your hand feels heavier. Let it drift back down." Her limp arm lowered to the counterpane.

As he readied himself for the next step, he found that he had the bizarre desire to ask her if she loved him. He suppressed the thought. This was not the time or place, and he was not sure he wanted to hear a truthful answer.

"Reach out to Kira," he said quietly. "She's tired and lonely and will feel better if she knows you're there. Can you feel her?"

Kit's gray eyes lit up. "Yes. Kira, Kira, love . . ."

Interlude

She was mortally weary when he left, but she found the strength to drag off her loathsome costume. Then she rubbed herself all over with a coarse towel, for though he had never used her sexually, she always felt soiled after a session. Tonight was worse than usual, for he had hinted at her fate and it was hard not to succumb to terror.

She donned the longest, most opaque chemise in her wardrobe and lay down to sleep. She had early vowed not to allow self-pity, but it was harder to banish despair.

As always, she used the thought of her sister as a shield. The knowledge that she was never truly alone was a balm.

Her mind was drifting toward sleep when she felt a warm presence in her mind and a gentle, questioning, "Kira?"

"Kit!" She was so startled that she jerked into wakefulness when she clutched for her sister. The sense of connection disappeared.

Alarm, loss, loneliness.

After a period of desperate mental thrashing, she realized that she must relax if she was to reestablish the contact. With the grim determination that had enabled her to keep her sanity, she made herself calm again. Then she opened her mind to her twin.

Chapter 28

Kit's face contorted. "She's gone!"

"Relax, be calm," Lucien said soothingly. "Kira was probably startled. Reach out and give her time to find you."

Several taut minutes passed before Kit gave a soft, relieved exhalation. She had connected with her sister again.

Lucien asked, "Is Kira in London or the country?"

Kit's brow puckered. "C-country."

"Does she know where?"

When Kit looked confused, he suggested, "Visualize a map of Great Britain with a cross where London is. Does she have any idea where she is in respect to London?" After a minute of silence had passed, he suggested, "North? West? South? East?"

"Don't *know*," Kit said fretfully. A long pause, then, "But . . . but not far from town. Maybe two hours or so."

If true, that narrowed the range considerably. "What is her prison like?"

"Dark. Always dark, only lamps. Silence. Guards." The sheet over her breasts rose and fell as her breathing roughened. "Not uncomfortable, but it's *ghastly* not to see the sun."

"Does she know who her captor is?"

Kit gasped and terror flashed across her face. "No! *No!*"

"It's all right, Kit, you're safe," he said quickly. "Tell Kira that we'll find her and she'll be safe, too."

Instead of soothing, his words produced more distress. "Not much more time! The sun . . . the sun is dying, and I'll not see the new year." Tears began flowing down her cheeks. she whispered desolately, "Don't cry, Kira, please don't cry, I can't bear it."

Her grief was wrenching. He set aside the candle and took her hand. "We're looking for you, Kira," he said forcefully. "When we find you, we'll bring you home as quickly as we can."

Kit's face twisted with agitation. "Want to come home *now*."

"The more you can tell us about your situation, the sooner we can find you, Kira. Is there anything at all you can tell us about your captor that might help us identify him?"

"A . . . a long devil from the fires of hell," Kit twisted her head in agitation. "Want to *leave*!"

It was time to end this, before one of the three of them broke down entirely. He inhaled deeply, then managed to say in an even voice, "Tell Kira that you love her, Kit. That you love her, and that she must not despair."

Kit's expression smoothed out. "Love you, Kira. Always."

"I'm going to count from one to ten, and when I reach ten, you'll wake up and remember what happened. One . . . two . . ."

After reaching ten, he said crisply, "Wake up, Kit."

She blinked, her eyes coming into focus. "It worked," she said in a barely audible voice. She rubbed her forehead with the heel of her hand. "But merciful heaven, I've never been so tired in my life. It was even more exhausting than the nightmares."

He lay down and put his arms around her, wanting to warm her shivering body. "You did wonderfully. Do you remember?"

"Yes. It was strange." Kit stopped and drew several jagged breaths. "She knew I wanted information, but it didn't seem possible to communicate words, no matter how hard we tried. Mostly it was emotions, with some images. Frustrating."

"I assume that 'a long devil' means that her captor is tall and probably thin. Does that fit your impression?"

"Yes, and it matches my vague memory of the man in

my nightmare. I'd forgotten until now." She rubbed her temple. "Did I say something about the fires of hell?"

"Yes. My guess is that is how your mind translated the idea of a Hellion. That's what we've assumed, but it's good to have confirmation. We've also learned that Kira is outside London, though not far away, and being held in a closed, isolated structure." He frowned. "That could be almost anything from a cottage with its windows boarded up to a genuine dungeon. Did you have any other impressions that you didn't speak aloud?"

"Only that she is afraid that something dreadful will happen to her soon." Kit shivered. "We are rapidly running out of time."

"But finally we are making progress. Starting tomorrow, I'll have all of your suspects watched. Perhaps the abductor will lead us right to your sister. I'll also try to learn what properties the men own within two hours or so of London, since she may be held at one of them." He considered his fingers gently stroking her upper arm. "I'll review the dossiers on the Hellions that I've assembled as part of my search for the spy. I don't think there is anything relevant, but one never knows."

"That would be good," Kit agreed. "I had to keep my search as narrow as possible because of limited resources, but I won't rule out the possibility that my quarry is someone I thought unlikely." She shivered again. "Even if we become convinced that one of the men is guilty, how do we actually find Kira?"

"We use you as a divining rod. From what you say, if we get close to where she is being held, you'll be able to find her."

Kit bit her lip. "If the distance isn't too great, but I think I would have to be within a quarter of a mile of her."

"We could search an estate by night, cutting back and forth in a pattern that would cover the whole property." He drew her closer, thinking how fine drawn and fragile she felt. It hurt to know that he could not protect her from what she feared most. Gravely he said, "It's asking a lot of you, kitten."

"I'll do whatever I have to," she said, stark shadows

under her eyes. "But once we find her, how will we get her out? I think she is guarded heavily."

"We will damned well go in and get her. Your cousin Jason will want to come, and he strikes me as an exceedingly capable gentleman. I'll also summon the most dangerous of my friends. With men like them, we could get Kira out of the Tower of London." He began massaging her back, wanting her to sleep away her exhaustion. "Try to relax, Kit. If it's humanly possible, we will get her back safely."

"You're very comforting." She closed her eyes and turned her face into the hollow between his neck and shoulder. Soon soft, regular exhalations were wisping against his throat.

He watched the shadow-splashed ceiling, his face somber. In spite of his show of confidence, he was deeply worried. There were too many possibilities, and, if the message from Kira was accurate, very little time. The kind of monster who had abducted her was quite capable of tiring of his plaything and killing her so that he could find a new woman to torment.

So much depended on Kit's gossamer bond with her sister. It was a devastating burden for her to carry; if they failed to find Kira in time, Kit would never forgive herself. She would be doomed to the guilt and loneliness, the sense of being incomplete, that had haunted Lucien most of his life. He wouldn't wish that on anyone, much less Kit. And selfishly, he feared that if her sister died, Kit would never want to see Lucien again because he had failed to rescue Kira. The mere thought made his muscles cramp with tension.

When he was sure she was asleep, he carefully disentangled himself from her arms, climbed from the bed, and went to his desk. There he penned a terse note. *Michael, I need your help. Can you come to London immediately? Lucien.*

On the outside he wrote "Lord Michael Kenyon, Bryn Manor, Penreith, Caermarthenshire, Wales." Then he dripped wax on the closure and pressed in the Strathmore seal with his signet ring. First thing in the morning he would send the note by special messenger. If a mili-

tary-style raid was needed, Michael would be invaluable.
But first, they had to find where Kira was.

As he slid into bed beside Kit again, he hoped to God
that he could live up to her trust.

Lucien paused in the open doorway. "Good morning,
Dolly. Your footman said to come straight up."

The flamboyant blonde who frowned over an account
book looked up, a smile wreathing her face. "Strathmore,
what an unexpected pleasure. Have you come to add
some spice to your bland life?"

He grinned and closed the door behind him. "Now,
now, remember our bargain. I don't call you a disgusting
pervert, and you don't tell me that I'm an unimaginative
puritan who would bore any reasonable woman
senseless."

She leaned back in her chair, laughing. "I've always
liked the way you joke about my business. Most men
either think I'm the wickedest creature since Eve, or they
take me and my work so seriously they forget they're
supposed to be having fun."

"Do you have a few minutes to spare?"

She waved airily. "I'm expecting a gentleman any minute, but he can wait. Frustration will help put him in
the mood." She lifted an enormous ostrich feather fan
from the desk, then stood and turned around, one hand
on her hip. "It's a new outfit. What do you think—will
I drive the lads all wild?"

Lucien solemnly inspected her spectacular red velvet
gown. She must be wearing a ferocious corset, for her
somewhat overabundant figure was cleverly shaped to
provide a maximum of stunning curves, some of which
were displayed by a décolletage that would make a stone
saint blush. As she turned, he saw that the skirt had
thigh-high slits that revealed riding boots, silver spurs,
and black lace stockings.

"Isn't it a bit conservative?" he asked. "I saw a duchess in a similar outfit several weeks ago, but hers was
more daring."

"Beast!" She swatted at him with her fan. It stung
across the back of his hand, and he saw that the frothy

feathers concealed narrow leather thongs that would hurt if applied with vigor. The pretty and the painful blended together, a perfect metaphor for Dolly's special skills.

"I'll admit that it isn't always easy to be more vulgar than some of your society ladies, but I'm the woman who can do it." She sat and crossed her legs so that the slit skirt exposed shapely, black lace-covered legs all the way to midthigh. "Take a seat. I don't suppose this is a social call."

"I'm afraid not." He sat down, his face becoming serious as he pulled out a slip of paper and handed it to her. "Are any of those men customers of yours?"

"You know I don't discuss such things, Strathmore," she said disapprovingly. "My gentlemen expect me to be discreet."

"I understand and respect that, but I'm hoping you might bend your rules this time. It's highly likely that one of these men has abducted a gently bred young actress and is forcing her to participate in the sort of activities your customers enjoy."

Dolly frowned. "That's not right. Games are only good if folks participate freely and respect each other's limits. It's best when done with real caring." She looked down at the list. "I don't think it would be this first one, Harford. I know of him, but he's never been in here. Sometimes he visits a regular brothel run by a friend of mine. I think he's a plain bread-and-butter type like you."

Lucien looked pained. "I would prefer that you not make comparisons between Harford and me."

She grinned and looked down again. "The others have all visited, though none are really regulars. They come more to add a bit of variety to their lives. Mace is strictly a dominant—quite good at administering discipline. Chiswick will do it either way, sometimes the master, sometimes the slave. Westley is strictly passive—fond of shackles and goes wild when his feet are tickled. Nunfield." She tapped a long, sharp fingernail on the paper. "He goes too far. After his last visit, I told him not to come back."

"Based on your knowledge of these men, is there one

you would pick as most likely to be behind an abduction?"

She hesitated. "Nunfield, maybe, but it's hard to say. They're all the sort who are too bloody used to getting their own way. That could include kidnapping and whipping some respect into a girl who hadn't been properly deferential."

"Actually, I have reason to believe the young woman is being forced to play the mistress."

Dolly pursed her lips. "Strange. I wouldn't expect a man who likes being dominated to try something as aggressive as abduction. Still, one never knows." She handed the list back. "I hope that helped."

"It did." He got to his feet. "Thank you, Dolly. I appreciate your cooperation."

"Let me know if you find the girl," she said somberly. "A bloke who would kidnap a young woman and force her to do something against her nature is capable of anything."

Lucien said softly, "That's what I'm afraid of."

Lucien was working in his study when Jason Travers emerged after a lengthy rest. Bathed, shaved, and dressed in his host's clothing, he looked quite presentable, though the garments hung loosely on his gaunt frame. Lucien gestured for him to come into the study. "Good afternoon. How are you feeling?"

The American entered and began prowling restlessly around the room. "Somewhat more sane than I did last night, though I haven't ruled out the possibility that I finally caught jail fever and this is all a hallucination."

"Have my servants been taking good care of you?"

"Very much so." Humor glinted in his dark eyes. "They all call me Lord Markland. I have trouble remembering that's me."

Lucien leaned back in his oak chair. "It seemed a reasonable precaution. Even if the authorities are searching for you, they won't connect an earl with an escaped prisoner of war."

"Certainly *I'm* having trouble making the connection." The American's gaze roved over the shelves of leather-bound books, graceful furniture gleaming with wax, the muted richness of the carpet beneath his feet. "Everything I see is a feast for the senses. After the grayness of a prison ship, it's rather overpowering. I had coffee, a soft-boiled egg, and toast for breakfast. Ambrosia." He touched the petals in a bouquet of fresh flowers that sweetly scented the room, his fingertips caressing the silky surface with reverence. "I gathered from your servants that you're a lord yourself."

Lucien inclined his head formally. "The ninth Earl of Strathmore, last in a long line of men who knew which side to back in a power struggle and how to quit a game of cards when they were ahead. Not the most heroic of traits, but they have given the family longevity."

Jason studied his host. "Perhaps being a lord doesn't mean a man has to be totally worthless."

Lucien grinned. "American directness is so refreshing."

The other man flushed. "Sorry, I didn't mean that the way it sounded. I've forgotten how to behave in normal society." He lifted an antique hourglass that sat in the bookcase and caressed the polished walnut, then turned it over and watched the white sand trickle from the top globe to the bottom. "Two years of my life gone, and not a damned thing to show for it."

"In time, the unbearable memories will fade," Lucien said quietly. "At least, that's what I'm told by a friend who spent several wretched years fighting the French on the Peninsula. You're welcome to stay here as long as you wish—as you can see, there is plenty of space. Or if you prefer, I can assist you to the Continent, where you can take ship to America or wait in safety until the war ends. There's an excellent chance that a treaty will be settled by the end of the year."

"Amen to that. But I'm not leaving England until I know about Kira." Setting the hourglass back on its shelf, he continued, "That being the case, I might as well enjoy your excellent hospitality, but you must keep an account of my expenses." He fingered the superfine wool of his blue coat. "I've transported enough fabric in my ships to know top quality when I see it."

Lucien said equably, "I'll keep track of every ha'penny and add a modest charge for interest."

"Thank you for humoring me." Jason's expression turned grim. "Now tell me everything about Kira's disappearance."

Lucien explained everything they knew or guessed. He ended with a description of Kit's nightmare and the fragmentary information received through mesmerism, repeating the exact words as closely as he could.

The American's face became rigid, only his eyes showing emotion. At the end of the recital he said with lethal precision, "When the man who abducted Kira is found, I am going to slice him into very small pieces with a very dull knife."

"You might have to wait in line for the privilege," Lucien said dryly.

"That part about her not seeing the new year—do you think she meant that literally? Christ, January isn't much more than a fortnight away!"

"In a few more days we should have enough information to act." Though his words were reassuring, Lucien's gaze went back to the antique hourglass. He could not escape the ghoulish thought that the hours of Kira's life were trickling away as inexorably as the sand. And if she died, he might lose Kit forever to grief.

Chapter 29

Lord Chiswick peered over the railing of the box. "Whenever I attend the theater, I have a nearly irresistible desire to throw rotten fruit at the low creatures in the pit."

"The actors wouldn't thank you for it," Lucien remarked. "The fruit would almost certainly end up being pitched at them."

Lord Mace took a pinch of snuff. "Only if the actors deserve it, I'm sure."

Nunfield said, "Perhaps we should summon an orange girl up here and buy all her stock in case it is needed."

"There shouldn't be much rotten fruit tonight," Ives said cheerfully. "I understand the play is quite amusing."

"I hope so," Nunfield drawled. "Otherwise, I may abuse your hospitality and leave in the middle, Strathmore. There's a new gaming club in Pall Mall that is supposed to be quite special, and I want to pay a visit tonight."

"If the play is a bore, I'll go with you," Lucien said casually. It was fortunate that all of his suspects except Harford had been free to accept his invitation to the theater. To avoid being too obvious, he'd also invited Lord Ives, who was always willing to visit the Marlowe so he could admire his Cleo.

Much of fashionable society had left town to spend the holidays on their estates, so a number of the best boxes were empty. The pit and gallery, however, were packed with Londoners anxious to see the first performance of *Scandal Street*.

To qualify as a concert, the program opened with the small orchestra playing a concerto grosso which was largely ignored by the audience. Conversation died down when the music ended and the first act began. The plot involved the nefarious attempts of a corrupt merchant to discredit an honest government official, Sir Digby Upright. (The very notion of an honest government official produced a roar of laughter.)

The dialogue was witty and topical, taking swipes at current issues from the Prince Regent's extravagance to the peace negotiations in Vienna and Ghent. The whole audience was amused, even the jaded sophisticates in Lucien's box.

The climactic scene of the first act was a ball that Sir Digby gave to announce his daughter's betrothal. Unbeknownst to him, his enemy had arranged to disgrace him in front of his guests, which included many important members of the government. The scene started when Sir Digby halted the dancing to introduce his blushing daughter, played by a very demure Cleo Farnsworth, and her handsome young betrothed.

No sooner had he made his announcement than two comic cockneys marched onto the stage, carrying an enormous roll of carpet. As the guests stared, the cockneys unrolled the carpet in the middle of the ballroom. Sinuous as a serpent, Kit emerged from the carpet, wearing a brassy blond wig and a crimson satin gown that was almost as outrageous as the one Dolly had worn. Not only was it low in front, but the back was cut almost to her waist, exposing an enticing swath of creamy skin.

Lucien had placed himself at one end of the box so he could observe his companions without being obvious. At Kit's appearance, Ives and Westley simply laughed along with the rest of the audience. Chiswick leaned forward and crossed his arms on the railing, his expression intent. Elaborately casual, Nunfield leaned back and drummed his fingers on his knee, his sharp gaze fixed on the stage. Mace showed no reaction at all, except perhaps for a tightening of the lips.

Lucien cursed the shadows that obscured nuances of expression. Though he hadn't expected the villain to leap up and cry, "Guilty!" he had hoped for some hint, some sign of amazement or discomfort at the sight of "Cassie

James." Not that the lack of reaction proved anything; all of the Disciples were expert gamesters, used to controlling their expressions.

To Sir Digby's horror, Kit kissed him with the appearance of long familiarity, insulted his wife and daughter, flirted with the entranced fiancé, and gaily told the guests that "Diggy" supported her in great style because he was making so much money by accepting bribes. When Sir Digby sputtered a protest, she shushed him with a languid wave of her hand, a splendid female creature reveling in her power over the male of the species.

Kit turned to face the audience, her gaze lingering fractionally on Lucien's box. Then, with a clash of drums, she whirled into a dance of floating petticoats and slender flashing legs. Lucien tried to watch his companions, but his gaze was irresistibly drawn to Kit. Her vitality and stage presence riveted every eye in the house.

There was a new sensuality in her movements. In *The Gypsy Lass* she had artfully mimicked passion. Now passion had become part of her. Every curve of her hand, every graceful arch of her neck, every slanted, beckoning glance, was a promise of earthy delights. His body tightened with longing. The two days since he had seen her seemed like an eternity.

Spontaneous applause burst out when her skirts lifted high enough to show the butterfly tattoo. He found himself torn between wanting to inflict grievous harm on every man in the audience who was lusting after her, and primitive masculine pride in the knowledge that he was the only one who had ever kissed that teasing butterfly, the only one who knew the secrets of her body and the bright clarity of her spirit.

He was also well on the way to becoming as mad as a March hare. Sanity was unlikely to return until Kit married him.

At the end of her dance Kit sank into a graceful posture of subservience at the feet of the mortified Sir Digby. His wife and daughter stormed off stage, the daughter dragging her reluctant fiancé. The outraged guests followed, leaving Sir Digby alone with his fraudulent mistress. Kit bounced to her feet, blew Sir Digby an airy kiss, and skipped away, leaving the poor public servant alone amidst the ruins of his life.

The act ended to thunderous applause. Lord Chiswick said with an unusual show of enthusiasm, "What a delicious actress."

"Indeed," Sir James said. "Does anyone know her name?"

"Cassie James." Nunfield inhaled some snuff, then proffered the box to Mace, who took a pinch. "I offered the girl a *carte blanche* once, but she turned me down, alas. Perhaps I shall try again with more generous terms." His gaze slid to Lucien. "Of course, she may have a protector already." The ironic amusement in his eyes showed that he had heard how Lucien had swept Kit from the green room, but there was no jealousy in his expression. Was his tolerance real or feigned? Impossible to tell.

Mace drawled, "I've had my fill of actresses. A greedy, self-obsessed lot. I prefer bored wives myself. They're much less expensive, and so grateful for the attention." He got to his feet. "I think I'll stretch my legs before the next act."

The other men also decided to go for refreshments or to visit people in other boxes, leaving Lucien alone to ponder what he had observed. He was about to go downstairs himself when a sixth sense made him look up as Kit entered his box. She wore a dark mantle with a hood drawn over her hair and looked chaste and modest, like a medieval nun.

For a moment they simply gazed at each other. Then they were in each other's arms. Her body was warm and pliant from her exertions, her kiss as hungry as his own. They embraced for a few mindless moments until she turned her head with a rueful laugh. "Actually, I came to find if you had learned anything."

Reminded of their surroundings, he said, "We shouldn't try to talk here. One of the others might return at any time."

"I know. I made inquiries before the performance, and the box at the end of this row should be empty. We can talk there." She peered into the corridor, then took his hand and swiftly led him to the empty box.

Kit had chosen well, for the box had an odd, deep shape and the interior was so shadowed that it was doubtful that anyone could see them. Nonetheless, for discretion's sake he drew her into his arms at the back of the box. If they were observed, it would be assumed they were lovers stealing an illicit kiss. Speaking quietly into her ear, he recounted what Dolly had told him and his own observations of his theater companions.

When he was finished, she said nothing, her disappointment palpable. "I'm sorry, kitten," he said ruefully. "Perhaps I missed something, but once you began dancing, I couldn't look away. Neither could anyone else. You were superb."

"I was dancing for you," she said in a voice so light it was nearly inaudible.

"That's what I hoped." He slipped his hands under her cloak. She still wore the low-backed costume, so he began to stroke her bare, velvety shoulders. Touching her underneath the garment gave him a delicious sense of doing something forbidden.

She gave a little shiver, and her gray eyes darkened. Speaking slowly, as if it were an effort to remember the subject, she asked, "If you had to make a guess, from pure intuition, which of the four would you pick as the abductor?"

"Mace." Though his reply was immediate, it took longer to analyze his reasons. "He showed the least reaction, to the point where it was a little conspicuous because every other man in the theater was intoxicated by your performance. And I don't doubt that he is capable of coldness and cruelty."

"Your friend Dolly said he was the sort who had to have the whip hand," Kit reminded him. "Why would he want to force a woman to abuse him?"

"I don't know." Lucien brushed her hood back a little. Heavy blond tresses were twisted up to the back of her head before falling in tangled ringlets. Barely visible below the flamboyant wig, her ear was small and delicate, as exquisitely formed as a spring blossom. He traced the curve with his tongue. A taste sweet and salt, a scent redolent of spice and woman. Reminding himself sharply to keep his mind on business, he added, "But Dolly also said that it was impossible to predict what such a man might do."

Kit exhaled breathily, her hands opening and closing on his back. "What . . . what about Nunfield? He admitted that he had wanted to make Kira his mistress."

His hands moved downward under the mantle, over smooth satin skin and tightly laced gown, to cup her firm buttocks. He squeezed gently, molding the tempting curves with his palms. "He didn't look like a persistent suitor who had become so obsessed that he had resorted to abduction. Of course, Nunfield might be a superb actor who is secretly gloating over the knowledge that he has Kira stashed away somewhere."

"And Chiswick?"

"He behaved as if he had never seen Cassie James before. Perhaps he hasn't—I don't think he is a regular theatergoer." Though Lucien knew he should release Kit, his hands refused to abandon their clasp. Half amused and half exasperated with himself, he said, "It's hard to be logical with you in my arms."

"I know exactly what you mean." Shyly, she leaned forward and ran the tip of her tongue along the angle of his jaw. Warmth tingled through him. He caught his breath, hoping she would continue.

Silently she obliged, her soft lips finding the hollow below his ear. Sharp little frissons of pleasure shot through him, a rising storm that splintered into lightning when she gave his lobe a light, experimental nip. He turned his head, and they kissed with lush, openmouthed abandon. She was reserved Kathryn and flamboyant Cassie and clear-eyed Kit all at once. His grip tightened, drawing them together, her feminine belly molding to his hardening flesh.

Somewhere far, far from their fevered embrace, theatergoers were returning to their seats with coughs and shuffling feet. Knowing this must end, he said breathlessly, "I suppose you must be going downstairs now for the next act."

After an uncertain pause, she said, "I ... I'm not on again until the end of the third act." Her breath was coming in quick puffs that teased the sensitive flesh below his ear.

He understood her fear of jeopardizing her bond with Kira and accepted her need to avoid the emotional firestorm of passion. Yet his hand, his wicked, selfish hand, slid around her hip and down between them, stroking over the luxuriant crimson satin and into the mysterious cleft between her thighs.

She gave a choked moan, her fingers curving into his waist like talons. "We ... we shouldn't be doing this."

"I know," he agreed, probing more deeply. Even through the layers of fabric, he felt luscious warmth. "But it is ... difficult to stop."

Her pelvis curled forward into his hand, and she gave a low whimper, the most enticing sound imaginable. He captured her mouth to swallow that telltale, rapturous noise.

A sharp exchange onstage precipitated a rumble of laughter all around them. He scarcely noticed, for astonishingly, her hand began to move around his waist and down his abdomen in a hesitant, exploratory caress. His hips moved forward, and he pressed into her palm. No longer tentative, her hand tightened around him. He stood paralyzed, his whole frame so rigid that he felt as if a move would shatter him.

Yet stillness was impossible. He caught a handful of skirt and petticoat and raised them upward. Under the foaming material her stockings were tied separately to her corset with dainty little bows. Ignoring the ribbons, he slid his fingers between her silk-covered thighs and found downy curls. Hidden within was hot, sweet female flesh, lavish with moisture.

She hid her face in his shoulder to keep from crying out when he first touched her. "We mustn't," she said weakly, not knowing whether or not she wanted him to be stronger than she. "What ... what if someone looks into the box?"

"It's too dark ... for anyone to see us," he said huskily, his words hazy, as if it was an effort to assemble a simple sentence.

She felt dizzy, no longer able to remember why they should not continue. Heat throbbed against her palm, the male power unmistakable even with layers of fabric between them. Her hand tightened as she remembered how it had felt to have him inside her. The thought made her go liquid with longing. Unconsciously she began stroking her hand up and down the taut ridge of flesh.

He groaned and reached for the buttons of his pantaloons, wrenching them open in his impatience. Then he stepped backward, tugging her with one hand while he reached behind with the other. He located a chair and sat, then drew her across his lap in a wide-legged straddle, guiding her down so that she impaled herself on him.

As he slid into her, she went still with surprise. There was an indecent intimacy in the way their bodies mated beneath the rippling, respectable folds of skirts and mantle. Indecent, and unbearably erotic.

He made a small thrust upward, and urgency scorched through her. She leaned forward, her torso flattening along his chest and her cheek pressing against his. He embraced her so tightly that she could scarcely breathe. They began rocking together with small, savage movements. The legs of the chair squeaked across the floor, the sound swallowed by more laughter.

Blood pounded in her temples like jungle drums, building to a tempo that was madness. Weight and pressure concentrated in a single nameless, internal place that burned with annihilating heat until sudden, violent spasms ripped through her. Her teeth sank into his shoulder, the dark wool rough against her lips.

"Dear God, Kit . . ." His fingers knotted into her hips, locking the two of them together as he ground upward, a raw, wordless sound rumbling from within his chest.

A potent throbbing deep inside her, then arrested moments when neither of them breathed. Slowly, taut muscles softened and burning lungs strained for air.

"Sweet . . . Jesus," he panted, "I'm sorry, Kit. I didn't mean for that to happen." He pressed his forehead against hers as he labored for breath. "Can you still feel your sister?"

"It was as much my fault as yours," she whispered with stark honesty. But merciful heaven, how could she have forgotten Kira like that? What kind of selfish woman would let herself indulge in lustful behavior that might threaten her twin?

She reached into her mind for Kira, fearful that their indefinable emotional bond could not have survived such scouring passion. This time she knew better than to panic when she could not immediately find the link to her sister. Patiently she focused her mind, blocking out the languid satisfaction of her body. Finally, she identified the subtle pulse of her twin's spirit. With a flood of relief she said, "It's all right. I can still feel Kira."

"In that case," he said with a breathless little laugh, "I'm not sorry that we forgot ourselves."

She lifted her head and said sharply, "This isn't funny. Passion scatters my wits dreadfully. I should never have permitted it."

"It's normal to feel scatter-witted after making love," he replied. "The effect is generally temporary. Don't be too hard on yourself—so far passion doesn't seem to have damaged your bond with your sister, and we've both enjoyed it immensely."

That was one reason she felt such wrenching guilt. Needing to lash out, she snapped, "And you don't want to give that pleasure up. Is my submission to your advances the price for your aid in finding Kira?"

His hands clamped painfully onto her upper arms, and she felt sheer rage crackling through him. They were still joined, and she felt utterly vulnerable, surrounded and invaded by his strength. Yet when he spoke, his voice was soft, lethally so. "Have I ever done or said anything to suggest that my help is conditional?"

"No." She looked down. "But I can't help feeling that I am very much at your mercy."

There was another explosive silence. Then, uncannily, he asked, "Are you trying to provoke me so that I'll stay at a safe distance?"

She stiffened, wondering how he could know her mind

better than she did. "Perhaps ... perhaps I am. I feel overwhelmed, Lucien, terrified about Kira, exhausted by the effort of living her life, and now by you. I'm like a leaf in a storm, with no control over my life. It's not a pleasant sensation."

"I don't suppose it is," he said quietly. His hard grip on her arms relaxed and he pulled her close again. "But it won't be for much longer. Soon you'll have your own life back again."

In the lull Sir Digby Upright's voice carried through the theater as he gave a monologue about what he would do to regain his position and punish his enemies. She could float in seductive contentment for a little while longer.

They had never separated, and as she lay in his arms, she realized that he was beginning to firm inside her. If they made love again, it would be slower and gentler than before. There would be more time to savor the growth of desire, the rich splendor of fulfillment....

The very last thing she needed was to become even more dependent on a man who turned her mind and body to butter. Summoning all her will, she disengaged herself and got to her feet.

As she withdrew she felt the shiver of protest in his muscles, followed almost instantly by acceptance. Silently he handed her a handkerchief so that she could dry herself, then stood and began to order his appearance.

Trying to sound more worldly than she was, she said, "As if there weren't already enough good reasons for me to behave myself, there is the risk of pregnancy. That is a possible complication so disastrous I don't even want to think about it."

"Not so disastrous." He smoothed the wrinkles from his coat. "Even if you have already conceived, by the time you are sure, we will be married."

Her hands clenched on the edge of her mantle as she said involuntarily, "I wish you would stop talking about that."

Chapter 30

As soon as the words came out of her mouth, Kit froze, wishing she could retract them.

It was too much to hope that he would let her remark pass. He fixed his too-observant gaze on her, his face unreadable in the dim light. "Is it the idea of having a child that bothers you, or is it marriage?"

Knowing that the only way to distract him was with a partial truth, she said, "I dislike the idea of being dragged to the altar to appease your notion of honor. It seems a poor foundation for a marriage."

He turned his head slightly, and a ray of light caught his eyes with a green, catlike flash. "So that's the problem. I should have guessed."

He took her hand, not pulling her toward him, but simply interlacing his fingers with hers. "I have been less than honest. Though I have talked about marriage as the right, honorable, and moral thing to do, I would not have offered if I hadn't wanted to marry you." He lifted their joined hands and kissed her fingertips. "There is already a great deal between us. I hope that in time there will be more."

She tried to pull her hand free. "But I don't think I want to be married."

His fingers locked on hers, preventing her retreat. "I'm not asking for your whole heart. A fairly small piece will do. I swear that I won't interfere with your work or try to come between you and your sister."

"Don't make promises you'll regret," she said miserably. "The less said now, the easier it will be to part later."

"I don't intend to part from you, my dear," he said

calmly. "Not unless you loathe me so much you can't bear to be in the same room with me, and that doesn't appear to be the case."

"You may want me now," she said in a brittle voice, "but you haven't met Kira. After you do, you'll lose interest in me."

His hand clenched hard on hers. As clearly as if he had spoken, she sensed his shock and a searing edge of anger.

A burst of applause filled the theater. Soon the second act would end. When the applause died, Lucien said with scathing humor, "I once knew a man who said that women are like rugs—both need to be beaten regularly to keep them in good condition. I never agreed, but perhaps he had a point. Where did you get the nonsensical notion that I am going to fall madly in love with Kira as soon as I meet her?"

"Because everyone does!" Kit snapped. "She is whatever you like in me, and so much more."

"Even if you are right, her affections are engaged. At least Jason Travers seems to think so," he pointed out dryly. "So I shall have to settle for marrying you."

Though she knew he meant the words ironically, they were too painful to be amusing. "Marriage is one place where I won't happily settle for being second best to Kira. I'd rather be a spinster. In fact, I've planned on it all my life."

She wrenched her hand free. "When the time comes, be willing to fight for Kira. Jason is quite a man, but you surpass him. If you want her, you may well be able to win her." She turned and headed for the door. "I must leave now. I have to change my costume for the third act."

Swift as a panther, he slid across the box and blocked her exit. "It's much easier to have a twin of the opposite sex. Less competition," he said, so much compassion in his voice that she wanted to weep. "You haven't a very high opinion of love, do you? It's not a contest to be won; it's a bond that is forged between two hearts. The fact that you and Kira are virtually identical in appearance doesn't make you interchangeable to those who care about you. And while I'm gratified that you find me more attractive than Travers, it's doubtful that your sister will share your opinion."

Wearily she said, "You think I'm talking nonsense, but you haven't met Kira. You don't know the impact she'll have on you."

"I don't need to—I already know the impact *you* have on me." He caught her waist and kissed her hard, imprinting his anger and his determination with an intensity that left her shaken.

Raising his head, he said, "I will make allowances for the fact that your sister's disappearance has scrambled your wits. But don't think this conversation is over. When Kira is safe, it will be resumed, and when I am finished, you will believe me. I swear it."

It was fortunate that he released her then, for she was incapable of answering. She pulled her hood over her hair and gathered her mantle around her, then fled. She was barely in time. The applause in the theater indicated that the act was ending, and in a few moments the corridors would fill with people.

A narrow stairwell took her down to a ground-floor service passage. As she made her way backstage, she should have been thinking about her next scene, but she couldn't. Her mind was too full of the man who wouldn't go away even when he was pushed.

Knowing he was unready to face his theater guests, Lucien lingered in the empty box as the second interval began. It was hard to believe that a few minutes earlier he and Kit had been coupling with mind-drugging intensity—in the middle of a theater! He was definitely losing his mind.

Why couldn't he have become involved with a simpler woman?

Because simple women didn't interest him; didn't challenge him; didn't make him so mad with desire that he could escape his restless, overactive mind. And of course intimacy with lesser women had always proved more painful than it was worth. Kit might leave him frothing, but at least he wasn't depressed.

It would be easier if he could dismiss Kit's misgivings outright, but he couldn't quite do that. His heart didn't believe he could want another woman more than her. However, his too-rational head pointed out that he had never met Lady Kristine Travers. Could she really be another Kit, only more so—more refreshing, more stimulating, more desirable?

Nonsense! Yet as long as Kit believed that he would inevitably prefer her twin, she would withhold her heart. It was one more reason to find Kira as quickly as possible.

He leaned on the railing and gazed down into the pit, not seeing the milling theatergoers below. The argument with Kit had brought him face-to-face with a hidden motive of his own. In the past he had always been very careful to avoid fathering a child. His near-celibacy in recent years had made that easy.

Yet with Kit, he had not been careful at all. The simple explanation was that she aroused him to a fever where restraint was impossible. But he knew himself well enough to recognize that he *wanted* to get her pregnant so that she would have to marry him. Instead of protecting the woman he loved, he was trying to coerce her, to trap her so securely that it would be impossible for her to fly away. Even worse, his selfish behavior might be endangering Kit's crucial bond with her sister.

It was not an insight he was proud of. Yet if he had another opportunity to make love to her, he suspected he would behave exactly the same way.

His mind skipped to an incident from his university days. An aristocratic bully at Christ Church College had issued a challenge to another student, a mild young man named Whitman who had had the temerity to disagree with the bully. Though Whitman had no experience of dueling, honor demanded that he accept the challenge even though injury or death was the likely outcome.

The approaching duel had become known among other students. Everyone deplored a match that would be so uneven, but because of the gentlemen's code, no one would intervene, except Lucien. A little investigation had revealed that the bully had sexual preferences that would have ruined him in society forever. Lucien had used that knowledge ruthlessly to blackmail the bully into dropping the challenge and issuing an apology to Whitman.

By chance Rafe had learned of Lucien's role in preventing the duel. Gray eyes cool and thoughtful, he had said, "You really are rather amoral, aren't you?"

The remark had not been offered as condemnation—Rafe had been glad when the duel was stopped—but as impartial assessment. Nonetheless, the words had stung. It was a tribute to the power of friendship that their relationship had been unaffected.

And, of course, Rafe had been right. Though Lucien did not consider himself to be without honor, he had never hesitated to set honor aside for what he considered a good reason. That trait had made him an excellent spymaster, but it was clear proof that being able to trace one's noble ancestors to the Norman Conquest and beyond did not make a man a true gentleman.

With a wry smile, he went into the corridor and headed toward his own box. Kit had the temperament of a reformer; he would provide her with ample opportunity to practice her skills.

Lucien entered his box just as the audience was settling down for the final act. Only Ives, Chiswick, and Westley were present. Chiswick cocked an amused eye at him. "You look as if you found better diversion than the second act of the play."

Not only was that true, but acknowledgment would enhance his rakish reputation. "I ran into a friend who wished to discuss politics," Lucien said blandly. "A most absorbing conversation."

"From the crushed look of your cravat, you must have entered into the discussion with enthusiasm," Sir James said slyly.

"Quite. Always an enthralling subject, politics." Lucien took his seat. "Did Mace and Nunfield lose interest in the play and leave?"

Ives said, "Yes, they asked me to offer their regrets for the defection. Nunfield said he felt an attack of luck coming on, and he had to get to a gaming table before it went away."

Lucien wondered if the departures were significant. Perhaps not, since the gentlemen in question were easily bored pleasure seekers. With a mental shrug, he turned his attention to Sir Digby Upright's clever revenge on his enemy.

At the climax of the play, Kit came on in a demure gown and tearfully confessed that the villain had forced her to appear at the ball and slander Sir Digby by threatening to send her dear old granny to debtor's prison. Her testimony sealed the villain's fate. Society applauded Sir Digby's ruthless destruction of his enemy; his comely wife welcomed him back with open arms; and the prime minister appointed him to a position with more power, prestige, and wealth than his previous one. A triumph for justice, and a very successful production for the theater. *Scandal Street* would probably be in the Marlowe's repertory for years to come.

Kit received special acclaim from the audience even though her part had been small. She had looked so convincingly weepy in her last scene that Lucien felt guilty. He didn't like being at odds with her, didn't like adding to the terrible strain she was enduring. He would call on her in the morning and go over some of the information on property ownership he had uncovered.

Surely, if he tried hard enough, he could keep his hands off her long enough for them to have a rational discussion.

Rather than stay for the brief farce that was to be performed after the main play, Lucien and his companions decided to go to Watier's, a club with good gambling and even better food. As their carriage clattered along Piccadilly, Lucien turned the conversation to Cassie James.

Chiswick made a number of admiring comments, sounding exactly like a man who had just seen her for the first time. Westley had also been impressed by her, though his attitude was more casual. Even to a listener as attuned to lies as Lucien, there was no hint that either man might be the kidnapper.

Lucien tried to concentrate on his subtle interrogation,

but he found himself becoming more and more anxious about Kit. Though he had made arrangements to see that she got home safely, he couldn't escape the feeling that he should have escorted her himself. That was doubly true because his conversation with the remaining Hellions was proving so fruitless.

His uneasiness continued to grow as they made their way along busy Piccadilly. They were almost to Watier's when Westley's voice penetrated his abstraction. "Strathmore, are you still with us?"

Lucien's attention snapped back to the present, and he realized that someone had asked him a question. He also realized that he didn't give a damn what it was. He must go to Kit *now*.

He rapped on the roof for the coachman to stop. As the carriage slowed, he said, "I just realized that I forgot another engagement. I'll have to give Watier's a miss. Sorry."

Before any of the other men could comment, he leaped from the carriage and bounded across the street to catch a hackney coach that was discharging passengers. "The Marlowe Theater, please," he snapped as he climbed inside. "And there's an extra five quid in it if you make the trip in less than ten minutes."

"You've got it, guv," the driver said enthusiastically.

The coach lurched forward so quickly that Lucien had to grab a ragged strap to keep from being pitched to the floor. As he braced himself, he wondered why the devil he was so concerned.

Kit stopped in the green room, scanning faces and watching reactions, just in case. But nothing significant occurred, so after a brief stay she went to her dressing room. She was bone-weary, and not only because of her exertions on stage. Passion was exhausting, and disagreeing with Lucien even more so.

By the time she had changed into her regular clothing, Henry Jones arrived. " 'Evening, miss," he said with a respectful nod. "Are you ready to go home?"

"I certainly am."

Henry consulted his pocket watch. "Lord Strathmore's

coach should be here in another fifteen or twenty minutes."

She pulled on her cloak. "I don't want to wait that long. Let's walk. It's not far, and I could use the fresh air." Brushing past the Runner, she headed toward the theater exit.

"His lordship was most particular that you should go in his coach. He's sending two armed footmen with it," Henry said as he followed her down the hall. "You might be in danger."

"If this were tomorrow night, I'd agree, but surely even the most efficient villain would have trouble organizing an abduction when he is right under Lord Strathmore's nose." When Henry showed signs of protesting again, she added, "If you will recall, *I'm* the one who hired you, and I want to walk."

The Runner frowned. "His lordship is not the sort I like to cross. A very forceful man."

She put on her fiercest face, the one she and Kira had perfected as children when they wanted to scare goblins under the bed. "And *I* am a very forceful woman, Mr. Jones. Are you coming with me or not?"

He chuckled, tacitly conceding defeat. "I'll tell the porter that we've gone so he can tell Strathmore's coachman."

The brisk air of the Strand dissipated some of her fatigue, but it could not alleviate her depression. She had been a fool to tell Lucien that he would fall in love with Kira when, God willing, they met. Of course he had been outraged; no man of honor or sensitivity could have accepted Kit's statement. But he didn't know. *He didn't know.*

Kit had never resented her sister's ability to effortlessly enchant every male between the ages of two and ninety-five, mostly because there had never been a man whom Kit had really wanted for herself. Except for Philip Burke, who had visited friends in Westmoreland the summer the twins had been sixteen. He had been a handsome, witty, university student of twenty. For the first time in her life Kit had desperately wanted a man to think she was special.

But in spite of her best efforts, it was Kira who had captured Philip's fancy. He had joined the eager crowd of admirers around her and scarcely noticed Kit's existence. That had hurt a little—more than a little—but Kit had not blamed her sister. It wasn't as if Kira had deliberately tried to win Philip's regard; she had merely been her usual charming self.

With Lucien it would be much harder. There was a good chance that Kira would choose Jason because of what was already between them. In that case Lucien would doubtless feel obligated to stand by his offer to Kit. However, she could never marry him, knowing it was her sister who he really wanted—and clever though Lucien was, he would be unable to deceive her about which sister he preferred.

For one of the few times in her life, Kit wished she was not a twin. The thought vanished as quickly as it had come, for it was impossible to imagine her life without her sister. When they were very small, they had resolved not to marry unless they could find suitable twin brothers. When they were older, they had discussed how dreadful it would be for the survivor when one of them died. Solemnly, they had decided that when they were very old and feeble, they would hold hands and jump off a cliff together so that they would die at the same time.

Oh, Kira, Kira . . .

She shivered and tightened her cloak around her throat, feeling suddenly chilled. If her sister died, Kit knew there was a very real chance that she would jump off that cliff alone.

Chapter 31

Given the bleakness of her thoughts, Kit was grateful Henry was not disposed to chatter. They turned from the Strand into a quieter side street.

Halfway down the block, the clatter of hooves and wheels sounded behind them. A battered hackney coach rumbled past, then stopped. Idly Kit noted that the horses were unusually good for a livery vehicle. Then the door swung open and three men in half masks barreled out and charged toward Kit and her companion.

Henry barked, "Run, miss!"

He gave her a shove back toward the Strand, then pulled a pistol from beneath his coat and moved purposefully between her and the newcomers. Two ruffians lunged at Henry, and one knocked the pistol from his hand before he could fire. The third and largest swerved around the scuffle and raced toward Kit.

She bolted. Before she had taken ten steps, her pursuer grabbed her arm, bringing her to a wrenching halt. She tried to shout for help, but before she could make a sound, he clamped a hand over her mouth.

His cruel grip tilted her head back. The eyes behind his mask were as dull as pebbles—the eyes of a man who would kill a human as easily as a spider. Had he helped to kidnap Kira? Furiously Kit sank her teeth into his leathery fingers.

"You little bitch!" He walloped the side of her head with an open-palmed blow that made her vision dim. "Try that again and I'll really hurt you."

Over her assailant's shoulder she saw that Henry was wrestling with one of the men while the other stood by with a pistol, unable to shoot for fear of hitting his comrade. Then she lost sight of him as her captor started dragging her toward the coach. She fought every inch of the way, kicking and clawing, but she was no match for him.

Another coach turned into the street and began rattling toward them. Making a supreme effort, Kit chopped her assailant in the throat with the side of her hand. He made a garbling sound, and his grip loosened. She wrenched herself away, her cloak coming off in his hands. Praying that the driver or passengers would help rather than turn and flee, she darted toward the oncoming vehicle, shouting for assistance. Behind her she heard the heavy footfalls of her pursuer.

The coach ground to a halt. Even before it stopped moving, the door swung open and Lucien leaped out, his expression as fierce as the fallen archangel he was named for. He snapped, "Get behind me, Kit!"

As she obeyed, the other man grinned nastily. "Aren't you the gallant fellow," he sneered. "I eat swells like you for breakfast."

Before he could say more, Lucien whipped his cane around like a quarterstaff. The heavy gold head slammed into the ruffian's skull with an ugly, pulpy sound and he dropped into an ungainly heap.

With movements as economical as a dancer, Lucien pivoted and went to aid the Bow Street Runner. Henry was down, and the man with the pistol was aiming it when Lucien cracked his cane over the barrel of the weapon. It spun away into the gutter. Even before it clattered onto the cobblestones, the third man leaped at Lucien in a flat dive that knocked them both to the ground.

The attacker landed on top. Rather than fight, he bounded to his feet and shouted, "Time to go, mates!" He grabbed the arm of his fallen comrade and hauled him toward the coach.

Lucien rose and lunged after them, but his ankle turned under him. As he stumbled, the three attackers piled into the vehicle. The driver cracked his whip over the horses, and they took off into the night, heading away from the Strand.

Lucien swore as he got to his feet. Then he turned and limped toward Kit. "Are you all right?"

"I think so," she said shakily. She took a step toward him, then another quicker one. A moment later she was in his arms, and he was embracing her with rib-bruising force.

Now that the danger had past, her knees turned to rubber. She hid her face against his shoulder and felt the hammering of his heart gradually slow to a normal tempo.

"They were trying to kidnap you?"

After she mastered the desire to break into hysterical tears, she replied, "I think so. It was no normal robbery."

He smoothed her mussed hair back from her forehead. "Did you recognize any of the men?"

"I'm sure that none were Hellions. I had the feeling they were hirelings." She tried to recapture those chaotic moments. "When the big one was dragging me toward the coach, I remember wondering if he had done the same with Kira. Perhaps he had taken part in her abduction, and I was vaguely sensing that."

"Mace and Nunfield left the theater during the second act. Possibly one of them could have arranged for an ambush in that short period of time if he knew where to go." Lucien's embrace tightened. "But it's also possible that the attack could be unrelated to your performing before your chief suspects tonight. There's simply not enough real evidence."

She raised her head so she could see his face. "How did you find out we were going to be attacked?"

He hesitated before saying, "I didn't. I just ... felt that I should find you."

He had said that he had had a sixth sense where his sister's safety was concerned. Apparently, that ability extended to other females in need. And he had known exactly where to come. She shook her head in amazement. "No wonder you're known as Lucifer—your instincts are uncanny. A good thing you're on my side."

"Always, Kit," he said quietly. "Don't ever doubt that."

Her lover, her protector. With a desire so strong it was pain, she wanted to melt into him, to shelter in his strength and kindness forever. A kind of shiver went through her, as if the invisible walls that separated one person from another were on the verge of dissolving. If that happened, she would sink into him so deeply that she would never be wholly free again.

Aching, she reminded herself that the more tightly she clung now, the more painful it would be to separate. She must maintain a safe distance, not only for the sake of finding Kira, but for her own sanity.

Stepping away, she asked, "Is your ankle badly hurt?"

As she spoke, she made the mistake of looking at him. He became utterly still, and the lamplight showed the warm gold fading from his eyes, leaving them a flat, pale green. He had recognized her subtle withdrawal for the rejection it was, and she was miserably aware how much she had wounded him.

Without a word more being spoken, something significant took place between them. A hardening, a wariness, that rebuilt the barriers between them. He had made himself vulnerable, but she had spurned him, and pride would not permit him to do that again.

His voice cool and uninflected, he said, "My ankle is only twisted. It will be fine tomorrow."

She retrieved her cloak, which had been dropped by her attacker, and wrapped it around her trembling body. Then she collected his hat and cane and silently handed them over. This time she avoided looking into his eyes.

Twenty feet away, Henry Jones had risen and was dusting himself off. A bruise was forming on his jaw, and his lip was split and bloody, but he didn't seem to be seriously injured. "A very timely appearance, my lord," he said genially, oblivious to the undercurrents throbbing between Kit and Lucien. "It was almost worth having my coat ruined to see you in action."

Lucien's head swung toward him. In a voice that could have scorched granite, he asked, "Might I inquire why you didn't wait for my coach to take you and Lady Kathryn home?"

Guessing that his anger toward her was being transferred to Henry, she said quickly, "It was my fault, Lucien. I didn't believe I was in danger, so I insisted on walking."

Ignoring her, he regarded the Runner with narrowed eyes.

Henry's face sobered. "I've no excuse, my lord. Her ladyship didn't understand the risk, but I should have."

"Yes, you should. If you're that careless with Lady Kathryn again, you'll have more to fear from me than from a whole gang of ruffians." Lucien's tone was still caustic, but his expression had relaxed at the Runner's honest admission of error. He gestured toward the coach. "Do you want the driver to take you home after he drops Lady Kathryn and me at Strathmore House? After the drubbing you took, I imagine you could use a ride."

"Thank you for the offer, my lord, but walking will keep me from stiffening up." Henry grimaced as he leaned over and scooped up his crushed hat. "When you've been in as many scrapes as I have, you learn what's best for the old bones."

After bidding Kit good night, the Runner walked away. As soon as he was out of earshot, Kit said, "If you don't think I would be safe at Kira's, take me to Aunt Jane's house. The villain can't possibly know where she lives."

"Don't talk rubbish," he said crisply. "You're staying with me for the duration. I never should have allowed you out of my sight." He held the door open for Kit, saying to the fascinated coach driver, "Hanover Square, please."

As he handed her into the coach, she opened her mouth to protest again, but Lucien cut her off. "Don't bother to mention the potential damage to your reputation. You've said that you are indifferent to such considerations."

He climbed in after her and slammed the door shut. "If you're concerned about propriety, Lady Jane can come and stay at Strathmore House. If you're going to say that your sister's Shakespearean cat needs tending, the creature can come, too." He sat on the opposite seat and braced himself as the coach lurched into motion. "And for the rest of the drive to Hanover Square, you can tell me what an overbearing beast I am."

She might have done exactly that, except that his last sentence disarmed her. Grateful that he was setting a casual tone to replace vanished intimacy, she said, "To be honest, I'm fresh out of arguments. I'll wait until to-morrow to point out your beastliness."

"Tomorrow you'll have better things to do. I've identified seven properties owned by the suspects that are within a couple of hours of London." He gave an exasperated sigh. "It's a start, but such information is not easily come by. There could be other locations that I don't know about."

"I'm sure you have discovered more than anyone else could have." She bit her lip, again feeling the sense of time flowing too rapidly. "I'm supposed to do *Scandal Street* tomorrow night, but if we're going to search for Kira, I can let the understudy take my part."

"That won't be necessary. The two properties closest to London can be visited during the day. Both are small, so it shouldn't be necessary to trespass for you to sense if Kira is being held at one of them."

"Thank heaven," she said fervently. "It will be good to be *doing* something."

A few minutes later they reached Strathmore House and Lucien escorted her inside after a lavish payment to the coach driver. There was no question of her sharing his bed; impeccably formal, he handed her into the keeping of a maid without so much as a good-night kiss.

As she wearily settled into a guest room, she told herself that sleeping alone was much wiser. She would have no ambivalence about whether to make love, nor the guilt that would come if she succumbed, which she probably would if Lucien seriously tried to persuade her.

What a pity that wisdom was so cold and lonely.

Because of her fatigue, Kit slept heavily and awoke only after prolonged knocking on her door. Groggily she looked around, at first not recognizing her luxurious surroundings. By the time she remembered where she was, the door had opened and her aunt swept in, followed by two familiar tabby cats and a maid carrying a tea tray. The cats jumped onto the bed and flopped on opposite sides of Kit, where they could glare mistrustfully at each other over her knees. Apparently Viola and Sebastian had forgotten that they were litter mates.

Ignoring the feline byplay, Jane said brightly. "Good morning, Kathryn. You're looking rather dreadful. Have some tea and currant muffins." She dismissed the maid and poured two cups of tea, adding sizable dollops of sugar to each.

Kit stifled a groan; her aunt had always been one of those regrettable creatures known as Morning People. "What are you doing here, Jane?" she asked as she accepted the tea cup and gratefully drank a scalding mouthful.

"That earl of yours called first thing in the morning and hauled Sebastian and me over here in the interests of propriety." Jane settled into a chair. "Though I suspect that trying to preserve your reputation is rather a case of closing the barn door after the horse has disappeared over the nearest horizon."

When Kit blushed, Jane added, "You needn't comment on that."

"I don't intend to." Though Kit had told Jane everything about her search for Kira, she had been rather less forthcoming about her relationship with Lucien. "And he's not my earl."

Jane grinned. "He seems to think he is. Since I'm not your legal guardian, he didn't bother to ask me for your hand, but he did inform me of your future nuptials."

"That has yet to be decided," Kit said sharply.

Her aunt frowned. "Is he bullying you, Kathryn? Men can be such brutes."

Kit stared into her steaming cup, "Lord Strathmore is not a brute. He simply feels that he has compromised me and we should marry. However, I doubt anything will come of it."

"If you say so, my dear," Jane said skeptically. "He

seems the determined sort. But I rather like him. You could do far worse for a husband."

Afraid to risk her fragile hopes by speaking them aloud, she said mildly, "I don't know that I want a husband, and I don't really think he wants a wife. After Kira is found, I expect that Strathmore and I will go our separate ways." Knowing the dangers of showing favoritism, Kit set aside her cup so she could pet both cats at once. "How did he get Viola from Kira's house?"

"Perhaps he woke Cleo Farnsworth and asked her to let him into the flat." Jane's eyes twinkled. "Then again, he may have picked the lock. I wouldn't put it past the gentleman."

"Neither would I. That sort of thing is what makes him so useful on a quest." Kit broke a muffin in half, automatically keeping it out of range of the cats' paws. "I don't care if the earl is a professional housebreaker. What matters is that he is helping me search for Kira."

Jane's expression sobered. Kira's disappearance was almost as hard on her as on Kit. "Have you learned something new?"

Kit outlined what had happened since she had last seen her aunt, concluding with the plan to visit two of the Hellion-owned properties that day.

Jane said doubtfully, "You really think you can detect Kira's presence if you're close to her?"

"I certainly hope so." Kit's fingers tightened on the muffin. It fragmented across the counterpane, eagerly pursued by the cats. "If I can't, I don't know what we'll do next."

Kit thought it would be less conspicuous to ride about the countryside dressed as a young man, so after eating, she delved into the clothing Jane had brought from home. Her aunt had wisely included her burglar's garb, so clad in boots and breeches, she, Lucien, and Jason Travers rode south into Surrey.

Their first destination was a small estate owned by Lord Chiswick and leased to a wealthy City merchant. With her escorts beside her, Kit circled the property on a series of lanes and small roads that came as close to the perimeter as possible. Then they tethered their horses in a copse and hiked across the estate on a public footpath.

The whole time she strained for a sense of Kira's presence. In the very center of the estate, she stopped and closed her eyes. Then she turned in a slow circle, like a hound scenting the wind, while the men watched in silence. The psychic space was as empty as the winter-blasted fields, with no trace of Kira's distinctive warmth and brightness.

Opening her eyes, she said bleakly, "Nothing."

His expression as strained as her own, Jason said, "It was too much to hope that she would be in the first place we looked."

"And this is not the most likely of the estates." Lucien laid a light hand on Kit's shoulder. "Come along to the next property. Nunfield owns it, and a couple of his aging relations live there. I think it's a better prospect."

Kit didn't answer. Not only was she disappointed at the lack of results at this location, but on a deeper level she was terrified. What if she was wrong, and she would be unable to sense Kira's presence even if her sister was near? What if the ability Kit had once possessed had failed under the pressure of her desperation?

If that was the case, her sister was doomed.

Interlude

She had not expected him to come for another session so soon, and she had little warning of his arrival. There was barely time to don her black wig, boots, and a red velvet shift that ended at midthigh. But clothing was simple compared to attitude. It was never easy to become the dominating bitch he craved; it took fierce concentration, all of her acting skill, and acute sensitivity to his desires. Not having had enough time to prepare meant that her portrayal was weak, which allowed her underlying fear to show.

For that reason she shackled him and secured his chains to the hook that hung suspended from the dungeon ceiling. Snarling a litany of abuse, she whipped him with all of her precisely gauged skill. It was a typical interchange, with her contemptuous and him groveling. But it took longer than usual to bring him to culmination, and there was a dark light in his eyes that alarmed her. Perhaps she was no longer enough of a novelty to arouse him. And when he tired of her . . .

Her fears were confirmed after she released him from his bondage. In the past she had always withdrawn to the other room, and he left when he was ready. This time he caught her wrists, trapping her at his side. "In time, the slave becomes the master, the mistress becomes the slave," he said with icy menace. "This will happen soon, my lady of the whip."

Like a wild beast he must be kept in his place. She jerked her knee up and knocked him in the chest, breaking his grip. "But a cur is always a cur," she sneered. "Like a dog that cringes before its master, you need what I give you, so you will accept any humiliation."

He grabbed her shoulders and slammed her against the wall, pinning her with his sweat-stenched body. Panic surged through her, for he had never physically assaulted her.

"Soon you will know the true meaning of fear, and I will savor every nuance." His breath was heavy with anticipation. "The last and most glorious performance of your life will occur when the tables are turned. But don't worry—you will not make your final bows alone."

As abruptly as the session had begun, it ended. He lifted the robe he had discarded and draped it over his welt-marked shoulders. Then he left, the heavy key grinding in the lock behind him.

She sank to her knees, shaking. How much longer did she have? She tried not to speculate about the evil hints he had made, but it was impossible not to wonder, even if the only real question was how long and horribly she would suffer before merciful death claimed her.

What had he meant when he said that she would not be alone?

Her stomach heaved as an unspeakable thought crossed her mind. No, that was impossible. Kit was too clever, and she knew the danger she faced.

But was she a match for pure evil?

Oh, Kit, Kit, she thought despairingly. In the name of God, be careful.

After he left the dungeon, he went to the sullen maid who tended his captive. "Make another of the bondage costumes with the slits and leather lacing," he ordered.

"Yes, my lord," she said incuriously. "How large should it be?"

"The same size as the one the mistress has now." He stopped for a moment as his mind filled with the intoxicating fantasy that would soon be fulfilled. "The costume must be *exactly* the same."

Chapter 32

It was late, almost midnight. After escorting Kit home from the theater and sending her off to bed, Lucien turned his attention to some of the work he had been neglecting in favor of the search for Kira. When a soft knock sounded on his study door, he answered absently, his mind full of the figures he had been analyzing.

As soon as he recognized the tall, travel-stained man who entered, he snapped back to the present. Leaping to his feet, he moved around his desk, his hand outstretched. "Good Lord, is that you, Michael, or am I hallucinating?"

Lord Michael Kenyon smiled and clasped Lucien's hand in both of his. "No hallucination. I knocked, but your servants have all retired so I used the key you gave me last year."

"Do you want something to eat?"

"No thanks, I had a substantial dinner in Berkshire. But I wouldn't say no to a drink."

Lucien waved his friend to a seat. "I didn't think you could possibly reach London for at least another couple of days. What did you do, hitch a ride with a passing falcon?"

Michael sprawled wearily onto the leather-upholstered sofa, his mud-spattered boots and breeches a mute testimony to his long journey from Wales. "I was rather disturbed by your message, so I decided to make all due speed. What's wrong?"

Thinking how fortunate he was to have friends who would come instantly, without questions, Lucien opened a cabinet and brought out a decanter of the Scottish whiskey that Michael favored. "A kidnapping, and time is running out." After pouring them each a generous measure of whiskey, he sat and succinctly told the story of Kira and Kit.

Michael listened without comment, his lean body relaxed, but his green eyes sharply alert. At the end of the recital he said, "I assume that you've considered cornering each of your suspects and beating the truth out of them."

Trust Michael to suggest the pragmatic solution. "Believe me, I've thought of that," Lucien admitted, "but we have too many suspects, and there is a distinct chance that the true villain is not among them. I'm afraid that it won't do to brutalize a number of wealthy, powerful men without more evidence."

Michael grinned. "One thing I've always liked about you is that you don't waste time being principled during a crisis."

"A characteristic we share," Lucien pointed out. "It is not generally considered a virtue."

"Principles are sometimes an unaffordable luxury." Michael eyed his host quizzically. "Though you didn't say as much, I get the impression that you are motivated as much by a desire to help Lady Kathryn as by general nobility."

"You guessed correctly. I have every intention of marrying her after we've found her sister."

Michael's dark brows rose. "You look rather glum for a prospective bridegroom."

"There are . . . complications." Lucien stared into his glass. Since the attempted abduction, he and Kit had been circling each other as warily as her two cats. He knew that she was under a terrible strain, and he accepted her desire to avoid physical intimacy while searching for her sister.

Nonetheless, he felt she was silently slipping away from him, and he had no idea how to stop that. In the beginning he had been confident that he could win her heart, but he was beginning to fear that when . . . if . . . she got Kira back, he would lose Kit entirely, for she would no longer need him. "Michael, why do men and women drive each other to distraction? And why do we keep reaching out to each other anyhow?"

Michael leaned forward and rested his elbows on his knees, cradling his whiskey glass between his hands. "I'm the last person to ask for advice about women, Luce," he said wryly. "My record in that area is dismal. But for what it's worth, women have something that men need—and I don't mean the obvious."

Lucien glanced up. "Then what do you mean?"

His friend hesitated before answering. "Males and females are complimentary. Often that means that we're opposites, with all of the conflict that implies, but it also means that we complete each other. A good woman has a warmth, an accepting quality, that is a blessed relief from all the sharp edges one meets in life." He smiled. "Think of Nicholas's wife."

"If only there were ten thousand more like Clare."

"I'll drink to that." Michael lifted his glass in a toast, then downed the rest of the contents. "But I gather there were a fair number of rocks in the road on their journey toward marital bliss. Nicholas and Clare have earned what they have."

Lucien's mind skipped back to a conversation he'd had with a worried Clare before her wedding. "I'd forgotten that. Thank you for the most encouraging words I've had in days."

"Wisdom offered free, and worth every penny."

Lucien laughed, his heart lighter. With Michael beside them, surely they would succeed in finding Kira. And then, by God, he would convince Kit that she needed him as much as he needed her.

Lady Jane's casual chaperonage extended only to spending her nights at Strathmore House. During the day she returned to her own home and went about her usual business. For that reason Kit breakfasted in her room so that she would not run the risk of being alone with Lucien. They were managing to rub along tolerably well during their surreptitious expeditions to Hellion-owned estates, and she didn't want to jeopardize that. She was also afraid what she might say, or do, if she spent too much time with him. Nonetheless, she missed his companionship dreadfully.

After breakfasting, she dressed and tried to work on an essay about the proposed Corn Laws, but she found it impossible to concentrate on protectionist trade policies. She had not written a decent article since Kira's abduction.

Restless, she left the room and went to the portrait gallery on the third floor, which she had been meaning to explore. It would be interesting to see if Lucien's relatives were all as handsome as he. She doubted that was possible.

When she entered the gallery, she saw a tall, brown-haired figure at the far end. Glad to have the company of her cousin, she called, "Good morning, Jason."

The man turned and she realized that he was a stranger, taller than Jason and not as thin. His hair was also a little lighter, with a touch of russet visible in the winter sun.

Coming toward her with a smile, he said, "Sorry, we haven't been introduced. I'm Michael Kenyon, a friend of Lucien's. You must be Lady Kathryn Travers."

"Indeed I am." She moved forward and offered her hand. "It's a pleasure to meet you. It's actually Lord Michael, isn't it? Lucien has mentioned you."

"To any friend of Lucien's, plain Michael will do." He bowed over her hand. As he straightened, she saw that his eyes were a remarkable shade of green, not Lucien's changeable green-gold but a true emerald.

"Then you must call me Kit." She studied his face. Even if she had not already known that Michael had been a soldier, she would have guessed that from his quality of steely, contained strength. "Lucien said he was going to send for his most dangerous friend. I gather that is you?"

"I suppose so, but if Luce wants someone who is dangerous, he need only look in a mirror. I'm merely a retired soldier who has gone to grass like an old cavalry horse."

She smiled, liking his dry sense of humor. "Yet you

are willing to come out of retirement for my sister's sake. You have my most profound gratitude."

"I hope I can be of service." He gave her a long, appreciative male glance. "There is really another like you?"

"Yes, only more so. You'll see soon, I hope." Since thinking of her sister would make her anxious, she continued, "I came down to take a look at the pictures. Are you familiar with Lucien's family?"

"Yes, and what I don't know, I can invent." He nodded toward the portrait of a blond gentleman in Cavalier dress. "That's Gareth, the third earl, I believe. He supported the Royalists during the Civil War, but took the precaution of having his brother become a Puritan. When the Royalists went into exile, the brother took over the family estates and swore his allegiance to Cromwell. After the Restoration, Gareth came back, reclaimed his lands, and made sure that his brother was amply compensated for his stewardship of the Fairchild interests."

Kit examined the cool, ironic face. "Lucien said once that he comes from a long line of pragmatists."

"It's why the Fairchilds have survived so many of the vicissitudes of British history." Michael indicated another portrait, this of a dandyish gentleman in the elaborate garments of a hundred years earlier. Beside him stood an elegant lady in flowing green silk. "That's the fifth earl, Charles, and his wife, Maria. He was quite dissolute and a heedless gamester. His son inherited at the age of six when Charles died under suspicious circumstances."

She glanced askance. "Is that true, or did you make it up?"

He chuckled. "That's the story Lucien told me. He claims that there was speculation that Maria had decided to preserve her son's patrimony at the price of her husband's life. Perhaps the story is true, or perhaps it is only Lucien's antic sense of humor. He doesn't take his elevated ancestors very seriously."

"That's better than taking them too seriously."

His levity vanished. "A failing of the Kenyons, I fear."

Kenyon ... Kit should have recognized the name sooner. "Your father is the Duke of Ashburton?"

"Yes," he said in a voice that made further questions impossible. He nodded to the portrait at the end of the wall. "Have you ever seen this painting? It's of Lucien and his family when he was nine or ten."

To look at the picture was to know that this had been a real family, not a mere dynastic union. The evidence was in the intimate way the countess's hand curved over her husband's arm; the fondness in the earl's eyes as he regarded his wife and children; the shared laughter of Lucien and the elfin girl with silvery blond hair flowing over her slender shoulders. Kit felt an ache in her throat at the sight. Lucien had lost so much, so young. Yet what could have destroyed him had made him strong. Softly she asked, "Did you know his family well?"

"Quite." He gazed at the canvas, his expression distant. "I didn't like spending holidays with my own family, so my friends usually took me home like a stray pup. Ashdown was my favorite place to visit because Lucien's parents were so happy together. That's not a common state among the nobility."

Kit's gaze went to the small blond girl whose radiant smile transcended the years. "And Lady Elinor?"

"She was enchanting," he said simply. "Bright and sweet and quick. She and Lucien had the most remarkable relationship. In my experience not all brother and sister twins are so close, but I think her delicate health drew them together. He was very protective of her. Her death devastated him."

There was a note in his voice that made her look quickly into his face. "And you as well?"

After a long silence he replied, "I missed them all, but especially Elinor. Though she looked like a spun-sugar angel, she was a very definite young lady. On my first visit to Ashdown, she decided that we would suit and informed me that we would marry when we were of age. I accepted her proposal quite willingly." After another long silence he said, "If she had lived . . ." He turned abruptly away from the portrait. "It was only childish fancy, of course. It meant nothing."

Obviously it had meant a great deal, even after so many years. The story brought Lady Elinor alive for Kit.

She must have been as clever as her brother, for even as a small child she had been able to identify a boy who would grow into an admirable man. "Thank you for telling me so much, Michael. I want to learn as much about Lucien's past as I can."

He gave her a piercing glance. "It's information that comes at a price. Try not to hurt him, Kit. Luce deserves better."

She caught her breath at the unexpectedness of his remark. "Believe me, the last thing I want to do is hurt Lucien."

Whatever he saw in her face must have satisfied him. Casual again, he said, "Down here is a portrait of the seventh earl. In the eyes of society he disgraced himself by dabbling in trade, but was redeemed by making pots of money in the process."

Eccentric relations were so much more comfortable than vanished happiness.

That night, her escort increased to three, Kit went to Blackwell Abbey, Mace's estate. It had been left until last because she had been there before and found no traces of Kira, but the estate was so large that there were areas that she could not have sensed from the house.

As with the other estates, Lucien had obtained a detailed map, this one drawn by a local man who had once worked there. It showed every cottage, every field, every footpath, as well as the stone wall that enclosed the entire property.

Before setting out, each of them had studied the map so that they could find their way unseen in the dark. Even so, the survey would have been impossible without Michael. Not only did he have the night vision of a cat, but he seemed to carry the map in his head. Like an army scout in hostile terrain, he led them on a weaving course carefully calculated to take Kit within a few hundred yards of every section of the estate.

Lucien traveled by her side, making sure she would not stumble because her attention was turned inward rather than on the rough ground. Behind them, moving with the soft-footed grace of a forest hunter, came Jason

Travers. In their dark clothing, all of them were shadows in a moonless night.

Blackwell Abbey disturbed her in ways she could not define. As they made a wide circle around the manor house, she stopped and stared at its dark, ominous silhouette. The men halted. "Do you sense something?" Lucien asked in a voice that would not have been audible ten feet away.

She was acutely aware that within those brick walls she and Lucien had become lovers, and she had the uneasy certainty that he was thinking the same thing. Yet that was not what had stopped her. "There is something about this place. Kira isn't there now. I don't think she ever was. Yet I feel that there is ... is some connection with her."

"Perhaps someone at Blackwell Abbey has been with her?"

"Perhaps." She bit her lip, wanting to shriek with frustration. "This is like being blindfolded and dropped into a crowd, then having to identify someone by scent."

Lucien's fingers touched her elbow. "Don't worry, Kit, you can do it. We need only get close enough to Kira."

He was mind-reading again. She released her breath, then reached out again, seeking the ineffable essence of her sister. They resumed their slow trek across the estate.

They had had no problems on the earlier searches, but this time their luck ran out. As they passed behind a row of tenant cottages, several dogs started barking furiously. Instead of assuming that a deer or rabbit had sparked the canine attention, men came out of several of the cottages, pulling on coats against the winter damp. A hoarse voice grumbled, "Probably nothin'."

"That's not for us to judge," a second one said sternly. "Could be poachers. Turn the dogs loose."

Kit's heart jumped in panic. Michael hissed, "There's a stream ahead. You three wade along it, and I'll draw them off."

Lucien grabbed her arm and guided her swiftly down a scrubby hill to the stream. Behind them the barking of the dogs increased as they were released from their chains.

On the bank of the stream she stumbled on a shifting rock, but Lucien kept her from falling. Together they waded into the water, Jason on her other side.

Trying to move soundlessly through the rushing current, they went up the stream and around a sharp bend. There they found a pool roofed with bare, arching branches. Lucien led them into the most heavily shadowed section and stopped. The icy water came to midthigh on Kit.

A hundred yards away at the place where they had entered the stream, the barking rose to hysterical excitement. "This way!" one of the pursuers shouted.

The frenzied baying of the dogs began to diminish. A little sick, Kit realized that Michael was leading them in the opposite direction by laying a trail downstream along the bank. She began shaking so hard that her teeth chattered.

Wordlessly, Lucien drew her into his arms, the warmth of his body countering the freezing water. "Don't worry, Michael will be all right," he said in a voice softer than a whisper.

And if he wasn't, it would be her fault. She wrapped her arms around Lucien's waist. Since the night of the street attack he had hidden his most private self behind a wall of reserve, but on a more mundane level he had never stinted with his support. If not for him, she would be raving by now.

He held her tightly, slowly stroking her back. Even here, in the presence of cold and fear and danger, desire stirred languidly through her veins, a teasing reminder of the passion they had shared. She wondered if they would ever be intimate again. It was hard to imagine such happiness.

When the barking of the dogs was only a distant echo, they clambered ashore on the opposite side of the stream and continued their trek. At the outer wall, Lucien said, "If we go west a quarter of a mile and cut across the estate one more time, we can cover the remaining ground. Can you manage, Kit?

"I can do it," she said with grim determination, even though her soaked feet were numb with cold.

"Invincible Kit," he said with a smile in his voice. "If I am ever abducted, I hope you come looking for me."

His vote of confidence raised her spirits a little. With Jason leading the way, they began their last trek across the estate. It seemed to take forever, and Kit was so cold that she was not sure how reliable her sensing was, but eventually they reached the far wall of the estate.

Lucien leaped and caught the edge of the wall so he could swing himself onto the top, then stretched a hand down to help her. Jason jumped up the same way Lucien had. Good food and regular riding exercise had restored much of the strength that the American had lost in prison.

After they lowered themselves down on the other side, they made their way to the horses. Michael was there waiting.

Kit asked, "You're all right?"

"Splendid," he assured her. "The best sport I've had since I left the army."

She shuddered as she heaved her weary body onto her horse. If being pursued through the dark by a pack of slavering dogs was his idea of sport, he was welcome to it.

It was a silent group that rode back to London. The mission had gone well, and they had gotten away safely. There was only one problem.

Kit had still not found a single trace of her sister.

Chapter 33

It was nearly three in the morning when they arrived back at Strathmore House, and Kit was reeling with cold and fatigue. She was intending to go straight to bed until Lucien said, "It's time for a council of war."

His expression was grim, the usual charm planed away to reveal the underlying steel. His gaze went to Michael and Jason, then to her. "Can we do it now, or is everyone too tired?"

"Now," Jason said harshly. "There is no time to be wasted." Michael agreed with a silent nod.

Knowing that they must be as tired as she, Kit squared her shoulders. "If you all can keep going, so can I."

"Good girl." Lucien gave her a smile that dispersed some of the chill from her bones. "Everyone go change to dry clothing. We'll meet in the kitchen."

Fifteen minutes later they were all seated in Windsor chairs around a trestle table. The kitchen was a comforting room, with tangy clumps of dried herbs hanging from the beams and light from the roaring fire glinting from copper pans. Lucien, bless him, had made arrangements to have food and drink ready when they returned. Kit drank her first cup of tea in two scalding gulps. Bread, cheese, sliced ham, and a bowl of thick lentil soup made her feel almost human.

After hunger had been slaked, Lucien pushed his chair back from the table and stalked to the fireplace. He tossed a shovel of coal on the fire, then turned to face the others as the flames rose behind him. So must Lucifer have appeared when addressing his hosts. "We've hit a dead end," he said flatly. "Does anyone have any suggestions of what we might do next?"

After a long silence, Michael said, "Only the one that you and I discussed—choosing the most likely suspects and forcing them to talk."

Horrified, Kit said, "You mean torture?"

Lucien looked at her. "If that's what it takes to find your sister."

He meant it, she realized. She bent her head and pressed her fingertips into the center of her forehead. Based solely on her unsupported word, these men—three strong, utterly competent men—were willing to harm someone who might be innocent. The thought was terrifying.

"It's an ugly idea, Kit, but it may be our only hope," Lucien said quietly. "Is there one man you would choose as your prime suspect? Nunfield, perhaps, or Mace?"

She had always thought of herself as a civilized woman, but apparently she was not, for she found herself seriously considering Lucien's suggestion. After all, Kira's life was at stake. The faces of the suspects passed before her mind's eye. After judging each carefully, she looked up. "I honestly cannot pick one as most likely. I'm sorry. If I could, I would."

"We're looking for a needle in a haystack," Michael said, exasperated. "The only thing we know for certain is that Lady Kristine was kidnapped off the street after a theater performance. For that, we have a witness. Everything else is speculation derived from Kit's intuition."

"Do you doubt her?" Lucien asked in a neutral tone.

"No. At its best, intuition can surpass logic. The question is, how can we use Kit's ability to find her sister?"

It was the same question Lucien had asked before, but this time, there was an unexpected answer. Jason Travers said tentatively, "There's a method of divination that might be worth trying here. It involves using a pendulum and a map to find a lost object. Perhaps Kit can locate Kira that way."

When the others stared at him, he said, "I know it sounds daft, but it's not that different from a dowser finding water with a divining rod."

"I've seen successful dowsing," Lucien said slowly.

"Though it makes no sense rationally, it often works. Kit?"

She shrugged. "I suppose it can't hurt. What should I use for a pendulum?"

"I don't know if it matters." Jason thought a moment, "Perhaps a piece of Kira's jewelry if you have one."

"I have her jewelry box upstairs." She got to her feet. "I'll see if there is something suitable."

"I'll get the most detailed maps of southern England that I have." Lucien lit two candles and gave one to Kit, then opened the door for her while Jason started to clear the table.

They climbed the stairs with Kit in the lead. When they reached the first landing, she turned to him. "Have I ever really said how grateful I am for what you are doing? You've believed me when anyone else would have sent me to Bedlam, and you have used your special skills to search for Kira with a thoroughness no one else could match."

"You can thank me after we've found her," he said with a tired smile.

His words caused her expression to change. For once, Lucien misinterpreted her. "Let me repeat that this is not a *quid pro quo*—your freedom in return for my assistance in finding your sister. You have my help no matter what you might decide later." His expression turned rueful. "Though I can be ruthless, there are limits. Finding Kira is a separate issue from my determination to persuade you that we should marry."

"I know that." She laid a gentle hand on his cheek. Whiskers too golden to be visible prickled teasingly against her palm. "This is not the time to worry about the future. Wait to decide what you want until the crisis has passed. Anything in my power, I shall give you willingly." Even if that meant saying good-bye, for it was not her freedom that she was concerned about, but his. Her hand dropped. After he met Kira, he would not be so determined to wed the plain, quiet twin.

Taking her words at face value, he said quietly, "I'll hold you to that." For the first time in days, he kissed her, cupping her chin in his hand—lightly, quickly, but still affecting her all the way to her marrow. The constraint that had been between them for days vanished, leaving peace. Then he turned toward his study while Kit continued up to her bedroom, her knees a little less steady than they had been.

Kira liked jewelry, and the velvet-lined chest that held her collection was a tangle of beads and baubles. Kit hesitated over the open box, wondering what to choose. Even if the divination attempt was absurd, she must try her best.

Not a bracelet or complicated necklace, or any of the brooches, for they would not swing easily. Her gaze fell on a pair of sapphire drop earrings. One of those suspended on a thread should do nicely.

Reaching for an earring, her hand halted in midair. There was an odd sensation of heat against her palm. No, not heat, and not really an itch, but . . . something.

Feeling foolish, she poked through the mound of jewelry until she discovered a heart-shaped locket at the bottom of the chest. It was a lovely trifle with a delicately etched pattern on the golden surface and a slender chain that would be perfect for a pendulum.

Beyond that, it *felt* like the right choice. Fatigue and anxiety were definitely making her a little strange. She closed the jewelry box and returned to the kitchen.

Jason was pacing restlessly about the long, flagstoned room. In sharp contrast, Michael was sprawled back in his Windsor chair, his legs crossed at the ankle with the calm of a man who had learned patience in the battlefield. Doubtless it helped that he had the least at stake; he scarcely knew Kit, and Kira not at all. Yet that made it all the more admirable he was willing to join a mission that could prove hazardous. She wondered what it would be like to have such courage. She was very tired of being afraid.

Lucien had returned before her and was opening an enormous book on the trestle table. As she drew closer, she saw that it was a folio of superbly drawn and colored maps of the British shires. She was admiring the quality of the printing when he calmly ripped out the page illustrating Surrey.

He glanced up when she made a sound of involuntary protest. "I don't know how a pendulum works, but it might have problems with a map that was bound in with other maps."

"That makes sense," she agreed. She opened her hand to show the locket. "Will this do, Jason?"

His face tightened when he saw what she held. "I gave that to Kira. Did ... did she ever wear it?"

Though Kit wished she could say yes, she had to shake her head. "No, but remember that I've seen her very seldom in the last several years."

He took the locket and opened it with a thumbnail. Inside was a wisp of dark hair that exactly matched his own. "At least she kept it. That must mean something."

Her heart ached for him. Not only did he fear for Kira's life, but he could not be sure of Kira's love. "Believe me, if my sister had wanted to forget you, she would have gotten rid of this." Kit took the locket back and turned it to the light so she could see the initials engraved inside. *K. T. + J. T.* Below was the horizontal hourglass figure that was the mathematical symbol for infinity. Kira and Jason, for always. Blinking back the emotion that was too close to the surface, she said, "Obviously I picked the right pendulum."

His expression raw, Jason said, "Let us hope so."

She snapped the locket shut. "How does this work? I just realized that I haven't the faintest idea."

"Take a chair and get comfortable. This will take time."

Obediently she settled into one of the Windsor chairs. Jason continued, "Prop your elbow on the table and let the pendulum swing freely from your right hand."

Lucien said, "Does it matter that Kit is left-handed?"

"In that case, use your left hand. Let the locket hang until it's absolutely still."

As Kit waited for the swinging to stop, Jason explained, "Generally a pendulum is used for questions that can be answered with a yes or no. However, the motions vary for different people. To find out how the pendulum works for you, ask questions for which you know the answer."

With a nod of understanding Lucien asked, "Are you in London?"

The hanging locket quivered. Then, to Kit's amazement, it began slowly swinging counterclockwise even though she was prepared to swear that she was doing nothing.

Jason said, "That direction must mean yes."

Intrigued, Lucien asked, "Have you ever been to India, Kit?"

The pendulum slowed to a stop, then began moving clockwise. "That must be no," the American said.

Michael spoke up. "Will the Congress of Vienna allow Napoleon to keep the throne of France?"

The locket twitched nervously and came to a halt.

"A pendulum isn't usually much good for telling the future," Jason said. "It seems to work best for finding lost objects, or to help people discover what they truly want in a situation that is confusing."

Lucien began asking Kit a series of questions with simple answers. It became clear that counterclockwise was always yes and the reverse was always no. Impressed in spite of her doubts, Kit asked, "Where did you learn this?"

"From my mother, who was a wild-eyed Irishwoman." Jason smiled with obvious affection. "According to her, the O'Hanlon females had been village wise women for generations, passing traditional knowledge from mother to daughter. My father died when I was young, and my mother never remarried, so she taught me the family lore with strict orders to pass it on to my own daughter." His smile faded. "If I ever have one."

He and his mother had obviously been close. Perhaps being raised by a "wild-eyed Irishwoman" was why Jason could fall in love with the sort of strong, unconventional woman who would dare to be an actress. The more Kit saw of her cousin, the better she understood why her sister had loved him in return.

Bringing her tired mind back to business, Kit asked, "Now that we've established how it answers for me, what do I do?"

"Think very hard about finding Kira," he replied.

"When you have your goal firmly in mind, keep the pendulum steady in your left hand while you slowly move the other hand above the map. If this works, you'll get a strong reaction from the pendulum when your right hand passes over the place where she is being held."

"Hang on a moment while I get the maps in order," Lucien said. "Shall we start with London itself?"

The others agreed, so he tore the city map from the folio. As she waited, Kit remembered what Jason had said about how a pendulum could help someone discover true feelings in a tangled situation. Mentally she asked, *"Am I in love with Lucien?"*

The pendulum jumped in her hand, then began whirling wildly in a counterclockwise direction. *Yes, yes, yes.*

She stared bleakly at the swinging locket. She had been a fool to ask. Of course she loved him; how could she not? But her cowardly mind had wanted to deny the truth because it preferred not to acknowledge how painful it would be to lose him. Actually, there was some relief in accepting that she was in love with him; denying the fact hadn't made her feel any better.

Before she could stop herself, her mind formed the words, *"Will he still think he loves me when this is over?"*

The locket slowed to a complete halt and hung motionless from the gold chain. Well, Jason had said a pendulum wasn't good at telling the future. Nor did she really want to know what would happen later; thinking about it already hurt too much.

Jason said, "Ready?"

Lucien set the map of London in front of her. She closed her eyes and thought of her twin, her other, better self. *Kira, where are you? Tell me where you are, love.* She repeated the sentences like a litany until her consciousness was saturated with the essence of her sister.

Then she began to move her right hand slowly above the city map. The tension in the room was suffocating. Surprisingly, she did not mind having an audience, for the three men gave her a feeling of protection against the unknown that she was seeking to penetrate.

Divination proved to be a slow, painstaking process.

As expected, London did not provoke a reaction, though she felt a faint tingling in her palm. Perhaps that was because Kira had spent so much time in the city.

Next Surrey, then Kent. Lucien was laying out the counties counterclockwise around the city. Essex next. Kit did not look closely at the maps. Instead, she did her best to keep her mind empty so that she was only an instrument for whatever mysterious power moved the pendulum.

Suddenly the locket began twitching, creating a flurry of excitement. In a voice trembling with hope, Jason asked, "Is Kira in or near Romford?"

The pendulum began swinging clockwise. *No.* Kit released the breath she had caught. "Kira used to visit friends in Romford. That's probably why there was a reaction."

"Still, it proves that the technique has value. You weren't even looking at the map, so you couldn't know that you were over Romford." Lucien studied her face and frowned. "Do you need to rest?"

Guessing that she was gray with exhaustion, she closed her eyes and leaned back in the chair, her hands loose in her lap. Lucien rested a hand on her shoulder and some of his strength and confidence flowed into her. When she felt a little stronger, she raised the locket and continued. After Essex, Hertford.

Now Middlesex. Still nothing. Her throat tightened. This wasn't working; she had covered all of the counties around London with no results.

Quietly, Lucien slid another map under her hovering hand. A quick glance showed that it was Berkshire, which lay just west of Middlesex. He was starting on the second ring of counties out from London.

Doggedly she passed her hand over Windsor, then north to Maidenhead. *Kira, where are you?* South again toward Bracknell.

The pendulum jerked like a hooked fish, then began wildly swirling counterclockwise. At the same time there was a sharp, almost painful, sensation in her right palm. Kit snapped back to wakefulness, excitement burning through her veins. She felt a strong sense of her sister's presence, not the barely conscious pulse that was always there, but the intense connection she had felt when Lucien had mesmerized her.

His voice choked, Jason said, "Is Kira near Basildon?"

The locket slowed a little, but continued circling in the same direction. Kit felt Lucien behind her. He said, "Is she closer to Hycombe?"

The pendulum began moving more rapidly. Kit was only half aware of it because she felt herself sliding into her sister's mind and emotions so deeply that she was unsure where one of them ended and the other began.

"You're over a small village, West Hycombe," Lucien said, his voice distant. "Is she near there?"

Kit's head was pounding, and she was dimly aware that the locket was again swinging wildly. *Swinging, swinging, the tip of the whip biting into glazed flesh. A guttural, animal sound of pain twisted with ecstasy. Maddened eyes filled with craving and menace . . .*

Far, far away, Lucien asked, "Is Kira in or near a place called Castle Raine?"

Reality splintered into a whirlwind of fear. *Sister . . . self . . . other . . . enemy . . . danger . . . danger . . . danger!*

As she fell into the vortex, she began to scream.

Chapter 34

As soon as Lucien said the words "Castle Raine," Kit cried out with a terror that froze his blood.

Michael vaulted from his chair and crossed the kitchen in two steps. "Bloody hell, what's wrong?"

Jason also said something, but Lucien ignored both of the other men. He moved in front of Kit and saw that she was oblivious to her surrounding, her eyes blind, her hands clawing, her tortured voice one long wail of distress. She was like a madwoman—or a woman trapped in madness.

He caught her hands and said urgently, "Wake up, Kit, you've succeeded. It's over."

She writhed frantically, trying to jerk her hands free. "I hate this, I hate it, I hate him, *I hate him, I HATE HIM!*"

Face pale, Jason said, "What do you think has happened?"

"I think she has become trapped in Kira's terror," Lucien said grimly. Pitching his voice more sharply, he said, "Come back, Kit. For God's sake, *come back*!"

The screaming stopped, but her eyes were still dazed, and she was panting like a deer that had been hunted to the point of collapse. He leaned down and wrapped his arms around her. She was shaking and as cold as when they had hidden in the stream to avoid the pursuing dogs. How much more could she stand before she shattered? Softly he said, "It's all right, Kit, you're safe here with me."

"Please ... please hold me, Lucien." She began to weep, but her voice was her own.

Thanking God that she was herself again, he lifted her

in his arms, then turned and sat in the chair. As he cradled her against him, he asked, "Is divining with a pendulum always so exciting?"

Face pale, the American said, "I've never seen anything like that happen before."

"Presumably, you've never worked with a woman who was searching for her lost twin." He stroked Kit's trembling shoulders. She seemed painfully fragile.

Hating the necessity of probing, he asked, "I gather that you connected with Kira's emotions?"

Kit swallowed hard. "Yes, just at the end of one of the whipping sessions. It was ghastly, like having a nightmare while still awake. I could see and hear everything and feel Kira's emotions, but I could do nothing. I felt paralyzed, like a fly trapped in a web with the spider approaching."

"Is Kira all right?"

Kit frowned, then relaxed. "Yes. He's gone now. She knew I was there. I think that helped."

"You think she's being held at a place called Castle Raine?"

Kit shuddered and hid her face again. "I believe so."

Lucien extended one arm, keeping the other around Kit. "Michael, give me the map."

His friend silently placed it in his hand. After studying the area, Lucien said, "Castle Raine is a ruined medieval fortress, and it's probably no coincidence that it falls roughly halfway between the estates of Mace and Nunfield."

"Probably not." Michael glanced at Kit. "A castle dungeon would fit your impression of a lightless underground prison."

She grimaced. "You're right. Even furnishing the place comfortably can't cover up that atmosphere."

Lucien was still frowning at the map. Not surprisingly for a medieval castle, a river ran nearby. What caught his attention was a nagging sense of familiarity. An image popped into his mind: standing on a hill amidst old stone walls, looking down at a curving, moonlit river. Stone walls and moonlight ... "Damnation, I think I've been there!" he exclaimed. "Castle Raine must be the place that the Hellions hold their rituals."

"You attended one of their infamous orgies?" Michael said, his brows raised.

Kit's head came up, her gray eyes narrowed as she waited for Lucien's answer. Uneasily he remembered the hard-faced whore, and the horrible desolation he had felt after allowing her to earn her fee. His arm tightened around Kit's shoulders. "Strictly in the way of business, not for pleasure."

She relaxed again. A good thing she was so tired, or she might have guessed that his answer was not the whole truth. The night was one Lucien preferred to forget.

Jason said, "Do you know if the castle has dungeons?"

"I didn't see any, but it's likely. The grounds are quite extensive. Almost anything, or anyone, could be hidden there."

Silence fell on the room until Michael said with quiet menace, "I assume that tonight we will go to Castle Raine and search for Lady Kristine."

"That we will," Lucien said. "But first we sleep. In the morning Kit and I will call on Lord Ives, who is one Hellion we can trust. He should be able to tell us more about the castle."

"One can never have too much information about the target of a raid." Michael ran a weary hand through his chestnut hair. "But the earlier we go to Berkshire, the better. There's a bad storm brewing. Freezing rain or sleet, I think."

"Then we'll need a place to go to ground near the castle. A private house would be better than an inn." Lucien tapped the map. "Rafe owns a small manor near Basildon. The tenant died recently, and it's still vacant. I'm sure he'll let us use it. We can ride there this afternoon. After the raid we can spend the night and not have to ride all the way back to London."

In spite of her fatigue, Kit's curiosity was piqued. She said to Michael, "You can predict a storm so accurately that Lucien accepts your word without a blink?"

"They used to call me the weather wizard. Even as a

child, I could always tell when a storm was coming, and how severe it would be." Michael flexed one arm. "After I took a ball in the shoulder, my predictions became even better." Getting to his feet, he added, "Sleep well for what is left of the night."

Jason covered a yawn. "Since tomorrow is the winter solstice, we still have a few more hours of darkness."

Lucien stood, Kit still in his arms. "Good night."

As he headed toward the stairs, she protested, "I can walk."

"I have my doubts," he said dryly. "Remember how drained you've been the other times you've reached Kira's mind?"

"Oh." Conceding the point, she closed her eyes and let her head drop against his shoulder.

He was struck again by how frail she seemed. Poor gallant, exhausted kitten. She must be operating on pure will.

He took her to her room and set her on the edge of the bed, then stripped off her outer clothing. She cooperated passively, her head drooping. When she was down to her shift, he pulled back the covers. Before he could tuck her in, she reached up and linked her arms around his neck. "Stay, Lucien," she said, her eyes starkly gray. "Please."

He hesitated, grievously tempted. But . . .

"I'd love to stay, but I can't swear that I'll behave with suitable propriety," he said, striving to keep his tone light. "Though I understand entirely why you must avoid the confusions of passion, when I'm close to you, sense goes out the window. Fatigue will protect you tonight, but I make no guarantees about tomorrow morning."

She gave a ghost of a smile. "I'm prepared to accept the consequences. Now that we know where Kira is, I no longer feel it is critical for me to avoid intimacy." She laid her head against his chest, then added in an exhausted whisper, "And tonight, I don't want to be alone."

He dropped a kiss on her forehead. "As long as I'm alive, Kit, you don't have to be."

Her face tightened, though she said nothing. He wondered if she would ever believe him, or if her unreliable father had forever destroyed her ability to take a man at his word. Well, Lucien could be as patient as he had to be. He undressed, then put out the candles and joined her under the feather comforter.

Kit settled against him with a soft sigh. The sheets were cold and so was she, but warmth slowly bloomed wherever their bodies touched. He smiled when a slim leg insinuated itself between his knees, followed by a chilly foot tucking under his ankle. He couldn't imagine why anyone would rather sleep alone.

Though fatigue had done a good job of deadening desire, it was still pleasant to stroke her from shoulder to hip. Her smooth, supple curves gradually warmed. When his hand drifted to a rest on her breast, he lazily thumbed her nipple. It tightened to a firm little nub under the lightweight chemise.

He leaned forward a few inches so that his lips touched hers. Their mouths clung, hers soft and welcoming. Tongue met tongue with velvet pleasure, and she made a muted, purring sound. After a long, leisurely kiss, he lifted his head away. "This is foolish," he said huskily. "We both need rest."

She murmured agreement, yet her hand slipped around his waist to the small of his back and began moving in languid circles, gently erotic. He felt a distinct throb of desire. Lowering his head, he kissed her breast, feeling the pebbly texture of her nipple through her shift. From the way her breathing changed, she was no more immune to desire than he.

His caresses became longer, his palm sliding down her thigh to her knee. On the return journey the hem of her shift caught on his thumb and slithered upward. He hadn't done that intentionally, but he couldn't resist drawing his head into the scented darkness under the quilt and kissing the tender satin curve of her belly. Her slim fingers moved to his neck and began toying with his sensitive nape. Delicious, utterly delicious.

They moved into the rhythms of mating with dreamlike ease, each not quite innocent step succeeded by another that was even less so—the friction of bare skin against crisply tufted hair, delicate nips along an arching throat; the crush of pliant femininity into angular maleness, subtle body scents enhanced by the darkness into intoxicating lures.

When her hand sought and found taut male flesh, he responded by an intimate exploration of her secret depths. Her thighs parted invitingly. Even when he lifted himself over her and they joined, there was no real sense of urgency. Passion, yes, and blood beating with a heat that kindled into pure flame. But no desperation, for their union felt deeply right, a sharing of cares that paradoxically strengthened each of them.

When they fell asleep in each other's arms, their rest was deep and dreamless.

Kit opened her eyes to the pearly light of dawn. The onset of winter made sunrise relatively late, but even so, she could not have slept more than four hours. Still, she felt amazingly rested, for which she must give full credit to Lucien. The intimacy of a shared bed seemed so right and natural that it was hard to imagine that it might never occur again.

But she would never regret loving him, no matter how much pain it cost her in the future. Nor would she forget that he had wanted her.

She studied his sleeping face, which was framed in tousled golden hair. He was heart-stoppingly handsome and more relaxed than she had ever seen him when he was awake.

A small, rebellious thought stirred in the back of her mind. Lucien was the cleverest man she'd ever met, and not at all prone to self-delusion. Perhaps she could believe that he truly loved her; maybe he really would prefer her to her sister.

She released her breath in a slow sigh. No one else ever had. Not only was Kira livelier, more charming, but she was stronger. She had blossomed in her independent life, unlike Kit, who had barely been able to function when she was no longer half of a larger whole. Lucien would admire Kira's strength as much as he would be enchanted by her vivacity.

It was deeply ironic. If Kira died, Kit might be so emotionally crippled that she would be of no use to anyone again, yet rescuing her twin might doom her hopes of love.

But for this poignant, ephemeral moment, Lucien was *hers*. Kit stretched her neck and pressed the lightest of kisses on his mouth. His lids opened a little, revealing a golden glow of contentment in his eyes.

"I warned you that I might not be able to behave properly if I stayed," he said with a wicked gleam. "Though I did think I could keep temptation at bay a little longer than I did."

"Nonsense," she said with a smile. "You only behave properly when it suits you."

"And it doesn't suit me now." He wrapped his arms around her and pulled her on top of him.

She gave a small squeak of surprise, then relaxed, her legs lying outside of his, her breasts flattened against his chest. She said with regret, "We really must get up soon. It's going to be a long day."

"Which means that it should start right." He silenced her with a kiss as his hands slid under her chemise and cupped her buttocks, his fingers kneading deep into the muscles.

As they kissed, she felt him hardening against her belly. She stretched with catlike litheness, enjoying the feel of his muscular body, and the way their bodies fitted together. As the kiss deepened, liquid heat began to burn through her veins.

She was about to roll onto the bed so that they could make love properly when he caught hold of her hips, then sheathed himself inside her with one swift movement. She inhaled sharply. "Oh, my. Now I understand why you put me on top of you."

He smiled and thrust upward. "Education is a wonderful thing."

"It certainly is," she said breathlessly. "L. J. Knight has written a number of provocative essays on the subject."

"As provocative as what we're doing?"

"This isn't provocation," she said with a choke of laughter. "It's blatant lechery."

"Mmm, lechery, my favorite deadly sin." He pushed upward again. She shuddered as heat coursed through her.

Carefully, she sat upright so that she straddled him. Then she peeled off her chemise with a deliberately seductive movement and tossed it over her shoulder. Lucien responded by raising his head and capturing her left breast with his mouth. As he suckled her, she moaned and rocked back and forth, driving him more deeply until he fell back on the pillows, panting for breath.

She leaned forward and trapped his wrists against the bed. Looking down into his face created the pleasing illusion that she was as strong as he. Wanting to see him helpless with longing, she slowly ground her pelvis against him. He gasped, his expression utterly open, every nuance of desire visible as he responded to her.

There was a profound intimacy about making love in the daylight with gazes locked. She discovered a whole range of delicious new ways for male and female to move together. Every movement by one of them was instantly reflected in the other's face, as if they were not two bodies but one.

She bent her head and kissed him with hot-tongued ardor. They were doubly joined, each inside the other. With painful intensity she yearned to merge emotionally as deeply as she had physically, to complete her ragged self with his powerful spirit.

No sooner had the thought formed then a clench of fear drove her back to the safety of humor. Breaking the kiss, she said lightly, "Now I understand a joke I overheard at the theater about a woman riding a man."

She saw a shadow—disappointment?—in his eyes and felt his subtle emotional withdrawal. Sadly, she recognized that in her need to protect herself, she had failed him again.

Swiftly masking his reaction, he answered humor with humor, saying drolly, "You should also be able to think of a whole new interpretation of the old nursery rhyme about riding a cockhorse to Banbury Cross."

"Lucien!" she exclaimed, laughing even as hot color flooded her face. "That's indecent. A cockhorse is just another name for a rocking horse."

"That's what they tell little girls, but little boys know better," he said darkly. "Since you're a writer, you might want to reevaluate phrases you've used without thinking. Cock of the walk. To feel cock-a-hoop. To go off half cocked. To be cocksure. The language is full of double entendres."

"Don't forget Scottish cock-a-leekie soup," she said primly, "where a tough old bird is stewed with a mess of leeks. And very good the cock tastes, too."

She didn't see a double meaning until he laughed. Whole new realms of bawdiness opened before her. Beet red, she closed his mouth with a kiss. Luckily, he took pity on her bruised modesty and teased her no further.

Kit had not known that passion could be so playful. She mastered the art of inflaming him by rolling her hips, and of keeping him simmering on the brink with her stillness. She found that she could behave like a wanton, and he would delight in her abandon. And she almost choked with laughter when he gasped, "Do you smell something burning? I think we're scorching the sheets."

But her levity swiftly died. In the next twenty-four hours everything would change. God willing, her sister would be free, but the price might be that never again would she know such intimacy with Lucien. And there was a very real element of danger; she felt it hovering around Kira like a dark London fog.

With sudden frenzy, she used her newfound skills to bring them both to culmination. There was no room for fear or regret in the violence of fulfillment.

The cure was a fleeting one. As she lay panting in his arms afterward, it was hard to conceal the melancholy that beat in her blood like a drum. *Never again, never again, never again.*

Lucien stared at the ceiling, feeling Kit's heartbeat as strongly as his own. She was pressed against him as pliant as taffy, and they had just made love with searing intensity. That being the case, why did he feel that she had been silently saying good-bye?

The closer they came to Kira, the more Kit detached herself emotionally; that had been blindingly clear when they made love and normal defenses dropped away. The logical result of this would be that when they found Kira, he would lose Kit entirely.

At the beginning he had been confident that physical intimacy would draw them ever closer, but that was no longer true. Though he didn't doubt that he could persuade her into marriage—gratitude was a potent force, and he was a master of subtle manipulations—he was no longer sure marriage would give him what he wanted.

He was no longer sure of anything.

It was a relief when Kit spoke. "I have a horrible feeling that rescuing her will be harder than you think," she said somberly. "Remember that Kira said there were guards? There's danger there, Lucien."

Glad to return to the mundane, he said, "How many guards can there be? We're not talking about laying seige to a sovereign city. The kidnapper is merely one wealthy, perverse man. The chances are there will be a single guard, two at most. If the villain is there himself, that would be three." He shrugged. "Even if there are half a dozen, which is hard to imagine, we'll still prevail because we have Michael."

"I'm awed that he is willing to risk himself when he has no stake in the outcome. Jason and I love Kira, and you are doing this for my sake"—Kit gave him a quick kiss—"for which I am deeply grateful, but Michael is acting from friendship for you and the goodness of his heart. Those are rather abstract motives."

"I suspect he is glad to use his warrior's skills for such a good cause. He would have made a fine medieval knight."

"Slaying dragons and rescuing damsels?"

"Precisely." Lucien looped an arm around her waist, wanting to hold her a little longer.

But time had run out. Kit pushed herself up. "If we hurry, we should be able to catch Lord Ives at Cleo's flat."

"Are they living together?"

"Very nearly." She smiled a little. "He wants to set her up in a larger, more luxurious house, but she keeps refusing. She says she'd rather be her own woman than merely a lord's mistress. It's ironic; she means every word of it, but it might result in him offering marriage to keep her."

"It wouldn't be the first time a lord had chosen his lady from the theater," Lucien remarked. "I've heard the way he speaks of her. They might do very well together." Losing interest in the subject, he caught Kit's wrist and pressed a kiss into her palm. "Twenty-four hours from now we'll be celebrating Kira's freedom. Then we can think about a wedding date. Personally, I favor a special license and an immediate marriage. Would that be agreeable to you?"

He wanted her to react as if she wanted that as much as he did—or if not that much, that at least she did want it. Instead, she gave a gentle smile that could not conceal the sadness in her eyes. "As I promised last night, I will agree to whatever you want."

If this was victory, it tasted remarkably like ashes.

Interlude

After he left, she was so drained that she could scarcely move. She fell into a mercifully dreamless sleep, then awoke with a jerk. How much time had gone by? With so little of that left to her, she shouldn't waste any. After achieving his satisfaction, he had told her with cruel glee precisely what her fate would be. The next time he came, it would be for her life.

Yet what could she do except pace frantically about her plush prison? She had looked for weapons before, but her captor had taken care not to furnish the rooms with anything that might be dangerous. The heavy furniture was bolted to the floor; her cutlery was made of soft, easily bent tin; and the plates and cup were of pewter, which could not be broken into sharp pieces.

She could use the thong of one of the heavier whips to try to strangle her adversary, but she doubted that she had the strength to overpower a grown man. Even if she did, she would be unable to get past the guard who waited outside. She would try, of course, for she would not go tamely to her death, but she had no illusions about her chances of success.

Her gaze fell on the nasty little whipping toy. With sudden rage, she raised it above her head and smashed it to the floor. Then she crushed the figures beneath her booted feet. If only she could do the same with her captor. . . .

A thought occurred to her, and she knelt to study the pieces. A number of metal gears had been exposed. She lifted the largest and tested the sharp-toothed edge. It was hardened steel. Used carefully, it should be able to rasp through wood.

She surveyed her three rooms thoughtfully. Ah, the bedside table. Given enough time, she could cut through one of the legs. When it was loose, she should have enough leverage to wrench it free of the bolt that held it to the floor. If not, well, she would cut the leg off a couple of inches above the floor.

She sat cross-legged by the table and grimly went to work. When she was done, she would have a club heavy enough to bash a man's skull in. That wouldn't be enough to free her, but if she was going to die, she would damned well take her captor with her.

Chapter 35

Cleo was slow to answer her door. When she did, she was laughing and her blond hair tumbled loosely over her shoulders. Seeing Lucien with Kit, she hastily pulled her green velvet wrapper more closely around her. "Cassie, my dear, you're up early this morning," she said in a voice pitched to carry to the back of her flat. Her speaking glance said that she had company. "I'm afraid this isn't the most convenient time for a cup of tea. Shall I come down for a good gossip later?"

Kit said, "We've come to speak to Lord Ives. Is he here? We think we know where my sister is being held, and he might be able to help us."

Cleo's eyes widened. "God be thanked." Raising her voice again, she called, "John, you have visitors."

A coatless Ives emerged from the bedroom, looking mildly surprised. When he saw who was waiting, he smiled and gave Kit a polite bow. "Strathmore, Miss James, what a pleasant surprise. I trust you are well."

"I'm not Cassie James, I'm her twin sister. She's been abducted, and I've been pretending to be her for weeks," Kit said bluntly. "I hope you can help us find her."

Incredulously, he said, "There are two of you who can perform like that?" He scrutinized her face for a long time before giving a slow nod. "I see. Come sit down. I suspect that this might be a long story."

Actually, Kit's description of Kira's disappearance and her own impersonation was brief because she omitted the most interesting details, such as her stalking of the Hellions and the fact that her sister had been located with a pendulum. She didn't even mention her stint as a barmaid, when she had whacked Ives with her bust improver. Since he hadn't recognized her, the subject was best left unmentioned for the sake of his dignity.

After she had outlined the situation, Lucien took over. "We think that Cassie is being held at Castle Raine in Berkshire. Am I correct that it is the site of the Hellion gatherings?"

"It is." Ives gnawed his lip unhappily. "You really think one of the Disciples has abducted her? Surely none of them would need to do anything like that. They can all afford as many women as they want."

Lucien said tersely, "There are men who prefer unwilling women. There are others who will not take no for an answer."

Ives's face become grave. Kit guessed that he was remembering comments that confirmed what Lucien had said. Looking up, he said simply, "What can I do to help?"

"We need to know as much as possible about Castle Raine," Lucien said. "For example, are there dungeons underneath?"

"I believe so, though I've never seen them," Ives replied. "The Disciples have a private sanctuary for their secret rituals. Lesser Hellions like me were never allowed to see that, but I think the entrance must be somewhere behind the chapel."

"Do you know anything about their ceremonies?"

"Not really. However, another junior Hellion stopped by the castle one night because he fancied seeing the ruins by moonlight. He left when he heard a woman screaming." Ives ran his fingers through his hair uneasily. "He thought that he must have imagined it all. He had been drinking, and that place is enough to give one odd fancies. But perhaps he was right."

"When did that occur?"

"Last summer. Around the end of June, I think."

Before Kira had been captured, Lucien thought with relief. But it raised the ugly possibility that other women had been victimized in the past. Since none had ever come forward to accuse the Hellions, the chances were that they had not survived the experience. "How does one get to the castle?"

After Ives had given a precise description of the roads and turns, Lucien asked a series of other questions. However, apart from some details of the layout, he learned nothing that he had not observed himself. At the end he asked, "Do you know if there are any guards there?"

"I believe there is a watchman when it is empty," Ives said. "Also, you might not have noticed the one time you attended, but at the Hellion banquets there are always several male servants dressed as Turkish harem guards. They're called eunuchs, though I'm sure they aren't. Actually, they look like boxers who had retired from the ring. They would make good guards, but I expect they're only there during services."

"I hope you're right." Lucien got to his feet. "Thank you for your help. I don't suppose I need to say that you must not mention this discussion to anyone."

"I won't." Ives stood also. "I assume you're going to go to Castle Raine to try to find the real Cassie James. Do you need another volunteer?"

"Thank you, but no. I've already enlisted several friends."

Ives glanced at Kit. "Is there is any chance of you and your sister performing together?" he asked. "It would be a night to remember."

She shook her head. "The moment she is free, I'm retiring from the stage permanently."

They said their farewells, then left the flat and went down to the carriage. When they were inside, Lucien muttered, "I wish you weren't going to Castle Raine with us."

"I have to be there to find Kira," she pointed out. "If the ruins are extensive, you might never find her without me."

"I know. That doesn't mean I have to like it."

Though her expression was troubled, Kit said lightly, "Why are you worrying? Remember, we have Michael, the warrior angel, leader of the hosts of righteousness, on our side."

Lucien gave a lopsided smile. "True, and there's no reason to expect trouble. We should be able to break in and get your sister out easily, but one never knows. I don't like the idea of exposing you to possible danger."

She sniffed. "*I* wasn't the one who almost fell off a roof from sheer clumsiness."

He smiled and took her hand. "I stand corrected. I'll need you there tonight to save me from myself."

Yet in spite of his joke, his concern did not go away. As they rode back to Strathmore, a couple of lines of Shakespeare kept circling in his head: *"By the pricking of my thumbs, something wicked this way comes."*

The man who had been watching the Marshall Street house for days swore as the actress climbed into the carriage with Strathmore and drove off. His employer had been furious that the abduction attempt had failed, and most insistent that the girl be taken by today. But it bloody wasn't possible. The silly chit hadn't been home in days. She'd finally shown her face, but only a damned fool would try to take her away from that languid earl who had turned out to be so much tougher than he looked.

The watcher shrugged and settled back into concealment in the room he had rented across the street from his quarry's house. He was being paid for his time, so he might as well sit and watch until it was time to report to his employer.

He yawned. If it was him, he'd kidnap a wench with more meat on her bones.

The hulking iron gates of Castle Raine were locked, with no watchman in sight. If there was one, he was probably inside, where it was warm and dry.

Michael had been right about the storm; as Kit waited by the gate, she was shivering from the freezing rain. If the temperature fell much further, the world would turn to ice. God willing, by then they would be safe and Kira would be free.

With a faint metallic jangle, Lucien bent over the lock of the man-sized door that was set into the larger gate. She could not see in detail what he was doing, but it seemed to involve a key ring with a broad assortment of keys and metal picks. She was not surprised when the door swung open with a faint squeal that vanished quickly amid the sounds of wind and rain.

Behind her Jason Travers said with a hint of laughter, "Am I going to have to learn to do that if I want to be a proper earl?"

"The real beauty of being a British peer," Lucien said as he ushered the others through, then closed the door behind them, "is that one can be as eccentric as one wishes."

"The issue isn't your eccentricity, Luce, but your unfortunate criminal tendencies," Michael said gently. The other men chuckled.

Her nerves strung drum-tight, Kit felt like swatting them for their frivolity. She refrained because she suspected that levity was a masculine way of coping with tension. It was easier to be female and allowed to show her fear. Lucien must have guessed at her state of mind, for he kept a light hand at the back of her waist as they moved soundlessly along the edge of the drive toward the main buildings.

The objective, writer part of her mind was taking notes, for this raid was giving her a sense of what war must be like. All four of them wore dark clothing, Kit in her burglar outfit again. Even the horses tethered in a nearby thicket were invisible because Michael had put blacking on the white markings that might have drawn attention at night.

She would never have thought of that; it was a small, comforting reminder of how much experience Michael had in covert missions. With his flinty expression, eyes that missed nothing, and a well-used carbine rifle slung over his shoulder, he was a formidable sight. Armed with pistols, Lucien and Jason looked equally dangerous. Though Kit prayed that violence would be unnecessary, if it occurred they were well-prepared.

Lucien had asked if she wanted a pistol, but she had refused with a shudder. It was one of the ways in which she differed from her twin; Kira was an excellent shot while Kit had always flatly refused to touch a gun, and it was too late to learn now.

The chapel was a dim outline, a blacker bulk against a stormy sky. Halfway there, she gasped and came to a stop, her fingers pressed to her temples.

"What is it?" Lucien asked in a low voice.

"She's here." Kit's voice trembled at the confirmation that her intuition had been correct. *"She's really here!"*

Jason made a sound that demonstrated how much his casual manner must be costing him. Cooler, Michael asked, "Can you tell what direction?"

Kit concentrated with an effort that made her temples throb. "Directly ahead, in the vicinity of the chapel. Below it, I think."

Heart hammering, she hastened toward the building, scarcely aware of her surroundings or the rain in her face. She reached the chapel and was fumbling for the knob when Lucien snapped, "Don't open the doors! There's light showing below."

She glanced down and saw that he was right.

As impatient as Kit, Jason said, "It's probably only the watchman. We can take care of one man."

"No doubt," Lucien replied. "Nevertheless, let's find another entrance. I believe that around to the right there's a side door that leads into the banquet hall."

They skirted the building until they found it. Lucien went to work on the lock, his movements so careful that Kit heard nothing even though she was less than six feet away. There was a faint click. He eased the door open, then ghosted through.

After a moment of listening he motioned for the others to follow. The banquet hall was a large room with the shapes of tables and chairs dimly visible in the faint glow that came from the far left corner. Wordlessly, he led the way toward the light, moving around the edge of the room to avoid the furniture.

At the entrance to the hall he pressed on Kit's shoulder in a silent order to stay. Leaving Jason with her, Lucien and Michael moved forward along the passage that went to the chapel.

The wait seemed endless. She clenched her hands into fists and forced herself to be still. Then, almost inaudible over the sounds of rain splattering against the windows, she heard a muffled cry, followed by a thud. A couple of minutes later, the men returned, Michael carrying a lighted taper that he used to ignite the two lamps Jason was carrying. The glass was shielded so that only narrow beams were emitted, but they were a great improvement over the dark.

"All clear," Lucien said. "There was only one guard."

"You didn't . . ." Kit said nervously.

"Merely knocked senseless and tied up," Michael assured her. "I never kill anyone without a reason."

She wondered if his nonchalance was bone-dry humor, then decided it wasn't. He had lived in a very different world from hers. As the men began searching through the small rooms and corridors that lay behind the chapel, she bent her head and probed inward to locate her sister.

She gasped when she succeeded. Kira's energy was scalding—not only close, but terrified. Though Kit tried to send a message of reassurance, she was unsuccessful; Kira was too distressed to feel her sister's presence.

Kit raised her head again, aware of a deep thrumming at the edge of her hearing. Unable to identify it, she went to Lucien. "What is that low, rumbling noise?"

He cocked his head and listened. From his expression she saw that he had not noticed it until she spoke.

"Machinery," he said with a frown. "Something like a steam boiler, I think. A very large one." If machines were running, there must be other people about. Kit had been right; this was going to be more difficult than anticipated.

"Over here," Jason called softly from around the corner.

When the other three reached him, Jason opened the door that he had discovered. Steps led down to an illuminated corridor and the sound of chanting voices filled the stairwell.

Lucien eased the door shut. "Damnation, the Disciples are holding one of their rituals tonight."

"Today is the winter solstice," Jason said tautly. "They probably play at paganism by celebrating the change of season."

Lucien thought back. "Very likely. It was around Midsummer Day when Ives's friend heard the screaming here."

"Didn't the Druids practice human sacrifice?" Michael asked.

Kit gave a gasp of horror and moved to open the door, ready to hurl herself downward. Lucien intercepted her. "Wait," he said sharply as he caught her upper arm. "Stay close to me."

She looked at him blindly, and he guessed that she was linked with her sister's mind again. He gave her a little shake. "Kit, if we are to rescue Kira, you must stay with us mentally as well as physically."

She gulped, then nodded, her eyes clearing. "I understand."

Michael opened the door again, then led the way down the stairs. The others followed, first Jason, then Kit, with Lucien bringing up the rear. The worn steps and rough walls were the coarse stone of medieval construction. As they descended, the chanting became much louder. A single deep voice would intone a phrase, followed by a chorused response. The language was largely unintelligible, but might be a bastardized form of Latin.

The thrumming intensified as well, vibrating through the stone. With every step, the sense of menace increased until Lucien wanted to jump from his skin.

He suspected that his unease was less a premonition of disaster than concern for Kit. Though he was not a stranger to mortal peril, in the past he had risked only his own life. Now he was far more worried about Kit's safety than he had ever been about his own.

It didn't help that Kit seemed ready to shatter from nerves. The bond between them might not be as close as he wished, but it was strong enough for him to be affected by her emotions. The depth of her fear struck haunting echoes of the desperate panic he had felt when trying to save Elinor.

His mouth tightened. He had failed his sister, but he would not fail again.

The corridor at the bottom of the steps ran in both directions, while the stairs turned and continued downward. To the right was more of the old stonework, but the chanting and light came from the left, where the passage seemed to have been carved directly from the chalk core of the hill.

Lucien touched Kit's shoulder inquisitively. She grimaced and pointed at the blank wall. Apparently, Kira was ahead of them and it wasn't clear which would be the best way to reach her.

Soft-footed, Michael went to investigate the light and disappeared around a corner. A few moments later he came back into view, surprise on his face, and made a gesture that ordered both caution and silence. The other three went after him.

What they found was astonishing. The corridor led to a shadowy wooden gallery that ran around all four sides of a huge chamber. It appeared to be a natural cavern that had been shaped into a roughly cubical space. Moisture glistened on the walls from the rain that was saturating the hill. Well below them, in the center of the chamber, stood the Disciples, garbed in scarlet robes and vaguely ecclesiastical headdresses. Lucien was surprised to see that there were only thirteen. The eerie echoes of the chanting had made it sound like a much larger group.

In each corner of the chamber stood a burly man in black robes and turban, holding a broadsword upright before him. Ives had been right; the guards looked like retired pugilists.

Most startling of all were the statues, a double circle within the square of the chamber. There were easily thirty figures, all of them larger than life, perhaps seven feet tall. Each effigy depicted a weapon-wielding warrior, with no two alike. A Roman gladiator with a short sword and round shield stood opposite a fierce African with a vicious throwing knife. A bearded Viking with a battle-ax snarled across the room at a menacing Turk with a scimitar while a foot soldier with a halberd glared at a mace-bearing medieval knight.

Made of metal and painted to look real, they were unnervingly lifelike. Lucien had a nightmarish vision of the effigies coming alive and using their weapons to destroy anyone who tried to pass through the rings to reach the Disciples.

In the very center of the chamber, standing between

two bonfires, stood the leader, the only one facing toward the intruders. It was Mace, his arms stretched high over his head. Above him hung a large chandelier and behind was a large, flat stone altar. Lucien's stomach turned; the altar looked as if it was designed for human sacrifice.

Kit must have guessed that, for she gave a shudder. Luckily, there was no sign of Kira. If she was scheduled to be the sacrificial victim of some barbaric rite, it hadn't happened yet.

Kit stepped back and pointed downward and back the way they had come. Kira must be on the same level as the ceremony. After a last look at the bizarre scene, Lucien followed the others as they returned to the stairwell and descended again.

The stairs ended on the next level. This time a passage led straight, as well as to right and left. Kit moved confidently into the middle corridor. Candles burned in niches along the walls, illuminating devils' masks that had been carved into the soft chalk. They leered with life, the faces glistening sweatily with the moisture exuding from the stone.

As they followed Kit, Lucien began to believe they might be able to extricate Kira without alerting the Disciples. That would be the safest course, though Lucien would regret not having the chance to wreak violence on the arrogant bastard responsible for the abduction. He comforted himself with the thought that justice might be delayed, but it would be done. He would make sure of that.

Kit was several feet ahead of him, looking neither left nor right as she strode along. The other two were behind, keeping a sharp eye on their surroundings. Ahead of Kit, Lucien saw that a band of darker stones crossed the corridor floor. Concealed within were holes several inches square. The dark band ran up the walls and continued across the ceiling. As he wondered what the purpose might be, Kit stepped on one of the dark stones.

The stone shifted with a clink, and all hell broke loose.

Chapter 36

Heavy bells began clanging, reverberating through the passage with ear-numbing power. Kit froze, her head whipping around to see what had happened.

Lucien heard a grating sound and looked up. A heavy iron portcullis was starting to fall from a slot masked by the dark stones—and Kit was standing directly below. He shouted her name and hurled himself forward, knocking her beyond the pointed stakes of the plummeting gate. She pitched to the floor, and he came tumbling after her.

With a boom that echoed through the passage, knocking chips of chalk from the ceiling, the portcullis crashed into the stone floor. Something grazed his right ankle, and he looked back to see that he had not jumped quite far enough to clear the path of the gate.

By sheer luck his leg lay between two of the viciously pointed stakes. A few inches to either side and his ankle would have been impaled, pinning him to the floor. As it was, his foot was caught in the narrow space between the floor and the bottom bar of the portcullis.

The bells were still tolling, and in the cavern a furious voice bellowed, "Intruders have entered. Find them!"

Bloody hell! Lucien wrenched his foot free, then scrambled up. If the portcullis couldn't be raised, Michael and Jason would be trapped between it and the angry Disciples.

Michael had already seen the danger. He heaved at the iron gate, then shook his head. "We'll never move this thing. Luce, you and Kit keep going." Calmly he unslung his carbine and cocked the hammer. "Travers and I can handle that lot."

Kit had risen and was staring at the other men, her face stricken. Lucien grabbed her arm. "We can't do anything. Don't worry, they're armed. Our job is to find Kira."

Kit gulped and nodded, then turned to continue along the corridor. "She's very close now."

The passage turned left. Fifty yards later, it split into four narrower tunnels that wound out of sight like Medusa's locks. Kit stopped and stared at the new obstacle.

Lucien asked, "Do you have any idea which of these passages we should take?"

Before she could answer, an exchange of gunshots and a shout of pain sounded behind them. Kit caught his arm, her face agonized. "Oh, God, that sounded like Jason. We must go back to help them."

"I'm not sure it was him." He frowned. "And I'll be damned if I'll take you into a tunnel where bullets are flying."

"Then go alone," she urged. "I'll stay here. Even if you can't get past the portcullis, you can shoot through it."

More shots, and another scream. Lucien winced. "Very well, I'll go look. Stay here—don't even *think* of moving unless someone attacks you from one of these small tunnels. If that happens, come for me."

As soon as she nodded, he raced down the tunnel, then rounded the corner, keeping low. The skirmish had generated eye-stinging clouds of acrid smoke, but once he blinked his eyes clear, he saw that Michael and Jason were unhurt. Both were crouched by the wall, weapons ready, while more distant figures were retreating. A black-turbaned guard lay unmoving on the floor, and a trail of blood showed that at least one fleeing man had been wounded.

Deciding that his friends had the situation well in hand, he pivoted and returned to Kit. As soon as he swung around the corner, he uttered a curse so blistering it should have brought down more fragments of chalk.

She was gone.

When Lucien left, Kit leaned against the wall, glad for

a chance to catch her breath. But when she relaxed, she became horribly aware of the clamoring bells. The clanging stabbed through her, triggering a panic more real than the outside world.

Oh, God, the bells must mean that he's coming for me! He said it would be tonight. I must be ready.

Kit pressed her hands to her temples, knowing that she was in Kira's mind, Kira's fear. Panting, she struggled to escape her twin's terror, for she could not afford to lose herself now.

She thought of Lucien, and managed to separate herself from her sister. When she was clearer, she sent out a mental call. *Where are you? We're very near. Show me how to find you, love!*

But she couldn't break through. Her twin's anguish was as blazing and impenetrable as a house on fire, and it threatened to drag Kit in again. Once more she struggled to maintain her clarity, but before she could free herself, fear struck again. This time it came from another source. In some impossible way, she could feel the abductor moving toward her sister.

Reason collapsed. Blindly, beyond thought, Kit shoved away from the wall and darted into the farthest left tunnel. In her head was a hazy mental map that showed her sister as a still white light and the abductor an oozing mass of darkness approaching from the left.

Her tunnel ended in a larger, brighter passage. She entered and swung left, then came face-to-face with Lord Mace. Tall and scarlet clad, with barbaric chains crossing his chest and supporting weapons at his side, he was a fearsome sight. He stopped dead when he saw her, astonishment on his narrow face.

Her chest heaving from her running, she said furiously, "I won't let you touch her again, you monster."

His eyes lit up. "Well, bless my wicked soul, it's the other one, Cassie the Second. Truly heaven is smiling on me." He began stalking toward her. "It appears that I shall be able to experience my fantasy after all."

Only then did Kit's mind throw off the dazed instinct that had brought her here. Good God, she had been insane to leave Lucien behind. Now she must confront a vicious madman without a weapon. She hadn't a prayer of defeating him.

But she could slow him down. The longer he was delayed, the better the chance that Lucien would find either her or Kira.

Knowing Mace would not expect her to attack, she hurled herself at him. Her sudden assault knocked him from his feet. She fell sprawling on top. Before she could extricate herself, he grabbed her shoulders and rolled over, trying to pin her beneath him. "What a quick creature you are," he said with queer, bone-chilling calm. "Every bit the equal of your twin."

She spat in his face.

A wild skirmish followed, with her kicking, punching, scratching, and kneeing. She hurt him and found savage pleasure that it was not the sort of pain he enjoyed. But her best efforts could do no more than delay the inevitable. When he slammed a fist into her solar plexus, she was stunned to the point where she could not resist when he tied her wrists behind her back with a handkerchief.

Jerking her to her feet, he said conversationally, "I had even prepared private quarters for you in anticipation of your abduction. Unfortunately, the men I hired were unequal to the task. I should have participated myself, as I did with your sister. But never mind, you are here now."

Half concealed in the folds of his robe were a scabbard on one side and a holstered pistol on the other. Though she guessed that the weapons were worn for ceremonial purposes, they were lethally real. He pulled the pistol from the holster and touched the cold barrel to the nape of her neck. "Come along, Cassie the Second. After you have changed into the costume I had prepared for you, it will be time for the ceremony. There you will see your sister again. I hope she will appreciate your gallantry in throwing your life away to find her. Most touching. I wonder if my brother, Roderick, would sacrifice himself for my sake. Somehow I doubt it, though he has always been happy to pimp for me."

Teeth gritted, Kit snapped, "You should give up and get out while you can, Mace. My companions will not be so easily captured as I was, and if I am injured, they will want justice."

He stopped and unlocked a door on the left side of the passage. "If they aren't dead yet, they will be soon. They are outnumbered and outgunned, and they know nothing of the traps I have scattered throughout my little subterranean kingdom."

He took a candle from one of the sconces, then with the pistol waved her into the room. When he lit a lamp, she saw it was furnished as a bedroom. He opened a cabinet and pulled out a collection of black garments. Kit recognized it as the decadent kind of outfit she had seen in her dreams of Kira.

He drew a curved, wickedly gleaming knife from the scabbard that hung opposite the pistol and sliced through her bonds. "Put these on," he ordered.

"No," she said flatly.

He brandished the knife so that the blade flashed ominously. "I would quite enjoy cutting off your clothing and dressing you by force."

The thought of him touching her intimately made her want to gag. Drawing on her acting skills, she said calmly, "That would be time-consuming. Won't your fellow perverts tire of waiting?"

He frowned. "You're right, I shouldn't neglect my guests. Still, I must insist on the costume. You have to look exactly like your sister when you go to the altar."

When he took a step toward her, she had to fight the instinct to bolt. Resigning herself, she said, "I'll put the outfit on voluntarily if you'll wait outside."

"A reasonable compromise. I can wrestle with you as much as I want later. Just make sure that you lace the costume tightly." He ran his tongue over his lips. "The effect is most enticing."

After he left the room and closed the door, Kit collapsed on a chair, shaking. As always when she was deeply distressed, she reached out for help. But this time she did not go to Kira, who was near the breaking point herself, but to Lucien. The thought of his strength and steadfastness brought her a measure of calm.

She got to her feet and surveyed the room in hopes

of finding a potential weapon, but there was nothing. Nor could the door be bolted or barricaded from the inside.

Lips tight, she began dressing as slowly as she could.

When Lucien found that Kit was missing, he reserved his choicest curses for himself. He should have known better than to leave her when she was in danger of sliding into that trancelike, sister-focused state.

She had to have entered one of the four passages, but which one? Mentally crossing his fingers, he went into the second from the left. It wound sinuously through the chalk, with gruesome, catacomb-style niches filled with animal bones.

Where the *hell* was Kit?

He rounded a bend and collided with someone coming the other way. Not Kit, unfortunately, but a burly guard with a pistol who must be on his way to investigate the gunshots. The impact knocked them both off-balance. By the time the guard recovered enough to raise his weapon, it was too late. Lucien kicked the gun from the other man's hand, then smashed him in the jaw with a hard right and an even harder left.

The guard dropped to the floor, unconscious. After confiscating the pistol and ammunition, Lucien tied the fellow up with his own shabby cravat. Then he stood and examined his surroundings. He was in a small chamber with another passage coming from the left. A table, two chairs, and a lamp were set in the center of the room, with cards splayed across the table, interrupted in the middle of a hand of solitaire.

No sign of Kit, but there was a heavy, iron-bound door on the opposite wall. He searched the guard and found a large brass key. It snicked neatly into the lock. As he turned the key, he prayed that Kira was inside. If she was, they could head for safety as soon as they located Kit again. She couldn't be far away.

The door swung open and he warily stepped inside, pistol in hand. He found himself in a well-furnished room that might have been a regular parlor except for the lack of windows. One door led to a bedroom while the other opened to a stone-walled dungeon. It matched Kit's description exactly.

As he moved forward, he saw a flicker of movement from the corner of his eye. He turned to see Lady Kristine Travers. For an instant, shock immobilized him. The fact that Kit and Kira were identical twins had been at the heart of this mission. Yet it was still deeply disorienting to see a woman who looked exactly like Kit, but who was at the same time a stranger.

And while he stared, she tried to bash his skull in.

Lucien reflexively dived sideways so that her cudgel only grazed his right arm, knocking the pistol from his hand. Swift as a cat, she wound up to try again, her gray eyes wild.

He backed across the parlor, saying urgently, "Kira, put that thing down. I'm a friend of Kit's."

She froze, poised between belief and lethal violence.

"My name is Lucien Fairchild." He spoke soothingly, as to a frightened child. "Kit is somewhere nearby, too. She got lost while looking for you. Let's go find her."

Voice shaking, Kira said, "Kit is *here*?"

He nodded. "I've misplaced her in the maze of tunnels out there, but she can't be far." He stepped forward and took the club from her unresisting hand.

For a moment she rubbed her temples exactly the way Kit did. "I . . . I'm sorry I hit you," she said, her voice cracking. "I thought you were Lord Mace."

"Mace is the one who abducted you?"

She nodded. "He saw me perform and became obsessed. When I refused to become his mistress, he kidnapped me after a performance. Since then, he's been forcing me to . . . to . . ."

He stopped her before she could break down again. Though she seemed physically well, months of captivity had left her emotionally fragile.

"You don't have to explain," he said quietly. "Kit learned the general outlines through her dreams of you."

That produced a faint smile. "She would, bless her."

He studied Kira's face. The resemblance between the twins was truly amazing. The same slim figure and soft brown hair, the same gray eyes and pure, striking profile that had enabled him to identify Kit again and again.

But there were also differences. Kira's face and lips were a fraction fuller, and the fact that she was right-handed had given a subtly different set to her features. And, of course, her spirit was uniquely her own.

He had also never seen Kit wearing a short black satin chemise laced together with leather thongs that revealed dramatic slashes of creamy flesh, or knee-high boots and lace stockings. However, he knew that Kit would look as alluring as her twin did.

Seeing the direction of his glance, Kira said wryly, "I swore that if I ever got out of here alive, I'd be happy to wear white muslin for the rest of my life."

He smiled. Obviously she was beginning to get her wits about her. "Do you have a cloak? The weather is wretched, and we'll have a ride of several miles after we leave."

Kira darted into the other room and returned with a sable cape fit for a princess. As she threw it around her shoulders, she examined Lucien as thoroughly as he had studied her. "Are you the reason Kit has been feeling happy lately?"

Startled, he said, "I'd like to think so. You can feel her emotions the way she can yours?"

"Not so well as she does, but I usually get the general drift. Lately she's been horribly anxious about me, but there have also been flashes of intense joy."

Interesting, very interesting. Putting that aside for a more appropriate time, he asked, "Is there anything else you want to take? The sooner we get out of here and find Kit, the better. Unfortunately, the Disciples are holding a ritual tonight, and they've discovered our little rescue operation."

Kira's face paled, and he saw that fear was still very near the surface. "The last time he was here, Mace explained that I was to be the main attraction for a gang rape by all of the Disciples," she said unevenly. "Afterward, there would be a private ceremony for him and his closest associates. The whole time I've been captive, he has been building toward tonight. Though he loved playing the role of sexual slave, the ultimate goal was for me to die at his hands."

Lucien caught her gaze with his. "Hang on a little longer, Kira," he said forcefully. "You can't fall apart just yet."

She closed her eyes, looking painfully brittle. Opening them again, she said, "I'll manage." She gave a crooked smile and brushed her hair with the back of her hand in a gesture that was purely her own. "There's nothing here I want. Except . . ."

She crossed the room and opened a cabinet. Inside were whips of different weights and materials. Taking the heaviest, she explained, "In case I need a weapon on the way out."

He retrieved the pistol, then ushered her out the door. In the guard room, he said, "I came from that direction, but I'm not sure we can leave the same way because a portcullis is blocking the main corridor that lies beyond. Also, Kit must be on this side of it. Do you know where that other passage goes?"

She shrugged. "Haven't the foggiest, but we might as well find out."

They entered the broader passage. Lucien hoped to God that they would find Kit quickly, because his anxiety about her was growing by the minute.

Chapter 37

A good thing the enemy was retreating, for the smoke made Michael choke so badly that for a time he was incapable of firing. When he could speak again, he said, "Close quarters are rotten for fighting—give me an open field any day."

"I prefer shooting cannon from a ship myself." Jason reloaded his pistol. "Lots of fresh air, and the enemy keeps his distance. Shall we get out of this corridor before they rally?"

"Excellent idea." After another fit of coughing, Michael gasped, "Back up to the gallery. There was a door on the far side that might take us down on the other side of the portcullis."

Moving fast, they retraced their path to the cross corridor. They were about to head for the stairs when they heard angry voices in that direction. The guards were planning another assault. Since the sanctuary, complete with Disciples, was the other way, they darted across the intersection into the corridor that was a continuation of the one they had come from.

When they were safely across and out of sight, they halted to consider the next step. Jason said, "Shall we try the stairs anyhow? I suspect that we can outfight any of this lot."

"Probably," Michael agreed, "but we came here to perform a rescue, not start a war. Let's see where this passage goes first. There's air moving through, so it's not a dead end. With luck, we'll find another way up or around to where Luce and the ladies are. This place may be a bloody maze, but it can't cover that great an area."

Jason nodded, and they went ahead with the lantern

that had survived the attack. As Michael had hoped, the passage turned and started to double back on itself. The soft chalk in this section was shored up with wooden props. As a mine owner, he recognized the technique. The stone must be particularly bad here, for rough boards had been laid for a floor.

He frowned. There was something odd about the prop ahead . . .

Because he was studying it, he saw the flash of light as something began whipping toward him at head level. He dived for the floor. "Down!"

The American followed his lead just in time to avoid being decapitated by a blade that swung across the corridor parallel to the floor. It looked like a giant reaper's sickle, with a blade sharp enough to cut an intruder in half.

"Christ!" Jason said breathlessly. "This place is full of nasty little devices. How did we set off this one?"

Michael watched as the blade swung back and disappeared into a slot in the wall. It must have been propelled by a giant spring concealed behind the wooden strut. "These boards weren't put down to cover holes, but to conceal the trigger. I think this light-colored board moved when I stepped on it."

He shoved on it with the heel of his hand. Again the blade swung over their heads with a wicked hiss. After it had folded demurely back into place, Michael said, "The triggers have to be obvious enough so that whoever devised these traps can avoid them himself. If we're careful, we should be able to spot them."

"I wish I shared your touching faith." Jason got cautiously to his feet and stepped over the trigger board. "Blockade running was never like this."

"One of the things I like about Lucien is that life is never dull in his vicinity." Michael stood and raised the lantern, which he had managed to avoid breaking. "Shall we see what lies ahead?"

Travers sketched a mock salute. " *'Lay on, Macduff, and damn'd be him that first cries, 'Hold, enough!' '* "

Kit tried to dally, but Mace forced the issue by opening the door before she had finished dressing. His avid expression made her hastily pull the high black boots over her lace stockings. She dared not push him too far. Though Mace might have enjoyed being whipped in the past, tonight he seemed primed for straightforward rape.

When she stood, he ordered, "Turn around."

She obeyed slowly, afraid of what a quick movement might do to her costume, which was the most indecent garment imaginable. In front it was slashed to the navel with leather thongs crisscrossing over bare flesh to hold the fabric together. The arrangement left her breasts and midriff half exposed. Similar slashes revealed provocative swathes of her backside. She felt more naked than if she had been truly nude.

Mace stared at the bright butterfly that was visible through the black lace stocking. "Wonderful! Even the tattoo is the same. But the laces are too loose. I'll tighten them myself."

She tried to back away when he approached her, but he whipped his knife from the scabbard and touched the tip to her throat. "Hold still," he hissed.

For some reason the knife, with its ability to slash and mutilate, was more frightening than the pistol. She stood rigid while he sheathed the blade, then grasped the thongs that laced the chemise over her breasts. He pulled them so tightly her that nipples showed clearly under the tight black satin. She could scarcely breathe, and the thongs would leave a lattice of crimson welts in her bare flesh, if she lived long enough.

"Yet surely you are not quite identical." He tied the bow, but instead of moving away he began to skim his hands over the satin-covered curves of her body. The heat of his palms on her breasts made her flesh recoil.

"Before I am done, I will discover the differences," he said huskily. "Since your sister is the wicked twin, I suppose you are the good one." He pinched her nipples with brutal force. "In some ways, that is even more titillating."

She bit her lip to keep from whimpering. She would not give him the satisfaction of showing her disgust, for she sensed that he would revel in a woman's fear.

He stepped back with visible regret. "Later. Now we must collect Cassie the First."

He bound her wrists behind her with a wide scarlet ribbon the exact shade of fresh blood. Then he gestured with his pistol for her to precede him.

The place was a rabbit warren of passages. After several confusing turns, they emerged into a guardroom containing a massive door. Slumbering peacefully on the floor was a bound man.

Mace's face darkened. "Stupid fool!"

Keeping Kit beside him, he threw open the door and gestured for her to enter first. She knew instantly that it had been Kira's prison; the very air was saturated with her twin's essence. But she was gone now; Lucien must have found her. Kit would have crowed with relief if she hadn't feared that doing so would trigger Mace's violence.

He swore viciously, then snarled, "I shall take you to the sanctuary. My associates can play with you while I recover your sister. Now *move*." He jabbed the pistol barrel into her ribs.

He gave her no opportunity to escape during the nightmare journey. As they neared the large chamber, she heard the buzz of excited voices. The talk ceased as soon as she stepped inside the sanctuary. Every man's gaze went to Kit. She wanted to cringe and cover herself with her hands. Since that was impossible, she thought of a play she had seen about Anne Boleyn, who went to the scaffold with unshakeable dignity.

She withdrew into herself as far as possible, as if she were on stage. This wasn't real, it was only a play. Head high, she walked toward the altar. The two roaring fires made the air very warm, which was welcome given her skimpy attire. She couldn't think of a single other advantage to her situation.

Her path took her through the rings of warrior statues Close up, they seemed even larger than they had appeared from above. She passed between a Red Indian with a spear and a mailed Crusader, without looking up But she could not ignore the crowd of scarlet-robed men with their hungry eyes and obscene comments. Worse some of them fondled her with outrageous intimacy as she walked through the group. She kept moving, her eyes straight ahead, until she reached the altar.

All of her chief suspects were at the forefront of the group. The men behind were other Hellions, but none had seemed important when she was investigating, and that was still true now; they were simply followers. The evil here came from the leaders—it was written on their faces.

Lord Nunfield and Roderick Harford studied her with frank lust. More detached, Chiswick drawled, "So you managed to engage Cassie James. Excellent, Mace. She's enough to titillate even the most jaded palate."

Sir James Westley said cheerily, "I prefer 'em a little meatier myself, but then, we've never sacrificed a female of such distinguished achievements. She'll do splendidly."

Voice portentous, Mace said, "It's even better than you think, gentlemen. This is not Cassie James, but her identical twin sister. Surely you have all dreamed of having twins, equally lovely, equally helpless." His lightless eyes flared with menace. "The real Cassie has become lost in the corridors, so I must go find her."

That aroused another babble of comments. Detachedly, Kit observed that all of the men wore the ceremonial scabbards and holsters. She wondered if the knives would be used on her.

Mace beckoned for his brother to come forward. "Take charge of this one while I find the other," he said in a low voice.

Harford frowned. "I've seen her before." He snapped his fingers. "This is the slut who tried to rob me at the ball!"

"Really?" Mace looked at Kit with respect. "So you braved Blackwell Abbey in your search for your sister. You're a bold wench." Turning back to his brother, he said, "Strathmore came with her, and he seems to have freed the sister. Did you manage to eliminate the other two men?"

Harford scowled. "Afraid not—the guards turned coward under fire, and while they were getting their nerve back, Strathmore's cronies slipped away. They're being hunted, but it could take a while to corner them."

Mace frowned. "I'll keep an eye out while I look for Strathmore and the twin. Since they don't know the passages, it shouldn't take long to find them. When I do, I'll take care of him and bring her here so we can start our ceremony."

Kit gave silent thanks that Mace seemed to be another one who underestimated Lucien. But it was unluckily true that Mace's knowledge of the terrain gave him an enormous advantage.

She opened her mind enough to search for her sister. As soon as she did, her heart spasmed with fear.

Lucien and Kira were close, dangerously close.

The twists and turns of the passages were hopelessly confusing. As they searched for a way through, Lucien's anxiety kept building. Then Kira stopped dead, her face ashen. "Dear God, he's got Kit!"

Her words confirmed Lucien's worst fears. "You're sure?"

"Positive." Kira pointed ahead and to the right. "She's that way." Her face crumpled and tears showed in her eyes. "She's frightened half to death."

The same hazy expression that he had seen so often on Kit's face was now clouding Kira's. Knowing he must catch her before she slid away, he asked, "Has she been physically harmed?"

"I don't think so." Kira exhaled, her face clearing a little. "It's my fault Kit is in danger. If I hadn't gone on the stage, this wouldn't have happened. Kit was right to object—she's always right."

He took her elbow, saying firmly, "You can feel guilty later. Now we have to find Kit and get her away from Mace."

Making a supreme effort, Kira focused herself and started forward. But knowing Kit's general direction was a far cry from finding the route. The corridors twisted infuriatingly, leading to dead ends, shrines to gargoylelike deities, and more bones. Neither of them spoke, for Kira needed all of her concentration to track her sister.

Finally they turned a corner and saw a pair of tapestry curtains ahead. On the other side was brighter light and rumbling voices. Lucien halted. "I think we've found Mace's sanctuary and his beastly associates. Wait here while I take a closer look."

Kira bit her lip. "Kit is that way."

"Yes, but not necessarily in the sanctuary itself," he said as he led her back around the corner. "If she isn't there, it will be safer to try to go around. Wait here and *don't move*." He hated leaving her, but if he was seen and captured, at least she would have some chance of escaping into the tunnels.

Remembering that Kit had said her sister was a good shot, he pulled out the pistol he had taken from the guard. "You should be safe for the few moments it will take me to investigate, but would you like this, just in case?"

She nodded and tucked her whip under her arm, accepting the gun with visible relief. As she expertly broke open the pistol to check that it was in firing condition, she said, "It's good to have a weapon after months of being helpless."

Feeling reasonably sure she would be safe, he rounded the corner and silently went down the passage to the tapestry curtains. He parted them a crack and looked through. As he had guessed, it was the sanctuary, complete with warrior statues, bonfires, and scarlet-clad Disciples. His gaze went immediately to Mace, who was striding arrogantly away from the center of the circle.

If Mace was present, Kit must be as well. He scanned the circle, and found her standing in front of the altar with Roderick Harford's knife at her breast. Even though she was dressed exactly like Kira, she managed to look as dignified as Marie Antoinette surrounded by peasants.

The sight sent berserker rage flaring through him. He wanted to hurl himself into the room and dismember every man there. Reminding himself that mindless impulse wouldn't save her, he clamped down his fury and weighed the possible courses of action.

There were at least a dozen men there, all carrying knives and pistols. Though they might not all be party to the full spectrum of Mace's evil, none could be counted on as allies. It took only a few seconds to reach the grim conclusion that there was nothing he could do that might not endanger Kit.

Intuition said that the longer she was in the hands of Mace and Harford, the greater the risk to her. Therefore, he must act immediately. A pity that Michael and Jason weren't here, but he dared not wait to find them.

There was a chance, slim but better than none, that he could free Kit by pure effrontery. Pistol in hand, he pushed aside the tapestry and stepped into the light. Pitching his voice so that it would dominate the chamber, he barked, "Let her go, Harford."

Everyone turned and stared at him with surprise. Kit's gaze met his, stark with relief. He hoped to God that her faith in him wasn't misplaced.

Recovering quickly from his shock, Mace said jovially, "Ah, Lucifer. You've come to join us. I was afraid that because of the weather, you might not get here in time to play your role." As he spoke, he edged back toward the altar.

"Stop pretending," Lucien said flatly. "This is no game, but criminal folly. If you don't release her, you or your brother will die." He started to move forward through the ring of statues.

Eyes sparkling with malice, Mace cried, "The time has come to seal the circle!" He leaned down and wrenched on a long lever that rose from the floor next to the altar.

The statues came alive.

Chapter 38

As Mace threw the lever, the chamber filled with the rumble of grinding gears and hissing steam. Instantly, the mechanical warriors were transformed into a race of ancient giants, swinging their weapons with vicious power.

The gladiator chopped down with his sword, the Viking cleaved the air with a battle-ax—and the knight, a yard away, slashed his sword straight at Lucien.

If it hadn't taken the mechanism a few moments to creak into motion, he would have died on the spot. As it was, he realized the danger and ducked barely in time.

Mace roared with laughter, as if the near-fatality was a great joke. "You of all men should appreciate my steam-powered warriors, Lucifer," he called. "There has never been anything like them in the history of the world!"

Lucien swore to himself as he retreated. The thrumming machinery and unusual warmth now made sense, for there had to be giant steam boilers nearby, with pipes running under the floor to power the movements of the statues. Each of the weapons swung rapidly back and forth through a single arc. Any single blade could be avoided, but the rings of figures had been placed so that the danger areas overlapped, some high, some low.

The arrangement completely blocked passage into the circle. Going around the path of the sword would put him in the range of the battle-ax on one side or a scimitar on the other. It was brilliant, and Lucien damned his enemy to hell for creating it.

"Very clever, Mace," he snapped. "But I can still shoot between the statues. Release her!"

"Do you want blood, Lucifer? If you don't cooperate,

the girl's will flow." Mace waved a grandiose hand at his brother.

His expression full of vicious excitement, Harford delicately drew the point of his blade in a line below Kit's collarbone. Scarlet drops of blood formed along the cut. She made a small, desperate sound, instantly suppressed.

Lucien felt his face go white. The glitter in Mace's eyes confirmed Kira's story; he was primed for the explosive release of sexual violence that he had planned for tonight. His brother must share his madness, for the air had the chancy, volatile aura of danger sometimes felt before a thunderstorm. Any provocation would serve as an excuse to slit Kit's throat.

"We have a stalemate, don't you think?" Mace's voice was eerily pleasant. "If you want your fancy piece to survive, drop your pistol."

Sickly, Lucien realized that he had no choice. He could shoot either Mace or Harford, but not both. Leaving one alive might be Kit's death sentence, for both brothers were capable of killing her without a moment's compunction.

Though he had little faith in Mace's trustworthiness, perhaps the presence of so many witnesses might keep his worst excesses in check. From what Kira had said, not all of them were murderers. Stony faced, he dropped his gun to the floor.

As he did, he saw a flicker of motion on the opposite gallery. He glanced up without shifting his head and saw Michael and Jason entering from a side passage. Summing up the situation in one keen glance, Michael raised his carbine and aimed it at Harford. Then he looked down at Lucien, waiting for a signal.

When Michael fired, Harford would be a dead man. However, Lucien would have to retrieve his gun and take care of Mace himself because Jason was too far away to be accurate with a pistol. It would be risky—but less so than leaving Kit in the hands of two madmen.

Once the shooting started, anything could happen. Thank God Kit had the intelligence and courage to react swiftly. Focusing his mind with furious intensity, Lucien tried to send a mental warning for her to be alert. She stared at him, ashen, but he thought he saw comprehension in her stark eyes.

Praying that Michael's aim would be true, Lucien looked up and gave a faint nod.

The carbine roared, the blast reverberating through the cavern with numbing force. Simultaneously Lucien dived for his pistol. Roderick Harford screamed and spun around from the impact of Michael's bullet, then collapsed. As he fell, Kit twisted away before his knife could slice into her throat.

Without rising, Lucien snapped a shot at Mace, but the instant it had taken to reach the gun gave the other man time to take shelter. Mace leaped behind the stone altar, which would protect him from the shots of both of his attackers.

Before Lucien could reload, he heard Kira scream, *"Kit!"*

In his concern for Kit, he had forgotten about her sister. Now, drawn by the sounds of gunshots, Kira burst into the chamber. He glanced up and saw that she was only a few feet away, her face frantic as she gazed at her twin.

Kit whipped around and stared at her sister, her soul in her eyes. *"Kira!"*

From his own understanding of the twin bond, he realized that having been separated by force, they now had a need to be together that was so fierce it was almost palpable. The rest of the world had vanished for the two of them.

Even so, he was unprepared when they began running toward each other. Kira dropped her whip and sable cape, then hurled herself into the midst of the slashing mechanical warriors. She safely ducked under the swinging sword, but Lucien gasped when he saw that she was moving into the downward arc of the battle-ax. She dropped to the floor and slithered under it. For an instant he thought her spine would be severed, but she was just slim enough to pass below unscathed.

So far, so good, but she would never be able to avoid the scimitar. He scooped up the whip she had dropped, then lashed it at the mechanical Turk with all his strength. The thong curled around the figure's arm. The steam-driven mechanism almost yanked Lucien from his feet, but he hung on grimly. With a shriek of metal, the arm twisted in its iron socket, slowing long enough to permit Kira to dart by.

As Kira ran her horrendous gauntlet, Kit dodged around Nunfield, who had made a grab at her. At the same time she was struggling with her bonds. She freed her wrists in time to run into her sister's embrace. They locked their arms around each other, clinging together in the midst of chaos.

Nunfield raised his pistol and swung it toward the two women, his face distorted with furious malice. Frantically, Lucien started to reload, praying that Nunfield's first shot would miss.

His eyes were caught by a movement above. He glanced up and saw Jason Travers grab the rope that ran from the gallery to the chandelier by way of a pulley. The rope was intended to lower the chandelier for cleaning and new candles, but Jason found a lethal new use for it. He leaped onto the railing, then swept to the floor of the chamber like an avenging eagle.

His weight caused the chandelier to fly upward and smash into the ceiling. Flaming candles rained onto the screaming Disciples below. The chandelier itself plunged downward after Jason released the rope, almost hitting Mace, who retreated farther behind the altar. Most of the candles went out when it hit the floor, leaving the cavern lit only by the bonfires.

As Jason landed, he whipped up his pistol and shot Nunfield at point-blank range. Even before the other man hit the floor, Jason grabbed the lever that controlled the statues. He yanked it and the effigies clanked to a stop, harmless again.

In the eerie silence that followed, Jason called hoarsely, "Kira?"

She looked up and gasped with shock, her face chalk-white. Slowly, incredulously, she broke away from Kit and walked toward Jason, whispering his name. She raised a hesitant hand to touch him, as if unable to believe he was real. He caught it and pulled her into his arms, desperate longing engraved on his face. She buried her face against him, her shoulders shaking.

Lucien noted the reunion as he dashed toward the center of the circle, but his main concern was for Mace, who was still free, still armed, and deadlier than ever. Pistol ready in his hand, Lucien started to circle the altar. A quarter way around, he came face-to-face with his quarry.

"I liked you, Strathmore," Mace said with fatalistic calm as he aimed his gun at Lucien's heart. "You're almost as clever as I am. A pity you're such a bloody middle-class puritan."

More experienced than his opponent, Lucien didn't waste time on talk. He pulled his trigger, diving sideways at the same time. The pistol sputtered and misfired. Mace's gun didn't, but Lucien's evasive maneuver saved him. The other man's ball blasted past his right ear, deafening but harmless.

Swearing viciously, Mace reached for his knife. Lucien scrambled to regain his balance, only to find that he had twisted his damned ankle again when he had dodged Mace's shot. As he fell to one knee, the other man moved in, blade glittering wickedly in the lurid light of the bonfires.

From the corner of his eye, he saw Kira break away from Jason. She raised the pistol that Lucien had given her—where the devil had she carried it in that revealing costume?—and pointed it at Mace, her eyes wild. Yet her hands were steady when she cocked the hammer, and her aim was true.

Her bullet caught Mace square in the chest. He gasped in astonishment, then slowly folded to the floor, his gaze on Kira. In a last, harsh whisper, he said, "You were the best, mistress. A pity . . ." Then he closed his eyes and died. The whole bloody altercation that left three men dead had taken place in well under two minutes.

Kira stared down at Mace for an endless moment. There was fury in her face, and the triumph of a woman who had taken power into her hands after a long hell of helplessness.

Slowly, her expression changed to a kind of horror.

Guessing her feelings, Lucien limped to her and put one arm around her shoulders in a brotherly hug. "Thank you, Kira," he said softly. "You're everything Kit said." Though he'd met her less than half an hour before, she seemed like an old friend.

He was looking around for Kit when danger reappeared. Most of the surviving Disciples were staring at the carnage, shocked and disbelieving. All except Lord Chiswick. In the lull after Mace's death, he had darted behind the altar and pulled out his own pistol. Keeping a wary eye on the gallery where Michael still stood, he pointed his gun at Lucien. "You've gone mad, Strathmore," he snapped. "Do you think we'll all stand still to be slaughtered?"

Lucien said under his breath, "Move away from me, Kira." While she withdrew from the line of fire, he dropped his useless pistol and raised his hands a little so that Chiswick could see that they were empty.

High above, Michael began to race around the gallery to a position where the altar wouldn't block his shot. But something in Chiswick's voice made Lucien think that the battle might be over. He said, "You think this is a senseless massacre?"

Pistol shaking, Chiswick said with an unconvincing show of nonchalance, "Christ, we were having a peaceful little orgy when you and your friends came and began shooting everyone in sight."

Michael reached a position where Chiswick was in his line of fire, but Lucien raised his hand in a signal to wait. To Chiswick he said harshly, "Are you claiming that you don't know that Mace kidnapped Cassie James two months ago and has kept her captive here? Or that he did his damnedest to kidnap her sister as well? Those things are facts, and he himself boasted to his captive that he had kidnapped, brutalized, and ultimately killed other women in the past."

Chiswick's jaw dropped. Across the room Sir James Westley exclaimed, "You've got it all wrong! The girls Mace hired for the solstice rituals were told to fight and scream and pretend to be captives. It was part of the fun. The rape of the Sabine women and all that, y'know."

His mouth trembled. "I thought you were part of the show, until you started killing people."

Lucien shifted his hard stare to the baronet. "Would you have known the difference between a real and a pretend captive?"

"You mean they *weren't* ...?" Westley's complexion took on a greenish hue. "I thought that Mace had hired Cassie James to entertain us for the evening. She's hardly the first actress to sell herself for the right price."

Kira had retreated into Kit's arms, but at Westley's statement she raised her head. "Not only did he tell me of his murders, but he said that my sister and I were to be the next victims," she said bitterly. "After the general rape, he and his closest cronies would have had a private little orgy of their own that would have ended with our deaths."

Her testimony left the surviving Disciples shaken. Chiswick's gaze went from Harford to Mace to Nunfield, and the shock in his eyes could not have been counterfeited. "I didn't know," he said with horror. "I swear to God that I didn't know."

Face implacable, Kira said, "Not consciously, perhaps, but by your cruelty and self-absorption, the whole rotten lot of you condoned Mace's behavior."

Chiswick's expression grayed.

Lucien said, "Think back and you may find it easier to believe."

After a painful hesitation, Chiswick nodded. "I always knew there was something a little strange going on with those three, but I thought it was merely family eccentricity between two brothers and their cousin." He straightened up, his gun sagging to the floor. "Though sometimes I wondered ..."

Fragments of fact from his own investigation clicked into place in Lucien's mind, bringing near-certainty. "Did it ever occur to you that one of them might be a French spy?"

Chiswick looked startled. "Strange you should say that. I once overheard something that made me consider going to the authorities. Nunfield had access to information, Mace enjoyed confounding authority, and Roderick always needed money. But they were my friends, and I was reluctant to accuse them. Then the war ended, and the matter didn't seem worth pursuing. It ... it never occurred to me that they might be murderers."

It made sense. Later Lucien would question Chiswick about the evidence of spying, but his intuition confirmed the other man's suspicion: the Phantom was not one man, but three, and all now lay dead. "I think their vices were multiple," he said dryly. "Though I didn't plan it this way, what happened tonight was justice, not slaughter."

Chiswick looked down at his pistol, then holstered it. "This wasn't loaded, you know. It was only part of the costume."

Which explained why he hadn't shot Lucien. It was also further evidence that Chiswick had not been part of Mace's violent inner circle.

Michael had descended from the gallery, alert but no longer in battle mode. He asked, "Has everything been resolved to your satisfaction?"

Lucien laid his hand on the other man's forearm. "It has. Thank you, Michael. God knows what would have happened without your marksmanship."

His friend smiled. "Think nothing of it. I'm always looking for a chance to atone for my sins." He moved away to look more closely at the warrior statues.

Now that the danger had passed, Lucien was physically and emotionally drained. His shoulder ached where Kira had clubbed him, his ankle hurt like the devil, and the prolonged anxiety of the night had taken a heavy toll. Instinctively he turned to Kit, needing to hold her.

She was with Kira, the identical faces like mirror images of each other. Though the twins were not clinging as desperately as they had earlier, it was obvious they were bound by an emotional intimacy that shut out everyone else.

Hesitantly he said, "Are you all right, Kit? Mace didn't hurt you?"

She looked at him, her gray eyes opaque and unreadable. "I'm fine, thank you. He didn't have time to do anything."

Worse than the formality of her words was the bitter

knowledge that she had deliberately cut the silent ties that had been growing between them. He had not realized how strong they had become until now, when they were gone, leaving an icy void.

It was his worst fear come true. She had become the center of his life, yet for her, he scarcely existed. She no longer needed him now that she had her twin again.

He wondered where Jason would fit into the equation. Perhaps he didn't want as much from Kira as Lucien needed from Kit; if so, he might be perfectly happy, not knowing what he was missing. But Lucien wanted more, and he felt bleakly certain that he would never get it. If pressed, Kit might agree to marry him, from gratitude if for no other reason. But in every meaningful way she was gone, for she had never really been his.

Damming the pain before it could drown him, Lucien looked back at Chiswick. "We're leaving now. Do you want to take care of this mess? You were part of it, so you and the others have the most to lose if a public scandal results."

Chiswick looked startled, then thoughtful. "If it was announced that Nunfield, Mace, and Harford died in a carriage accident because of the icy weather, it would be sad, but not scandalous." He glanced at his fellows. "Do you agree?"

There were murmurs of relief. Judging by the faces of the other Disciples, the night's events had persuaded this particular lot of rakes to stick to more conventional vices in the future.

"Speaking of carriages," Chiswick said, "mine has special wheels that make it travel well in ice and snow. If you like, you can borrow it for the ladies." He glanced at Kit and Kira. "I think they have endured quite enough for one night."

Lucien accepted the offer, and within a quarter of an hour they were on their way. Even when he helped Kit into the carriage, she would not meet his gaze. She couldn't have been more reserved if they had just been introduced.

Michael drove the carriage while Lucien and Jason rode behind with the extra horses. The sleet and freezing rain had stopped and the temperature had fallen, turning the world to a glittering fantasy land of ice.

Lucien welcomed the biting cold, for it matched the chill in his heart. He thought back to the night at Eton when he had decided to become Lucifer—cool, ironic, detached, as far above the pain of loss as the clouds sailing through the sky. It had worked then, and it would work now, for he had had so many years of practice.

After the pain was firmly locked away, he discovered a weary sense of peace. Though Kit had slipped away, taking his dreams with her, tonight he had found a measure of absolution for his failure to save his sister's life.

Chapter 39

At first Kit and Kira did not speak, content merely to hold hands as the carriage rumbled through the icy ruts. Rather than try to find her lost clothing in the maze of tunnels, Kit wore her outrageous costume under a warm cloak that Chiswick had given her. His usual cynical detachment had vanished; she guessed that he was trying to make amends for his failure to recognize the full depravity of his fellow Hellions.

Ruthlessly she suppressed her memory of the moment when Lucien had hugged Kira and said that she was everything Kit had described. After all, she had expected something like that. If she allowed herself to feel the pain, she would disintegrate, and for that she would rather be alone. Now she would rejoice in her sister's survival. There would be time enough for anguish later.

The silence was broken when Kira said in a shaking voice, "I just killed a man. I keep seeing the blood, and his face ..."

"Good riddance," Kit said tartly. "Quite apart from Mace's other sins, he was in the process of trying to knife Lucien. It's all very well to forgive one's enemies, but not until after they've been safely hung."

Her sister's faint smile faded quickly. "He never raped me, he never even kissed me. I suppose he was saving that for his grand finale. But being forced to play his loathsome games was almost as bad. I felt helpless, soiled."

"Yet you survived and kept your sanity as well," Kit said quietly. "Few women could have been as strong."

"I never could have done it without you. No matter how dreadful things were, I knew that on some level you were always with me. When it became unendurable, I drew on your strength. I also knew that if I could stay alive long enough, you would find me." Kira's clasp tightened. "And you did."

"I had help." Kit glanced at her sister, seeing the familiar profile outlined against the window. Though in principle she didn't believe in revenge, in this case she applauded it. Surely Kira's act of vengeful justice had restored some of what Mace had taken away.

"And very impressive help it was," Kira said, sounding more like herself. "Tell me everything that happened."

For her twin Kit recounted everything, except for her relationship with Lucien. That was too painful to discuss.

Kira swore when she learned about Jason's imprisonment and escape, but didn't interrupt. At the end she exclaimed, "My shy, straitlaced little sister played in *The Gypsy Lass*?"

"*And* cut my hair and got tattooed with that damned butterfly so that no one would notice any difference," Kit said acerbically.

Kira chuckled. "How were your notices?"

"The critics said I was in good form." Kit shrugged. "I merely pretended that I was you. The audience saw what they expected of Cassie James."

"Maybe you should take my place permanently," Kira suggested. "I'm not going to continue acting, but it would be a pity to retire Cassie right when fame is there for the plucking."

Startled, Kit said, "You're going to leave the stage?"

"I've had enough. Sometimes it was wonderful— there's nothing like knowing you hold an audience in the palm of your hand. But the theater world is narrow and self-absorbed and takes itself far too seriously. I was often impatient with it."

"You never hinted at that before."

Kira's fingers moved restlessly within her sister's. "I didn't want to admit that it was a mistake to become an actress. And it wasn't a complete mistake—having done it, I can now walk away with no regrets." A warmer note entered her voice. "A good thing I've had enough, because continuing to act wouldn't be fair to Jason. Theater people should marry only other theater people."

"So you are going to marry him?"

"There's nothing on earth I want more. After I met him, damn his stubborn American hide, no one else would do. I assume he feels the same, or he never would have come for me." An anxious note sounded in her voice. "You like him, don't you? It would be dreadful if you didn't."

"I like him very much. The two of you should suit wonderfully."

"He has the ability to be emotionally intimate. That's rare in a man. I think it was because his mother raised him—he takes women seriously." Kira chuckled. "He probably didn't mention it, but he's also done rather well with his shipping business. Can you believe it? A Travers male who knows how to make money instead of wasting it! Papa would have considered that heresy."

"Obviously, two generations in America have improved the stock," Kit agreed. "But why did you refuse him three years ago? He said that you didn't want to leave England, but surely, since you loved him so much ..."

"I couldn't bear to be so far from you, of course." Kira's clasp tightened again. "It was bad enough being separated when we were both in England, but to have a whole ocean between us ... As much as I loved Jason, I simply couldn't go with him."

Kit was so moved that at first she couldn't reply. "I would have felt that way," she said quietly, "but I didn't know you did." She hesitated, wondering if she should ask the question that had nagged at her since she met Jason.

Inevitably, Kira noticed. "What are you not saying?"

"Why didn't you tell him about me?" Kit asked, trying to repress the hurt. "He knew I existed, but not that we were twins, much less what that means. Were you ashamed of me?"

"Kit, no! How could you think such a thing?"

"Why else would you keep silent?"

After a long silence Kira said haltingly, "I hate having to admit this—it sounds so horribly petty. But ... I was afraid he would prefer you to me."

Kit sat bolt upright. "Have you run mad? No man has ever preferred me to you!"

"'It's not a joking matter," Kira snapped. "I hate your false modesty. It's bad enough that you can out-think and out-talk me—you don't have to out-humble me as well."

Kit gasped at the sheer unfairness of the remark. "If I'm humble, it's because I have plenty of reason to be," she said, her voice trembling as she thought of Lucien. "I've spent my whole life trailing around in your shadow. The quiet twin. The dull twin. The twin who isn't Kristine, who looks exactly the same except that for some reason she isn't as pretty. I haven't minded that, but you have no right to accuse me of hypocrisy!"

Kit bit her lip. "Oh, Kit, I'm so sorry. My nerves are a wreck, but I shouldn't take it out on you of all people."

They went into each other's arms again, tears very close to the surface. Kit thought of their childhood, when they would creep into the same bed and sleep together like kittens. Impossible to imagine her life without her twin.

Eventually Kit disengaged herself. "Have you ever noticed that when we've been apart, we always have some stupid little disagreement shortly after we're reunited?"

Kira settled back and took her sister's hand again. "You're right, it happens every time. Why do you think that's so?"

"Because we miss each other so much." After a peaceful silence, Kit added, "I still can't believe you thought I could ever be a rival for Jason. Firstly, I would never, ever do that to you, and secondly, that man adores the water you walk on."

"I knew you wouldn't deliberately try to win him away, but men are always so intrigued by you," Kira said ruefully. 'I'm such a frivolous creature. You're wiser, stronger, and you have a quality of female mystery that drives men wild. I didn't really doubt either Jason or you—but because you're both so important to me, I couldn't help worrying a little."

"Are we talking about the same person?" Kit said incredulously. "*Me* as a mysterious enchanter of men? You're off your head, big sister! Back in Kendal, you were always the one who was surrounded three dep by admirers."

Kira shrugged. "They were boys, not men, and they

found it easier to talk to a chatterbox like me. Oh, some of them fancied me, but half were hanging about as a way to get closer to you. Your intelligence intimidated them all fearfully, you know. I always knew you would come into your own when you were older and could meet men who were mature and confident."

"What about Philip Burke?" Kit asked, feeling a faint twinge even now. "I wanted desperately for him to notice me, but he didn't know that I was alive."

"Him? Oh, he was just one of *those* people, the sort that can't deal with identical twins," Kira said dismissively. "Since he needed something to do while visiting Kendal, he decided to dangle after me. So he did, which meant that you became invisible to him. I'm sorry that upset you, but honestly, he wasn't worth it. *Those* people never are."

"To think that I pined over him for one whole summer, yet missed something so obvious! You overrate my intelligence."

"No, I don't." Kira sighed. "I'm not as strong as you, Kit. I knew that Jane was right when she insisted that we separate and learn to lead independent lives after Papa died. I tried my best, but I just couldn't manage as well as you. Professionally, you became an influential writer, read and respected by the most prominent men in the kingdom. Even more important, you were always so calm, so confident, so comfortable with yourself. Not at all like me."

"But you were a much greater success!" Kit retorted. "You made ten times the money I did. It was you who paid off most of Papa's debts, and you had so many friends and admirers."

Kira shrugged. "I did well enough as an actress, but as a person I was a fraud—incomplete. I desperately wanted to find someone who would love and take care of me. That was why it was so dreadful to fall in love with an American. It was unthinkable to leave England, yet sending Jason away was almost as bad."

Again Kit had the sense that they were talking about two different people. "You really thought that I was successfully independent? I love Jane, and living with her has been very comfortable, but I would have accepted her offer of a home even if she'd been Caligula. When I left Westmoreland, I couldn't endure the thought of living alone or going among strangers. I had such respect for your courage in entering a whole new world. I spent four years lurking in my room, writing essays, which is about as far from real life as one can get."

"I needed the distraction of being constantly busy," Kira said simply. "I knew I would have a terrible time without you, but activity and novelty would help."

Understanding struck them simultaneously. They stared at each other in the darkness. "Jane kept emphasizing how well you were doing on your own," Kit said. "When she wrote you, did she go on about my success?"

"Yes!" Kira exclaimed. "I suppose she was only trying to be encouraging, but by telling each of us that the other was doing so well, she made us both feel like failures!"

"Though her intentions were good, the results weren't," Kit said half laughing, half exasperated. "For four years I've been blaming myself for my weak character."

"I did until I met Jason. That's when I realized it isn't in my nature to be frightfully independent like Jane. Oh, I can survive on my own, I know that now, but I'm far happier being with someone I love."

Her sister's words triggered a series of insights in Kit. She had been resisting Lucien with all her might. Part of that was her genuine fear that he would prefer Kira and leave her devastated, but she had also believed she shouldn't need him so much. Her experience had been that it wasn't safe to rely so much on men, and that had been reinforced by Jane, who was so splendidly independent herself.

But Lucien was not a Travers, and Kit should not doubt him because of her father's failings. Nor should she read so much into the way he had hugged Kira after she had shot Mace. Kit had been disposed to assume the worst, but apparently she and her sister had been misjudging each other for years. If she could do that with her twin, she could certainly be wrong about Lucien.

It was also high time for her to accept that it was no more her nature to be emotionally self-contained than it was Kira's. Thoughtfully she said, "We haven't talked like this in four years, Kira. Thank you for giving me a new perspective on life and love."

"Speaking of love, are you going to marry Lucien Fairchild? He's rather magnificent."

"So he is. As to marriage . . ." Kit hesitated, not wanting to discuss what was still so horrendously unresolved. "That remains to be seen. He thinks we should marry, but that's mostly because he feels guilty about all of the times we were in compromising situations. Since that was my fault, not his, it seems rather silly that he should have to marry me for the sake of my reputation."

"That's just an excuse—the truth is that he's another victim of your fatal charm." After a short pause, Kira inhaled sharply with surprise. "Kit, you sly thing, are you pregnant?"

"What?" Kit gasped. "That's impossible!"

"Is it?" Kira asked with interest.

Kit felt herself blushing so violently that the interior of the carriage should have warmed several degrees. "Well, not actually impossible. But certainly improbable."

Kira chuckled wickedly. "Nonetheless, I think it's true. I shall prepare myself to become an aunt."

Perhaps she was right; it was the sort of thing one twin would know about another. Kit thought about the possibility of having Lucien's child. Warmth sparked in her heart and spread through her whole body. It was a wonderful prospect—yet it complicated her situation enormously.

For the rest of the ride they chattered back and forth comparing notes, finishing each other's sentences, washing away four years of subtle estrangement in a flood tide of words. Then Kira glanced out the window and saw the manor house outlined against the night sky. "Incidentally, where are we going? I didn't think to ask."

"A small estate owned by a friend of Lucien's. It's vacant at the moment, so we've temporarily taken it over. Some of Lucien's servants came along to keep us comfortable."

"Did you bring some decent clothing? As soon as we get inside, I want you to help me take off this ghastly costume so that I can burn it."

"I packed several of your gowns," Kit assured her. "Warm, conservative ones because I knew that was what you would want."

Kira glanced down at herself. "Actually, Jason would enjoy seeing me in this outfit, but I can't bear having anything that Mace forced on me. Speaking of which, would you switch cloaks with me? You can have the sable cape; I don't want it anywhere near me."

Awkward in the cramped quarters, they exchanged their outer garments. As she wrapped the sumptuous fur around her, Kit remarked, "Since Mace is hardly one of my favorite people, I don't want to keep the cape either. Maybe we should give it to Cleo. She was wonderfully helpful, and she would love it."

"Good idea." A touch of defiance in her voice, Kira continued, "After I change, I'm going to find Jason and drag him off to his room for the night. We have a lot to catch up on."

Kit realized that her sister expected a scold. Once prim Lady Kathryn would have been scandalized at such immoral behavior, but not now. Not since she had learned something about passion and the bond it would forge between a man and a woman. "You certainly do. Having each survived a terrible captivity, I expect you'll be closer than ever."

"I hadn't thought of that, but you're right." After a slight hesitation, Kira said, "You needn't be jealous of Jason, you know. The connection between you and me has changed and evolved over the years, but it will always be there. Always."

Trust Kira to know and understand. Her heart full of love, Kit said, "And you say *I'm* clever. When it comes to the most important things in life, you've always been ahead of me."

"Only by ten minutes or so." The carriage rumbled to a halt in front of the manor. Already beginning to put her experience behind her, Kira continued buoyantly, "Now come help me out of this beastly outfit!"

Chapter 40

Lucien had been unsurprised to see Kit and Kira enter the manor house, then dart upstairs together. He guessed that for the next few days it would take a crowbar to separate them. Quite understandable under the circumstances.

He kept his distance, not trusting himself near Kit. It was one thing to intellectually accept that their affair was over, another for him to stop craving her. But surely, in time, that would pass.

After drinking half his glass of brandy, he stood and wandered restlessly across his bedroom. The other two men were relaxing over supper and a celebratory drink, but he had chosen not to join them. He had no appetite, nor did he feel much like celebrating. Michael had frowned when he had excused himself, but had known better than to comment. Friendship was as much a matter of knowing when *not* to speak as when one should.

He opened the French doors and went out onto the small balcony. The wind was brutally cold, but the storm had blown away, and the moon rode high in the sky. Its cool light refracted brilliantly through the ice that sparkled on every twig and branch. Ice everywhere, especially in his heart.

He leaned against the railing and gazed into the crystalline night, consuming his brandy in slow sips. Perhaps when he was done, he would be able to sleep.

Kit helped her sister change from the bondage costume to a plain blue gown. With her hair brushed out and falling simply over her shoulders, Kira was beautiful, with the special glow that was uniquely her own. She looked exactly as a woman going to her lover should. Kit guessed that the next time she saw her sister and Jason, the two would be at peace for the first time in years. Certainly Kira would be.

She wanted to change her own clothing, but as soon as her sister left the bedroom, sharp anxiety washed through her. Something was very wrong where Lucien was concerned.

It wasn't until Kit reached out and found silence that she realized that she had become accustomed to feeling him in the background of her mind, rather as she did with her sister. His current blankness was unlike the time when she had feared Kira was dead. Instead, it was as if he had closed a door that had been gradually opening to her.

Suddenly worried, she grabbed the cape and headed though the icy hall toward Lucien's room. Perhaps he was angry because she had wandered off and gotten herself captured. At the time she'd had as little volition as a sleepwalker, but her behavior had complicated events dreadfully. If she and Lucien had stayed together, Kira might have been rescued without any bloodshed—not that Mace and the other two were any great loss to society.

Her steps slowed as she approached his room. What if he really didn't want her? What if . . .?

Before she could lose her nerve, she rapped firmly on his door. No answer. Quietly she turned the knob and went inside.

The lamp was lit and the bed turned down, but he wasn't in it. Cold air gusted from the open French doors. She looked out to see Lucien standing on the balcony, his back to her.

He must have heard the knock, for he said without turning, "No need to check up on me, Michael. Nothing ails me that a night's sleep won't cure."

Uncertainly, she said, "Are you feeling unwell, Lucien?"

His broad shoulders became rigid. After a long pause, he turned and leaned casually against the railing of the balcony. He looked cool and elegant, with no trace of warrior remaining. "Only tired, Kit. It was a busy night."

She walked toward him, tugging the cape closer against the fierce cold. As she did, she realized that she was dressed exactly as her sister had been earlier. Needing to know if he could tell them apart, she offered him Kira's smile and Kira's glow. "Are you sure I'm Kit?"

Guessing that he was being tested, he said ironically, "Of course, even if you are still playing the role of Cassie James." His gaze went to the cape. "I assume that you and Kira exchanged cloaks because she didn't want anything that had come from Mace."

It was a relief that he could unerringly tell them apart. Equally clearly, he still knew how her mind worked. But his expression was as remote and unapproachable as the fallen archangel of his nickname. The silent communication that had been growing between them had vanished as absolutely as if it had never existed.

For an instant she felt a sick certainty that Kira really had dazzled him to the point where he was hoping Kit would quietly fade from his life. Of course, if she told him she was pregnant, he would certainly marry her. But that was not the marriage she wanted.

Her mouth tightened. She had never given up on finding Kira, and she was not going to give up on Lucien until she was absolutely sure he didn't want her.

The sable cape swirling about her calves, she joined him on the balcony. The house was L-shaped. with a formal garden lying in the angle between the wings. Not daring to look directly at him, she studied the frozen fountain, which the moonlight had transformed into an opalescent ice sculpture. "I said that when the crisis was over, I would be happy to give you anything you wished that was in my power. Have you decided what you want?"

There was a stillness so profound that she could hear the brittle sound of ice-crusted twigs tapping against each other in the wind. Finally, he said, "What I want is something that can't be given. You're under no obligation to me, Kit. I'm glad I could help find Kira. In the process

I found the spies I was seeking, so the scales are balanced. Go and be happy."

It was blatant dismissal. She caught her breath, the frigid air searing her lungs. "You've changed your mind about wanting marriage?"

"Ever since Linnie died, I've been looking in vain for the other half of myself," he said in a voice as bleak as the winter night. "Whenever I sought it in a woman, I found loneliness instead. I hoped that with you, there was a chance of having the emotional intimacy I craved. You are a twin, you know how to give, how to make yourself vulnerable, and how to love without reservation. I wanted all of that."

He braced his hands on the railing and raised his face to the sky. The moonlight gilded his face to impossible handsomeness. Bright star of the morning, most beautiful of God's host, beyond the ken of man—or woman.

"But I was a fool to think it possible to have that kind of closeness with anyone else," he continued. "Elinor and I were born in the same hour, of the same blood. Together we learned to play, to talk, to laugh—to share all our thoughts and emotions. And even with Linnie, that would have waned when we grew up. Perhaps it's as much a curse as a blessing to be a twin, because it gives one an appetite for what can never again be attained."

After a long pause he said in a scarcely audible voice, "I suppose that what I really wanted was to recapture the golden days of my childhood, before I discovered what a painful place the world is. You can't give that time back to me. No one can, any more than I could have replaced Kira in your heart if she had died. She comes first with you. She always will. Tonight I realized that I would not be content with any shreds that are left over, and it's better not to try."

He looked at her then, his eyes a pale, moonstruck green. "It has been a pleasure knowing you, Lady Kathryn. I learned many useful things about myself."

She shivered, the chill of his distance far worse than the bitter wind.

Noticing, he said, "You should go inside. After surviving so much, it's foolish to risk lung fever."

Before she could reply, a light came on in a bedroom in the wing of the house that ran at right angles to the section they were in. Kira was visible in silhouette going to the window to draw the curtains. Before she could, Jason came up behind her and wrapped his arms around her waist. She leaned back against him, her head falling against his shoulder with complete trust.

Lucien had seen also, and his hands tightened on the railing. When Kira turned in Jason's arms and they kissed with an intensity that blazed through the night, Lucien turned sharply away and ushered Kit into the bedroom. She agreed entirely; that tableau of tenderness was too private to be seen by any outsider, even a twin.

"I'm sorry you had to see that, Kit. It must hurt to be excluded." He looked at her, that green in his eyes intensifying. "Did you come to me because you felt rejected and wanted company while Kira went to her lover?"

"Good Lord, no!" She took a deep breath, knowing that to break through his barrier of distance, she must be as insightful as he had been in building it. "You're right that being twinborn sets a very high standard for closeness, but I think you're wrong that only a blood tie and a shared childhood can create true intimacy. Being a twin is wonderful, and Kira and I are as close as two sisters can be. Obviously, you and Elinor shared an equally special love.

"But twins are siblings, with all of the advantages and limitations that implies. I hope—I believe—that passion can create a different kind of bond that may be even deeper. I want closeness as much as you do, Lucien. I assumed I would never marry because I didn't think I could find that kind of emotional bond with a man, and I didn't want to settle for less." Her voice broke. "I . . . I never imagined a man like you. In the last few weeks I've learned there is a kind of intimacy that a woman can find only with a man."

Raw anguish showed in his eyes. He wanted her. Of that she was certain, for it showed in every line of his body. But she knew intuitively that he had already surrendered hope for the black peacefulness of defeat. To reach out for what she was offering was to open himself to loss again. By letting her own fear and confusion come between them, she had made love a risk he no longer dared take.

Since thoughts and fears had become an impassable barrier, it was time to invoke the awesome power of passion. She raised her hand to her throat and unhooked the sable cape, then let it slide from her shoulders in a cascade of lustrous dark fur. Underneath she still wore Mace's satin, leather, and lace.

Lucien tensed as the sexual awareness that was always between them crackled into fire. "Don't do this, Kit," he said tightly. "Sex creates an illusion of closeness, but it vanishes as quickly as ice in the sun. I found out years ago that coupling without the possibility of something deeper was a sure route to desolation."

"You would know that better than I, but surely physical fulfillment is part of what we both want."

His face hardened. "If it's a bedmate you want, look somewhere else. You don't need me."

"You're wrong," she said, voice shaking. "All of my life, Kira was the essential person. Oh, I have loved my mother and Jane and others, but I could and did survive their losses. Only Kira's death would have left me so diminished that I would no longer be the person I once was." She caught her gaze with his. "Now there are two essential people in my life. I need you as much as I need Kira, but in a different way. You will never be second in my heart, Lucien. There is room enough there for two."

He shook his head, desolation in his eyes. "Even if we both want the same thing, wishing isn't enough to make it happen."

"You're right, wishing isn't enough. We must *make* it happen." Reaching into herself, she conjured up the sensual allure she had learned as Cassie James. Then she moved toward him, the high-heeled boots making every step an exercise in provocation. Black satin shimmered over the curves of her body and her breasts swayed within the lattice of leather laces. "Can't we at least try one more time?"

"I don't know if I can endure another failure." He stared at her, his chest rising and falling as if he had been running.

In his eyes was fierce longing, yet when she extended her hand, he made no move to accept it. For a moment she despaired. Then she realized what was lacking. She opened her heart, then reached out again. This time she silently offered her love.

Later she could never remember which of them moved first, but they came together with savage abandon. His mouth slanted hard over hers in a wordless cry of yearning, loneliness, and hope. She recognized his tortured emotions, for they found echoes deep inside her. When she kissed him back, it was a plea and a promise.

The desperation between them eased, leaving more room for the primal blaze of passion. "Dear God, Kit," he said huskily as his deft fingers undid the lace thongs, releasing her breasts into his hands. "You're more than mortal man can resist."

"Then don't . . . resist." Fabric ripped, buttons popped, garments fell as they instinctively sought to bare their bodies as thoroughly as their minds. The bed creaked with protest at the force of their arrival. Then flesh against flesh, musky scent and liquid heat, taut muscle and harsh breath. Passion was the instrument, and intimacy the goal.

When they had made love before, she had pulled away, fearing that she would lose herself in him beyond recall. This time she did not retreat. Instead, she dropped all the barriers, concealing nothing of herself. In that surrender she found fulfillment. If Kira was her other self, Lucien was her soul.

He had feared this fevered mating almost as much as he had craved it, terrified that it would be only of the body, leaving his deeper self unsatisfied. Yet this time she was there, her love lighting the dark corners of his mind, her tenderness a balm to his aching heart. She knew his strengths and failings, his fears and hopes, as surely as he knew hers. And the love that joined them was as unmistakable as the sun.

The physical climax was shattering, a fiery symbol of the melding of their spirits. Afterward they lay face-to-face in each other's arms, her forehead against his cheek, her ragged breath stirring wisps of his hair. He was half afraid to move in case this was only a dream and he risked waking.

But she was more real than any dream when she tilted he head back and said lazily, "Did you know that your eyes turn to transparent gold when you're happy?"

He gave a slow smile, knowing only Kit would say something like that. "I think of them as a rather ordinary hazel."

"Nothing about you is ordinary," she said with conviction.

He ran his hand down the naked curve of her back, loving her lithe strength. "Though you've suspected me of being a rake, for years I've been nearly celibate because the satisfactions of coupling were brief compared to the loneliness I felt after. But making love with you is as soothing as it is intoxicating." He bent his head and gave her a light kiss. "I feel so content right now that it's hard to believe we'll ever need to speak a word aloud again. We can simply read each other's minds."

"We might not *have* to talk, but we'll want to. I love talking with you." She caressed his cheek with the back of her hand. "I love looking at you. I love making love with you." She blinked pensively. "Have I mentioned yet that I just plain love you, body and soul?"

"No, but after the way we made love, you don't have to." He lifted her hand and kissed it. "The feeling is entirely mutual, as you know."

"Yes," she said with perfect contentment. "I know."

He brushed a kiss on her forehead. "You and I suit each other perfectly, my little tiger kitten. We both prefer lurking behind the scenes to being on center stage."

She laughed. "That's true, isn't it? Kira and Jason are both more sociable types."

He wound a silky strand of her hair around his forefinger. "The estate that borders Ashdown will soon be coming on the market. I had intended to buy it and farm the land, then lease the house, but perhaps Jason might be interested in the place. It's a fine property and convenient to Bristol, which would be a good base for his shipping business."

"And Kira and I can be neighbors for the rest of our lives," she said quietly. "What a wonderful, generous thought."

"I'm being entirely selfish. The happier you are, the happier I'll be."

Her quick smile soon faded. "I'm still astonished that you love me. And . . . I think I'm a bit afraid you'll be disappointed when you see me in more mundane circumstances. So much of what you've seen has been me pretending to be Kira, rather than the real me."

"Nonsense," he said calmly. "It isn't only the world that tends to define identical twins as opposites—twins do it to themselves as well. You could never have impersonated Kira so effectively if you didn't have the same qualities in yourself. In the last few weeks you haven't been playing a role, you've been discovering your own nature."

She blinked at him. "You really think so?"

"I *know* so." This time he kissed the tip of her nose. "I'm glad you're retiring as Cassie James, but I hope you'll still dance for me. You make a delightfully wicked Gypsy."

"You may have a private performance whenever you want."

"I still like the idea of a special license. We can be married before Christmas."

"An excellent idea—the best of all possible presents." She stretched languidly, then settled closer to him. "Very practical, too. Kira claims that I'm pregnant." She laid a gentle hand on her belly. "Another essential person might be on the way."

That startled him out of his lassitude. "Indeed? If she's right, that's wonderful news." He propped his head on his hand and studied her face. "Why didn't you tell me earlier?"

"I wanted you to marry me because you loved me, not because you had to."

He smiled ruefully. "You're more honorable than I, Kit. For much of what might be laughingly called our courtship, I had a thoroughly selfish desire to get you with child so that you would have no choice but to accept my offer." He laid his hand over hers on her abdomen. "I'm not a very admirable character, you know."

"*I* am," she said in her primmest, most Kathryn-ish voice. "I have every intention of devoting the rest of my life to your physical and spiritual upliftment."

"Speaking of physical upliftment . . ."

She laughed as he rolled her on top of him, and she discovered that the physical was definitely uplifting. After settling over him with a provocative wiggle of her hips, she asked in a voice husky with love, "Do you think we'll have twins?"